Ryan lowers his lips to my ear. "Dance with me, Beth."

"No." I whisper the reply. I hate him and I hate myself
for wanting him to touch me again....

* * *

Praise for Katie McGarry

DARE YOU TO

Katie McGarry

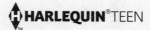

HARLEQUIN®TEEN

ISBN-13: 978-0-373-21098-5

DARE YOU TO

www.HarlequinTEEN.com

Printed in U.S.A.

"It is the beautiful bird which gets caged."

—Old Chinese Proverb

RYAN

I'M NOT INTERESTED in second place. Never have been. Never will be. It's not the style of anyone who wants to play in the majors. And because of my personal philosophy, this moment sucks. My best friend is seconds from scoring a phone number from the chick working the Taco Bell counter, placing him in the lead.

What started as a simple dare twisted into a night-long game. First, Chris dared me to ask the girl in line at the movies for her number. Then I dared him to ask the girl at the batting cages for *her* number. The more we succeeded, the more momentum the game gained. Too bad Chris owns a grin that melts the hearts of all girls, including the ones with boyfriends.

I hate losing.

Taco Bell Chick blushes when Chris winks at her. Come on. I chose her because she called us redneck losers when we ordered. Chris rests his arms on the counter, inching closer to the girl, as I sit at the table and watch the tragedy unfold. Shouldn't she be having an epiphany right about now? If not, can she find some self-respect and tell Chris to beat it?

Every single muscle on the back of my neck tenses as Taco Bell Chick giggles, writes something on a piece of paper, and slides it over to him. Dammit. The rest of our group howls with laughter and someone pats me on the back.

Tonight isn't about phone numbers or girls. It's about enjoying our last Friday night before school begins. I've tasted everything—the freedom of hot summer air in the Jeep with the panels down, the peace of dark country roads leading to the interstate, the exciting glow of city lights as we took the thirty-minute drive into Louisville, and, lastly, the mouthwatering taste of a greasy fast-food taco at midnight.

Chris raises the phone number like a referee holding up the glove of the prize champion. "It's on, Ryan."

"Bring it." There's no way I've gotten this far to have Chris outdo me.

He slouches in his seat, tosses the paper into the pile of numbers we've collected over the evening, and tugs his Bullitt County High baseball cap over his brown hair. "Let's see. These things have to be thought through. The girl chosen carefully. Attractive enough so she won't fall for you. Not a dog because she'll be excited someone gave her a bone."

Mimicking him, I shift back in the chair, extend my legs, and fold my hands over my stomach. "Take your time. I've got forever."

But we don't. After this weekend, life changes—my life and Chris's. On Monday, Chris and I will be seniors starting our last fall baseball league. I only have a few more months to impress the professional baseball scouts or the dream I've been working toward my entire life will dissolve into ashes.

A shove at my foot brings me back to the here and now.

"Stop the serious shit," Logan whispers. The lone junior

at the table and the best damn catcher in the state nods toward the rest of the group. He knows my facial expressions better than anyone. He should. We've been playing together since we were kids. Me pitching. Him catching.

For Logan's sake, I laugh at a joke Chris told even though I didn't hear the punch line.

"We close soon." Taco Bell Chick wipes a table near ours and gives Chris a smile. She almost looks pretty in the glow of the red neon Drive-Thru Open sign.

"I may call that one," says Chris.

I lift a brow. He worships his girlfriend. "No, you won't."

"I would if it weren't for Lacy." But he has Lacy, and loves her, so neither one of us continues that conversation.

"I have one more try." I make a show of glancing around the purple Tex-Mex decorated lobby. "What girl are you choosing for me?"

A honk from the drive-thru announces the arrival of a car full of hot girls. Rap pounds from their car and I swear one girl flashes us. I love the city. A brunette in the backseat waves at me. "You should pick one of them."

"Sure," Chris says sarcastically. "In fact, why don't I hand you the title now?"

Two guys from our table hop out of their seats and go outside, leaving me, Logan, and Chris alone. "Last chance for hot city girls before we drive back to Groveton, Logan."

Logan doesn't say anything one way or another, nor does his face move an inch. That's Logan for you—unmoved by much. Unless it involves a feat associated with death.

"There she is." Chris's eyes brighten as he stares at the entrance. "That's the girl I'm calling as yours."

I suck in a deep breath. Chris sounds too happy for this girl to be good news. "Where?"

"Just came in, waiting at the counter."

I risk a look. Black hair. Torn clothes. Total skater. Damn, those chicks are hard-core. I slap my hand against the table and our trays shift. Why? Why did Skater Girl have to wander into Taco Bell tonight?

Chris's rough chuckles do nothing to help my growing agitation. "Admit defeat and you won't have to suffer."

"No way." I stand, refusing to go down without a fight.

All girls are the same. It's what I tell myself as I stroll to the counter. She might look different from the girls at home, but all girls want the same thing—a guy who shows interest. A guy's problem is having the balls to do it. Good thing for me I've got balls. "Hi. I'm Ryan."

Her long black hair hides her face, but her slim body with a hint of curves catches my attention. Unlike the girls at home, she isn't wearing marked-down designer labels. Nope. She has her own style. Her black tank top shows more skin than it covers and her skintight jeans hug all the right places. My eyes linger on a single rip in them, directly below her ass.

She leans over the counter and the rip widens. Skater Girl turns her head toward me and the drive-thru. "Is someone going to take my fucking order?"

Chris's laughter from our corner table jerks me back to reality. I pull off my baseball cap, mess my hand through my hair, and shove the hat back in place. Why her? Why tonight? But there's a dare and I'm going to win. "Counter's a little slow tonight."

She glares at me like *I'm* a little slow. "Are you speaking to me?"

Her hard stare dares me to glance away, and a lesser guy would. I'm not lesser. *Keep staring, Skater Girl. You don't scare me.* I'm drawn to her eyes though. They're blue. Dark blue. I never would have thought someone with such black hair could have those brilliant eyes.

"I asked you a question." She rests a hip against the counter and crosses her arms over her chest. "Or are you as stupid as you look?"

Yep, pure punk: attitude, nose ring, and a sneer that can kill on sight. She's not my type, but she doesn't have to be. I just need her number. "You'd probably get better service if you watched your language."

A hint of amusement touches her lips and dances in her eyes. Not the kind of amusement you laugh with. It's the taunting kind. "Does my language bother you?"

Yes. "No." Girls don't use *fuck*. Or they shouldn't. I don't care for the word, but I know when I'm being tested and this is a test.

"So my language doesn't bother you, but you say—" she raises her voice and leans over the counter again "—I could get some *fucking* service if I watched my language."

Wouldn't hurt. Time to switch tactics. "What do you want?"

Her head snaps up as if she had forgotten I was there. "What?"

"To eat. What do you want to eat?"

"Fish. What do you think I want? I'm at a taco joint."

Chris laughs again and this time Logan joins in. If I don't salvage this, I'll be listening to their ridicule the entire way home. This time I lean over the counter and wave at the girl working the drive-thru. I give her a smile. She smiles back.

Take lessons, Skater Girl. This is how it's supposed to work. "Can I have a minute?"

Drive-Thru Chick's face brightens and she holds up a finger as she continues with the order from outside. "Be right there. Promise."

I turn back to Skater Girl, but instead of the warm thank-you I should be receiving she shakes her head, clearly annoyed. "Jocks."

My smile falters. Hers grows.

"How do you know I'm a jock?"

Her eyes wander to my chest and I fight a grimace. Written in black letters across my gray shirt is Bullitt County High School, Baseball State Champions.

"So you are stupid," she says.

I'm done. I take one step in the direction of the table, then stop. I don't lose. "What's your name?"

"What do I have to do to make you leave me alone?"

And there it is—my opening. "Give me your phone number."

The right side of her mouth quirks up. "You're fucking kidding."

"I'm dead serious. Give me your name and phone number and I'll walk away."

"You must be brain damaged."

"Welcome to Taco Bell. Can I take your order?"

We both look at Drive-Thru Chick. She beams at me, then cowers from Skater Girl. With her lids cast down, she asks again, "What can I get you?"

I pull out my wallet and slam ten dollars on the counter. "Tacos."

"And a Coke," Skater Girl says. "Large. Since he's paying."

"Oookaay." Drive-Thru Chick enters the order, slides the money off the counter, and returns to the order window.

We stare at each other. I swear, this girl never blinks.

"I believe a thank-you is in order," I say.

"I never asked you to pay."

"Give me your name and phone number and we'll call it even."

She licks her lips. "There is absolutely nothing you can do to ever get me to give you my name or number."

Ring the bell. Playtime ended with those words. Purposely invading her space, I steal a step toward her and place a hand on the counter next to her body. It affects her. I can tell. Her eyes lose the amusement and her arms hug her body. She's small. Smaller than I expected. That attitude is so big I hadn't noticed her height or size. "I bet I can."

She juts out her chin. "Can't."

"Eight tacos and one large Coke," says the girl from behind the counter.

Skater Girl snatches the order and spins on her heel before I can process I'm on the verge of losing. "Wait!"

She stops at the door. "What?"

This "what" doesn't have nearly the anger of the one before. Maybe I'm getting somewhere. "Give me your phone number. I want to call you."

No, I don't, but I do want to win. She's wavering. I can tell. To keep from scaring her off, I bury my excitement. Nothing sends me higher than winning.

"I'll tell you what." She flashes a smile that drips with a mixture of allure and wickedness. "If you can walk me to my car and open the door for me, I'll give you my number."

Can.

She steps into the humid night and skips down the sidewalk to the back parking lot. I wouldn't have pegged this girl as a skipper. Skip she does and I follow, tasting the sweet victory.

Victory doesn't last long. I freeze midstep on the sidewalk. Before she can prance past the yellow lines confining an old rusty car, two menacing guys climb out and neither appears happy.

"Something I can do for you, man?" the taller one asks. Tattoos run the length of his arms.

"Nope." I shove my hands in my pockets and relax my stance. I have no intention of getting into a fight, especially when I'm outnumbered.

Tattoo Guy crosses the parking lot, and he'd probably keep coming if it wasn't for the other guy with hair covering his eyes. He stops right in front of Tattoo Guy, halting his progress, but his posture suggests he'd also fight for kicks. "Is there a problem, Beth?"

Beth. Hard to believe this hard-core girl could have such a delicate name. As if reading my thoughts, her lips slide into an evil smirk. "Not anymore," she answers as she jumps into the front seat of the car.

Both guys walk to their car while keeping an eye on me, as if I'm stupid enough to jump them from behind. The engine roars to life and the car vibrates like duct tape holds it together.

In no hurry to go inside and explain to my friends how I lost, I stay on the sidewalk. The car slowly drives by and Beth presses her palm against the passenger window. Written in black marker is the word signaling my defeat: *can't*.

BETH

THERE'S NOTHING BETTER than the feeling of floating. Weightless in warmth. Comforter-out-of-the-dryer warmth. The warmth of a strong hand against my face, running through my hair. If only life could be like this...forever.

I could do forever here, in the basement of my aunt's house. All walls. No windows. The outside kept outside. The people I love inside.

Noah—his hair hiding his eyes, keeping the world from seeing his soul.

Isaiah—a sleeve of beautiful tattoos that frightens the normal and entices the free.

Me—the poet in my mind when I'm high.

I came to this house for safety. They came because the foster care system ran out of homes. We stayed because we were stray pieces of other puzzles, tired of never fitting.

One year ago, Isaiah and Noah bought the couch, the king-size mattress, and the TV from the Goodwill. Shit thrown away by somebody else. By yanking it down a flight of stairs into the depths of the earth, they made us a home. They gave me a family.

"I wore ribbons," I say. My own voice sounds bizarre. Echoing. Far away. And I speak again so I can hear the strangeness. "Lots of them."

"I love it when she does this," Isaiah says to Noah. The three of us relax on the bed. Finishing another beer, Noah sits at the end with his back propped against the wall. Isaiah and I touch. We only touch when we're high or drunk or both. We can because it doesn't count then. Nothing counts when you feel weightless.

Isaiah runs his hand through my hair again. The gentle tug urges me to close my eyes and sleep forever. Bliss. This is bliss.

"What colors?" The normal rough edges of Isaiah's tone disappear, leaving smooth deepness.

"Pink."

"And?"

"Dresses. I loved dresses."

It feels as if I'm turning my head through sand in order to look at him. My head rests on his stomach and I smile when the heat of his skin radiates past his T-shirt onto my cheek. Or maybe I'm smiling because it's Isaiah and only he can make me smile.

I love his dark hair, shaved close to his scalp. I love his kind gray eyes. I love the earrings in both ears. I love...that he's hot. Hot when he's high. I giggle. He's tragically hot when he's sober. I should write that down.

"Do you want a dress, Beth?" Isaiah asks. He never teases me when I remember my childhood. In fact, it's one of the few times he asks endless questions.

"Would you buy me one?" I don't know why, but the thought lightens my heart. The teeny sober part of my brain reminds me I don't wear dresses, that I spurned ribbons. The rest of my mind, lost in a haze of pot, enjoys the game—the prospect of a life with dresses and ribbons and someone willing to make my wildest dreams come true.

"Yes," he answers without hesitating.

The muscles around my mouth become heavy and the rest of my body, including my heart, follows suit. No. I'm not ready for the comedown. I close my eyes and will it to go away.

"She's baked." Noah's not baked and part of me resents him for it. He quit pot and being carefree when he graduated, and he's taking Isaiah with him. "We waited too long."

"No, it's perfect." Isaiah moves and places my head on something soft and fluffy. He gave me a pillow. Isaiah always takes care of me.

"Beth?" His warm breath drifts near my ear.

"Yes." It's a groggy whisper.

"Move in with us."

Last spring, Noah graduated from high school and the foster system. He's moving out and Isaiah's going with him, even though Isaiah can't officially leave foster care until he graduates next year and turns eighteen. My aunt doesn't care where Isaiah lives as long as she keeps receiving the checks from the state.

I try to shake my head no, but it doesn't work too well in sand.

"The two of us talked and you can have a bedroom and we'll share the other one."

They've been at this for weeks, trying to convince me to leave with them. But ha! Even stoned I can foil their plans. I flutter my eyes open. "Won't work. You need privacy for sex."

Noah chuckles. "We have a couch."

"I'm still in high school."

"So's Isaiah. In case you didn't notice, you're both seniors this year."

Smart-ass. I glare at Noah. He merely sips his beer.

Isaiah continues, "How else are you going to get to school? You gonna ride the bus?"

Hell no. "You're going to get your sorry ass up early to pick me up."

"You know I will," he murmurs, and I find a hint of my bliss again.

"Why won't you move in with us?" Noah asks.

His direct question sobers me up. *Because,* I scream in my mind. I flip onto my side and curl into a ball. Seconds later something soft covers my body. The blanket tucked right underneath my chin.

"Now, she's done," says Isaiah.

My ass vibrates. I stretch before reaching into my back pocket for my cell.

For a second, I wonder if pretty boy from Taco Bell somehow managed to score my number. I dreamed of him—Taco Bell Boy. He stood close to me, looking all arrogant and gorgeous with his mop of sandy-blond hair and light brown eyes. This time he wasn't trying to play me by getting my number. He was smiling at me like I actually mattered.

As I said—just a dream.

The image fades when I check the time and the caller ID on my cell: 3:00 a.m. and The Last Stop bar. Fuck. Wishing I never sobered up, I accept the call. "Hold on."

Isaiah's asleep beside me, his arm haphazardly thrown

over my stomach. Gently lifting it, I squeeze out from underneath. Noah's passed out on the couch, with his girlfriend, Echo, pulled tight against him. Shit, when did she get back in town?

Quietly, I climb the stairs, enter the kitchen, and shut the door to the basement. "Yeah."

"Your mother's causing problems again," says a pissed-off male voice. Unfortunately, I know this voice: Denny. Bartender/owner of The Last Stop.

"Have you cut her off?"

"I can't stop guys from buying her drinks. Look, kid, you pay me to call you before I call the police or bounce her out to the curb. You've got fifteen minutes to drag her ass out."

He hangs up. Denny really needs to work on his conversational skills.

I walk the two blocks to the strip mall, which boasts all the conveniences white trash can desire: a Laundromat, Dollar Store, liquor store, piss-ass market that accepts WIC and food stamps and sells stale bread and week-old meat, cigarette store, pawn shop, and biker bar. Oh, and a dilapidated lawyer's office in case you get caught shoplifting or holding up any of the above.

The other stores closed hours ago, placing the bars over their windows. Groups of men and women huddle around the scores of motorcycles that fill the parking lot. The stale stench of cigarettes and the sweet scent of cloves and pot mingle together in the hot summer air.

Denny and I both know he won't call the cops, but I can't risk it. Mom's been arrested twice and is on probation. And even if he doesn't call the cops, he'll kick her out. A burst of male laughter reminds me why that's not a good thing. It's not happy laughter or joyous or even sane. It's mean, has an edge, and craves someone's pain.

Mom thrives on sick men. I don't get it. Don't have to. I just clean up the mess.

The dull bulbs hanging over the pool tables, the running red-neon lights over the bar, and the two televisions hanging on the wall create the bar's only light. The sign on the door states two things: no one under the age of twenty-one and no gang colors. Even in the dimness, I can see neither rule applies. Most of the men wear jackets with their motorcycle gang emblem clearly in sight, and half the girls hanging on those men are underage.

I push between two men to where Denny serves drinks at the bar. "Where is she?"

Denny, in his typical red flannel, has his back to me and pours vodka into shot glasses. He won't talk and pour at the same time—at least to me.

I force my body to stay stoically still when a hand squeezes my ass and a guy reeking with BO leans into me. "Wanna drink?"

"Fuck off, dickhead."

He laughs and squeezes again. I focus on the rainbow of liquor bottles lined up behind the bar, pretending I'm someplace else. Someone else. "Hand off my ass or I'll rip off your balls."

Denny blocks my view of the bottles and slides a beer to the guy seconds away from losing his manhood. "Jailbait."

Dickhead wanders from the bar as Denny nods toward the back. "Where she's always at."

"Thanks."

I draw stares and snickers as I walk past. Most of the laughter belongs to regulars. They know why I'm here. I see the judgment in their eyes. The amusement. The pity. Damn hypocrites.

I walk with my head high, shoulders squared. I'm better than them. No matter the whispers and taunts they throw out. Fuck them. Fuck them all.

Most everyone in the back room hovers over a poker game near the front, leaving the rest of the room empty. The door to the alley hangs wide-open. I can see Mom's apartment complex and her front door from here. Convenient.

Mom sits at a small round table in the corner. Two bottles of whiskey and a shot glass sit beside her. She rubs her cheek, then pulls her hand away. Inside of me, anger erupts.

He hit her. Again. Her cheek is red. Blotchy. The skin underneath the eye already swelling. This is the reason why I can't move in with Noah and Isaiah. The reason I can't leave. I need to be two blocks from Mom.

"Elisabeth." Mom slurs the *s* and drunkenly waves me over. She picks up a whiskey bottle and tips it over the general area of the shot glass, but nothing comes out. Which is good because she'd miss the glass by an inch.

I go to her, take the bottle, and set it on the table beside us. "It's empty."

"Oh." She blinks her hollow blue eyes. "Be a good girl and go get me another."

"I'm seventeen."

"Then get you something too."

"Let's go, Mom."

Mom smoothes her blond hair with a shaky hand and glances around as if she just woke from a dream. "He hit me."

"I know."

"I hit him back."

Don't doubt she hit him first. "We've gotta go."

"I don't blame you."

That statement hits me in ways a man can't. I release a long breath and search for a way to ease the sting of her words, but I fail. I pick up the other bottle, grateful for the pitiful amount remaining, pour a shot, and swig it down. Then pour another, pushing it toward her. "Yes, you do."

Mom stares at the drink before letting her middle-aged fingers trace the rim of the shot glass. Her nails are bitten to the quick. The cuticles grown over. The skin surrounding the nails is dry and cracked. I wonder if my mom was ever pretty.

She throws her head back as she drinks. "You're right. I do. Your father would never have left if it wasn't for you."

"I know." The burn from the whiskey suppresses the pain of the memory. "Let's go."

"He loved me."

"I know."

"What you did...it forced him to leave."

"I know."

"You ruined my life."

"I know."

She begins to cry. It's the drunk cry. The type where it all comes out—the tears, the snot, the spit, the horrible truth you should never tell another soul. "I hate you."

I flinch. Swallow. And remind myself to inhale. "I know."

Mom grabs my hand. I don't pull away. I don't grab her in return. I let her do what she must. We've been down this road several times.

"I'm sorry, baby." Mom wipes her nose with the bare skin

of her forearm. "I didn't mean it. I love you. You know I do. Don't leave me alone. Okay?"

"Okay." What else can I say? She's my mom. My mom.

Her fingers draw circles on the back of my hand and she refuses eye contact. "Stay with me tonight?"

This is where Isaiah drew the line. Actually, he drew the line further back, forcing me to promise I'd stay away from her altogether after her boyfriend beat the shit out of me. I've kind of kept the promise by moving in with my aunt. But someone has to take care of my mom—make sure she eats, has food, pays her bills. It is, after all, my fault Dad left. "Let's get you home."

Mom smiles, not noticing I haven't answered. Sometimes, at night, I dream of her smiling. She was happy when Dad lived with us. Then I ruined her happiness.

Her knees wobble when she stands, but Mom can walk. It's a good night.

"Where are you going?" I ask when she steps in the direction of the bar.

"To pay my tab."

Impressive. She has money. "I'll do it. Stay right here and I'll walk you home."

Instead of handing me cash, Mom leans against the back door. Great. Now I'm left with the tab. At least Taco Bell Boy bought me food and I have something to give Denny.

I push people in my quest to reach the bar, and Denny grimaces when he spots me. "Get her out, kid."

"She's out. What's her tab?"

"Already paid."

Ice runs in my veins. "When?"

"Just now."

No. "By who?"

He won't meet my eyes. "Who do you think?"

Shit. I'm falling over myself, stumbling over people, yanking them out of my way. He hit her once. He'll do it again. I run full force out the back door into the alley and see nothing. Nothing in the dark shadows. Nothing in the streetlights. Crickets chirp in surround sound. "Mom?"

Glass breaks. Glass breaks again. Horrible shrieks echo from the front of Mom's apartment complex. God, he's killing her. I know it.

My heart pounds against my rib cage, making it difficult to breathe. Everything shakes—my hands, my legs. The vision of what I'll see when I reach the parking lot eats at my soul: Mom in a bloody pulp and her asshole boyfriend standing over her. Tears burn my eyes and I trip as I round the corner of the building, scraping my palms on the blacktop. I don't care. I need to find her. My mom...

My mom swings a baseball bat and shatters the back window of a shitty El Camino.

"What...what are you doing?" And where did she score a baseball bat?

"He." She swings the bat and breaks more glass. "Cheated."

I blink, unsure if I want to hug her or kill her. "Then break up with him."

"You crazy ass bitch!" From the gap between the two apartment buildings, Mom's boyfriend flies toward her and smacks her face with an open palm. The slap of his hand across her cheek vibrates against my skin. The baseball bat falls from her hands and bounces three times, tip to bottom, against the blacktop. Each hollow crack of the wood heightens my senses. It settles on the ground and rolls toward my feet.

He yells at her. All curses, but his words blend into a buzzing noise in my head. He hit me last year. He hits Mom. He won't hit either one of us again.

He raises his hand. Mom throws out her arms to protect her face as she kneels in front of him. I grab the bat. Take two steps. Swing it behind my shoulder and...

"Police! Drop the bat! Get on the ground!" Three uniformed officers surround us. Damn. My heart pounds hard against my chest. I should have thought of this, but I didn't, and the mistake will cost me. The cops patrol the complex regularly.

The asshole points at me. "She did it. That crazy ass girl took out my car. Her mom and I, we tried to stop it, but then she went nuts!"

"Drop the bat! Hands on your head."

Dazed from his blatant lie, I forgot I still held it. The wooden grip feels rough against my hands. I drop it and listen to the same hollow thumping as it once again bounces on the ground. Placing my hands behind my head, I stare down at my mom. Waiting. Waiting for her to explain. Waiting for her to defend us.

Mom stays on her knees in front of the asshole. She subtly shakes her head and mouths the word *please* to me.

Please? Please what? I widen my eyes, begging for her to explain.

She mouths one more word: *probation.*

An officer kicks the bat from us and pats me down. "What happened?"

"I did it," I tell him. "I destroyed the car."

RYAN

SWEAT DRIPS FROM MY SCALP and slithers down my forehead, forcing me to wipe my brow before shoving the cap back on. The afternoon sun beats down on me as if I'm simmering in hell's roasting pan. August games are the worst.

My hands sweat. I don't care about my left hand—the one wearing the glove. It's the throwing hand I rub repeatedly on my pant leg. My heart pounds in my ears and I fight off a wave of dizziness. The smell of burnt popcorn and hot dogs drifts from the concession stand, and my stomach cramps. I stayed out too late last night.

Taking a look at the scoreboard, I watch as the temperature rises from ninety-five degrees to ninety-six. Heat index has to be over one hundred. In theory, the moment the index hits one-o-five, the umps should call the game. In theory.

It wouldn't matter if the temperature was below zero. My stomach would still cramp. My hands would still sweat. The pressure—it builds continually, twisting my insides to the point of implosion.

"Let's go, Ry!" Chris, our shortstop, yells from between second and third.

His lone battle cry instigates calls from the rest of the team—those on the field and those sitting on the bench. I shouldn't say *sitting*. Everyone in the dugout stands with their fingers clenched around the fence.

Bottom of the seventh, we're up by one run, two outs, and I screwed up and pitched a runner to first. Damn curveball. I've thrown one strike and two balls with the current batter. No more room for error. Two more strikes and the game's over. Two more balls and I walk a batter, giving the other team a runner in scoring position.

The crowd joins in. They clap, whistle, and cheer. No one louder than Dad.

Grasping the ball tightly, I take a deep breath, wrap my right arm behind my back, and lean forward to read Logan's signal. The stress of this next pitch hangs on me. Everyone wants this game done. No one more than me.

I don't lose.

Logan crouches into position behind the batter and does something unexpected. He pulls his catcher's mask onto the top of his head, places his hand between his legs, and flips me off.

Damn bastard.

Logan flaunts a grin and his reminder causes my shoulders to relax. It's only the first game of the fall season. A scrimmage game at that. I nod and he slides his mask over his face and flashes me the peace sign twice.

Fastball it is.

I glance over my shoulder toward first. The runner's taken a lead in his hunt for second, but not enough to chance a steal. I cock my arm back and throw with a rush of power and adrenaline. My heart thumps twice at the sweet sound of the ball smacking into Logan's glove and the words *Strike two* falling out of the umpire's mouth.

Logan fires the ball back and I waste no time preparing for the next pitch. This will be it. My team can go home— victorious.

Logan holds his pinkie and ring fingers together. I shake my head. I want to close this out and a fastball will do it, not a curve. Logan hesitates before showing me two peace signs. That's my boy. He knows I can bring on the heat.

Keeping his hand between his legs, he pauses, then points away from the batter, telling me that my fastballs have been straying outside. I nod. An understanding to keep place- ment in mind with my speed. The ball flies out of my hand, punches Logan's glove right in the middle, and the umpire shouts, "Ball!"

I stop breathing. That was a strike.

The fence rattles as my teammates bang on it, screaming at the injustice. Shouting at the umpire, Coach stands on the verge of no-man's-land between the dugout and the field. My friends on the field whistle at the bad call. The crowd mur- murs and boos. In the bleachers, with her head down and lost in prayer, Mom grasps the pearls that hang around her neck.

Dammit. I yank hard on the bill of my hat, trying to calm the blood racing in my veins. Bad calls suck, but they happen. I've got one more shot to close this out. One more...

"That was a strike." Dad steps off the bleachers and heads to the fence right behind the umpire. The players and the crowd fall silent. Dad demands fairness. Well, his version of fair.

"Get back in the stands, Mr. Stone," the ump says. Every- one in this town knows Dad.

"I'll return to my seat when we have an ump that can call fair. You've been calling bad this entire game." Even though he said it loud enough for the entire park to hear, he never raised his voice. Dad's a commanding man and someone this entire town admires.

From behind the fence, Dad towers over the short, fat ump and waits for someone to make right what he views as a wrong. We're carbon copies of each other, my dad and I. Sandy hair and brown eyes. Long legs. All shoulders and upper arms. Grandma said people like Dad and me were built for hard labor. Dad said we were built for baseball.

My coach steps onto the field along with the coach from the other team. I agree. The ump's been calling bad, on both sides, but I find it ironic that no one had the guts to say anything until Dad declared war.

"Your dad's the man." Chris walks onto the pitcher's mound.

"Yeah." The man. I glance over to Mom again and at the empty space where my older brother, Mark, used to sit. Mark's absence stings more than I thought it would. I extend my glove out to Logan, who has inched away from the four men discussing the fairness of the calls. He automatically pitches the ball back.

Chris scans the crowd. "Notice who came to the game?"

I don't bother looking. Lacy always attends Chris's games.

"Gwen," he says with a canary-ate-the-cat grin. "Lacy heard she's into you again."

I react without thinking and turn my head to search the bleachers for her. For two years, Gwen and baseball were my entire life. The breeze blows through Gwen's long blond hair and, as if she could sense my stare, she looks at me and smiles. Last year, I loved that smile. A smile once reserved for me. Several months have passed since that time. Mom still loves her. I'm not sure how I feel anymore. A guy scales the bleachers and puts his arm around her. Yeah, rub it in, asshole. I'm well aware Gwen and I are done.

"Play ball!" The voice of a new ump booms from the batter's box. The old ump shakes hands with Dad on the other side of the fence. As I said, Dad believes in fairness and also thinks justice should be served with a man's pride still intact. Well, for every man that isn't my brother.

Everyone off the field claps and watches my father return to his seat. Some people extend their hands to him. Others pat his back. Off the field, Dad's the leader of this community. On the field, I'm the man.

Out of the batter's box, the batter takes a few practice swings. Two strikes. Three balls. And the kid knows I can bring heat. I whistle and gesture for Logan.

Beside me, Chris laughs. He knows I'm up to no good. Logan approaches with his catcher's mask on top of his head. "What's up, boss man?"

"Talk to me."

This is what a great catcher does. "The batter was sluggish, but he's had a break, which means he'll give it everything he has. Your fast has been wandering outside and he knows it."

I roll the ball in my fingers. "He'll be expecting fast?"

"If I was him, I'd expect you to throw fast," says Chris.

I shrug my shoulder and the muscles yell in protest. "Let's do a changeup. He'll read it as fast and won't have enough time to readjust."

A smile slides across Chris's face and he places his glove over his mouth. "You're popping him out."

"We're popping him out," I repeat, hiding my own lips with my glove.

I turn toward the field and whistle to get everyone's attention. Chris goes back to short, slides his open hand across his chest, and taps his left arm with his right hand twice. The center fielder runs up, and our second baseman passes on the message. By the time I face the batter, Logan's already sent the message to first and third.

Logan flips his mask over his face, crouches into position, and holds his glove out for the pitch. Yeah, I'm closing this out.

"See you tonight, dawg." Chris kicks my foot as he walks past. He cradles his bat bag in one hand and Lacy's hand in the other. Chris and I met Lacy when our schools combined in sixth grade. I liked her the day she skinned her knee playing football with the boys. Chris fell in love with her the day she pushed him on the playground after he tagged her out in baseball. They've been a couple since sophomore year—the year he grew a pair and finally asked her out.

Lacy pulls a rubber band off her wrist and twists her brown hair into a messy bun. I love that she isn't a girly girl. In order to keep up with me, Chris, and Logan, a girl has to have thick skin. Don't get me wrong—she's hot as hell, but Lacy doesn't give a damn what others think of her. "We're going to the party tonight. I want conversation and people and dancing. There is more to life than batting cages and dares."

With our fingers frozen on unlacing our cleats, Logan and

I snap up our heads. Chris's face blanches. "That's sacrilegious, Lace. Take it back."

Next to me, Logan shoves his feet into his Nikes and tosses his cleats into his bag. "You don't know the thrill of winning a good dare."

"Dares aren't fun," she says, the reprimand thick in her tone. "They're crazy. You set my car on fire."

Logan holds up his hand. "I opened the window in time. In my defense, the upholstery is barely singed."

Chris and I chuckle at the memory of Lacy screaming as she was doing forty on a curve. The short story: a hamburger wrapper, a lighter, a stopwatch, and a dare. Logan accidentally dropped the blazing wrapper and it rolled under Lacy's seat. One patented I'll-kick-you-until-you-drop glare from Lacy shuts us both up. "I wish you'd get a girlfriend so she can drive your insane ass around."

"I can't." Logan waggles his eyebrows. "I'm Ryan's wingman."

"Wingman." She spits the word, then points a sparkly fingernail at both me and Logan, but I don't miss how it lingers on me. "One of you needs to find a girl and commit. I'm tired of this testosterone bull."

Lacy hates the string of girls I've dated over the summer. She's terrified I'll influence Chris to drop her, though she should know better. Chris reveres her as his own personal religion.

"You didn't approve of the one I committed to last time," I say. "Why should I try again?"

"Because you can do better than evil."

I drop my tone. "Gwen's not evil." Gwen and I broke up, but there's no reason to talk trash about her.

"Speak of the devil," mumbles Logan.

"Hi, Ryan." I turn my head to witness Gwen in all her glory. A blue cotton dress swishes around her tanned legs, and she wears a new-to-me pair of cowboy boots. Hand-curled ringlets bounce at the ends of her long blond hair. Surrounded by her three best girlfriends, she floats right past, but keeps her green eyes locked on me.

"Gwen," I say in return. Reaching the concession stand, she sweeps her hair over her shoulder as she refocuses her attention. I keep staring, trying to remember why we broke up.

"Drama!" Lacy purposely blocks my view of Gwen's ass. "She was nothing but drama. Remember? You said, 'Lacy, there's nothing real about her,' and I said, 'I know,' and I happily threw an 'I told you so' in your face. Then you said, 'Don't let me go back to her,' and I said, 'Can I rip off your balls if you attempt it,' and you said..."

"'No.'" I said no because Lacy would actually do it, and I prefer my balls attached, but I did ask her to remind me of that conversation if I became weak. Logan and I should ask some girls to the movies next weekend. Hell, if Skater Girl had given me her number, I might even have considered calling her. God knows she was sexy as hell and when it comes to Gwen, a distraction always helps.

"Come on, Logan," says Chris. "I'll give you a ride home."

Near the dugout, Dad wraps an arm around Mom as the two of them chat with Coach and a man dressed in a polo shirt and khakis. I wonder if anyone else notices how Mom leans slightly away from Dad's body. Probably not. Mom's in homecoming-court mode, all smiles and laughs.

From over his shoulder, Dad indicates I should join them by giving me one of his rare I'm-proud-of-you smiles. It makes me unbalanced. Yeah, we won, but we win a lot. It's what state champions do. Why the outpouring of pride now?

As I said, Dad and I are clones, except for the age and the skin. Years of rain, sun, heat, and cold have seasoned his face. Owning a construction company requires a lot of time in the elements. "Ryan, this is Mr. Davis."

Mr. Davis and I both offer our hands at the same time. He's tall, thin, and possibly my father's age, except Mr. Davis doesn't look weathered. "Call me Rob. Congratulations on a well-played game. You have a hell of a fastball."

"Thank you, sir." I've heard it before. Mom tells everyone God gave me a gift, and while I'm not sure what I think of that, I won't deny I've enjoyed the ride. Too bad Dad and I couldn't garner any interest at pro baseball tryouts.

I'm used to meetings and introductions. Because Dad owns his own company and has a seat on the city council, he's into networking. Don't get me wrong—Dad's not the power-hungry sort. He declined running for mayor several times, even though my mom has been begging him to consider it for years. He's just real into the community.

Rob tilts his head to the field. "Do you mind throwing a couple for me?"

Mom, Dad, and Coach share knowing grins and I feel like someone told a joke and left me out of the punch line. Or maybe I am the punch line. "Sure."

Rob pulls a radar gun and a business card out of the bag. He keeps the radar gun in his left hand and hands me the card. "I came here today to watch a player from the other team. Didn't see what I was looking for with him, but I think I found something promising with you."

Dad claps my back, and his public showing of affection

has me looking at him. Dad's not a touchy guy. My family—we aren't like that. I grip the card in my hand, and it takes everything I've got not to swear in shock in front of my mother. The man heading to the area behind home plate is Rob Davis, scout for the Cincinnati Reds.

"Told you that spring tryouts weren't the end of it." Dad motions for me to follow Rob. "Go blow him away."

BETH

THE OLDER PRISON GUARD, the nice one, walks beside me. He didn't put the cuffs on supertight like the other dickhead guard. He isn't in my face, trying to scare the shit out of me. He's not trying to reenact a scene from *Cops*. He just walks next to me, ignoring my existence.

I'm all for silence after listening to a girl come down from a bad acid trip last night.

Maybe it was today.

I don't have a clue what time of day it is.

They gave me breakfast.

They discussed lunch.

It must be morning. Maybe midday.

The guard opens the door to what I can only describe as an interrogation room. Other than the holding cell I've shared with the fifteen-year-old who's way too strung out for my taste, this is where I've spent the majority of my time since they arrested me for destruction of property. The guard relaxes his back against the wall. I sit at the table.

I need a cigarette.

Bad.

Unbelievably bad.

Like I would rip off my own arm if I could get one drag.

"What are you coming down from?" The guard stares at my fingers.

I stop tapping the table. "Nicotine."

"That's rough," he says. "I never kicked it."

"Yeah. It fucking blows."

The police officer who arrested me last night—this morning—steps into the room. "She speaks."

Yeah. Didn't mean to. I clamp my mouth shut. Last night, this morning—who the hell knows—I managed to keep silent when they grilled me on my mom, my home life, my mom's boyfriend. I refused to talk, refused to say one word, because if I did, I could have said the wrong thing and sent my mom to jail. There's no way I could live with that.

I have no idea what happened to her or her boyfriend after they snapped the handcuffs on my wrist and sat me in the back of the squad car. If God's hearing prayers from me, then maybe Mom's in the clear and the asshole's sharing a urinal with the other felons-of-the-month.

The officer resembles a twenty-year-old Johnny Depp, and he smells clean—soap with a hint of coffee. He's not the one who tried to talk to me last night. Just the guy that arrested me. He settles into the seat across from me and the guard leaves.

"I'm Officer Monroe."

I glare at the table.

Officer Monroe reaches over, unlocks the cuffs, and slides them to his side of the table. "Why don't you tell me what really happened last night?"

Just one drag. Oh God, it'd be better than a deep kiss from

a really hot guy. But I'm not kissing a hot guy and I don't have a cigarette because I'm currently being questioned in purgatory.

"Your mom's boyfriend, Trent—we know he's bad news, but he's smart. We've never gotten enough to put him away. Maybe you can help us and yourself. Help us put him in jail, then he'll be away from you and your mom."

I agree—he's Satan. Other than the fact that he's a washed-up has-been of a football player who traded tackling men on the field for beating the shit out of women though, I have nothing to tell them beyond rumors I've heard on the street. The cops who walk the south-side beat are well aware of our bedtime stories regarding The Asshole Known as Trent. The tantalizing tidbit that he hits me and Mom could get us a flimsy piece of paper with the words *Emergency Protection Order* on the header, but domestic violence offenders rarely sit inside jail cells for long, plus Trent burns EPOs and puppies for fun.

Even before my mother got involved with Trent, the police were after him, but he's the walking, talking real-life version of an oil spill—impossible to pick up once he's been released. Helping the police will only bring the ooze and his sickening wrath quicker to our doorstep.

"He lives in the same apartment complex as your mom, right? Wouldn't it be nice to live with her again and not have to worry about him?"

Having no idea how he knows I don't live with my mom, I fight hard not to glance at him. Refusing to indicate he's right.

"We didn't even know he was dating your mom. He, uh, sees other women."

I keep from rolling my eyes. There's a shock.

"Elisabeth," he says after my nonresponse.

"Beth." I hate my given name. "My name is Beth."

"Beth, your one phone call has been standing in the lobby since five a.m."

Isaiah! My eyes flash to Officer Monroe's. The walls I built to protect myself crumble and fatigue sets in as the iciness I've clung to all night melts. Fear and hurt rush to take its place. I want Isaiah. I don't want to be here. I want to go home.

I blink, realizing the stinging sensation is tears. Wiping at my face, I try to find my strength—my resolve, but I only find a heavy emptiness. "When can I go home?"

Someone knocks. Officer Monroe cracks the door open and exchanges a few heated whispers before nodding. Seconds later, my aunt, an older and cleaner version of my mother, walks in. "Beth?"

Officer Monroe leaves, closing the door behind him.

Shirley comes straight to me. I stand and let her hug me. She smells like home: stale cigarettes and lavender fabric softener. I bury my face in my aunt's shoulder, wishing for nothing more than to lie in the bed in her basement for a week.

A cigarette is a close second.

"Where's Isaiah?" Though I'm grateful for my aunt, my heart was set on seeing my best friend.

"Outside. He called me the moment he heard from you." Shirley squeezes me before breaking our embrace. "What a mess."

"I know. Have you seen Mom?"

She nods, then leans in and whispers in my ear, "Your mom told me what really happened."

The muscles around my mouth tighten and I try to stop my lower lip from trembling. "What do I do?"

Shirley runs her hands up and down my arms. "Stick with your story. They brought Trent and your mom in for questioning. With you not talking, they couldn't find anything to arrest them on. Your mom's twitchy though. If you talk, they'll send her to jail for breaking probation and the destruction of property. She's scared of going to jail."

So am I, but Mom can't hack jail. "What's going to happen to me?"

Her arms drop to her sides and she places the table between us. It's only a few steps, but it creates a gap resembling a canyon. I turned seventeen last month. Before tonight, I felt like an adult: old and big. I don't feel so big anymore. Right now I feel small and very, very alone. "Shirley?"

"Your uncle and I don't have money for a lawyer. Isaiah and Noah, even that girl Noah brings around, they offered what they had, but your uncle and I got scared once the cops told us you took a bat to Trent. Then I had an idea."

My heart sinks as if someone yanked a trapdoor right below it. "What did you do?"

"I know you don't want anything to do with your dad's side, but his brother, Scott—he's a good man. Left that baseball team and became a businessman. He has a lawyer. A fancy one."

"Scott?" My mouth gapes. "How...what..." My breathing becomes shallow as I try to make sense of the insanity falling out of my aunt's lips. "Impossible. *He* left."

"He did," she says slowly. "But he moved back to his hometown last month and he called me to find you. He wanted you to go live with him and his wife, but we blew him off. Your mom talked to him when he got persistent and she told him you ran away."

My lip curls at the thought of him anywhere near me. "Good choice. So why involve Scott now? We don't need him. We can figure this out without him or his fancy lawyer."

"They said you were going to hit Trent with a bat," Shirley repeats as she wrings her hands together. "That's serious and I thought we needed help."

"No. Tell me you didn't." I'm in hell. Or pretty damn close.

"We would have respected your wishes about him, but then this happened and...I called him. Listen to me, he has a great life now. Lots of money and he wants you."

I start to laugh. Only it's not funny. It's not even close to funny. It's the saddest damn thing I've ever heard. I collapse into the seat and rest my head in my hands. "No, he doesn't."

"He got the charges dropped." Not a hint of happiness can be found in her voice.

I keep my face hidden, unable to look at her to see whatever truth she's been building toward. "What did you do?" I ask again.

Shirley kneels beside me and pitches her voice low. "When I called him, your uncle Scott went to your mom's apartment. He saw things he shouldn't have seen. Things that can hurt your mom."

I sway to the side as if I've been hit by a wave and the rushing sound of being sucked into the ocean whirls in my ears. My world is crashing around me. He went into my old room. Mom told me never to go in there after I left to live with Shirley. I never have. There are things even I don't want to know.

"He didn't tell the police," she says.

Shocked by her revelation, I peek at her through my fingers. "Really?"

Shirley's lips turn down and she scrunches her forehead. "Your mom had no choice. He walked into the station with his lawyer and made the demand—she either turned over custody of you to him, or he would tell the cops what he saw."

My aunt stares at me, her eyes bleak. "She signed over custody. He's your legal guardian now."

RYAN

THANKS TO THE SHOWERS at the community center, there's no need to head home. Clean and dressed in street clothes, I return to heaven.

Everyone has left the ballpark. The bleachers are empty. The concession stand closed. Kenny Chesney blares from the parking lot, meaning that Chris ignored me when I told him I'd catch up with him later. Chris is really good at three things—playing shortstop, loving his girl, and knowing what I need even when I don't know it myself.

At least most of the time.

From the community pool, little kids squeal in delight in time to the sounds of splashing and the bounce of the diving board. My brother, Mark, and I spent most of our summers swimming in that pool. The other part, we spent playing ball.

I stand on the pitcher's mound, except this time I'm in blue jeans and my favorite Reds T-shirt. The early evening sky fades from blue to orange-and-yellow. It's no longer a million degrees and the breeze shifts from the south to the north. This is my favorite part of the game—the time alone afterward.

The rush of winning and the knowledge I have a scout interested in me still linger in my blood. My lungs expand with clean oxygen and my muscles lose the tension that weighed me down during the game. I feel relaxed, at peace, and alive.

I stare at home plate and in my mind I see Logan crouched in position and the batter taking a practice swing. My fingers curl as if I'm clutching the ball. Logan calls for a curve; I accept, except this time I...

"I knew you'd be here." In her brown leather cowboy boots and blue dress, Gwen swings around the gate into the dugout.

"How?" I ask.

"You screwed up the curve." In one smooth motion, Gwen sits on the bench in the dugout and pats the wood beside her. She's playing a game. One I'll lose, but damn if my feet don't move toward her.

She looks good. Better than good. Beautiful. I ease down beside her as she tosses her blond ringlets behind her shoulder. "I remember you explaining the bases to me in this dugout. The best baseball conversation we ever had."

I lean forward and clasp my hands together. "Maybe you missed part of the conversation, because I wasn't explaining baseball."

Gwen flashes her bright smile. "I know, but I still enjoyed the demonstration."

Our eyes meet for a moment and I glance away when heat crawls along my cheeks. Gwen's the only girl I've had any real experience with. She used to blush when she talked about anything sexual, but she doesn't today. Nausea rolls through my gut. What new bases has Mike taught her?

"You seemed out of it during the game." The material of her dress swishes as she crosses her legs and angles her body toward mine. Our thighs touch now, creating heat. I wonder if she notices. "Are you having problems with your dad again?"

Gwen and I spent countless afternoons and evenings in this dugout. She always knew when Dad pushed me too far with the refs or that if I played like crap, I'd come here for clarity. "No."

"Then what's wrong?"

Everything. Mom and Dad fighting. Mark's absence. Me and pro ball. My friends/not-friends relationship with Gwen. For a moment, I think about telling her about Mark. Like the rest of the town, she remains blissfully unaware. I stare into her eyes and search for the girl I first met my freshman year. She wouldn't have messed with me then. Unfortunately, I've since become her favorite pastime. "I'm not in the mood to be played, Gwen."

Gwen raises her hand and twirls her hair around her finger. The glint of a large red-stoned ring strikes me like an ice pick. I shift so that our thighs no longer touch. "Mike gave you his class ring."

She drops her hand and covers it with the other, as if hiding the ring will make me forget it's there. "Yeah," she says quietly. "Last night."

"Congratulations." If I could have let more anger seep out I would have.

"What was I supposed to do?"

"I don't know." My voice rises with each word. "For starters, not be here screwing with me."

She ignores my comment as her own voice hardens. "Mike's a good guy and he's always around. He's not gone all the time and doesn't have a thousand commitments like you."

In all of our breaks and breakups, we never fought. Never raised our voices at each other. Before, I never considered yelling at Gwen; now it's the only thing I want to do. "I told you that I loved you. What else could you want?"

"To be first. Baseball always came first with you. God! How much clearer a picture did you need? I broke up with you at the beginning of your seasons."

I stand up, unable to sit next to her. How much clearer a picture? Obviously I needed detailed drawings with written directions. "You could have told me that's how you felt."

"Would it have changed anything? Would you have given up baseball?"

I curl my fingers into the metal of the fence and stare out at the field. How could she ask that type of question? Why would any girl ask a guy to give up something he loves? Gwen's playing games right now and I've decided to throw the pitch that ends the inning. "No."

I hear her sharp intake of air and the guilt of hurting her punches me in the stomach.

"It's just baseball," she rushes out.

How can I make her understand? Beyond the fence is a raised mound, a trail of dirt leading to four bases all surrounded by a groomed green field. It's the only place where I've felt like I belonged.

"Baseball isn't just a game. It's the smell of popcorn drifting in the air, the sight of bugs buzzing near the stadium lights, the roughness of the dirt beneath your cleats. It's the anticipation building in your chest as the anthem plays, the adrenaline rush when your bat cracks against the ball, and the surge of blood when the umpire shouts *strike* after you pitch. It's a team full of guys backing your every move, a bleacher full of people cheering you on. It's...life."

The clapping of hands to my right causes me to jump out of my skin. In pink hair and a matching swimsuit cover-up, my junior English teacher and soon-to-be senior English teacher stops the annoying sound and raises her hands to her chin as if in prayer. "That was poetry, Ryan."

Gwen and I share a what-the-hell look before returning our stares to Mrs. Rowe. "What are you doing here?" I ask.

She picks her beach bag up off the ground and swings it. "The pool closed for the night. I saw you and Ms. Gardner and decided to remind the two of you that your first personal essay is due to me on Monday."

Gwen's boots stamp on the ground as she switches legs again. A month ago, Mrs. Rowe tried to ruin everyone's vacation with a summer homework assignment.

"I'm so excited to read them," she continues. "I'm assuming you've completed yours?"

Haven't even started. "Yeah."

Gwen stands and readjusts Mike's ring on her finger. "I've gotta go." And she does. Without another word. I shove my hands in my pockets and rock on my feet, waiting for Mrs. Rowe to follow Gwen's lead. I've got a ritual to complete.

Obviously having no intention of leaving, Mrs. Rowe leans her shoulder against the dugout entrance. "I wasn't kidding about what you said, Ryan. You showed a lot of talent in my class last year. Between that and what I just heard, I'd say you have the voice of a writer."

I snort a laugh. Sure, that class was more interesting than math, but... "I'm a ballplayer."

"Yes, and from what I hear, a fine one, but it doesn't mean you can't be both."

Mrs. Rowe is always looking for a book convert. She even started a literary club at school last year. My name isn't on that roster. "I've got a friend waiting for me."

She glances over her shoulder toward Chris's truck. "Please tell Mr. Jones that his paper is also due on Monday."

"Sure."

Again I wait for her to leave. Again she doesn't. She just stands there. Uncomfortable, I mumble a goodbye and head for the parking lot.

I try to shake off the irritating itch embedded in my neck, but I can't. That moment on the mound is hallowed ground. A need. A must. My mother calls it a superstition. I'll call it whatever she wants, but in order for me to win the next game, I have to stand on that mound again—by myself—and figure out the mistake I made with my curveball.

If not, it means bad mojo. For the team. For my pitch. For my life.

With his head tilted back and eyes closed, Chris sits in his old black Ford. His door hangs wide-open. Chris worked his ass off for that truck. He plowed his granddaddy's cornfield this summer in return for a leaky truck that rolled off the line when we were seven.

"I told you to head home."

He keeps his eyes closed. "I told you to let the bad throw go."

"I did." We both know I didn't.

Chris comes to life, closes the door, and turns over the motor. "Hop in. We've got a party to go to that will make you forget."

"I've got a ride." I motion to my Jeep, parked next to his truck.

"My goal is to make sure you ain't gonna be fit to drive home." He revs the engine to keep it from stalling out. "Let's go."

BETH

OFFICER MONROE PUSHES OFF the wall the moment I slip out of the girls' bathroom. "Beth."

I don't want to talk to him, but I'm not real giddy for the long-lost uncle reunion either. I pause, folding my arms over my chest. "I thought I was free."

"You are." Officer Monroe has clearly mastered the Johnny Depp puppy-dog eyes. "When you're ready to tell me what happened last night, I want you to call." He holds out a card.

Never going to happen. I would rather die than send Mom to jail. I brush past him and walk into the lobby. Hurting my eyes, the sun glares through the windows and the glass doors. I blink away the brightness and spot Isaiah, Noah, and Echo. Isaiah leaps to his feet, but Noah puts a hand on his shoulder and whispers something to him, nodding to the left. Isaiah stays still. His steely-gray eyes implore me to come to him. I want to. More than anything.

Two people cross in front of Isaiah, and pain slices my chest. It's my mom. Like some sort of deranged baby monkey, she clings to her asshole boyfriend. Her eyes are desperate. She sucks her cheeks in as if she's trying to hold back tears.

That bastard has engulfed her in his disgusting life. I swear to God, I'm going to drag her back out.

Trent yanks her out the door. *It's not over, asshole. Not even close.*

I'm about to step toward Isaiah when I hear it. "Hello, Elisabeth." A shiver snakes down my spine. That voice reminds me of my father.

I turn to face the man who's hell-bent on destroying my life. He resembles my father in looks as well: tall, dark brown hair, blue eyes. The main difference is that Scott's built like an athlete, whereas my father had the body mass of a meth head.

"Leave me alone."

He gives Isaiah the judgmental once-over. "I think you've been left alone for too long."

"Don't pretend to care. I know your promises are worth shit."

"Why don't we get out of here, now that you're free to go. We can talk at home."

Scott puts a hand on my arm and is unmoved when I jerk away. "I'm not going anywhere with you."

"Yes," he says in an annoyingly even tone. "You are."

The muscles in my back tense as if I'm a cat arching its back to hiss. "Did you just tell me what to do?"

Fingers wrap around my wrist and gently pull me to the left. Isaiah hovers over me and speaks in a hushed tone. "Do you need a reminder you're in a police station?"

I sneak a peek and notice Officer Monroe and another cop watching our dysfunctional family reunion. My uncle regards Isaiah and me with interest, but keeps his distance.

My body is nothing but anger. Rage. It beats at my lungs,

wreaks havoc with my blood. And Isaiah is standing here telling me to rein it in? I have to let it go because it's consuming me. "What do you want me to do?"

Isaiah does something he's never done sober. He touches his hand to my cheek. His palm feels warm, strong, and safe. I lean into it as the anger drains from his simple touch. Part of me craves that anger. I don't care for the frightening emptiness left behind.

"Listen to me," he whispers. "Go with him."

"But—"

"I swear to God I'm going to take care of you, but I can't do it right here. Go with him and wait for me. Do you understand?"

I nod as I finally comprehend what he's attempting to tell me without saying the words. He's going to come for me. A shimmer of hope breaks through the emptiness and I fall into the safety of Isaiah's protective arms, our bodies pressed tight to one another.

RYAN

IN THE BACK FIELD that borders three farms, a field party rages without me, Logan, and Chris. Parties are great. They have girls, girls who drink beer, dancing, girls who like dancing, and guys who hate dancing but do it anyway in the hope of laying the girls who drink beer.

Lacy's in the mood to dance, Chris is in the mood to avoid dancing, I'm still burnt from Skater Girl last night, and Logan's always game for the stupid and insane. Ten minutes into the party, Lacy was dancing and the three of us took on a dare. Actually, I took on a dare. I lost last night and I don't lose. Chris and Logan are along for the ride.

"You can't pull this one off." Chris walks beside me as we head toward the cars parked neatly in a line. The full moon gives the field a silver glow and the scent of bonfire smoke hangs in the air.

"That's because you have no imagination." Thankfully, I have plenty and I know a few guys who get a kick out of screwing with friends.

"This is going to be sweet," Logan says when I change

course and head toward a group of defensive linemen enjoying their own private party.

Tim Richardson owns a mammoth-size, ozone-killing truck, which is good, because the four guys sitting on lawn chairs on the back of it easily weigh 275 pounds each. Tim liberates a can of beer from his cooler and tosses it to me. "What's going on, Ry?"

"Nothing." I put the cold can on the tailgate. No drinking for me. I've got business to take care of. "Not in the mood for the party?"

His truck is one of the few that can make it over the hill into the back field. "A girl over there is pissed at me," Tim mutters. "Anytime I go near her, she won't keep her mouth shut."

Logan snorts and Chris smacks him on the back of the head. *Pissed* would be an understatement. Rumor at school said Tim's ex-girl caught him making out with her twin sister. Tim throws a warning glare at Logan before focusing on me. "How's your brother? The team's ticked at him. He promised he'd help with summer practice while he was home from college."

Hating these kinds of questions, I shift my stance and shove my hands in my pockets. Dad made it clear that we tell no one what happened with Mark. "He's been busy." Before Tim has a chance to probe further, I switch to the problem at hand. "How would you guys like to help me with a... situation?"

Tim leans forward as his fellow linemen snicker. "What dare did you sign up for this time?"

I bob my head back and forth like what I'm preparing to

ask isn't a big deal. "Nothing fancy. Rick dared me to move his car."

Tim shrugs because it doesn't sound like a big deal.

"Without the keys," says Chris.

Tim lowers his head, and deep chuckles resonate from his chest. "You three are the definition of insane. You know that, right?"

"Says the guy that tackles other dudes for fun," I say. "Are you in or out?"

Tim's lawn chair moves with him as he stands. As he reaches his full height, the chair plunges onto the bed of the truck with a loud clank. "In."

Curled fingers miserably clutch metal and my back and thighs burn with pain. Seven guys, one 2,400-pound car, and one more inch to go.

"On three," I say through clenched teeth. "One..."

"Three," yells Logan and I barely unwedge my fingers from the bumper of the two-door Chevy Aveo when the six other guys drop the car to the ground. The frame of the blue car bounces like a Slinky before coming to a rest.

"Sweet shocks," says Logan.

Sweat soaks my shirt. Gasping for air, I bend over and place my hands on my knees. The rush of the win races through my veins and I laugh out loud.

Logan admires our handiwork. "Six feet over and nicely parallel parked between two trees." *Nicely* meaning the front and rear bumpers currently kiss bark.

Tim's chest heaves as if he's experiencing a heart attack. "You're a crazy son-of-a-bitch, Ry." Pant. "How the hell is Rick going to move this piece of shit?"

"Chris, Logan, and I will stick around. Once he gets done freaking, we'll lift the back end and move it so he can wedge out."

Tim laughs while shaking his head. "I'll see you at school on Monday."

"Thanks, man."

"Anytime. Let's go, guys. I need a beer."

I sag to the ground and lean against the tree near the bumper. Chris slides against the passenger door until his butt hits the dirt. We both stare at Logan, waiting for him to join us, but he's busy studying the two oak trees pinning in our third baseman's car.

In any circle that doesn't involve me, Chris, and Lacy, Logan is known for silence and his constant state of boredom. At the moment, so-called silent, bored boy's mind is spinning like a toddler on a sugar high. It's ironic: at school, people think I'm the adrenaline junkie because I admire a good dare. Hell, I'm not looking for a high—I just like to win. Logan, on the other hand, thrives on the edge. Gotta love a guy like that.

I'm not the only one who's noticed Logan's insane infatuation with the tree. Chris eyes him warily. "What the hell are you doing, Junior?"

Logan winks at me. "Be back in a second, boss man." He scrambles up the old oak tree. Small dead limbs that can't hold his weight fall through the branches and onto the ground.

Chris grows restless. He won't admit it, but heights scare the shit out of him and Logan's fear of nothing scares the shit out of him more. "Get your ass back down here."

"Okay," calls Logan from somewhere high in the tree.

I shake my head. "You shouldn't have said that."

From above, tree limbs crackle and snap and leaves whoosh as if a strong breeze rushes through them. It's not wind. It's Logan, and one of these days he's going to get himself killed. A swirl of dirt accompanies the thud on the ground. Logan's body presses against my foot. On his back, with his black hair full of torn leaves, Logan convulses with laughter. Obviously this isn't the night he was meant to die. He turns his head to look at Chris. "Here."

I kick Logan hard when I remove my foot from under his ass. "You're the crazy son-of-a-bitch, not me."

"Crazy?" Logan rolls over to sit up. "I'm not the one following a psycho chick into a parking lot for a phone number. Those guys could have kicked your ass."

Damn. I hoped they had forgotten. "I could have taken them." They would have eventually handed my ass to me, but I would have given them some bruises as payback. Two versus one are bad odds.

"Not the point," says Logan.

"Since you mentioned it." Chris takes his baseball cap off and holds it over his heart. "I'm going to take this moment and remind everyone of the following—I won."

"I won tonight. So we're even again."

Chris shoves his hat back on. "Doesn't count."

He's right. It doesn't. The only dares we keep track of are the ones we give to one another. "Enjoy the brief taste of victory. I'll be winning next time."

We lapse into silence, which is fine. Our silences are never uncomfortable. Unlike girls, guys don't have to talk. Every now and then, we hear laughter or shouting from the party.

Every now and then, Chris and Lacy text. He likes to give her space, but doesn't trust drunk guys near his girl.

Logan fiddles with a long branch that fell to the ground. "Dad and I headed into Lexington this morning to check out U of K."

I hold my breath, hoping that the conversation doesn't turn to where I think it's heading. Logan's had this visit scheduled for weeks. He's a damn genius and will have every college knocking on his door next year, including the University of Kentucky. "How'd it go?"

"I saw Mark."

I rub the back of my head and try to ignore the nagging ache inside. "How is he?"

"Fine. He asked about you. Your mom." He pauses. "Your dad."

"He's fine. That's it?"

"No offense, but it was weird. I'm cool that he's your brother and that he's made his choices, but I'm not sticking around to play head shrink over your family problems, especially when he had an audience."

"An audience?" I echo.

"Yeah," says Logan. "His boyfriend, I guess."

The twisting pressure usually only reserved for games pummels my stomach. I pull my knees up and lower my head. "How do you know it was his boyfriend?"

Logan's face scrunches. "I dunno. He was standing next to another dude."

"It could have been a friend," says Chris. "Did the guy look gay?"

"Mark didn't look gay, asswipe," Logan snaps. "Who would have guessed the damn defensive lineman had it for the home team. And sure, the other dude could've been straight. But how the hell should I know?"

Listening to them discuss my gay brother's possible gay boyfriend is just as comfortable as convincing my mom over and over again that I prefer girls and their girl parts. Nothing makes you think you might need years of therapy like having to say the word *breasts* in front of your mother. "Can we end this conversation?"

I consider walking back to Tim's truck and collecting that beer. I've only been shit-faced drunk twice in my life. Once when Mark told the family he was gay. The second time when Dad kicked him out for that announcement. Both incidents happened in the span of three days. Lessons learned: don't tell Dad you're gay, and getting drunk doesn't make anything untrue. It just makes your head hurt in the morning.

With a loud crack, Logan breaks the twig in his hand. He's looking for courage, which means I'm going to hate the words coming out of his mouth. "Mark was all cryptic, but he said you'd know what he meant. He said he can't come and he hoped you'd understand why."

The muscles in my neck tighten. My brother didn't even have the balls to tell me himself. I texted him last week. I outright defied my parents and texted him. I asked him to come home for dinner tomorrow night and he never texted back. Instead, he took the coward's way out and used Logan.

Earlier this summer, Dad gave the ultimatum: as long as Mark chooses guys, he's no longer a part of our family. Mark walked out, knowing what leaving meant: leaving Mom... leaving me. He never considered trying to stay home and fight to keep our family together. "He made his choice."

Logan lowers his voice. "He misses you."

"And he left," I snap. I kick the back tire of the car. Angry. Angry at Dad. Angry at Mark. Angry at me. For three days straight Mark talked. He said the same thing over and over again. He's still Mark. My brother. Mom's son. He told me how he spent years confused because he wanted to be like me. He wanted to be like Dad.

And when I asked him to stay, when I asked him to stand his ground...he left. He packed up his shit and he left, leaving me and the destruction of my family behind.

"Screw the serious talk," says Chris. "We won today. We'll win fall season and spring. We're going to graduate victorious and when we do, Ryan's going pro."

"Amen," says Logan.

From their lips to God's ears, but sometimes God chooses not to listen. "Don't get your hopes up. The scout today could be a one-time deal. Next week they could find somebody else to love." I should know. That happened at the pro tryouts this past spring.

"Bullshit," says Chris. "Destiny is knocking, Ry, and you need to get your ass up to answer."

BETH

I FELL ASLEEP. Either that or my dear old uncle Scott drugged me. I'm going with *fell asleep*. Scott may be a dick, but he's a dare-to-keep-kids-off-drugs kind of dick. I should know. He once brought red ribbons and a police mascot to my preschool.

I love irony.

Moonlight streams through white lace curtains hanging from an artsy brown metal rod. I sit up and a pink crochet blanket falls away. The bedding beneath me is still perfectly made and I'm wearing the same outfit I wore on Friday night. Someone has neatly laid my shoes on the wooden floor next to the bed. Even sober, I wouldn't have done that. I don't do neat.

I lean over and turn on a lamp. The crystals decorating the bottom edge of the shade clink together. The dull light draws my focus to the painfully cheery purple paint on the wall. Closing my eyes, I count the days. Let's see. Friday night I went out with Noah and Isaiah and put Taco Bell Boy in his place. Early Saturday, Mom tried to become a felon. Saturday morning, Scott ruined my life.

I pretended to fall asleep in the car so I wouldn't have to talk to Scott, but I sucked and actually fell asleep. Scott woke me, I think, and half carried me into the house. Crap. Why don't I put a sign on my head and announce I'm a loser girl who needs help.

I open my eyes and stare at the ticking clock on the bedside table. Twelve fifteen. Sunday. This is early Sunday morning.

My stomach growls. I've gone a full day without eating. Wouldn't be the first time. Won't be the last. I slip out of bed and slide my Chuck Taylor wannabes onto my feet. Time to have a coming-to-Jesus moment with Uncle Scott. That is, if he's awake. It may be better if he went to bed. That way I can slip out without the fight.

Maybe I'll score some food before I call Isaiah. With a room like this, I bet he buys brand-name cereal.

The house has that newly built, fresh sawdust smell. Outside the bedroom is a foyer instead of a hallway. A large staircase, the type I thought existed only in movies, winds to the second floor. An actual chandelier hangs from the ceiling. Guess baseball pays well.

"No..." A woman's voice carries from the back of the house. I can tell she's still talking, but she's lowered her tone. Did he marry or does he keep a fuck on hand like he did when I was a kid? Gotta be a fuck. I overheard Scott tell Dad once that he'd never marry.

I follow the low voices to the brink of a large open room and pause. The entire back of the house—excuse me, mansion—is one enormous wall of windows. The living room flows right into the eat-in kitchen.

"Scott." Exasperation eats at the woman's tone. "This is not what I signed up for."

"Last month you were on board with this," says Scott. Part of me feels vindicated. He's lost that annoyingly smooth calm from yesterday.

"Yes, when you told me you wanted to reconnect with your niece. There is a difference between reconnecting and invading our life."

"You were fine with it when I called last month from Louisville and said I wanted her to live with us."

The woman snaps, "That was after you said she ran away. I didn't actually think you would find her. When you described the hellhole she lived in, I figured she was long gone. She's a criminal. You expect me to feel safe with her in my home?"

Her words slice me open. I'm not that bad. No, I'm not kittens and bunnies, but I'm not that bad. I glance down at my outfit. Jeans. Tank top. My black hair falls in front of my face. It doesn't matter. She made her decision before she met me. I bury the hurt, step into the room, and welcome the anger. Screw her. "You might want to listen to her. I'm a fucking menace."

The shocked expression on their faces is almost worth being here. Almost. I press my lips together to keep from laughing at Scott. He wears a pair of chinos and a short-sleeved button-down shirt. It's a far cry from the outfits he used to wear when I was a kid: gangsta jeans that showed his underwear.

The woman is nothing like the girls Scott dated when he was eighteen. Her hair is a natural blond instead of bleached. She's thin, but not alcohol-diet thin, and she looks kind of smart. Smart as in she probably finished high school.

She sits at a massive island in the center of the kitchen.

Scott leans on the counter across from her. He glances at her, then talks to me. "It's late, Elisabeth. Why don't you go back to bed and we'll talk in the morning."

My stomach cramps, and a light wave of dizziness fogs my brain. "Do you have food?"

He straightens. "Yes. What do you want? I can fix some eggs."

Scott used to make me scrambled eggs every morning. Eggs—the WIC-approved food. The reminder hurts and creates warm fuzzies at the same time. "I hate eggs."

"Oh."

Oh. The man's a conversational genius. "Do you have cereal?"

"Sure." He enters a pantry and I plop onto a stool at the island as far from Scott's girl as possible. She stares at a spot right in front of me. Huh. Funny. I'm in arm's reach of a butcher block full of knives. I can imagine the thoughts running through her single-celled brain.

Scott places boxes of Cheerios, Bran Flakes, and Shredded Wheat in front of me.

"You have got to be fucking kidding." Where the hell are the Lucky Charms?

"Nice language," the woman says.

"Thanks," I respond.

"I didn't mean it as a compliment."

"Do I look like I fucking care?"

Scott slides a bowl and spoon to me, then goes to the refrigerator for milk. "Let's tone it down."

I choose the Cheerios and keep pouring until a few toasty circles trickle onto the counter. Scott sits in the chair next to mine and the two of them watch me in silence. Well, sort of silence. My crunching is louder than a nuclear bomb blast.

"Scott told me you had blond hair," says the woman.

I swallow, but it's hard to do when my throat tightens. The little girl I used to be, the one with blond hair, died years ago and I hate thinking about her. She was nice. She was happy. She was...not someone I want to remember.

"Why is your hair black?" The lawn ornament at the other end of the island has officially become annoying.

"What are you exactly?" I ask.

"This is my wife, Allison."

The Cheerios catch in my throat and I choke, coughing into my hand. "You're married?"

"Two years," says Scott. Ugh. He does that googly-eye thing Noah does with Echo.

I slide another spoonful of Cheerios into my mouth. "When I'm done—" crunch, crunch, crunch "—I'm going home."

"This is your home now." Scott has that calm tone again.

"The hell it is."

Allison's eyes dart between me and the knives. Yeah, lady, a couple of hours in jail and I've moved from destruction of property to sociopath.

"Maybe you should listen to her," she says.

"Yeah," I say through more crunches, "maybe you should listen to me. Your wife's worried I'm going to go all Manson and slit her throat while she sleeps." I smile at her for effect.

Color drains from her face. At times, I really enjoy being me.

Scott gives me the once-over—starting with my black hair, then moving on to my black fingernails, the ring in my nose, and finally my clothes. Then he turns to *his wife.* "Will you give us a few minutes alone?"

Allison leaves without saying a word. I shovel in more cereal and purposely talk with my mouth full. "Did you have to purchase the leash for her or did it come as a package deal?"

"You won't disrespect her, Elisabeth."

"I'll do as I fucking please, Uncle Scott." I mimic his fake haughty tone. "And when I'm done eating my shitty cereal, I'm calling Isaiah and I'm going home."

Him—silence. Me—crunch, crunch, crunch.

"What happened to you?" he asks in a soft voice.

I swallow what's in my mouth, put down the spoon, and push the bowl of half-eaten Cheerios away. "What do you think happened?"

Scott—the master of long silences.

"When did he leave?" he asks.

I don't have to be a mind reader to know Scott's asking about his deadbeat brother. The black paint on my fingernails chips at the corners. I scrape off more of it. Eight years later and I still have a hard time saying it. "Third grade."

Scott shifts in his seat. "Your mom?"

"Fell apart the day he left." Which should tell him a lot, because she wasn't exactly the poster child for reliability before Dad took off.

"What happened between them?"

None of his business. "You didn't come for me like you promised." And he stopped calling when I turned eight. The refrigerator kicks on. I scrape off more paint. He faces the fact that he's a dick.

"Elisabeth—"

"Beth." I cut him off. "I go by Beth. Where's your phone?

I'm going home." The police confiscated my cell and gave it to Scott. He told me in the car that he tossed it in the garbage because I "didn't need contact with my old life."

"You just turned seventeen."

"Did I? Wow. I must have forgotten since no one threw me a party."

Ignoring me, he continues, "This week my lawyers will secure my legal guardianship of you. Until you turn eighteen, you will live in this house and you will obey my rules."

Fine. If he won't show me the phone, I'll find it. I hop off the chair. "I'm not six anymore and you aren't the center of my universe. In fact, I consider you a black hole."

"I get that you're pissed off I left...."

Pissed? "No, I'm not pissed. You don't exist to me anymore. I feel nothing for you, so show me where the damned phone is so I can go home."

"Elisabeth..."

He doesn't get it. I don't care. "Go to hell." No phone in the kitchen.

"You need to understand...."

I walk around his fancy ass living room with his fancy ass leather furniture looking for his fancy ass phone. "Take whatever you have to say and shove it up your ass."

"I just want to talk...."

I lift my hand in the air and flap it like a puppet's mouth. "Blah, blah, blah, Elisabeth. I'll only be gone a couple of months. Blah, blah, blah, Elisabeth. I'll make enough money to get us both out of Groveton. Blah, blah, blah, Elisabeth. You'll never grow up like me. Blah, blah, blah, Elisabeth. I'll make sure you have some fucking food to eat!"

"I was eighteen."

"I was six!"

"I wasn't your father!"

I throw my arms out. "No, you weren't. You were supposed to be better than him! Congratulations, you officially became a replica of your worthless brother. Now where the fuck is the damn phone?"

Scott slams his hand on the counter and roars, "Sit your ass down, Elisabeth, and shut the fuck up!"

I quake on the inside, but I've been around Mom's asshole boyfriends long enough to keep from quaking on the outside. "Wow. You can take the boy out of the trailer park and pretty him up in a Major League Baseball uniform, but you can't take the trailer park out of the boy."

He takes a deep breath and closes his eyes. "I'm sorry. That was uncalled for."

"Whatever. Where's the phone?"

Noah told me once that I have a gift that borders on supervillain status—the ability to push people past the edge of sanity. The way Scott releases another breath and rubs his forehead tells me I'm pushing him hard. Good.

Scott tries for that obnoxious, level tone again, but I can hear the edge of irritation in it. "You want trailer park, I can go trailer park. You are going to live in my house with my rules or I'll send your mother to jail."

"I broke out the windows of the car. Not her. You have nothing on her."

Scott narrows his eyes. "Wanna discuss what's in your mom's apartment with me?"

My body lurches to the left as the blood seeps out of my face, leaving behind a blurry and tingling sensation. Shirley already warned me, but hearing it from him is still a shock. Scott knows what I don't want to know—Mom's secret.

"Push me, Elisabeth, and I'll have this same exact conversation with the police."

I stumble as I try to stay upright. The back of my legs collide with a coffee table. Losing the battle, I sit. Right beside me is a phone and as much as I want to, I can't touch it. Scott has me. The bastard traded my life for my mom's freedom.

RYAN

I LEAN AGAINST the closed tailgate of Dad's truck and listen from two parking spots away as Dad recounts to a group of men loitering outside the barbershop every detail of our meeting with the scout last night. Some of them heard the story at church this morning. Most of the listeners are generational farmers and this kind of news is worth hearing again, even if it means standing in the type of August heat where you can smell the acrid stench of blacktop melting.

In my peripheral view, I notice a man stop on the sidewalk and assess the ring of listeners and my storytelling father. I don't pay attention to tourists and if he were a local, he'd join the group. It's better to leave the tourists alone. If you look at them, they talk.

Groveton's a small town. To appeal to tourists, Dad persuaded the other councilmen to call the old stone buildings dating back to the 1800s *Historic* then add the words *Shopping District.* Four B-and-Bs and new tours of the old bourbon distillery later, and the city folk brave the fifteen-mile winding country road from the freeway. It can make parking a bitch on the weekends, but it gives lots of good people jobs when money gets tight.

"What's the local gossip?" the man asks.

He's speaking and I didn't even make eye contact. That's bold for a tourist. I fold my arms across my chest. "Baseball."

"No kidding." There's a drop in his tone that catches my attention.

I turn my head and feel my eyes widen in slow motion. No way. "You're Scott Risk."

Everyone in this town knows who Scott Risk is. His face is one of the few to peer at the student population from the Wall of Fame at Bullitt County High. As a shortstop, he led his high school team to state championships twice. He made the majors straight out of high school. But the real achievement, the real feat that made him a king in this small town, was his eleven-year stint with the New York Yankees. He's exactly what every boy in Groveton dreams of becoming, including me.

Scott Risk wears a pair of khakis, a blue polo, and a good-natured grin. "And you are?"

"Ryan Stone," Dad answers for me as he appears from out of thin air. "He's my son."

The circle of men outside the barbershop watch us with interest. Scott holds out his hand to Dad. "Scott Risk."

Dad shakes it with a badly suppressed smug smile. "Andrew Stone."

"City Councilman Andrew Stone?"

"Yes," Dad says with pride. "I heard rumors you were moving back to town."

He did? That's the sort of news Dad should have shared.

"This town always did love gossip." Scott keeps the friendly look, but the light tone feels forced.

Dad chuckles. "Some things never change. I heard you were looking at buying some property nearby."

"Bought," says Scott. "I purchased the old Walter farm last spring, but asked the Realtor to keep the sale quiet until we moved into the home we built farther back on the property."

My eyebrows shoot up and so do Dad's. That's the farm right next to ours. Dad takes a step closer and angles his back to make the three of us into our own circle. "I own the property a mile down the road. Ryan and I are huge fans of yours." No, he's not. Dad respects Scott because he's from Groveton, but loathes anyone from the Yankees. "Except when you played the Reds. Home team takes precedent."

"Wouldn't expect anything else." Scott notices my baseball cap. "Do you play?"

"Yes, sir." What exactly do I say to the man I've worshipped my entire life? Can I ask for his autograph? Can I beg him to tell me how he stays calm during a game when everything is on the line? Do I stare at him like an idiot because I can't find anything more coherent to say?

"Ryan's a pitcher," Dad announces. "A major-league scout watched him at a game last night. He thinks Ryan has the potential to be picked up by the minors after graduation."

Scott's easygoing grin falls into something more serious as he stares as me. "That's impressive. You must be pitching in the upper eighties."

"Nineties," says Dad. "Ryan pitched three straight in the nineties."

A crazy gleam hits Scott's eyes and we both smile. I understand that spark and the adrenaline rush that accompanies it. We share a passion: playing ball. "Nineties? And you're just now getting the attention of scouts?"

I readjust my hat. "Dad took me to Reds' tryout camp this past spring, but..."

Dad cuts me off. "They told Ryan he needed to bulk up."

"You must have listened," Scott says.

"I want to play ball." I'm twenty pounds heavier than last spring. I run every day and lift weights at night. Sometimes, Dad does it with me. This dream also belongs to Dad.

"Anything can happen." Scott looks over my shoulder, but his eyes have that far-off glaze, as if he's seeing a memory. "It depends on how badly you want it."

I want it. Badly. Dad checks his watch, then extends his hand again to Scott. He's itching to pick up some new drill bits before supper. "It was nice officially meeting you."

Scott accepts his hand. "You too. Would you mind if I borrowed your son? My niece lives with me and she'll be starting Bullitt County High tomorrow. I think the transition will be easier for her if she has someone to show her around. As long as that's okay with you, Ryan."

"It would be an honor, sir." It would. This is beyond my wildest dreams.

Dad flashes me his all-knowing smile. "You know where to find me." The crowd near the barbershop parts like Moses commanding the Red Sea as Dad strolls toward the hardware store.

Scott turns his back to the crowd, steps closer to me, and runs a hand over his face. "Elisabeth..." He pauses, rests his hands on his hips, and starts again. "Beth's a little rough around the edges, but she's a good girl. She could use some friends."

I nod like I understand, but I don't. What does he mean by rough around the edges? I keep nodding because I don't care. She's Scott Risk's niece and I'll make sure she's happy.

Beth. A strange uneasiness settles in my stomach. Why does that name sound familiar? "I'll introduce her around. Make sure she fits in. My best friend, Chris, he's also on the team." Because I'll try to work Chris and Logan into any conversation I have with Mr. Risk. "He has a great girl who I'm sure your niece will love."

"Thanks. You have no idea how much this means to me." Scott relaxes as if he dropped a hundred-pound bag of feed. The bell over the clothing shop chimes. Scott places a hand on my shoulder and gestures at the shop. "Ryan, I'd like you to meet my niece, Elisabeth."

She walks out of the shop and crosses her arms over her chest. Black hair. Nose ring. Slim figure with a hint of curves. White shirt with only four buttons clasped between her breasts and belly button, fancy blue jeans, and an eye roll the moment she sees me. My stomach drops as if I swallowed lead. This is possibly the worst day of my life.

BETH

"IT'S NICE TO MEET YOU," Arrogant Taco Bell Boy says as if we never met. Maybe he doesn't remember. Jocks usually aren't smart. Their muscles feast on their brains.

"You have got to be fucking kidding me." I'm in hell. No question about it. This bad version of the town from *Deliverance* is certainly hot as hell. The heat in this forsaken place possesses a strangling haze that envelops me and seizes my lungs.

Scott clears his throat. A subtle reminder that *fuck* is no longer an acceptable word for me in public. "I'd like you to meet Ryan Stone."

Once upon a time, Scott used to say words like *s'up* and *sick*. Variants of *fuck* were the only adjectives and adverbs in his vocabulary. Now he sounds like a stuck-up, suit-wearing, cocky rich guy. Oh wait, he is.

"Ryan's volunteered to show you around at school tomorrow."

"Of course he has," I mumble. "Because my life hasn't sucked enough in the past forty-eight hours."

God must have decided He wasn't done screwing with

me yet. He wasn't done screwing with me when Scott black-mailed me into living here. He wasn't done screwing with me when Scott's wife bought these tragically conservative clothes. He wasn't done screwing with me when Scott told me he was enrolling me at the local redneck, *Children of the Corn* school. No, he wasn't quite done screwing with me yet. The damn icing on this cake is the conceited ass standing in front of me. Ha fucking ha. Joke's on me. "I want my clothes back."

"What?" Scott asks. Good—I messed with him without cursing.

"He's not dressed like a moron, so why should I?" I motion to the designer jeans and starched Catholic-schoolgirl shirt disgracing my body. Per Scott's request to play nice with Allison, I stepped out of the dressing room to look at this atrocity in the full-length mirror. When I returned, my clothes were gone. Tonight, I'm searching for a pair of scissors and bleach.

Scott censures me by subtly shaking his head. I have close to a whole year of this bull in front of me, and the woman I'm trying to protect I can't even see—my mom. A part of my brain tingles with panic. How is she? Did her boyfriend hit her again? Is she worried about me?

"You're going to love it here," says Taco Bell Boy—I mean Ryan.

"Sure I am." My tone indicates I'm going to love this place as much as I'd love getting shot in the head.

Scott clears his throat again and I wonder if he cares that people will assume he's diseased. "Ryan's father owns a construction business in town and he's on the city council." Underlying message to me: don't screw this moment up.

"Of course." Of course. Story of my freaking life. Ryan's

the rich boy that has everything. Daddy who owns the town. Daddy who owns the business. Ryan, the boy who thinks he can do anything he wants because of it.

Ryan flashes me an easygoing grin and it's sort of hypnotizing. As if he created it just for me. It's a glorious grin. Perfect. Peaceful. With a hint of dimples. It promises friendship and happiness and laughter and it makes me want to smile back. My lips start to curve into an answer and I stop myself abruptly.

Why do I do this to myself? Guys like him don't go for girls like me. I'm a toy to them. A game. And these types of guys, they all have the same rules of play: smile, trick me into thinking that they like me, then toss me to the side once I've been used. How many countless losers do I have to stupidly make out with only to regret it in the morning? Over the past year—too many.

But while listening to Ryan easily digress into a conversation with Scott about baseball, I swear that I'm done with loser guys. Done with feeling used. Just done.

And this time, I won't break the promise—no matter how lonely I get.

"Yeah," Ryan says to Scott as if I'm not standing right here, as if I'm not important enough to involve in conversation. "I think the Reds have a shot this year."

God, I hate Ryan. Standing there all perfect with his perfect life and perfect body and perfect smile, pretending he never laid eyes on me before. He glances at me from the corner of his eye and I realize why he's pouring on the charm. Ryan wants to impress Scott. Guess what? Misery definitely loves company. My life shouldn't be the only one that sucks. "He hit on me."

Silence as my words kill the moronic baseball conversation. Scott rubs his eyes. "You just met him."

"Not now. Friday night. He hit on me and he stared at my ass while he did it."

Joy. Utter joy. Okay, not utter, but the sole joy I've had since Friday night. Ryan yanks off his hat, runs his hand through his mess of sandy-blond hair, and shoves the hat back on. I like him better with his hat off.

"Is this true?" Scott asks.

"Y-yes," stutters Ryan. "No. I mean yes. I asked for her phone number, but she didn't give it to me. But I was respectful, I swear."

"You stared at my ass. A lot." I turn and lean over a little so I can give a demonstration. "Remember, there was a rip right along here." I slide my finger along the back of my leg. "You bought me tacos afterward. And a drink. So I'm assuming you must have enjoyed the view."

I hear muffled male comments and I peek at the crowd of men farther down the sidewalk. The first genuine smile slips across my face. Scott's going to love a show. Maybe if I push hard enough I'll be home in Louisville by dinner.

"Elisabeth." Scott drops his voice to trailer-park pissed. "Turn around."

Twelve different shades of red blotch Ryan's cheeks. He doesn't even look at my ass, but at my uncle. "Okay...yes, I asked her out."

Scott does a double take. "You asked her out?"

Hey now. Why's he surprised? I'm not a dog.

"Yes," says Ryan.

"You wanted to take her on a date?"

Uh-oh. Scott sounds happy. No. I'm not going for happy.

"Yes." Ryan holds out his hands. "I thought...I thought..."

"That I would be easy?" I snap, and Scott winces.

"That she was funny," Ryan says.

Yeah. I'm sure that's exactly what he thought. "More like you thought it would be fun to screw with me. Or just plain screw."

"Enough," snapped Scott. His narrowing blue eyes rage at me as I thrust my hands in the stiff pockets of the new jeans. Scott lowers his head and pinches the bridge of his nose before forcing that fake relaxed grin into place. "I apologize for my niece. She's had a rough weekend."

I don't want him to apologize for me to anyone. Especially not to this arrogant ass. My mouth drops open, but the brief white-trash glance Scott gives me shuts it. Scott becomes Mr. Superficial again. "I understand if you don't want to help Elisabeth at school."

Ryan has this blank, way too innocent expression. "Don't worry, Mr. Risk. I'd love to help *Elisabeth*." He turns to me and smiles. This smile isn't genuine or heartwarming, but cocky as hell. Bring it, jock boy. Your best won't be good enough.

RYAN

THE WALLS OF OUR KITCHEN used to be burgundy. As kids, Mark and I would race home from the bus stop and when we'd burst into the kitchen we'd be greeted by the aroma of freshly baked cookies. Mom would ask us about our day while we dunked the hot cookies in milk. When Dad came home from work, he'd sweep Mom into his arms and kiss her. Mom's laughter in Dad's arms was as natural as Mark's and my constant banter.

With an arm still wrapped around her waist, he'd turn to us and say, "How are my boys?" Like Mark and I didn't exist without each other.

Thanks to the renovations Dad finished last week, the kitchen walls are gray now. And thanks to my brother's announcement and my father's reaction to the announcement this summer, the loudest sound in the kitchen is the clink of knives and forks against china.

"Gwen came to your game," says Mom. It's only the third time she's mentioned it in the past twenty-four hours.

Yeah, with Mike. "Uh-huh." I shove a hunk of pot roast into my mouth.

"Her mom said she still talks about you."

I stop mid-chew and glance at Mom. Proud for earning a reaction from me, she smiles.

"Leave him alone," Dad says. "He doesn't need a girl distracting him."

Mom purses her lips and we enter another five minutes of clinking forks and knives. The silence stings...like frostbite.

Unable to stomach the tension much longer, I clear my throat. "Did Dad tell you we met Scott Risk and his—" psychotic "—niece?"

"No." My mother stabs at the cherry tomato rolling around in her salad bowl. The moment she spears the small round vegetable, Mom glares at Dad. "He has a niece?"

Dad holds her gaze with irritated indifference and follows it up with a drink from his longneck.

"I gave you a wineglass," Mom reminds him.

Dad places the longneck, which drips with condensation, next to said glass right on the wood of the table—without a coaster. Mom shifts in her seat like a crow fluffing out its wings. The only thing she's missing is the pissed-off caw.

For the last few months, Dad and I have been eating our dinners in the living room while watching TV. Mom gave up food after Mark left.

Mom and Dad began marriage counseling a few weeks ago, though they have yet to directly tell me. The need to project perfection won't allow them to admit to a flaw like their marriage needing help from an outside source. Instead, I found out the same way I discover anything in this house: I overheard them fighting in the living room while I lay in bed at night.

Last week, their marriage counselor recommended that

Mom and Dad try to do something as a family. They fought for two days over what that something should be until they settled on Sunday dinner.

It's why I invited Mark. We haven't had a dinner together since he left and if he'd showed, maybe the four of us could have found a way to reconnect.

I wonder if Mom and Dad feel the emptiness of the chair next to mine. Mark possessed this charm that kept my parents from fighting. If they were annoyed with each other, Mark would tell a story or a joke to break the chill. The arctic winter in my house never existed when he was home.

"Yeah, he has a niece," I say, hoping to move the conversation forward and to fill the hollowness inside me. "Her name is Elisabeth. Beth." And she's making my life hell—not too different from suffering through this dinner.

I tear a biscuit apart and slather on some butter. Beth embarrassed me in front of Scott Risk and I lost a dare because of her. I drop the biscuit—the dare. A spark ignites in my brain. Chris and I never set a time limit on it, which means I can still win.

Mom straightens the napkin on her lap, disrupting my thoughts. "You should be friendly with her, Ryan, but maintain your distance. The Risks had a reputation years ago."

Dad's chair scrapes against the new tile and he makes a disgusted noise in his throat.

"What?" Mom demands.

Dad rolls his shoulders back and focuses on his beef instead of answering.

"You have something to say," prods Mom, "say it."

Dad tosses his fork onto his plate. "Scott Risk has some

valuable contacts. I say get close to her, Ryan. Show her around. If you do a favor for him, I'm sure he'd do one for you."

"Of course," says Mom. "Give him advice that goes directly against mine."

Dad begins talking over her and their combined raised voices cause my head to throb. Losing my appetite, I slide my chair away from the table. It's gut-wrenching, listening to the ongoing annihilation of my family. There is absolutely no worse sound on the face of the planet.

Until the phone rings. My parents fall silent as all three of us look over at the counter and see Mark's name appear on the caller ID. A rocky combination of hope and hurt creates a heaviness in my throat and stomach.

"Let it go," Dad murmurs.

Mom stands on the second ring and my heart beats in my ears. *Come on, Mom, answer. Please.*

"We could talk to him," she says as she stares at the phone. "Tell him that as long as he keeps it a secret he can come home."

"Yeah," I say, hoping that one of them will change their minds. Maybe this time Mark would choose to stay and fight instead of leaving me behind. "We should answer."

The phone rings a fourth time.

"Not in my house." Dad never stops glaring at his plate.

And the answering machine picks up. Mom's cheerful voice announces that we're away at the moment, but to please leave a message. Then there's a beep.

Nothing. No message. No static. Nothing. My brother doesn't have the balls to leave me a message.

And I'm not stupid. If he wanted to talk to me, he could have called my cell. This was a test. I invited him to dinner and he was calling to see if I was the only one who wanted him home. I guess we all failed.

Mom clutches the pearls around her neck and the hope within me fades into an angry clawing. Mark left. He left me to deal with this destruction on my own.

I jerk out of my seat and my mother turns to face me. "Where are you going?"

"I've got homework."

The corkboard over my computer desk vibrates when I slam my bedroom door shut. I pace the room and press my hands against my head. I've got a damn homework assignment and the clarity and calm of a boat being tossed by the waves. What I need to do is run off the anger, lift weights until my muscles burn, throw pitches until my shoulder falls off.

I shouldn't be writing a damn four-page English paper on anything "I want."

The chair in front of my desk rolls back as I fling myself into the seat. With one press of a button the monitor brightens to life. The cursor mockingly blinks at me from the blank page.

Four pages. Single spaced. One-inch margins. My teacher's expectations are too high. Especially since it's still technically summer vacation.

My fingers bang on the keys. *I've played ball since I was three.*

And I stop typing. Baseball...it's what I should write about. It's what I know. But the emotions churning inside of me need a release.

Dad and Mom would turn into raging bulls if I wrote about the real status of my family. Appearances mean everything. I bet they haven't even told their marriage counselor the truth about why they see her.

A dawning realization soothes some of the anger. I shouldn't do it. If anyone figured it out, I'd be in deep, but right now I need to dump all the resentment. I erase the first line and give words to the emotions begging for freedom.

George woke up with a vague memory of what used to be, but one glance to the left brought on a harrowing realization of what his new reality was. Of what, specifically, he had become.

BETH

"THEY MIGHT REMEMBER ME." Mondays suck and so does the first day of school in Hicksville, USA. I lean against the windows in the guidance counselor's office and look around. Décor circa the 1970s: faux wood paneling, desk and chairs bought from the Wal-Mart bargain basket. The scent of mildew hangs in the air. This is backwoods schools at their finest.

"That's the point, Elisabeth." Scott flips through a thick schedule booklet. "Your old elementary school is one of three schools that feed into here. You'll know some people and rekindle old friendships. What about Home Ec? You and I baked cookies a couple of times, remember?"

"Beth. I go by Beth." It's like the man is learning impaired. "And the last time I baked anything, it was brownies and I put..."

"We'll put Home Ec in the No section. But I prefer the name Elisabeth. What was your best friend's name? I used to drive you to her house."

And we played with dolls. Over and over again. Her mom let us use her real cups for tea parties. They had a real house with real beds and I loved staying for dinner. Their food was hot. It becomes hard to swallow. "Lacy."

"That's right. Lacy Harper."

The door to the office opens and the guidance counselor pops in his head. "Just a few more minutes, Mr. Risk. I'm on the line with Eastwick High."

Scott drops that cheesy grin. "Take your time. Is there a Lacy Harper at this school?"

Somebody shoot me. Now. Right now.

"Yes, there is."

The fun doesn't stop coming. Scott glances at me. "Isn't that great?"

I overly fake my response. "Awesome."

He either chooses to ignore my sarcasm or believes my excitement. "Mr. Dwyer, could you place Beth in one of Lacy's classes?"

Mr. Dwyer practically falls to the floor in admiration. "We'll certainly try." He withdraws from his own office and shuts the door.

"Were you smacked upside the head with a bat?" I can't believe Scott expects me to attend this school.

"Only when I was five and on days that end in *y*," he mumbles, still flipping through the catalog. His response pricks my chest. I've done my best to block out that portion of my childhood. Grandpa, his dad, used to beat the crap out of him and my dad. Scott kept him from doing the same to me. "What about Spanish?"

I actually smile. "My friend Rico taught me some Spanish. If a guy's too touchy I can say..."

"Strike Spanish."

Damn. That could have been fun. "Seriously, Scott. Do

you really want me going to school here? Have you thought this through? Your pet with a wedding ring..."

"Allison. Her name is Allison. Let's say it together. All-i-son. See, not so hard."

"Whatever. She loves how everybody worships you. How long is that going to last when they remember that you're low-life trash from the trailer park a couple miles out of Groveton?"

He stops flipping through the catalog. Even though his eyes fix on the paper, I can tell he's no longer reading. "I'm not that kid anymore. People only care about who I am now."

"How long do you think it will take before people remember me or Mom?" I meant to say it nasty, like a threat, but it came out soft and I hate myself for it.

Scott looks at me and I loathe the sympathy in his eyes. "They'll remember you the way I do—a beautiful girl who loved life."

Pissed that he keeps discussing that poor pathetic girl, I break eye contact. "She died."

"No, she didn't." He pauses. "As for your mom, she moved into town her sophomore year and dropped out when she was still fifteen. People won't remember her."

Nausea strikes and my hand drops to my abdomen. Scott wasn't there when the police came to the trailer and he wasn't there to dry my tears. This is a small town and everyone knows everyone else. Even though they promised to keep that night a secret, I'm sure someone told.

"What happens to both of us when someone remembers Dad?" I ask. "No one's going to worship you then. This is a bad mistake, Scott. Send me home."

"Mr. Risk." The guidance counselor from Hicksville pokes

his head into the office. Worry lines clutter his overly large forehead and his fingers white-knuckle a fax. I told him I majored in detention while at Eastwick. "Can I have a moment?"

I tilt my head, knowing the words to say to make Mr. Dwyer uncomfortable. "What was that class you wanted to put me in? Hmm." I tap my finger to my chin. "Honors English?"

"Sit down, Elisabeth." Scott's getting really good at demanding things in a low voice. "Okay, Mr. Dwyer, let's discuss Beth's schedule."

RYAN

LADIES AND GENTLEMEN, bow your heads and give an amen. Scott Risk's niece is attending Bullitt County High and the dare is back in play. I weave through the crowded hallway with an extra spring in my step. *Defeat* is a nasty word. A word I no longer have to accept.

My mood crashes when I spot Chris backing Lacy against a locker. His head angles down as hers inches up. Not a good position to be in with the assistant principal exiting his office. Last year, he lectured the junior class on our hormones, carnal impulses, and the consequences for those who break the body boundary barrier. In plain English: if you're caught standing close to a person of the opposite sex, then you'll spend a day in detention. Back-to-back state championships require practice, not detention.

"Backseats of cars work." I ease to the other side of Chris and Lacy to block the oncoming assistant principal's view. "Preferably off campus."

Chris groans when Lacy places her hand on his chest and pushes him until they're an "acceptable" distance apart. She lets out a frustrated sigh. "Morning, Ry."

"Go away," Chris says flatly.

"The assistant principal is on the prowl and we are not moving practice like we did last year because you're sitting in detention."

Chris lets out a sigh identical to Lacy's. "You need a girlfriend."

"Exactly!" Lacy throws her arms out. "I've been saying that for months. Not an evil girlfriend. We are not doing evil again. I was tired of wearing crucifixes. I considered carrying holy water, but then I would have had to sneak into a church and then—"

"Shut it down," I tell her. There has always been bad blood between Gwen and Lace, but I dated Gwen once. I won't tolerate anyone disrespecting her.

The first warning bell rings, and the three of us head to English. Standing by himself, oozing perpetual boredom, Logan waits for us at the line between the seniors' lockers and the juniors'. The four of us take as many classes as we can together. For fun. For camaraderie. For Lacy and Logan to help me and Chris with homework.

Because the boy is smarter than Einstein and most of the kids in this school are dumber than dirt, Logan takes senior courses. Next year, they won't have any classes advanced enough for him, so odds are they'll shove him in a dark corner of the library and pretend he doesn't exist.

I glance around the hallway, trying to spot Beth. "So, about that continuing dare from Friday."

"You mean the bet you lost on Friday." Chris enters English and claims our usual seats by the window. Lacy stays in the hallway to do her girl-talk thing.

"No, the bet I'm going to win."

Chris flashes a disbelieving grin. "Logan, do you hear the smack he's talking?"

Logan drops into his seat and slouches. "You lost, Ryan. Badly."

"Badly?" I ask.

"The most fun I've had in weeks," Chris says. "In fact, let's relive the moment. Hi, I'm Ryan, I want your phone number." He holds out his hand to Logan.

"Let me think," Logan says. "She had this elegant way of talking. Oh yeah, I believe her response was 'Fuck you.'"

"Her name is Beth."

"Getting her name wasn't the dare." Determined to keep Mrs. Rowe from taking into her possession every hat he owns like last year, Chris shoves his cap into his back pocket. "You lost. Be a man. Suck it up. Or let us continue to make fun of you. Either way works."

"I like making fun of him," says Logan.

I lower my voice and lean into the aisle so only Logan and Chris can hear. I have a small window of opportunity and the longer people stay in the dark regarding her uncle, the better my odds of scoring her number. Scott is a god at this school, which automatically makes her a demigod. "Her real name is Elisabeth Risk and she's Scott Risk's niece."

"Beth." Books slam on my desk and the three of us flinch and look up. Black hair, nose ring, and a formfitting white shirt unbuttoned recklessly close to areas where guys stare. Well, at least where I stare. Good God almighty, the girl's hot.

"I'm going to say this slowly and use little words in the hope you can follow along. If you call me Elisabeth again, I'll make sure you can never father children. Tell anyone else whose niece I am and you'll be sucking air out of a tube in your throat."

Chris laughs and it's the deep, throaty kind that tells me the shit we're entering is bad. "It's nice to meet you. Ryan just told us how badly he wanted to call you, didn't you, Ry?"

Ding-ding, Chris rang the bell for round two and he's in direct violation of game play by interfering. Well played, because I would have done the same damn thing. "I tried looking for you this morning, but the secretary said you were in a meeting with Mr. Dwyer."

Her blue eyes pierce me, and an eyebrow slowly arches toward her hairline. The silence stretching between us becomes excruciating. Chris shifts in his seat and Logan slouches lower by an inch. I will her to leave, but I need her presence to win the dare. I focus on keeping my face relaxed. If I even breathe, Skater Girl will know she has the upper hand.

"Uh-huh," she finally responds. "I'm sure you did. Suck-ups do that type of thing. Here's the deal. I avoid you, you avoid me, and when my uncle asks if you helped me today I'll giggle like one of those pathetic girls standing in the hallway and gush about how poor, defenseless me couldn't make it in the big, mean school without big, strong Ryan to help me out."

"You can giggle?" asks Logan.

She glares at him. He shrugs. "You don't strike me as the giggling type—just saying."

Damn, Logan entered game play too, which means he'll want to place money on the dare. Time to salvage. "This is Chris and Logan. They play baseball with me. Chris has a girlfriend who I'm sure you'll love and if you want, you can sit with us today during lunch."

"Dear God, you really are brain damaged."

The bell rings and Skater Girl goes to the opposite side of the room and holes up in the corner. That went well. My friends both wear smiles that make me want to kick their asses.

"Twenty she curses you out by lunch," says Chris.

"Thirty she kills you by lunch," adds Logan.

"I'm getting her number." The two of them laugh, and the muscles in my biceps tighten at the thought of another loss. The paper in my notebook crinkles in my fist. "You don't think I've got game?"

"Not enough game for that," says Logan.

"I'll prove you wrong." Out of the corner of my eye, I glimpse Beth. With her head down and her long black hair hiding her face, she doodles in a notebook with a pen in her left hand. Huh—a southpaw.

Chris shakes his head. "Sorry, dawg. Beth attending Bullitt High is a rule-changing event. See, phone numbers are for those we will never see again. You have months to work her. You want a win, then the stakes are raised—you have to ask her out and she has to accept."

"And the date has to be at a public venue for no less than an hour," adds Logan. "You know, to keep it legit."

I shouldn't do it. If I mess this up, I could tick off Scott Risk; but then again, if I work this right, I could have Scott Risk eating out of the palm of my hand. He all but begged me to become friends with the spawn of Satan over there. Plus, if I walk away from this opportunity, it means I lost and I don't lose.

"Fine," I say. "Dare accepted."

Game on, Skater Girl. Game on.

BETH

I NEED A CIGARETTE and a smoker who will trust me. Unfortunately, I haven't come across either of those in my four hours of living the teen version of *Deliverance*. From a distance, while the juniors and seniors head to lunch, I follow two guys with long hair and sagging jeans. I hope I can convince one of them to give me a drag.

They round a corner and I give them a sec. If I approach before they light up, they'll try to act cool like they aren't doing anything. Then there will be nothing I can say to convince them I won't snitch.

Hell, I wouldn't believe me. The new girl in a white button-down shirt.

I've given them long enough. I turn the corner, prepared to tell them to chill, but the words catch in my mouth. They aren't there.

It's a short hallway with double doors leading out. I hurry to the window and watch as the two guys duck and weave through the parking lot. My head smacks the door. Damn. I never thought they'd skip. First day. That's hard-core.

At the sound of a knock, my heart kicks out of my chest

and with one glance out the window it melts. It's him. My body sags with relief. It's really him. I press the door open and the moment the warm summer sun caresses my face, Isaiah gathers me into his arms. Normally, I wouldn't do this—touch him so aware. Today, I don't mind. In fact, I bury myself in him.

"It's okay." Isaiah kisses my hair and his hand cradles the back of my head, keeping me close. He kissed me. This embrace should bother me and I should push him away. We don't connect like this. Not sober. Today, his touch entices me to hold him tighter.

"How did you know?" I mumble against the material of his shirt.

"Figured you'd come out for a smoke at some point. This is the only place anyone has been doing it."

His heart has a strong, steady rhythm. There were times, in my search for weightlessness, that I pushed too hard. Drank too much. Inhaled more than I should. Became physical with guys who were no good for me. I would go beyond weightlessness as a balloon on a string that had been snapped—left alone in a frightening abyss. With one touch, Isaiah could ground me. Keep me from floating away with his arms as my anchor. His steady beating heart the reminder he would never let go.

With reluctance, I put space between us. "How did you know I'd be at this school?"

"I'll explain it to you later. Let's go before we get caught." He holds his hand out to me.

"Where?" I play along, knowing what my answer will be. I want the fantasy—if only for a second.

"Wherever you want. You once said that you wanted to see the ocean. Let's go to the ocean, Beth. We can live there."

The ocean. The scene comes alive in my mind. Me in a pair of old faded jeans and a tank top. My hair blowing wildly in the breeze. Isaiah with his hair buzzed short and shirt off, his tattoos frightening the tourists as they stroll by. I'll sit barefoot on the warm sand and watch the crashing waves while he watches me. Isaiah always keeps his eye on me.

I wrap my arms around myself and clutch the hem of my shirt to prevent myself from grasping him. "I can't."

He keeps his arm extended, but the weight of my words causes it to waver. "Why not?"

"Because if I run away, if I break Scott's rules, he'll send my mom to jail."

Isaiah's hand clenches into a fist and his arm drops to his side. "Fuck him."

"My mom!"

"Fuck her too. In fact, why were you even with her Friday night? You promised me you'd stay away from her. She hurts you."

"No, it was her boyfriend. Mom would never hurt me."

"She let you take the fall for her bullshit and she sat back while he used you as a fucking piñata. Your mom is a nightmare."

A car door slams in the parking lot, and we slink to opposite corners by the door.

"We need to talk, Beth."

I agree. We do. I nod toward the pinewoods. "Let's go over there."

Isaiah pokes his head out and scans the area. He waves his hand for me to go. We don't run. We walk in absolute silence. Once we're deep enough in, I turn, waiting for the question that has to be tearing him apart.

"You lied to me." Isaiah shoves his hands into his jeans pocket and stares at the brown pine needles on the ground. "You told me you never knew your dad."

Okay. Not a question, but an accusation. One I deserve. "I know."

"Why?"

"I didn't want to talk about my dad."

He keeps looking at those damn needles. A few years ago, I told Isaiah the same lie I gave everyone else regarding my father. Isaiah was so moved that he told me something he'd never told anyone else: that his mother had no idea who his father was. The lie I told Isaiah bonded him to me for life. By the time I figured out what cemented our relationship, that he believed we both had huge question marks on the paternal side, it was too late to tell him the truth.

"You know how people are." I hate the desperation in my voice. "They love gossip and if there's a story, they'll dig, and I never wanted to think about the bastard again. When I told you I never knew who my father was, I had no idea that was your reality. I didn't know that was the story that would make us friends."

His eyes shut at the word *friends* and his jaw jumps as if I said something to hurt him. But we are friends. He's my best friend. My only friend.

"Isaiah…" I have to give him something. Something that will let him know what he means to me. "What happened with my dad…" It hurts to breathe. "When I was in third grade…" Say it already!

Isaiah's gray eyes meet mine. The kindness in them fades

as they turn a little wild. "Is your dad around?" In the predatory movement of a panther, he takes several steps toward me. "Are you in danger?"

I shake my head. "No. He's gone. Uncle Scott and Dad hated each other. Scott didn't even know Dad left."

"Your uncle?"

"He's a dick, but he'd never lay a hand on me. I swear."

He blinks and the wildness fades, but his muscles still ripple with anger. "I trusted you." His three simple words gut me.

"I know." I can give him honesty now. "I wish I could go with you."

"Then do it."

"She's my mom. I expected you to understand." It's a low blow. I stay silent, unmoving, waiting for him to swallow his demons.

"I get it," he says in a hard voice, "but it doesn't mean I agree."

Good. He's forgiven me. Guilt still eats at me, but at least my stomach muscles relax while the guilt feasts.

"Nice shirt," he says, and I smile at his playful tone.

"Fuck you."

"There's my girl. I was wondering if they sucked out your personality in first period."

"You're not far off." Time is running short. I've lost so much already. I can't lose him. "What do we do?"

"What are your uncle's terms?"

"No running away and no more seeing you or Noah." Scott said he wanted me to completely forget my old life. That the only way I'd have a fresh start was to make a clean break and if I wouldn't willingly amputate the past, then he'd do it for me.

Isaiah grimaces. "And?"

"No ditching school. No being disrespectful to his wife or teachers or people."

"You're screwed."

"Fuck you again."

"Love you too, Sunshine."

I ignore him. "Good grades. No smoking. No drugs. No drinking. And...no contact with Mom."

"Hmm. I agree with the last one. Can you make it happen this time?"

I glare at him. He flips me off. God, he's aggravating. "No more cursing. Keep curfew."

His head pops up. "He's letting you out?"

"Probably with a GPS stitched under my forehead. I have to clear every second of every outing through him. What are you thinking?"

"I'm thinking you're a bright girl who could manipulate the devil for a passage out of hell. You get out of that house and I'll come get you. Any day. Any time. And I'll have you safely home by curfew."

Hope fills me, yet it's not enough. I need more than Isaiah. I need something else. I fiddle with the ends of my shirttail. "Will you take me to see my mom?"

He sighs. "No. She's no good for you."

"He'll kill her."

"Let him. She made her choices."

I stumble back as if he punched me. "How can you say that?"

The anger returns to his eyes. "How? A few months ago,

she let you bleed in front of her. How could she go back to that bastard? How could she let you take the fall for her? Don't play the sympathy card on me. No one fucks with you. Do you understand me?"

I nod to placate him, but I'll find another way. Isaiah's right. I can play Scott, keep Isaiah, and find a way to take care of Mom.

He pulls something out of his back pocket and tosses it to me. I slide open a shiny new gray cell phone. "We saw Scott trash your cell so I bought a new one for you and put you on my plan."

I quirk up a smile. "You got a plan?"

He shrugs. "Noah and I got a plan and we put you on it. Cheaper that way."

"How..." Echo inspired. "Grown-up."

"Yeah. Noah's been doing a lot of that."

"How did you know? That I'd be here? In Groveton? At school?"

Isaiah focuses on the trees. "Echo. At the police station, she sat close enough to your uncle and your mom to overhear what was going down. Then Echo talked Shirley into giving us the rest of the information. Scott told Shirley his plans."

"Great," I mumble. "I'm in debt to psycho bitch." The moment I say it, I feel a twinge of remorse. She's not entirely crazy, but the truth is our relationship is strained. She's sweet and she's nice and she makes Noah happy, but she's brought change...too much change...and how can I like that?

He shifts from one side to another. That's not good. "What else, Isaiah?"

"Echo sold a painting."

I raise my eyebrows. "So?" Echo's been selling her paintings since last spring.

He reaches into his back pocket again and produces a wad of cash. Holy Mother of God, I'm going to start painting. "It was one of her favorites. Something she painted for her brother before he died. Noah was ticked when he found out." He holds out the money. "She did it for you."

Pissed. I'm beyond pissed. "I don't want her charity." She didn't do it for me. She did it for Noah and Isaiah, but she mainly did it so I'd have to owe her and she knows that pride is one of the few things I rightfully own.

Isaiah closes the distance between us and shoves the bills in my back pocket before I have a chance to step away. "Take it. I want to know you have cash in case you need to bail quickly. It's my debt to pay."

The wad of cash feels heavy in my back pocket. Even though I'm determined to see this year out, I also know that life sucks. It's best to be prepared.

The bell rings, signaling the end of lunch. "I gotta go."

As I walk past him, Isaiah wraps a hand around my arm. "One more thing." His eyes darken into shadows. "Call me. Anytime. I swear to you, I'll answer."

"I know." It takes a second to work up the courage to say it, but he's my best friend and worth the words. "Thank you."

"Anything for you." Isaiah releases me, and as I walk back to school my fingers trace the area where my skin still burns from his touch. He's my friend...my only friend.

I pull on the handle of the same door I'd snuck out of and my heart sinks as the door stays shut. No. I broke the cardinal rule of ditching: always make sure you can sneak back in. I wiggle the handle. Nothing. I wiggle the other door's handle. Same result. The dread sparks deep in my stomach and becomes a flash fire of panic in a heartbeat. I can't get back in, which means I'll be busted when I don't show for next period. When Scott finds out, he'll burst a blood vessel.

With both hands, I grab the handle again. "Come on!" I yank. The door gives. A hand flies out, snatches my arm, and drags me into the building.

I glance up at my rescuer and my insides become liquid when I see the most beautiful light brown eyes staring down at me. Ruining the moment, their owner speaks. "I'm not sure this is what your uncle meant by showing you around."

"Damn, my life sucks," I mutter.

It's Ryan. I really hate this town.

RYAN

SKATER GIRL IS ON THE losing end of this moment. She snaps her arm out of my hand and glares at me with those unblinking blue eyes. "I don't want your help."

Winning feels great. Awesome. Drives me higher than anything else in the world. The twisting and pressure that I so often feel—gone. Winning leaves my muscles loose, makes me lift my head higher, and damn if it doesn't bring on a smile. "You may not want it, but you need it."

The second bell rings and Beth slams into my arm as she stalks past. Twenty bucks she thinks she's late for class. "It's only second bell."

She hesitates and her spine goes rigid. "How many are there?"

"After lunch?" I casually walk up to her. This is too much fun. "Three. One to release lunch. A two-minute warning bell. Then the tardy bell."

She releases a slow stream of air from her perfectly shaped lips, and relief relaxes her cheeks. This girl is sexy, but she's also a handful. If I hadn't accepted the dare, I'd toss her into avoid-like-the-plague territory. "What's your next class?"

"Go to hell." Beth rushes down the hallway and I pursue her at a leisurely pace.

Lockers lurch open and clang shut. Chatter fills the hallway. People stop and stare as Beth moves. Moves—that's exactly what the girl does. She holds her head high and owns the middle of the hallway. A few kids have transferred to this school since my freshman year, but they spent their first couple of weeks trying to blend into the paint. Not Beth. Her hips have this easy sway that catches the eye of every guy, including me.

Beth checks out the numbers over the doors, no doubt searching for her fifth-period room. I pick up the pace and fall in step with her as she pulls a badly folded schedule out of her back pocket. Her thumb skims the list until it finds its target: Health/Physical Education.

The odds of winning just increased in my favor. That's my next class too. "I can show you where it is."

"Are you stalking me? If so, you'll get your ass kicked."

"By who? The guy you made out with in the tree line?" I have a hard time believing that a man as great as Scott Risk would allow his niece to date Tattoo Guy, but maybe that's why he switched her schools. You gotta love a man who takes care of family. "Sorry to tell you, but I can hold my own."

Beth wears a scowl that could kill on sight. "Threaten Isaiah again and *I'll* kick your ass."

I chuckle at the thought of the tiny, black-haired threat throwing swings at me. Punches from her would feel like a bunny biting a lion. By the way she pinches her lips together, I can tell my laughter pisses her off. Time to end this bull. "I'm just trying to be helpful."

"Helpful? You mean you're trying to help yourself. You're a walking hard-on for my uncle."

A muscle near my eye ticks. On rare occasions, bunnies can develop rabies, and Scott did warn me she was rough around the edges. He failed to mention that razor blades are her softest layer. My mouth snaps open to ask what the hell is wrong with her when Lacy sidles between us. She shoots me a warning glare. "I got this."

"Come on, dawg." Chris waggles his eyebrows and I realize he sent in Lacy to disturb us, thinking he interrupted me making a play. "Let's go to class."

"Yeah." Class. I want to win the dare, but that won't happen if I lose my temper. I follow Chris, willing to do anything to get away from Beth.

BETH

THE MOMENT RYAN TURNS his back, I sag against a purple locker. The acrid smell of fresh paint fills my nose. Watch— the damn locker is newly painted and I'll have purple on my ass.

A hallway full of strange teenagers gawk at me like I'm an animal caged at the zoo. I swallow when two girls giggle as they pass. Both crane their necks to get a better glimpse of the new school freak.

People judge. They're judging me now.

"Your hair used to be blond," says Lacy.

What is the deal with the people in this town and my hair? I barely recognize the girl I once claimed as a friend. We sized each other up in English, trying to figure out if the other was really who we thought she was. Lacy has the same chestnut-brown hair as when we were kids. Just as long, but not as stringy. It's thick now. She nods at Ryan's friend Chris, indicating that he should follow Ryan into the classroom and he does.

"You used to hang out with cool people," I say.

The right corner of her lips tilts up. "I used to hang with you."

"That's what I just said."

The bell rings and a few remaining stragglers race to class. Lucky me, I share another class with Ryan. I push off the wall, check for paint, and feel off-balance when Lacy follows.

The cliques split off as fast as cockroaches when a light shines. Ryan and a couple other guys relax at a table near the back as if they're God's gift to women. Their expensive jeans and T-shirts that sport their favorite moronic teams scream total jock. I hand my enrollment sheet to a teacher deep in conversation with two more jocks. They discuss baseball, football, basketball. Blah, blah, blah. It must be a male thing to talk about playing with balls.

Lacy plops down at an empty table and kicks out a chair for me to join her. "Ryan says you go by Beth."

I fall into the chair and glance over at Ryan. He quickly averts his eyes. My blood tingles—was he really staring at me? *Stop it.* The tingling fades. *Of course he was. You're the freak, remember?* "What else did Ryan tell you?"

"Everything. Meeting you Friday night. Yesterday with Scott."

Fuck. "So the whole damn school knows."

"No," she says thoughtfully. Lacy looks me over and I can tell she's searching for that pathetic girl from a long time ago. "He only told me, Chris, and Logan. The one with dark hair sitting next to Ryan is my boyfriend, Chris."

"My apologies."

"He's worth it." She pauses. "Most of the time."

For four classes, people have ignored me. I helped the situation by sitting in the back of each room and glaring at anyone who looked at me for longer than a second. Lacy drums her fingers against the table. Two thin black ponytail holders wrap her wrist. She wears low-rider jeans and a green retro T-shirt imprinted with a faded white four-leaf clover.

"How many people have you told?" I ask her.

The drumming stops. "Told what?"

I lower my voice and pick at the remaining black paint on my nails. "Who I am and why I left town." I'm fishing. Because of the enrollment slip, no one has called my name out in class and no one's mentioned my uncle. For today, I'm anonymous, but how long will that last? I'm also testing the waters for the town gossip. Lacy's dad was a police officer and he was the first one to walk into the trailer that night.

"No one," she says. "You'll tell people about your uncle when you're ready. It's sickening. No one gave a crap about Scott until the World Series. Now everyone worships him."

A group of girls break into laughter. The same type of purse rests on the table in front of each perfectly manicured girl. Sure, the colors and sizes of the purses are different, but the style is the same. The blonde laughing the loudest catches me looking and I toss my hair over my shoulder as a shield. I know her, and I don't want her to remember me.

"Gwen's still staring," Lacy says. "It might take a few days for the hamster wheel turning her brain to make the full circle, but she'll figure you out soon enough."

I might appreciate her sarcasm if I wasn't distracted by the blonde. Gwen Gardner. The summer before kindergarten, Lacy's mom suggested to Scott that I go with Lacy to Vacation Bible School. I put on my favorite dress, one of two that I owned, pinned as many ribbons as I could in my hair, and skipped into the room. A group of girls in beautiful fluffy dresses surrounded me as I introduced myself. To the tune of giggles and whispers from the other girls, Gwen proceeded to point out every hole and stain on my beloved dress.

That was the high point in my relationship with Gwen. From there, it went downhill.

"She still a bitch?" I ask.

"Worse." Lacy's tone drops. "Yet everyone believes she's a saint."

"And I thought third grade sucked."

Lacy snorts. "Imagine what middle school and training bras were like with her. I swear the girl blossomed into a C-cup between fifth and sixth grade. Thank God Ryan finally broke up with her last spring. I couldn't stand being within a foot of her a moment longer."

Of course Ryan dated Gwen. I'm sure the break-up is temporary and they'll marry soon and create tons of other little perfect spawns of Satan in order to torture further generations of people like me.

We lapse into an awkward silence. It's strange talking to Lacy. It used to be the two of us against the world. Then I left. I assumed, in my absence, she'd become one of them—the girls who were perfect. She had the potential to be one. Her parents had money. Her mom would have bought her the clothes. Lacy was pretty and fun. For some insane reason, she stuck with me—the girl who had two outfits and lived in the trailer park.

I scratch off the remaining paint. Yesterday Allison bought me nail polish in the annoying shade of mauve. How can anyone look at me and think mauve? "What did your dad tell you?"

Lacy's pinkie taps the table repeatedly. "That he was called to your home and that you later moved to another city."

Surprised, I glance up to catch sincerity in her dark eyes. "That's it?"

"Everyone thinks Scott swooped in and saved you. Daddy and the other guys that responded that night let that rumor stand." Her forehead crinkles. "It's what happened, right? You've been living with Scott?"

I scratch my cheek, trying to hide whatever reaction she might see. I could lie and tell her yes, but that would be like I'm embarrassed about Mom. And I'm not embarrassed. I love her. I owe her. Yet there are times...

"I cried for three months when you left," Lacy continues. "You were my best friend."

I cried too. A lot. Thanks to me and my stupid decisions, I cost my mom everything and I lost my best friend. Typical me—a hurricane that leaves nothing but destruction. "Go sit with your friends, Lacy. I'm bad news."

"In this classroom, those two guys sitting over there are the only real friends I have." Lacy drums her fingers once more. "And you."

I raise an eyebrow. "Your life must suck then."

She laughs. "Not really. It's a good life."

The teacher calls the class to order and I inch my seat away from Lacy's. An unseen, uncomfortable vise tightens my chest. Normal people don't like me. They don't want to be my friend, and here is someone offering friendship willingly.

As the teacher calls attendance, Ryan's name is read and he answers with a deep, soothing, "Here."

Taking a chance, I peek in his direction and find him staring at me again. No smile. No anger. No cockiness. Just a thoughtful expression mixed with confusion. He scratches the back of his head and I'm drawn to his biceps. My traitorous stomach flutters. God, the boy may be an ass, but he sure is built.

And guys like him *don't* go for girls like me. They only use me.

I force my eyes to the front of class, pull my knees to my chest, and wrap my arms around them. Lacy invades my space and whispers to me, "I'm glad you're back, Beth."

A sliver of hope sneaks past my walls and I slam every opening shut. Emotion is evil. People who make me feel are worse. I take comfort in the stone inside of me. If I don't feel, I don't hurt.

RYAN

WAITING ON SUNDAY DINNER, I can observe a lot from my seat on the couch in the living room of the mayor's house. For instance, the serious set of Dad's mouth and the angle of his body toward Mr. Crane suggests that Dad's talking business. Serious business. Mom, on the other hand, is laughter and giggles as she stands next to the mayor's wife and the pastor's wife, but the way she fingers her pearls tells me she's anxious. That means someone asked a question about Mark.

Mom misses him. So do I.

The power of observation. It's a skill I need to play ball. Is the runner on base going to chance a steal? Is the batter going to hit the ball out of the park or is he going to hit a sacrifice fly in order to score the runner on third? Is Skater Girl the hard-nosed chick I believe her to be?

For the last two weeks, I've watched Beth roam the school. She's interesting. Nothing like the girls I know. She sits by herself at lunch and eats a full meal. Not salad. Not an apple. A full meal. Like an entrée, two sides, and a dessert. Even Lacy doesn't do that.

Beth sits in the back of every class, except for Health/

Gym, where Lacy patiently makes small talk even though Beth stays quiet. Sometimes Lacy can get Beth to crack a smile, but it's rare. I like it when she smiles.

Not that I care if she's happy or anything.

What I find the most interesting is that even though she's Ms. Antisocial, she doesn't avoid people. Yeah, plenty of kids hide in plain sight. They duck into the library before school or during lunch. They evade eye contact and walk in the shadows as if they can go to school and never be detected. Not Beth. She stands her ground. Owns the space around her and smirks if someone comes too close, as if she's daring them to take her on. A smirk that dares turns *me* on.

"Are you ready for the quiz tomorrow?" Mrs. Rowe, my English teacher, rests against the arm of the couch. She also happens to be the mayor's daughter. While everyone else wears suit pants, ties, or conservative dresses, Mrs. Rowe wears a daisy-print hippie dress. Today, her hair is purple.

Considering the fights my family has had over Mark, I'm curious about the brawls that happen behind closed doors at this house. Or maybe other families find a way to accept one another.

"Yes, ma'am." To discourage small talk, I shove a bacon-wrapped shrimp into my mouth. Dad likes me to be at these occasional Sunday gatherings. I come in handy when the men discuss sports. I used to come in handier when I dated Gwen. Her dad is the police chief, plus my mother's friends thought we were "cute together."

"I hated these things when I was your age," Mrs. Rowe continues. I pop in another shrimp and nod. If she hated them, I would think she'd remember that useless conversation is physically painful. "My dad made me attend every dinner he threw."

I swallow and realize that not once in my four years of being old enough to represent the family have I seen Mrs. Rowe attend one of these functions. I consider asking why she's here tonight, then remember I don't care. In goes a meatball.

"I read your paper," she says.

I shrug. Reading my paper is her job.

"It's good. In fact, it's very good."

My eyes dart to hers and I curse internally when she smiles. Dammit, it shouldn't matter if it was good. I want to play ball, not write. I make a show of staring in the opposite direction.

"Have you thought about expanding it into a short story?"

This I have an answer for. "No."

"You should," she says.

I shrug again and begin to search the room for a viable reason to escape—like the curtains catching on fire.

A sly smile spreads across her face. "Listen, I received good news and I'm so glad I don't have to wait until tomorrow to share. Do you remember the writing project we worked on last year?"

It'd be tough to forget. We spent the year devouring books and movies. Then we tore them apart as if they were machines so we could see how the parts worked together to create the story. After that, Mrs. Rowe snapped the whip and made us write something of our own. Hardest damn class I ever took and I loved every second. Hated it too. When I became too interested or too eager in class, the guys from the team rode me hard.

"Do you remember how I entered everyone into the state writing competition?"

I nod a yes, but the answer is no. Just because I loved the class didn't mean I listened to everything she said. "Why? Did Lacy win?" She had a hell of a short story.

"No..."

In goes another meatball. That sucks. Lacy would have been excited if she won.

"You finaled, Ryan."

The meatball slips into my throat whole and I choke.

Ditching the formal clothes for a pair of athletic pants and a Reds T-shirt, I lean back in the chair at my desk and stare at the homework assignment I turned in to Mrs. Rowe. In four pages, poor George woke up to discover he had become a zombie. My favorite sentence is the paper's last:

Staring down at his hands, hands that someday would likely kill, George swallowed the sickening knowledge that he had become absolutely powerless.

Why it's my favorite, I don't know. But every time I read it something stirs inside me, some sort of sense of justification.

I run a hand over my hair, unable to comprehend that I finaled in a writing competition. Maybe later tonight hell will freeze over and donkeys will start flying out of my ass. It all seems possible at this point.

I swivel the chair and survey my room. Trophies and medals and accolades for playing ball are scattered on the wall, the shelves, my dresser. A Reds pennant hangs over my bed.

I know baseball. I'm good at it. I should be. It's been my entire life.

I'm Ryan Stone—ballplayer, jock, leader of the team. But Ryan Stone—writer? I chuckle to myself as I pick the paperwork up off the desk. All of it describes in detail how to continue to the next phase of the writing competition, how to win. Not once in my life have I backed down from a challenge.

But this...this is beyond what I am. I toss the papers down again. I need to stay focused on what's important and writing isn't it.

BETH

GYM IS AN ABOMINATION to self-esteem. While changing out of the white ruffled shirt into the required gym attire of a pink Bullitt County High T-shirt and matching shorts, I take stock of the other girls. They gossip as they change. Most brush their hair. Some fix their makeup. All thin. All fit. All beautiful. Not me though. I'm thin enough, but I'm not pretty.

The girls who really irritate me are the ones God gave everything to: money, looks, and a C-cup chest. Gwen is the worst. The moment she enters the locker room, she strips her shirt and walks around freely in her lace bra. Her non-verbal reminder that us B-cups are inferior.

Busting out of the locker room, I relax when I see the gym is empty. Most of the school is a no-cell zone, but not the gym. I desperately need to speak to Mom. It's been two weeks since the last time I talked to her and her last words to me were that pathetic "please...probation" in the parking lot. Trent wouldn't permit her to say goodbye to me at the police station. God, I hate him.

I duck under the bleachers, pull the phone out of my shorts

pocket, and dial Mom's number. I've called several times over the last two weeks, but she's never answered. Anytime after four she'd be at the bar. Mom told me once that you're only an alcoholic if you drink before noon. Good thing for Mom she never wakes before three.

The phone rings once then three loud beeps answer. A calm, annoying voice states a message of doom: "Sorry, the number you have dialed has been disconnected."

Regret becomes a weight in my stomach. Last month, I could pay the electricity bill with Mom's disability check or I could pay the phone bill. The electricity company sent a disconnect notice. I thought I had more time on the phone. I picked the electricity bill.

My throat becomes thick and my eyes burn. Crap—my mom. I messed up. Again. Imagine that. I should have paid the phone bill. I should have found a way. I could have taken on more hours stocking at the Dollar Store. I could have sucked up my pride and asked Noah or Isaiah for money. I could have done so many things and I didn't. Why am I such a screwup?

I suddenly wish it was ten at night. Isaiah and I talk then— every night. Usually, it's not for long. Just a few seconds or so. He's not a phone talker by nature, but the first time I called he asked me to check in nightly and I do. His voice is the only thing keeping me sane.

I slip the phone into my pocket as everyone files into the gym. They chatter and laugh, oblivious to the real problems of the real world. I need to find a ride into Louisville and I need to find one fast. A sharp pain slices through my head and threatens to form into a headache when Lacy breaks away from Chris and Ryan to join me. I'm not in the mood for this—not today.

"You changed quickly," Lacy says. "Are you okay? You look upset."

"I'm fine." But I itch to wipe my eyes. Somehow, they're wet and full, and I refuse to touch them around Lacy or anyone else. I never cry and I'll never let anyone believe that I'm capable of the moronic act.

"Five-minute round up!" Mr. Knox, our health teacher, calls.

He wears a shiny whistle around his neck. "On the bulletin board is every exercise you are required to perform in order to receive credit for this class. We will be spending three days in the gym and two in the classroom. Some exercises you can do on your own. Others require teamwork. You have two opportunities to impress me, so I suggest that you use your time wisely and do not come to me for credit unless you have practiced the item to perfection."

We stare at him in silence. Mr. Knox jerks his thumb behind him. "Get to work."

I lag behind the others, praying that most of the exercises can be done on my own. My insides twist as I watch people pair off into twos and threes to complete their assignments. Left alone, I sidle up to the board and sigh so heavily that the posted paper moves. Surely I can convince Mr. Knox that I am, within myself, a four-layered pyramid.

"You can work with me."

My heart stutters at the sound of Ryan's voice. Damn, why do I have to find everything about this boy attractive? His voice, his face, his biceps, his abs... *Stop it!* I cross my arms over my chest and turn to face him. "I thought we had an agreement."

"No. You threw a hissy fit on the first day of school. That doesn't constitute an agreement."

Ryan isn't wearing his baseball cap and I love it. His sandy-blond hair has a golden tone. It's styled-yet-not-styled into the disarray of not quite curls that kick out in various directions. Get a grip, Beth. Hot guys don't go for loser girls. "Leave me alone."

I walk away from Ryan because he shows no sign of leaving me. Stacks of equipment line the wall on the other side of the gym. One of the four items that can be completed on my own is jumping rope. I can do that. I think. I used to jump rope when I was a kid.

I grasp one of the ropes and twenty others tumble out of the box along with it. All of them knotted and intertwined. Gwen and a group of girls giggle as they gawk at me. I wonder if they'll still be giggling when I turn and beat them with the jump-rope knot from hell.

"Trust fall." Lacy magically teleports in front of me.

Still holding the train of ropes, I glance up at her. "What?"

"Trust fall. Me and the boys are doing it and you're going to do it with us."

"No, I'm not."

"Yes, you are. Requirements say that we have to have at least two girls in the group."

I blink twice. "Go ask one of the girls grooming each other like monkeys."

"Those aren't girls. They're vultures."

Ryan and Chris watch us. The other one studies the five-foot platform we're supposed to "fall" from. I ask, "What's the guy with black hair doing in this class?" He wasn't last week, but he is in my English class and had the balls to tease me on my first day. Platform guy is lucky to be alive.

Lacy waves him off. "That's Logan. He tested out of his math and they switched his schedule and the rest is totally not important. Let's go." She snatches my hand and the rope drags with me until I remember to drop it.

She releases me when we reach the platform. Ryan gives me a condescending smile. "Changed your mind? Don't worry, most girls do when it comes to me."

I wish I had a jacket that I could pull around myself and hide in. I don't, so I do the next best thing. "Did you have to bribe those girls with tacos or was that reserved for me?"

Chris and Logan chuckle and Ryan angles his shoulders away from me. On the other side of the gym, Lacy kicks at a huge foam mat. The boys rescue her by lifting the gigantic mat into the air like it weighs nothing, then tossing it in front of the platform. A spark of panic hurts my lungs. "What's that for?"

"In case we drop you," says Logan.

"In case you what?" Frantically, I eyeball the wooden platform that reminds me of a diving board at a public pool. I can't swim and I don't jump.

"Drop you," he repeats.

Lacy smacks the back of Logan's head. "Stop it. We won't drop you."

Of course they won't, because I'm not jumping. I step backward.

"What's the plan, Boss Man?" asks Logan as he looks at Ryan. I snort and Ryan glances at me. Of course, they see perfect Ryan as their fearless leader.

Ryan rearranges the mat to center it with the platform. "Each of us takes one practice run. We perfect our technique and then we show Coach. Logan, you're first. That way if we have the wrong technique, we drop a guy, not a girl."

Chris, Ryan, and Lacy gather around the mat. I stay planted in my spot. "If you're the boss, then why don't you go first?"

"Because Logan's crazy and would go first even if I didn't ask. At least now someone's here to catch him."

"It's true," adds Lacy. "Logan's too smart for common sense."

"Fear." Logan sits on the platform. His legs dangle over the side. "Too smart for fear."

Lacy shrugs. "Potayto, potahto. Same thing."

"No, it's not."

"Yes, it is."

"Shut it down," says Ryan. "Come on, Beth. You and Lacy take the area toward his feet. Chris and I will handle his back."

"Why, so we can get kicked in the head? That's real gallant."

"No," says Ryan with forced patience. "Logan's all upper body. Chris and I are going to take the heavier part."

Logan pumps his chest with his fist. "Solid wall, baby."

"Less talking, more jumping," says Chris. "Let's go, dawg."

I take my place across from Lacy. Without giving me much of a choice, Lacy grabs hold of my hands and seconds later we grip each other tighter when heavy legs plop onto our arms.

"Son-of-a-bitch, Junior," swears Chris. "You were supposed to count down before you jumped. Drop his sorry ass."

Okay. Lacy and I let go and Logan falls the remaining way

onto the mat. He laughs as he scrambles up. "You caught me just fine."

"My turn!" Lacy hops over the mat and climbs the platform.

Ryan takes Lacy's place across from me and offers me his hands. I stare down at them. I don't touch people and they don't touch me. I mean, Lacy has, but it's different. We used to be friends, even if was a long time ago. Sweat forms on my palms and I rub them against my shorts and place my hands over Ryan's. His fingers clutch mine. His skin is the right mixture of strength and warmth, and his touch sends shivers through my body. I've gone two torturous weeks without a cigarette and I really crave one right now.

"All right, Lace," Ryan says in that deep, soothing voice. "Whenever you're ready."

Ryan and I have been holding hands for five seconds.

"It's kind of high." Lacy stands on the edge of the platform. A bit of the fire that constantly lives in her eyes diminishes.

Ryan gives me that glorious smile—the cute one with a hint of dimples. A curling heat spreads in my bloodstream. Damn, I like that smile.

"You can do this, baby," says Chris.

Ryan's thumb moves across the top of my hands and every single cell of my being becomes a live electrical socket. We've been holding hands for ten seconds.

"I know." Lacy doesn't look like she knows. She looks as unsure as I feel about catching her. "Maybe one of you guys should go."

"Turn around, Lace, and fall backward." Ryan uses a gentle yet commanding tone. Even though he speaks to Lacy, he keeps those brilliant light brown eyes locked on me. His thumb does another heart-skipping sweep across my hand. "You've got this and you know we got you."

I wonder what it would be like if he held me in his arms? Would I feel as alive as I do now?

"You're right." She sighs. "Give me a sec."

My hands sweat again and I don't want any more thoughts of my body lying next to his or visions of his hands on my skin or hope that his smile is for me. I don't want anyone touching me anymore. Especially guys that are strong and warm and slightly cute and can make my heart stutter. I try to pull away, but Ryan tightens his grip. "What are you doing?"

"She can't do it," I say. "And she shouldn't have to."

Ryan studies me for a second. "Yes, she can. Lacy can do anything she puts her mind to."

I try to jerk my arms away again, but Ryan's hold is too tight.

"This is stupid." Panic floods my brain and makes me feel a little crazy. "All of this is stupid. What's the stupid point?"

"To learn how to work together as a team and to put our trust in one another." Ryan's voice becomes a calming balm on my panic until I figure out how much I want to listen. This isn't good. Not good at all. Isn't that how the pied piper worked? Didn't he play something soothing and all the rats drowned?

"I'm not a part of your stupid team."

"I know, but let's pretend for a few seconds that you are."

"She's ready," says Chris.

A split second later Lacy's Nikes are inches from my face. Resting safely in our hands, Lacy laughs. "That was great. Let's do it again."

Ryan releases me and helps the guys lower Lacy to her feet. I step back and try to rub any trace of Ryan off onto my clothes. I don't want strong hands holding my arms. I don't want to be part of a team, and I sure as hell don't have to prove anything by jumping off a ledge.

"You're next, Beth," Ryan says.

"No." The word comes out automatically.

"You're going to have to go sometime, so let's do it now."

"I swear it's not that bad." Lacy flies to my side. "At first I was like 'no way' and then Ryan was like 'You can' and then I thought 'I can't' and then I thought 'These guys would never drop me' and I was like 'Okay' and then I did it and it was such a rush."

Logan and Chris warily look at me. They'd drop me. Just like Ryan would definitely drop me. "What type of game are you playing?" I ask of Ryan.

He narrows his eyes. "What?"

"You used Lacy to lure me over here. Was your plan to make me believe I could trust you and then drop me so everyone can laugh?" With each word, my voice becomes higher and my heart pounds faster in my chest.

Ryan shakes his head. "No."

I turn on my heel and head to the locker room. I'll claim cramps and blood and periods and tampons and keep saying words like *menstruation* until the teacher lets me out of class. Right on the verge of entering the locker room, Ryan's large figure looms in front of me. "Where do you think you're going?"

"Go away," I say.

He points at me. "You are a part of this team and you will help us until this task is done."

"No," I bite out. "I'm not part of your perfect team."

"Get back over there."

"Here's the beauty of living in America. You can't make me do a damn thing." I slam my body into his and enter the safety of the locker room.

RYAN

COACH KNOX MADE US hit the locker rooms early and I rushed to get dressed. Beth will be one of the first girls out since she was the first in. Me and her—we have unfinished business. She left my team in a bind plus she ruined my plan to ask her out.

At the top of the wooden bleachers, she sits by herself with her back against the cinder-block wall and her legs stretched out. Her black hair rests behind her shoulders and she types into a cell phone with her thumbs. A small smile curves her lips. There's a look about Beth, one I haven't seen before... something almost peaceful.

Scaling the bleachers, I take the rows two at a time. The hollow thumping of my steps echoes in the empty gym. Beth snaps the phone shut and shoves it in her back pocket. The small smile and peacefulness fade as she officially extracts the claws. "Aren't you popular people supposed to be gracing the masses with your presence in the locker room, leaving us losers to hide in peace?"

"We need to talk."

"Well, I want to be alone."

Noted, but her being alone won't help me win the dare. "This is going to be a long year if you keep pushing everyone away. I can help you fit in, you know."

In a slow, sexy motion, Beth slides her silky hair behind her ear. "I see. You're into charity work. Admirable, but I think I'll pass."

How she does it, I don't know, but she has this hypnotizing sway and seductive voice that can make me forget for a few seconds why I don't like her. Then my brain replays her snide comments. Ignoring my admiration of her body and that I love the sound of her voice, I sit on the row below her.

Beth flutters her fingers in the air. "Go on," she says as if she was talking to a dog. "Shoo."

Play it cool. I've done it plenty of times. Pull out the charm. Overlook the fact she dismissed me when I asked her to hang with me during gym. Pretend I didn't have to resort to using Lacy in order to accomplish my goal. Repeat over and over again that I don't care that she left a team depending on her. "You look nice."

She glances at her outfit: black pants—stylish, form-fitting—and another white button-down shirt, except this one has puffed sleeves. Definitely not the style she wore when I first met her. On Gwen, those clothes would look like they came out of a fashion show. On Beth...it makes me miss the jeans with holes.

"Nice for a clown in a traveling circus. What angle are you playing?"

For her to give me a damn break. "Go out with me."

"Are you trying to snag the niece to impress Scott or a fuck to impress your friends?"

A muscle in my jaw jumps and her all-seeing eyes catch

it. I've come to detest that wicked grin. Be nice. Even if she isn't. Getting mad won't help me win her over. Plus, she's not far off the mark. "There's a field party Friday night. It would be a good chance to meet people instead of blowing them off."

She leans in and I inhale the distinct scent of roses. "I'll let you in on a secret. I kind of enjoy blowing people off. It goes well with my attitude of this-school-can-eat-shit-and-die."

What the hell is wrong with this girl?

Beth relaxes back onto the bleacher. "I'll ask again, what's the game, Jock Boy?"

"No game," I say too quickly and try to slow it down. The door to the locker rooms opens and I hear laughter as people enter the gym. I have seconds to impress her before the bleachers fill. "You're pretty, Beth." Suddenly it's hard to look at her. She is pretty. More than pretty. I stare at my shoes. Get a grip, Ryan. She's a dare.

"I'm pretty?" Beth raises her voice and I glimpse the other students climbing the bleachers and taking their seats. Their chatter stops and they watch the two of us. This is not how this moment is supposed to go.

"I'm pretty," she repeats loud enough for the entire gym to hear. The evil sparkle in her eye informs me that she's enjoying the social lynching. "Is that the best line you can come up with? Let's fast-forward this entire conversation so you can stop wasting my time." She holds up the palm of her hand and even though the word is gone, I still see my defeat: *can't*.

Tim Richardson imitates the whistle of a bomb dropping from the sky and uses his hands to create the explosion. "Crash and burn, Ry. Good to hear that the new girl has some standards. When you're done playing with the ballplayer, Beth, you can come play with me."

"Back off, Tim," I say in a low, clear warning. If Tim wants to cut me down—fine, but he leaves Beth out of it. Girls will be treated with respect.

"Don't pretend you're trying to defend me." Beth's eyes narrow. "You're pissed off that I'm not falling at your feet in worship like the rest of this pathetic school."

More laughter from the crowd. Idiots. She also put them down.

"You can't keep up," she whispers. "Stay the hell away from me."

Screw this. I can do anything.

Coach Knox blows his whistle and the entire class turns to face him. "Last order of business for the day. We need one senior girl and one senior guy nominated for the homecoming court. We'll start with guys."

Several hands rise. I can't keep up? She's so wrong.

"Raise your hand if you want Tim Richardson." Coach nods with each hand he counts.

I'm the king at this school. I can win any dare, any time. Win any game. If she wants to play, we'll play. She doesn't want the world to know she's Scott Risk's niece. Skater Girl humiliated me and she's about to learn that turnabout is fair play.

"Now for the girls," says Coach.

My hand rises in the air at the same time as everyone else's, but I'm not giving anybody else the opportunity to supply another name. "Beth Risk."

Hands drop. All gazes flicker between me and Beth. Her feet fall off the seat, one right after another—clomp, clomp. "What did you say?"

"Did you say Risk?" asks Tim. "As in Scott Risk? As in the baseball god who just moved back to our town?"

A wave of whispers crashes among the students sitting on the bleachers, Beth's name the topic of each hushed conversation. Ignoring Tim, I face Beth. Her blue eyes blaze like twin flames from a blowtorch. Who's not keeping up now? "I nominate you, Beth Risk, for homecoming court."

"No." She shakes her head. "You can't."

"Yes." I love winning. "I can."

"I second it," says Gwen with a bright smile plastered on her face, and red flags rise. She's wanted the homecoming crown since she was three.

Beth jerks up and stamps her foot against the bleacher like a toddler throwing a fit. "No, you can't. Nominate yourself."

"It's okay," says Gwen, "I was already nominated in first and second period."

"So was I." I waggle my eyebrows at Beth. "We could walk on the field together. Won't that be fun?"

Beth stands completely still, mouth slightly slack, her hands held out to her sides with her fingers spread. I finally nailed the girl who's been nailing me for weeks.

Coach Knox claps his hands to get our attention. "All in favor of adding Beth to the football homecoming court raise their hands."

With every eye on Beth, the entire class raises their hands. Everyone except for Lacy. Her stare burns holes through me, but she keeps her mouth shut.

"All opposed," says Coach Knox.

"Me," Beth yells. I smile. I love winning.

"Congratulations," Coach Knox says in a bored voice. "You're on the homecoming court."

"What the fuck is wrong with you people?"

Coach Knox points at her. "Take a seat and watch your language."

The bell rings. Beth grabs her backpack and leans into my face. "You are so fucking dead."

BETH

ARROGANT BOY—HE'S GOING DOWN. Blah. It's aggravating the way they worship him. Ryan this. Ryan that. Ryan's a god. Ryan's a goddamn moron. I've met guys like him before. Hell, I screwed one. Rather, one screwed me over. I'm not a stupid little girl anymore and I will no longer fall for things that look pretty.

Our Calculus teacher, with teased eighties hair, peers at us over her gigantic glasses. "When I call your name, come to the front and write out your work on the board." She scans the class. "Morgan Adams, Sarah Janes, Gwen Gardner, and Beth Risk."

The back of my head hits the wall behind me. Damn. This is Scott's fault. The stupid guidance counselor told Scott I couldn't keep up in this class, but Scott insisted I be placed in the honors program. Scott explained to me later that night, over the tofu and green crap his wife insisted on calling dinner, that he was raising my expectations of myself.

"So, it's true," someone says from the front of class. "Your last name is Risk."

Clank. Clank. The sound of the chains squeezing my lungs

echoes in my head. Since Ryan's little performance in Gym, the entire school has whispered as I pass and this time it isn't because I'm the school freak. No, they whisper for reasons way worse. Their envious, judging eyes survey me because they want to know me—or rather, my uncle.

"Are you related to Scott Risk?" asks a girl with short brown hair.

Everyone in the class watches me. My hands start to sweat.

"Ms. Risk?" prods our teacher. I'm not sure what she's prodding me on: that I'm the only one who hasn't come to the front or because I haven't answered the question. I stare at my empty notebook. Panic pushes my heart past my rib cage. What do I do?

My teacher's lips edge into a cheesy grin. "Why don't you go ahead and satisfy the curiosity of your fellow classmates." On the first day of school, Scott met privately with my teachers to "ensure I was in the best possible hands." The witch flirted with Scott until he gave her an autograph. She probably has his face tattooed on her ass.

Sweat forms along the hairline on my neck as the world sways. It's been too much: the changes. Losing Mom. Losing Isaiah. Losing my home. I've tried. Really I have. I've roamed the halls as the reclusive freak show. This answer will change everything again. "Yes."

Whispers and comments rush through the class like wind from an oncoming thunderstorm. Our teacher becomes uncharacteristically cheery. "I'm sure Beth would love to answer your questions about her uncle outside of class. Now, Ms. Risk, would you please come and write out your solution to today's equation?"

"No," I say without thinking. No to both of her statements.

I'm not answering anyone's questions and I'm not writing out a solution. My reply silences the class.

"Excuse me?" she asks.

I look at my blank sheet again. There is no way in hell I'm going to that dry-erase board and have the entire school witness the niece of the great Scott Risk fail because I'm an idiot. "I'm not writing out my solution."

The bell rings and my teacher's expression gives new meaning to the term *wrathful*. A couple more pounds of chains settle in my stomach. I've gone and done it—I've broken Scott's rules in a very public fashion. How could I do this to Mom?

"Ms. Risk," she calls from her desk as the rest of the class files out. I go, knowing the level of shit I'm in is too deep for her to allow an audience. "Let's discuss a few rules."

She "discusses" for a long time, and when she finally lets me go, I race down the stairs. Scott made it perfectly clear I was never to miss my bus. The idling buses greet me through the window when I reach the bottom floor. I have seconds before they leave.

A high-pitched whistle catches my attention. Ryan leans against the last locker with a shit-eating smirk on his face. He lifts his right hand and shows me his palm. Written there is the word that makes me want to vomit: *can*.

The buses roll out of the lot. Ryan withdraws his hand, and strides out the door.

RYAN

DEEP, THROATY LAUGHTER fills the school's weight room when Chris rips off the Kick Me sign Logan planted on his back. The laughter grows when Chris wads the paper up, throws it at Logan, and flips him off.

"All right, girls." Coach bangs his hand against one of the lockers to gain our attention. "I've got this week's study hall list."

The laughter switches to groaning. Coach is serious about our grades. Each week he pesters our teachers for a progress report and if he sees our grades slightly teeter, we end up in after-school tutoring. I wipe my hands on a towel and prepare to lie back to finish my reps. I'm no Logan, but I keep my grades at a decent level.

"Allen, Niles, and Jones."

Chris tilts his head back and moans. "Damn science."

I snap the towel at him. "Have fun." Nothing can lower this mood. I finally got the better of Beth. And it's about damn time. No one has bested me this long.

"Screw you, Ryan." Without another glance, Chris leaves the room.

"Stone!" calls Coach.

"Yeah?"

Coach stares at me oddly and hitches a thumb in the direction Chris just went. "Study hall."

"For what?" My grades are fine.

He shrugs. "Your English teacher requested you."

Back talk will get me push-ups or laps, so I suck up any commentary and head out of the room and down the empty hallways. When I finally reach study hall, I'm immediately greeted by Chris's chuckles. He leans back in his chair, ignoring the science book in front of him. "My life just got better."

If it weren't for the tutors and teachers in the room, I'd tell him where to shove it.

"Over here, Ryan." Mrs. Rowe waves at me as if I'm across a stadium. Her hair has a green tint today. I acknowledge her with a movement of my chin and walk over to her desk.

I slide into the chair next to her. "I passed the quiz and I've turned in my papers."

Her hand flutters in the air. "Oh, you're not here because of your grades."

My eyes narrow as my muscles tighten. "Then why am I here?"

She shuffles through a stack of papers, searching for something. Possibly her mind. "Your coach said we could request you for any academic reason. It doesn't have to be a bad reason. Stop being so pessimistic."

Pessimistic? "I'm missing weight training."

"So you are," she says as she pulls my George the zombie tale out of the stack. "You haven't turned in your paperwork for the writing competition. What you should be worried about is missing your opportunity at a college scholarship.

If you win this competition, you'll receive money toward any Kentucky school of your choice. It's not a full scholarship, but it's something."

"I'm not going to college," I say plainly.

She freezes and stares at me as if I'd announced her impending death. "Why not?"

I gesture at my shirt. Is this lady for real? "I'm a ballplayer. I'm going to play ball."

"You can play ball at college. Ryan...." She falters, then places my story in front of me. "This is the most magnificent piece of writing I've seen from a high school student. Ever. Have you considered that you're more than a ballplayer?"

My mouth opens to respond, but absolutely nothing comes out and that shocks me into closing it. My mind's blank. I'm a ballplayer. A damn good one. Isn't that enough?

"Did you even read the information I gave you about the state competition? For three years I've watched you obsess over winning. Aren't you interested in winning this too?"

I say nothing as my face reddens. Mrs. Rowe just called me out and she has a right to. I didn't read the paperwork. I haven't even considered the competition since the other night when she first told me I finaled.

"I have a feeling you enjoyed writing this. It's too good for you not to have."

She's right again. I did enjoy it. Finding those words, being in George's head...I stare down at the printed-out pages...it felt freeing. Just like when I step on the pitcher's mound before the game and the pressure begins. The moment when it's just me, a ball, and a mitt to throw into.

And he wondered what happened to the world around him. Did it also collapse into chaos? Had everything ceased to exist as it was, just like how his life spiraled into nothingness? Or had the rest of the world continued on like normal, because in the end his position within it never really mattered?

The words I wrote glare at me in accusation. A nagging ache pulls at my insides. I'm proud of those words and denying the competition is like denying part of me. In front of my computer, there were no secrets, no complications—just a world that I could control.

"In order to be considered for the award," Mrs. Rowe continues, "you need to complete a short story and turn it in a week prior to the event. Your attendance is still required that day, however, as that's when you'll get critiques of your work and meet with faculty members from universities across the state. It's one day. Just one Saturday."

I hear my dad in my head. "I have games Saturdays." And I glance over at Chris, who's eyeing me warily. How much of this conversation can he hear? "My team's depending on me."

She pats the pages resting in front of me. "Let's start off small, okay? Turn this four-page beginning into a true short story. I can yank you out of every weight training, or you can promise me that you'll write it in your free time at home. The choice is yours."

And it's a no-brainer. "I'll do it in my free time."

"Good." Her eyes light up. "But I'm still keeping you for the next hour. I want you to get started now."

BETH

ALLISON OWNS A MERCEDES. Leather interior. Jet-black on the outside. Isaiah would get all hot and bothered about the junk under the hood. She drives fast on the backcountry roads and a couple of times my stomach drops like we're on a roller coaster.

"You smell like smoke." Allison wears a red business suit and black stilettos. She's slicked her blond hair into a painfully tight bun. Maybe that's why she's uptight.

While waiting for Allison to drag herself away from the Ladies' Planning Committee, I smoked one of the cigarettes I bummed from a stoner boy before the incident in Calculus. I hoped it would help me get over the fight I had with Ryan. I don't know why, but yelling at him made me feel like crap. Kind of like I do after I fight with Isaiah. "Must be in your head."

"You smell like smoke when you come home from school. Scott may choose to ignore it, but he's not ignoring your little stunt in class." Allison pulls into the massive driveway surrounded by woods and notices when I glance at her. "That's right. Your teacher called."

Crap. I don't have any idea how to get myself out of this.

Scott and Allison live in a two-story white house with a wraparound porch. It resembles something you'd see in a Civil War movie full of rich plantation owners. Part of the house is surrounded by woods. The other part faces an open pasture with a barn.

Allison parks the car outside the four-car garage and grabs my wrist before I have a chance to bolt. "Do you have any idea how embarrassed I was to leave the meeting because you called? This is a small town. Your teachers belong to our church. How long do you think it will be before everyone knows what a menace you are? I won't permit you to ruin our life."

"Get your hands off of me." My eyes flicker from her fingers on my wrist to her eyes. No one touches me.

She drops my wrist like she was handling fire. "Why don't you leave? Even Scott knows you're miserable."

I bet Scott knows she's miserable too. I'd never have imagined him with someone like her. Manicured. Polished. Heartless. "Were you surprised he wasn't hard to trap?"

"What?"

"When you—" I do the mock quotation marks in the air "—'told' him you were pregnant, were you surprised how quickly he proposed? Scott always had a soft spot for babies. Why else would he marry you?"

Blood flushes her collarbone and her hands flutter up to her neck. "I don't know what you're even asking me." She clears her throat, obviously flustered. "Scott doesn't have a soft spot for babies."

Has she had a conversation with the man she married? "If it weren't for my mom, he would have married half of the girls knocked up in our trailer park." And he wasn't even the daddy.

Her hands slowly lower to her lap and I swear she quits breathing. "What did you say?"

"You heard me."

Her lips twist into a snarl. "Get out."

"Gladly." I open the door to her car, slam it shut, and repeat the process with the front door of Scott's house. Before I can even reach the guest bedroom Scott declared as mine, Allison stalks in behind me, slamming the front door with as much, if not more, force than I did.

Scott opens the door to his office—the room across the foyer from my bedroom. He wears his crisp button-down shirt. Shit. He came home early from his "sales job" at the bat factory in Louisville. His eyebrows scrunch together. "What the hell is going on?"

Allison points at me. "Get rid of her."

Scott places his hands on his hips. "Allison..."

"You knocked up girls in trailer parks?"

In my defense, that isn't what I said, but even I know when to keep my mouth shut. Scott's face turns red, then purple. "No."

Allison clutches the hair on her head and the perfect bun loosens. "Forget the trailer parks. I can't believe you told her. You promised you would never tell anyone." One hand descends to her abdomen.

Damn. I was right—sort of. She did tell him she was pregnant, except she wasn't lying like I'd assumed. She *was* pregnant, and then she lost it. If I'd known, I never would have said those things. Guilt makes me nauseous.

"Wait. I didn't tell her." Scott reaches out to Allison and his hand freezes in the air when she steps back. He extends his hand again and when she remains still he wraps his arms around her, pulling her close to him. Scott lowers his head to her ear and I can tell he's whispering to her. Allison's shoulders shake and I feel like a Peeping Tom intruding on this intimate moment.

I slip inside the bedroom and try to close the door without making a sound. Sun shines from the two walls of windows. Crawling onto the middle of the bed, I draw my knees up and curl into myself. I hate this house. There are too many windows. All floor-to-ceiling. All open. All of them make me feel...exposed.

RYAN

IN THE GARAGE, I stand outside Dad's office and prepare myself for the impending conversation. The enrollment papers for the writing competition are rolled tightly in my left hand. I rap twice on the door and Dad tells me to come in.

Except for the chair he sits in, Dad made everything in this room: the chrome desk and matching cabinet, the printer stand, the large art table that displays the stack of blueprints for his current clients. He shot the two deer mounted on the wall. The central air kicks on and a couple of papers near the vent on the floor crinkle against each other.

Dad keeps the office neat, tidy, and controlled. His eyes flick to me then back to the bound manual on his desk. He's disposed of his tie, but he still wears his white work shirt. "What can I do for you, Ryan?"

I sit in the chair across from him and search for words. Before Mark left, I never had a hard time talking to Dad. The words came easily. Now words are hard. I stare at the papers bound together in my hand. That's wrong. Since Mark left, writing words has made life slightly tolerable. "Do you remember last year's short-story assignment?"

He gives me a blank look and scratches the back of his head.

"You were upset because it was due during spring play-offs," I remind him.

The lightbulb goes on as he nods and returns to the manual. "Didn't you write about a pitcher that came back from the dead or something?"

Actually it was a pitcher that sold his soul to the devil in return for a perfect season, but I'm not here to argue.

"Did your English teacher give you a hard time? Too much gore?"

My mouth grows dry and I swallow. "No. I...uh...finaled in a writing competition."

That caught his attention. "You entered a writing competition?"

"No, Mrs. Rowe entered the entire class in the state writing competition. It was open to any high school student not graduating that spring. They read the entries this summer and I finaled."

He blinks and the smile is slow to appear, but it finally manages to form. "Congratulations. Have you told your mom? She loves it when you do well in school."

"No, sir, not yet. I wanted to tell you first." I would have told them together, but since Mark left, they can barely be in the same room.

"You should tell her." The smile slips and he glances away. "It'll make her happy."

"I will." I suck in air. I can do this. "There's another round of the competition in a couple of weeks in Lexington. I have to be there to win."

"Will Mrs. Rowe be providing transportation or will the school let you drive yourself?"

"It's on a Saturday so I can drive myself."

"A Saturday," Dad repeats. "Was Mrs. Rowe upset when you told her you couldn't make it? If so, I'll talk to her. There's no reason why she should hold this against you. Maybe one of her other students can take your place."

He relaxes in his chair and folds his hands over his stomach. "I saw Scott Risk at your game yesterday. He didn't stay long because of family obligations, but he saw you pitch and he was real impressed. He mentioned a camp the Yankees may be doing this fall. I know what you're going to say—'not the Yankees,' but once you've proved yourself you can trade teams."

My mind swirls. Scott Risk watched me play. Which is great and odd. Great because Scott knows people—specifically scouts. Odd because I'd have bet Beth would crucify me to her uncle.

Not important. Or it is, but not now. I came in here to discuss the writing competition. A competition Dad never considered. "I think I should compete. I can play the Thursday game and let one of the other two pitchers on the team play for me on Saturday."

Dad's forehead wrinkles. "Why would you want to do that? The teams worth playing are scheduled on Saturdays."

I shrug. "Mrs. Rowe said that a lot of college recruiters will be at the competition and that a lot of the finalists win scholarships. I figure I can get some sort of an athletic scholarship and combine that with whatever scholarship I could win from this writing event, and that way you won't have to pay much."

Dad lifts his hand. "Wait. Hold on. College recruiters and scholarships? Since when do you care about that?"

Until my conversation with Mrs. Rowe, never. "You and Mark visited colleges. We haven't discussed it, so I thought this would be a good opportunity to..."

Dad's face flushes red and he spits the next words. "He was different. You can't go into the NFL straight out of high school. He had to go to college first. You can go straight to the minors out of school. Hell, Ryan. You can go straight to the majors."

"But Mark said..."

"Do not say that name in my presence again. You're not doing the competition. End of story."

No, it's not the end of the story. "Dad..."

Dad picks up an envelope off his desk and tosses it at me. "A two-hundred-dollar-a-month car payment so you can make practices and games."

The envelope lands on my lap and my throat tightens.

"Your insurance on the car, the booster fees, the uniforms, the travel costs, the league fees—"

"Dad—" I want him to stop, but he won't.

"Gas for the Jeep, the private coaching lessons...I have supported you for seventeen years!"

The anger inside me snaps. "I told you I'd get a job!"

"This is your job!" Dad pounds his fist against the desk, exactly how a judge ends all discussion in court. A stack of papers resting on the edge falls to the floor.

Silence. We stare at each other. Unblinking. Unmoving. A thick tension fills the air.

Dad's eyes sweep over his desk and he inhales deeply. "Do you want to waste four years of your life going to school when you could be out on that field playing baseball for money? Take a look at Scott Risk. He came from nothing and see what he's become? You're not starting with nothing. You have a jump on opportunities he never had. Think of what you can make of your life."

My fist tightens around the enrollment papers in my hand and they crackle. Is it fair? Is it fair of me, even if it's just for one game, to walk away from something that my parents have sacrificed and worked so hard for?

Besides, it's baseball. Baseball is my life—by my choice. Why are we even arguing?

"Ryan..." Dad's voice breaks and he rubs his hand over his face. "Ryan...I'm sorry. For yelling." He pauses. "Things at work...things with your mom..."

My dad and I—we've never fought. Strange, I guess. I know plenty of guys who go rounds with their fathers. Not me. Dad's never given me a curfew. He believes I'm responsible enough to decide what trouble I want to get in and says if I go too far, I'm smart enough to dig myself out. He's encouraged me every step of the way with baseball. More than most parents ever would. Dad watches out for me and this... this is him looking out for me again.

I nod several times before speaking, agreeing to something, but I don't know what. Anything to make this confusion stop. "Yeah. It's okay. This was on me." I crumple the papers in my hand. "You're right. This..." I lift the wadded paper. "It's nothing. Stupid, even."

Dad forces a smile. "It's all right. Go in and tell your mom. She'll be thrilled."

I stand to leave and try to ignore the emptiness in my chest.

"Ryan," says Dad. At the door, I turn to face him.

"Do me a favor—don't tell your mom about the last round of competition. She's been on edge lately."

"Sure." What would be the point of telling her? Mom has a way of knowing when I'm untruthful, and I'm not eager to discover that the words I just uttered to Dad are a lie.

BETH

THE CLOCK READS NINE FORTY-FIVE and Isaiah gets off work at ten. My finger, paused against the speed dial button, goes numb. The sun set a while ago, leaving the room dark. I haven't moved from my spot on the bed. Scott hasn't come in. Neither has Allison. Not to lecture me on school or to scold me for yelling at Allison or to call me to dinner.

I've dry heaved twice. Scott's going to send Mom to jail. He probably already called the police. The ironic part of this whole nightmare? I tried. I tried and I failed. Imagine that.

At ten, I'll call Isaiah and tell him to come and get me. We'll go to the beach. We'll run away. Too bad I can't convince Mom to go with us. Isaiah and I could get her before the cops do.

I raise my head and a wave of hope floods my body, making me dizzy. I could convince Mom to go. We could go away—together.

Someone knocks on the door. I slip the phone under the covers. "Yeah."

Scott enters the room and turns on the light. He wears a black T-shirt and a pair of blue jeans. For the first time, I see a hint of the kid that took care of me when I was younger and, foolishly, my heart responds. I move off the bed. I have to tell him I'm sorry. "Scott..."

Focusing on the carpet, he cuts me off. "I'm not in the mood to hear you bitch. If you ever talk to Allison like that again, I'll make sure you regret it. She's my wife and I love her."

I nod, but Scott doesn't look at me to see it.

He pulls his wallet out and slaps a card onto the dresser. The name and number belong to Mom's probation officer. "I talked to him this evening. Nice guy. Did you know your mom will serve a ten-year sentence if she screws up probation? Ten years. That's not even counting what they'll charge her with when I tell them what I know. Your choice, Elisabeth. Either way you're living here until you turn eighteen. Your actions decide if your mom goes to jail."

The relief sweeping through my body makes me weak. He hasn't sent my mom to jail. Not yet. I still can make this work. The possibilities have my mind racing. I'll have to find a way into Louisville, to convince Mom to leave with me, and then get Isaiah on board....

"Last chance." Scott breaks into my thoughts. "I want perfection this time."

He smacks his hand against the dresser and the last cigarette I bummed rolls out of a folder and onto the floor. Shit.

Scott crouches and stares at the cigarette before picking it up. He acts like it's a joint instead of tobacco. Crap. It might as well be a needle full of heroin. "I can explain." Actually, I can't. But I heard Noah use that phrase with Echo once and it bought him time.

As he stands, his hand shakes. Dad's hands used to shake.

"This is bullshit. I bring you to my home." He falters and I can see him trying to rein in the anger. It scares me that he won't look at me. "I give you a home and you don't even have the decency to try to follow my rules."

Quiet anger frightens me. The drunks, the idiots, the ones that rage easily—them I can handle. I know when to step out of their way. It's the ones that hold the anger in, the men that think about what they do and how they do it, that scare me. They're the ones that cause damage. A small voice, a voice that sounds a lot like me when I was a child, sweetly murmurs that Scott would never hurt me. That he was our protector. Once. I don't know this man.

"I tried," I whisper.

"Bullshit!" Scott yells so loudly that the crystals on the lampshade tinkle. I flinch and step back. "You've done everything you can to make Allison and me miserable."

I swallow. Mom's boyfriend, Trent, started this way. He walked into the apartment all calm and cool, with anger seething underneath. Then he yelled. Then he hit.

Dad had this anger too. So did Grandpa. My heart beats wildly in my chest as Scott crushes the cigarette in his hand. For the first time, he looks at me. "Jesus, you're shaking."

He moves toward me and I take a retreating step. My back hits the window and my hands fly out, searching for something—anything—to protect myself with. "Get out."

The anger—it's gone, calls the little girl in my head, but I ignore her. She died along with my love of ribbons and dresses and life. She's nothing but a ghost.

"I'm sorry," he says slowly and places space between us. "I didn't realize I scared you. I was mad. Allison was upset.

I hate to see her cry and your teacher called...but I'm calm. I swear."

I tried. Really, I did. I tried and this is where it got me. Trapped in a room full of windows with a man who resembles my father. Dad also used to say he was calm, but he never was. "Get out!"

"Elisabeth..."

"Out!" My hands wave air in front of me, motioning for him to leave. "Get out!"

Scott's eyes grow abnormally wide. "I am not going to hurt you."

"This is your fault!" I yell and I want to stop, but if I stop I'll cry. A strange wetness burns my eyes. My lip is so heavy it trembles. I can't cry. I won't cry. Embracing the anger, I open my mouth again. Damn him if he makes me cry. "You're the one that dragged me here. Is it not enough to take me away from home? You have to humiliate me at school?"

"Humiliate you? Elisabeth, what are you talking about?"

"I am not Elisabeth! Look at me!" I grab at the clothes on my body with one hand and yank my Calculus book off the bedside table with the other and fling the book straight at his head. He ducks and the book makes a loud thud when it smacks the wall. "You want me to be somebody else. You don't want me to be me. You're just like Dad! You want me gone!"

My chest is heaving and I gasp for air. The silence that falls between us is heavy and I'm drowning under its weight.

"That's not true." Scott pauses as if he's waiting for a reply. He picks up the textbook and sets it on the dresser. Right beside Mom's parole officer's card. "Get some sleep. We'll talk in the morning."

No, we won't. He leaves for work before I wake for school. Scott gently closes the door. I race across the room, lock it, turn off the lights, then toss the covers off the bed, searching for the phone. My fingers shake as I press the numbers. My pulse beats in my ears in time to the name of the person I need: Isaiah. A heartbeat. Isaiah. The phone rings. Isaiah.

"Hey." At the sound of his easygoing voice I lean against the closet door. "You had me worried. It's five after ten. You're late for our one-minute talk."

Hoping my lip will quit trembling, I close my eyes and will the tears to stay away. It's all in vain. If I speak, I'll cry and I don't cry.

"Beth?" Worry creeps into his tone.

"Here," I whisper back and that one word is almost my undoing. Isaiah and I—we don't do phone conversations. Never have. We watched TV. We partied. We sat next to each other—existed. How do you just be on a phone? And that's what I need. I need Isaiah to just exist.

"Beth..." He hesitates. "Is that Ryan guy messing with you again?"

I swallow a possible sob. I won't cry. I won't. "Sort of." And Allison and my uncle and school and everything and I feel like the walls are caving in, an avalanche preparing to bury me.

Silence from Isaiah.

I bite my lip when one tear rolls down my face. "Do you want me to let you go?" Dammit. Just dammit—I don't cry. "Because I know you don't talk. I mean us. We. We don't talk." I swear under my breath. My voice shook. He'll know I'm upset. He'll know.

Silence again. Air crackling on the line. When he lets me

go, I'll fall apart. I'll have nothing to hold on to. Nothing to anchor me. I'll be exactly what everyone wants me to be—nothing.

"I'm okay with silence, Beth."

I'm still here in this house in the room with too many windows. I'm still exposed—raw—and living in hell. But I have Isaiah and he's anchoring me. I slide down the wall until I can curl into a tight ball on the floor. "I need you."

"I'm here." And we sit in silence.

RYAN

SITTING ON MY BED, I read the text message. First the fight with Dad, then, at ten at night, Gwen sends me this: Beth Risk???

She waits on the other end for my reply. At least when I play baseball, I can catch the balls being thrown at me. Dad and Gwen? I'm getting the hell pounded out of me.

I shouldn't answer Gwen. I should pretend I never read the message. She loves drama. I love baseball. She hated my games and I hated hers. We stopped kissing and touching and dating, yet somehow, like that night at the dugout, we've never stopped the games.

I text back: what about her?

The wait for her answer stretches into eternity. I glance away from the phone as if that will make her respond faster. This summer, after Mark left, Mom repainted my room blue. She loves to redecorate as much as Dad loves to build. They used to work together on projects, but that was before our world fell apart.

Gwen: you tell me

I hate texting. You never know what the person is really

trying to say. I take a risk. One that will make me an idiot and her dangling monkey if she ignores my request.

Me: call me

My heart picks up a few beats. Will she do it or will she leave me hanging? Since our breakup, when we play the text game, I call her.

My cell rings and I smile. On the third ring, I answer. "Gwen."

"Stone," she says without much emotion.

"What's going on?" It's an awkward dance. One I despise. We used to spend hours on the phone talking and now we overanalyze every word and pause.

"You knew who she was the entire time." There's a hint of accusation in her voice.

I work at staying nonchalant. "And if I did?"

"You could have told me."

I stare at the posters of my favorite teams. Why would I have told her that Beth is Scott Risk's niece? They share classes together. They went to the same elementary school. She could have talked to Beth herself.

"Why did you nominate her?" she asks.

I hear ruffling. The sound is Gwen lying back onto her pillows. She has five of them on her bed and she sleeps with every last one. I can picture her golden hair fanning out.

"You know how much homecoming queen means to me," she says.

I do. I used to listen as she rattled on about her dream of winning that sparkly tiara. Actually, I faked interest, then pretended to listen. "You seconded the nomination."

"Because I'd look like a sore loser if I didn't, and now I have to scramble for votes. This would have been a lot easier if you told me sooner she was Scott Risk's niece. Really, Ryan, I thought we were friends."

"What do you care? No one knows her and she doesn't want friends."

Her frustrated sigh sets my muscles on edge. "She's an instant celebrity and for some insane reason certain people think she's cool. You nominated her and everyone at school knows you've asked her out, so you give her credibility. If you had told me who she was from the beginning, I could have done some damage control. Befriended her or something. Because of you, she has a shot at winning."

We broke up and I shouldn't have to deal with this. I go with the old standby answer: "I'm sorry for ruining your life, Gwen. The next time I do anything I'll be sure to get your permission."

Gwen blurts out, "She's not your type."

I blink. "What?"

"Beth's a little, I don't know, freakish. I mean, she is kind of pretty if you like the weird my-life-is-a-dark-room sort of pretty. I guess I'm saying you won't be able to give her the attention she needs. You know, because of baseball. I guess I'm just saying...not her."

Not her. Anger strangles my gut. And we're back to the conversation from the dugout—baseball ruined our relationship. "We broke up and now you're with Mike."

I can hear Gwen's smile. "But you promised we'd be friends. I'm being a good friend."

Friends. I hate that word. "You're right. Beth is pretty."

"She has a nose ring." Gwen's lost the smiling voice.

"I think it's sexy." I do.

"I heard she smokes cigarettes."

"She's trying to quit." Yeah, I made that up.

"I heard she has a tattoo on the small of her back."

Interesting. "I haven't gotten that far, but I'll let you know if I do since we're friends and all."

An image plays in my mind of lifting the back of Beth's shirt to reveal her skin, my caress causing her to smile. I bet her skin is smooth, like petals. My fingers fidget with the desire to touch Beth and my blood warms with the idea of her whispering my name. Damn. The girl really does turn me on. I run a hand over my head, trying to rid my mind of the thought. What the hell?

"Ryan. I'm not kidding. She's not your type."

"Then tell me who is." I say it with more anger than intended, but I'm tired of the game.

"Not her, okay?" Gwen pleads.

The image of touching Beth taunts and confuses me. Three quick raps on my door and Mom enters. "I've gotta go."

"'Night," Gwen says with disappointment.

Mom wears a matching blue blazer and skirt. She attended a women-only dinner with the mayor's wife this evening. "Am I interrupting?"

"No." I toss my phone onto the bedside table.

"You sounded a little upset." Mom walks over to my dresser, appraises her reflection in the mirror, then readjusts her pearl necklace. "I could hear you in the hallway."

I shake my head. "Just Gwen."

Her hands freeze on her necklace and a smile curves her lips. "Are you together again?"

"No." Mom loved Gwen and I think the breakup was hardest on her.

She continues her grooming. "You should consider it. I

heard that both you and Gwen were nominated for home-coming court."

News travels at lightning speed in our town. "Yeah."

"You know, your father and I were nominated for home-coming courts. Both fall and winter."

"Yep." She mentioned it. A million times. They won both times too. If her continued retelling of the events didn't refresh my memory, the pictures hanging in the family room of them dancing with crowns on is a good reminder.

"I also heard that Scott Risk's niece was nominated."

"Uh-huh." If Mom knows everything, then why is she bothering me?

"What are your thoughts on the niece? Her aunt, Allison Risk, has asked to be nominated for the empty seat on the church event committee."

And there's my answer. Respectability. If Beth is an outcast, then Beth's guardians will be considered bad parents. Mom wants the prestige of nominating Scott Risk's wife, but she doesn't want the scandal of nominating the guardian of the "bad girl." Both Mom and Dad's families have been members of this community since the first foundations of home and church were laid hundreds of years ago. The Stones are a legacy.

"She's interesting."

Mom turns. "Interesting. What does that mean?"

I shrug. It means that Beth's in the way of my winning a dare. It means she tries my patience. It means I want to see her tattoo. "Interesting."

Mom rubs her forehead in frustration. "Fine. She's interesting. If you discover another word, you know where to find me."

Yep, I do. If in public, she'll be right next to Dad. In private, the exact opposite of where Dad will be. Mom pauses at the door frame. "And, Ryan, I talked to Mrs. Rowe this evening."

I dip my head and briefly close my eyes. Not good. Not good at all. "Uh-huh."

"She's curious as to when you'll be turning in your paperwork for the final writing competition in Lexington."

Damn. I raise my head, but my shoulders stay slumped as I look at Mom. "I'm not doing it. It interferes with ball."

Mom stiffens. "Was that your father's decision or yours?"

"Mine." The word comes out fast. The last thing I want is for them to get into another twelve-round fight, especially over me.

"I'm sure it was." Mom gives a dismissive wave.

Something inside me snaps. "Logan saw Mark in Lexington a few weeks ago. He asked about us."

Mom becomes uncharacteristically still.

"Logan knows, Mom. So does Chris."

Fury flashes over her face. "If your father finds out you told anyone… If anyone in town finds out…"

"They won't tell."

She closes her eyes for a second as she releases air. "Please remember what happens in this house stays in this house. Chris and Logan are your friends. They are not family."

A simmering anger settles at the bottom of my stomach. How can she shut out her emotions for her oldest son? "Don't you miss him?"

"Yes." Her immediate answer catches me off guard. "But there's too much at stake."

"What does that mean?" I ask.

Mom scans my room. Her eyes linger on my posters. "I think I'm going to redo your room. Blue isn't your color."

BETH

THUMP, THUMP, THUMP. My eyes flash open and my heart
pumps in my ears. The cops. No, the boyfriend. Sometimes
he knocks in the morning to confuse me into opening the
door. I blink when I see the shadow of curtains against a
window. Curtains. I'm not home. I inhale and the fresh
oxygen mixes with the adrenaline in my bloodstream. Old
habits die hard.

"Elisabeth," Scott says from behind the door. "Wake up."

Shit. Six in the morning. Why can't he leave me alone? The
bus doesn't arrive until seven-thirty. A half hour is plenty
of time to get ready for school. I roll out of bed and pad on
bare feet to the door. The bright light from the foyer hurts
my eyes so I squint and barely comprehend that Scott's shoving a bag into my hand. "Here. I got your stuff."

I wipe the sleep from my eyes. Scott wears the same
T-shirt and jeans from last night. "What stuff?"

He drops his I-mean-business glare and my lips tug up.
It's a look he gave me when I was little, especially when I
wouldn't eat my vegetables or when I begged him to read
to me.

Scott's answering smile is hesitant. "I went by your aunt's and picked up your clothes. That Noah guy was there last night and he showed me what was yours. I'm sorry if I left anything behind. If you tell me something specific maybe I can swing by one day after work."

I stare at the bag. My stuff. He got me my stuff and he talked to... "How's Noah?"

The hesitant joy on his face fades. "We didn't have a heart-to-heart. Elisabeth, this doesn't change any of my rules. I want you to settle here in Groveton and let your old life go. Trust me on this one, okay, kid?"

Okay, kid. It's what he always said to me, and I find myself nodding without realizing it. A habit from childhood—a time when I believed that Scott hung the moon and commanded the sun. A bad habit for a teenager. I stop nodding. "I can wear my clothes?"

"Skin has to be covered and no rips in indecent places. Push me on this and I'll burn every stitch in that bag." Scott inclines his head toward the kitchen. "Breakfast in thirty."

I cradle the bag in my hands like a newborn. My stuff. Mine. "Thanks." The gratitude is stiff and awkward, but give me credit—I said it.

I slide the low-rise, faded blue jeans to my hips and a contented sigh escapes my lips. How I missed you, old friend. Jeans that hug a little too tight. Small rips on the thighs. The other pair, the pair I really love that has rips right below my ass, Scott would soak in gasoline. I carefully fold them on a hanger and store them in the closet.

For the first time in two weeks, I feel like me. Black cotton tee that clings to my waist. Silver hoop earrings in my ears.

I change the hoop in my nose for a fake diamond stud. As I check myself out in the mirror, I revel in the lightness because I know the moment I step into that kitchen, I'll grow heavy again.

Right at six-thirty, I enter the kitchen. The red breaking of dawn splatters across the sky. Scott fries bacon at the stove and the smell makes my mouth water. Allison is perfectly absent.

I take a seat at the bar that has a glass of orange juice and a plate. I assume the other place setting is for him. In between the plates is a stack of buttered toast and sausage patties. "Is it turkey or tofu or whatever you try to pass off as food?"

Everything in this house is healthy. I pick up the toast and smell it. Hmm. White bread and it smells like butter. I stick out my tongue and barely lick it to see if it is. Scott laughs. Embarrassed, I roll my tongue into my mouth and close my eyes in ecstasy. Mmm. Real butter.

"No, it's not turkey. It's real. I'm tired of watching you not eat." He places a plate of bacon and eggs between us as he sits. "If you'd try Allison's cooking, you'd see it's not half-bad."

I bite into the toast and talk between bites. "That's the point. Food shouldn't be half-bad. It should be all good."

Scott assesses my outfit before spooning some scrambled eggs onto his plate. "I like the stud. When did you pierce your nose?"

"When I turned fourteen." I help myself to bacon and sausage while staring at the eggs. Scott made great eggs when I was a kid. Too bad I told him I hate them.

"Your mom wanted one. She talked about driving into Louisville to get one several times." Mom liked to talk to Scott while Scott raised me. She moved into Grandpa's trailer when Dad knocked her up and her mom kicked her out. Scott was twelve when I was born.

My heart sinks. Mom never told me she wanted a nose ring. She never even noticed when I pierced mine. Why it bothers me, I don't know. Mom doesn't tell me a lot of things. I tap my fork against the counter. Screw it. I'm eating the eggs. Who knows when I'll get another decent meal. Scott flashes a smug smile when I fork eggs on my plate.

"Is that a baseball thing?" I ask.

"What?"

"Ryan has that same I-know-everything smirk when he thinks he's one-upped me."

Scott sips his orange juice. "Have you and Ryan been hanging out at school?"

I shrug. Hanging out. Annoying the piss out of each other. Same thing. "Kind of."

"He's a good kid, Elisabeth. It would do you good to make more friends like him."

Noah's a good guy. Isaiah is the best, but Scott doesn't want to hear that. "I go by Beth."

As if I hadn't said anything, he asks another question. "How's school?"

"I'm gonna fail."

He stops eating and I shove food into my mouth. I'm beginning to hate these silences.

"Are you trying?" he asks.

I contemplate my answer while savoring a piece of bacon. On my last bite, I decide to go with the truth. "Yes. But I don't expect you to believe me."

He tosses his napkin onto his empty plate and stares at me with sincere blue eyes. We both have Grandma's eyes.

Dad did too, except Dad's never looked kind. "I'm not smart. I can throw a ball, catch a ball, and hit a ball. It made me a rich man, but it's better to be smart."

"Too bad for me, I can't do any of that. Smart included."

"Allison's smart," he says and he holds up his hand when I roll my eyes. "She's real smart. Has a master's in English. Let her help you."

"She hates me."

Scott falls into one of his long silences again. "Let me handle that. You focus on school."

"Whatever." I glance at the clock: six forty-five. We managed to have a conversation without yelling for fifteen minutes. "Shouldn't you be heading to work?"

"I'm working from home today. We're going to do this every morning. I want you up at six and out here for breakfast by six-thirty."

If he's going to cook, I'm not going to argue. "Okay."

Scott gathers his dishes and goes to the sink. "About last night."

And things were going so well.… "Let's not discuss last night."

"You were shaking."

I stand, feeling suddenly fidgety. "I should get my backpack together."

"Has someone hurt you? Physically?"

The dishes. The dishes should go in the dishwasher. I pick them up. "I really need help with Calculus. I want to drop it." Why am I telling him this?

Scott takes the dishes from me and I don't like being empty-handed. He places them on the counter and crosses his arms over his chest. "What happened after I left town?

My dad was dead and buried. Did my brother take his place as residing bastard?"

I'm shaking again. It's either that or we're having an earthquake. My head jerks back when the reality of what I let happen smacks me head-on like a Mack truck. I'm an idiot. He maneuvered expertly around my walls. "Fuck you."

I expect Scott to yell at me or reprimand me. Instead, he chuckles. "You're still as stubborn as you were at four. Go get your stuff ready for school. I'll drive you in today."

I hate him. "I'll take the bus."

Scott turns his back to me and loads the dishwasher. "I'm making pancakes tomorrow."

"I won't eat."

He laughs again. "Yes, you will. Allison's making goat cheese tofu casserole tonight."

RYAN

I PULL MY JEEP into the student lot and park behind Chris's car. He leans against the bumper while Lacy stands a good three feet away from him near the hood. She holds her books close to her chest and snubs me by angling her body toward the school when I shut off the engine. Not a good sign. I take a deep breath and ready myself. Lacy has a hell of a temper. My ears rang for two days after the last time I ticked her off.

Chris greets me when I open the door. "She's pissed at you, dawg."

"I can see that."

Before I can reach her, Lacy wheels around. "A dare? You humiliated Beth in gym yesterday over a dare? I'm trying to make friends with her and you and Chris and Logan have made her the target of a dare?"

Dammit all to hell, Chris. "You sang like a little girl with her hand caught in the cookie jar, didn't you?"

"Sorry," he says, repentant. "Her tactics are brutal. The Marines could employ her."

Lacy rushes between us, her hand waving in the air. "Don't

you laugh this off. You don't know Beth. You don't know what life was like for her. You don't know what type of friend she was to me. You are ruining everything!"

I stare at her, shocked. Tears swim in her eyes. She's not just angry. She's upset. "It's only a dare, Lace. I asked her out. She has the choice to say yes or no. I'm not hurting anyone."

"Yes, you are." She glances away. "You're hurting me." The girl I consider one of my best friends bolts into school.

"I gotta go after her," Chris says.

"I know." I want him to.

"She's wrong about this. Don't worry though, I think she's PMS-ing."

Yeah. Lacy is emotional at times, but a nagging in my gut tells me that she could be right.

"Ryan?"

Chris and I both turn to see Beth. My heart stops. It's her. Skater Girl from Taco Bell. Gone are the trendy clothes. Back is her own style. Skin-hugging black shirt, jeans with holes. All knee-dropping curves. She looks every bit as sexy as she did the first night I met her.

"Can we talk for a second?" Sweet and seductive, her voice purrs over my skin and I'm absolutely hypnotized. The girl must be a magician.

"Sure." I wait for Chris to remember that he needs to go after his own girl, but he's too busy admiring Beth's ass to notice that Beth and I want him to leave. I give the blatant reminder. "Lacy needs you."

"Yeah," says Chris like he's waking from a dream. "Lacy. See you later, dawg. You too, Beth."

She drums her fingers against her thigh as a dismissal. Chris wanders into the building while I try to understand

Beth's attitude switch. Yesterday, the girl would have been the main suspect in my murder. This morning, she's hot and friendly. Talk about mood swings.

Guilt becomes a whisper in my brain. I humiliated her at school. Time to make amends. "Yesterday, in gym—"

"Whatever." Beth cuts me off. "I was thinking that you're right. I should make friends and I'd really like you to be the one to help me."

Can.

I suppress the smile edging onto my face. No need to rub it in. Why couldn't Lacy be here to see this? "You'll go with me to the party on Friday?"

"Yes, but there's a catch."

"What type of catch?" I should be focusing more on the word *catch*, but I can't when Beth nibbles on her bottom lip. I love those lips.

"My uncle is a little control-freakish and he'll want to talk to you."

This day keeps getting better. I win the dare and I get to talk to my hero. Plus, I get to spend time with Beth. Maybe Lacy's right. Maybe there is more to her. "Sure. I can come by early on Friday."

Beth readjusts the pack hanging on her shoulder. "Actually, I was wondering if you could come over tonight and meet him. Maybe we could hang out after."

I love my life. The girl is asking *me* out. "Yeah, sure." Damn. My mind becomes chaos as I remember my plans. "Wait. I would love to, but I have ball practice with the team and then pitch practice in Louisville tonight."

She lowers her head. "Oh. Okay, I guess. If you can't, you can't, but tonight's the only night Scott's going to be home."

I am not blowing off this change of heart. If she's anything like Lacy, she could have a total mood reversal in three minutes. "I can come over after ball and meet your uncle and then you could ride with me into Louisville. We could go out to eat after practice. That is, if you're okay with sitting through an hour of me pitching."

She raises her head and flashes this glorious smile. "If you don't mind."

Mind? I can't think of anything I want more. I just won the dare.

Standing on Scott Risk's front porch, I yank the bill of my baseball hat and wipe my hands on my athletic pants. This is it. I'm about to walk into my hero's home. Two knocks and the door swings open. Staring back at me, wearing jeans and a T-shirt, is Scott Risk.

"Good afternoon, Ryan." His eyebrows rise to give the impression he's surprised.

"Good afternoon." I rub the back of my head when the tension starts to form in my neck. "Is, uh, Beth here?"

An easy grin spreads across his face. "She'd better be, but I did just piss her off. It might not be a bad idea to check to see if she snuck out the window."

Having no idea what to say back, I shove my hands in my pockets. He laughs. "Elisabeth and I don't work well together on her homework. Come on in. She said you two made plans, but I have to admit I was wondering if she was messing with me."

"Is she ready, Mr. Risk?" Amazed and starstruck, I walk in. This place is huge.

"Call me Scott," he says, then hollers, "Elisabeth!"

Something hard smacks the door to our right. "Fuck you!"

I sigh heavily and a knot forms between my shoulder blades. The pendulum swings on the mood spectrum. Guess we're back to crazy. Can't wait to see what Friday night will bring.

"You have company!"

Silence. The door squeaks as it slowly opens.

"Hello, Ryan." Beth rests her hip against the door frame and my heart stutters. She changed from the T-shirt to a black tank top, exposing a hint of beautiful cleavage. "See. I told you he stares."

Damn. I do. And I did it right in front of Scott Risk.

Scott claps my back. "It's okay. But try not to stare too hard in front of me. At some point I'll stop finding it amusing and might have to kick your ass. And, Elisabeth? *Fuck* isn't allowed."

She shrugs, clearly not caring what's allowed.

"Get yourself together," Scott says to Beth. "I'm going to talk to Ryan for a bit, then you can go."

Beth glances at her clothes. "I am together."

"I see skin. Lots of it. Come back out when there is less skin."

She sighs and does this slow pivot. As she walks into her room her hips have this easy sway that makes me stare— once again.

"I received something yesterday that you'll appreciate." Scott crosses the foyer to the room opposite Beth's and motions for me to follow.

The moment I enter the large office I'm in awe. Baseball. Everywhere. Jerseys in glass frames. Balls. Bats. Cards in display cases. Scott pulls out a see-through box and hands it to me. My mouth gapes. "Babe Ruth. You have a baseball signed by Babe Ruth?"

"Yes." Scott flashes a smile, the kind I understand; this office is hallowed ground. The phone on his large mahogany desk rings. "Give me a sec."

I start to head out when Scott stops me. "Stay. This won't take long."

I love this man. I could spend hours in this office drooling over his stuff. Speaking in correct grammar and a business voice, Scott chats on the phone. I hover over a bat signed by Nolan Ryan. This could be my office someday. Hell no. This will be me.

Across the room is a table of framed pictures. Scott and Pete Rose. Scott and Albert Pujols. The picture frames are angled slightly toward the center of the table. Each person in the frame more important than the last. When I get to the middle, I see a wedding picture of Scott and his wife and my respect for the man grows. He values his family.

I frown when I spot the small 4 x 7 photograph. It's of a child and Scott. At least I think it's Scott. I pick it up. He's young and looks dorky wearing the old-school version of the Bullitt County High baseball uniform. He holds a girl. Barely out of toddler years. Maybe five. Entwined and pinned everywhere in her long blond hair are pink ribbons. The white fluffy dress makes her look like a princess. She has her arms squeezed tight around Scott's neck. Her smile is contagious and her eyes are the deep blue of an ocean, almost exactly like...

"Elisabeth loved ribbons," Scott says behind me. "Bought them for her every chance I could."

No way. "This is Beth?"

He takes the frame from me and gently places it back as the very center picture on the table. "Yes."

He says it with the heaviness of a man mourning. Hell, I guess he is grieving. Beth is a far cry from the happy child in that photo.

Scott's lighthearted tone returns. "I picked Allison up from a dinner last night and ran into your mom. She said you finaled in a state writing competition."

My eyes flicker away. Dad must love that everyone in town now knows. "Yeah."

"Your dad said you're bent on going pro out of school, but there are a lot of colleges that would die to have a pitcher with your potential. Especially if you have academic talent."

"Thanks." I don't know what else to say.

"Want to tell me what's going on with you and my niece?"

I freeze. And that is what I call throwing a changeup. Scott loses his easygoing grin and I notice he shares Beth's eyes. He doesn't blink either. Time to man up. "I asked her out." Because of a dare. "And she said yes. She said that you'd want to meet me first."

"Where are you taking her tonight?"

"To my pitch-coaching lesson, then to wherever she chooses to eat. There's a..." Taco Bell—I should skip that one. "McDonald's and an Applebee's nearby."

Scott nods as if he's processing how to perform brain surgery. "Where are you taking her Friday?"

"Not far. Actually, it'll border your property and my dad's. My best friend lives on the other side of you and we invite friends over to hang out."

Scott fights amusement and tenses at the same time. "You're taking my niece to a field party."

I swallow.

"I grew up fifteen miles from Groveton," says Scott. "I know what a field party is, having attended more than a few myself."

Busted. "I thought it would be a good opportunity for her to spend time with my friends."

Scott rubs his jawline. "I don't know."

I have to give him more. Lots more. "I like Beth. She's pretty." Yeah, she is. "She's more than pretty. She's not like any girl I've ever met before. Beth keeps me on the edge. With her, I have no idea what's coming next and I find that..." Amazing. Thrilling. "Fun."

Scott says nothing back and I'm glad. Until I said the words—words I thought I was creating to impress him—I had no idea they were true.

A sexy voice, one I know all too well, causes my stomach to levitate like I'm at the top of a roller coaster, then plummet. Beth heard every word. "You're kidding."

"It's impolite to eavesdrop." Scott keeps his back to her and his eyes glued on me.

"I didn't say *fucking* kidding," she responds.

He inclines his head to the right as if to agree that was a major concession. "When?"

"When what?" I ask.

"When are you picking her up on Friday?"

"Seven."

"I want her home by nine tonight. Midnight on Friday."

"Yes, sir."

Scott turns to Beth. "What are you going to do while he's practicing?"

"Watch."

Scott dips his head in disbelief.

Beth sighs heavily. "Fine. I'll do homework. I'll become studious and add 'big fat dork' to my 'freak' label. It's what you want, right?"

"It's all I dream about. Go on. Enjoy yourselves." He enters the foyer and Beth's lips twist into that evil smirk. What the hell did I walk myself into?

BETH

EVERY NOW AND THEN, fate smiles in my favor. Yes, I know, hard to believe, but today is one of those rare days. Last week, Lacy told me Ryan drove into Louisville for coaching lessons on Wednesdays, and yesterday she told me that the facility is located in the south side of Louisville, sweetly tucked away a half mile from my home.

Outside of a large metal warehouse, Ryan plucks a bag full of his baseball crap out of the back of his Jeep and I do my best to keep from fidgeting. My nerves make it difficult to stay still. I'm so close to my mom that I can almost taste the cigarette. *Be cool, Beth. This is a hand you have to play carefully.* "How long is practice?"

"An hour. Maybe a little longer." Ryan slings his bag over his shoulder. I swear, this guy has the broadest shoulders of any high school kid I have ever met. He wears a tight T-shirt and my stomach performs tiny flips when his shirt rides up, exposing his abs.

I sigh and push the thoughts away. The characteristics of gorgeous and decent don't mix with wanting me. And while

Ryan can be a jerk, he is...decent. It doesn't take a rocket scientist to figure out that what I'm doing to him is wrong.

Wrong but necessary.

Besides, whatever is going on between us is a game of some sort. I just haven't guessed his angle yet. Not that it matters. By the end of the night, Ryan will hate me and so will Scott. I won't feel bad about Scott though. He's the one that dragged me into this mess and he'll be much happier without me. In an hour I will have reached Mom, contacted Isaiah, and we'll be out of town. The schedule is tight, but doable.

"Where do you want to go to dinner? There's an Applebee's close by and a T.G.I. Friday's. Hopefully our dinner conversation will be a lot better than the silence on the way in." He pauses. "We can do fast food if you prefer. I know how you love tacos."

The first cool breeze of fall blows across the parking lot and goose bumps rise on my arms. In an hour, I'll be heading to the beach.

"I said tacos, Beth. Where's the 'eff you' that typically follows?"

I stare up at him and blink. I'm doing this. I'm actually going to run away.

Ryan's eyebrows furrow together and he comes closer to me, blocking the breeze, or maybe it's the heat radiating from his body warming me. "Are you okay?"

"Yeah, I'm fine." He's taller than me. Gigantically. I'm not going to see him again so I let myself notice Ryan as he really is. He's sexily hot with his broad shoulders, curved muscles, cute mess of sandy-blond hair kicking out behind his baseball cap and adorable warm brown eyes. I pretend for a second that the sincerity in them is real—and for me.

The wind blows again, harder this time, and several strands of my hair move across my face. Ryan focuses on them. His fingers whisper against my cheek, then down the sensitive skin on my neck as he brushes the strands over my shoulder. His touch tickles and burns at the same time.

Heat races to my face and my hands immediately cover my cheeks. What the hell? I'm blushing. Guys don't make me blush. Guys don't want to make me blush. Confused by my reaction, I step away and reach into my back pocket to pull out a cigarette I bummed from stoner boy at school. "Give me a few, okay?"

"If you get bored in the waiting area and you want to watch, I'll ask Coach if you can..."

I shake my head. "No."

Ryan presses his lips together and heads toward the entrance. I sneak a peek at his retreating form and my heart drops. Whatever messed-up moment we just experienced doesn't change anything. Ryan goes for girls like Gwen and screws over girls like me. You can't change destinies already written. That only happens in fairy tales.

I do feel sorry for him. Scott's going to kill him by the end of the night. "Ryan?"

He glances over his shoulder. What do I say? You've been fun to mess with, but I have to save my mom. I'm sorry that when you return to Groveton tonight without me, my uncle will rip off your balls and my aunt will serve them for dinner with a side of seaweed?

"Thanks." The word tastes weird in my mouth.

He removes his baseball cap, runs his hand through his hair, and smashes it back into place. I look away to keep the guilt from killing me.

"I'm sorry," he says.

I blink, unsure what he's apologizing for, but I don't ask for an explanation. I said my piece. He said his. We're even.

A teenage boy leaves the building and holds the door open for Ryan. He goes in while the other boy jingles his car keys. Thank you, fate, for lending me a hand. I tuck the cigarette into my back pocket and smile in a way that makes the boy assume he has a chance. "Can I bum a ride?"

Nerves vibrate in my stomach and I keep taking deep breaths. No matter how many times I inhale, I still have a hard time filling my lungs with air. Please, God, this one time, please let the asshole be gone. And please, please, please let Isaiah agree to my crazy plan once I show up with my mom in tow.

I thought about telling him about my plan beforehand, but, in the end, I knew he wouldn't agree to Mom tagging along. He blames her for the problems in my life, but I know Isaiah. When I show up with her, begging to leave, he won't let me down. He'll take us—both.

The Last Stop is empty, but give it another hour or two and the bar will be filled. Even in daylight, the place is as dark as a dungeon. In his typical jeans and flannel shirt, Denny sits at his bar and hovers over a laptop, giving his face a bluish glow. Out of the corner of his eye, he spots me. "Heard your mom lost custody."

"Yeah."

He sips a longneck. "Sorry, kid."

"How has she been?" My mouth dries out and it takes everything I have to act like his answer doesn't matter to me.

"Do you really want to know?"

No. I don't. "What do I owe you?"

He closes the laptop. "Nothing. Go back to where you came from. Anywhere has to be better than here."

I go out the back. It's the fastest way to Mom's apartment. At night, the place is creepy in the shadows. During the day, the run-down apartment complex just looks sad and pathetic. Management spray-painted parts of the 1970s orange brick white to hide the graffiti. It's a useless effort. The elementary kids paint their swear words back on the next night.

Since most of the windows are broken, the residents use cardboard and gray tape to cover the glass, except for the windows with the roaring air-conditioning units that leak water like faucets. Mom and I never had one of those. We were never that rich or lucky.

Asshole Trent lives in the complex across the parking lot from Mom. The only thing sitting in his parking spot is the large pool of black oil that seeps from his car when it's parked. Good. I inhale again to still my internal shaking. Good.

After Dad left, Mom moved us to Louisville and we officially became gypsies, moving into a new apartment every six to eight months. Some were so bad we left voluntarily. Others kicked us out after Mom missed rent. The trailer in Groveton and my aunt Shirley's basement are the only stable homes I've ever known. The apartment near Shirley's is the longest Mom has ever stayed in one place and it sucks that Trent is the reason why. I knock softly.

The door rattles as Mom unlocks the multiple dead bolts and, like I taught her to, she leaves the chain on when she opens the door an inch. Mom squints as if her eyes have never seen the sun. She's whiter than normal, and the blond hair on the back of her head stands upright as if she hasn't brushed it in days.

"What is it?" she barks.

"It's me, Mom."

She rubs her eyes. "Elisabeth?"

"Let me in." *And let's get you out.*

Mom closes the door, the chain jiggles as she unlocks it, and the door flies open. In seconds, she wraps her arms around me. Her fingernails dig into my scalp. "Baby? Oh God, baby. I thought I'd never see you again."

Her body shakes and I hear the familiar sniffling that accompanies her crying. I rest my head on her shoulder. She smells like a strange combination of vinegar, pot, and alcohol. Only the vinegar seems out of place. Part of me is thrilled to see her alive. The other part beyond annoyed. I hate that she's high. "What did you take?"

Mom pulls back and runs her fingers through my hair in very fast successive motions. "Nothing."

I note her red eyes and dilated pupils and tilt my head.

"Okay, just some pot." She smiles while a tear runs down her face. "Do you want a bowl? We have new neighbors and they're into sharing. Let's go."

Snatching Mom's hand, I push past her and into the apartment. "You need to pack."

"Elisabeth! Don't!"

"What the hell?" The place is trashed. Not like normal trashed. This is beyond dirty dishes, mud-caked floors, and fast-food wrappers on the furniture. The cushions of the couch lie on the threadbare carpet, both ripped open. The coffee table could now be used as kindling. The insides of Mom's small television lie exposed near the three-foot kitchen.

"Someone broke in." Mom shuts the door behind her, locking one of the dead bolts.

"Bullshit." I turn and face her. "People who break in steal shit and you don't have shit to steal. And what the hell is that stench?"

I dyed Easter eggs with Scott once and our trailer smelled like vinegar for days.

"I'm cleaning," Mom says. "The bathroom. I got sick in there earlier."

Her words hit me hard. Puking can mean an OD. My worst nightmare for my mother. "What did you take?"

She shakes her head and nervously laughs. "I told you, pot. A little beer. I'm barely buzzing."

Ah, hell. "Are you pregnant?"

I hate it when she has to think for an answer. "No. No. I'm taking those pills. It's good you found a way to have them sent to me in the mail."

Kneading my eyes with my palms, I gather my wits. None of this matters. "Get your stuff together. We're leaving."

"Why? I haven't received an eviction notice."

"We're gypsies, remember?" I say, trying to lighten the mood. "We never stay still."

"No, Elisabeth. You have the gypsy soul, not me."

Her statement stops me short and I wait for her to explain. Mom sways from side to side. Whatever. She's high and I don't have time for this. I step over the shredded coffee table. "Isaiah offered to take me to the beach and you're coming with us. We'll lay low until I turn eighteen next summer and then we'll be home free."

"What about Trent?"

"He beats you. You don't need that asshole!" I spot a couple of plastic shopping bags in the corner. Those will do. Mom owns few items worth packing.

"Elisabeth!" Mom kicks the remains of the coffee table as she bolts after me. She grabs my arm. "Stop!"

"Stop? Mom, we have to go. You know if Trent comes back and finds me here..."

She cuts me off and runs her fingers through my hair again. "He'll kill you." Her eyes pool with tears and she sniffles again. "He'll kill you," she repeats. "I can't go."

My entire body bottoms out like a fast sobering from a high. "You have to."

"No, baby. I can't go now. Give me a few weeks. I got some business to take care of and then we'll leave together. I promise."

Business? "We're leaving. Now."

Her fingers curl in my hair and tighten, yanking to the point of pain. She leans down and places her forehead to mine. The stench of beer rolls off her breath. "I promise. I promise I'll go with you. Listen to me. I have to clean some stuff up. Give me a couple of weeks, then we'll go."

The doorknob wiggles and my heart kicks into high gear. He's back.

Mom grips my hand painfully. "My bedroom." She drags me through the apartment and loses her balance as she trips over the pieces of broken furniture. "Go out the window."

Bile rises in my throat and I begin to shake. "No. Not without you."

Leaving Mom here is like watching sand run out of an hourglass while I'm chained to the wall, unable to flip it back over. Someday, Trent will go too far and it won't just be a bruise or a broken bone. He'll take the life out of her body. Time with Trent is an enemy.

"Sky!" Trent shouts when he enters the apartment. "I told you to keep the door unlocked."

Mom hugs me tightly. "Go, baby," she whispers. "Come and get me in a few weeks."

She rips the cardboard off the glass and I jump back when a hand shoots through the already-open window. "Give her to me."

Isaiah pokes his head in and both of his hands latch onto my body. I stop breathing and realize one way or another, one of these guys is going to kill me.

RYAN

I SNAP MY ARM FORWARD. With a thump, the ball hits outside the orange box taped onto the black tarp bag that serves as a target. My mind's not in it today and I need it to be. Placing my pitches is the priority. If Logan calls inside— I need to hit inside. If Logan calls outside—I need to hit outside. If he calls straight down the plate—I need to smack that mother too.

I keep thinking about Beth. She looked so damn small and lost that I wanted to gather her in my arms and shield her from the world. Definitely not a reaction I ever thought I'd have with Skater Girl. I slap my glove against my leg. I'll find out what's going on with her at dinner. Silence will no longer be accepted.

I roll my shoulder in an effort to find some life in it, but I come up empty. I've pitched for the past hour and the muscles in my arm are as useful as jelly.

The training facility isn't much, just a warehouse with green turf carpeting and an air conditioner welded to the ceiling. The unit buzzes overhead and every few seconds a bat cracks.

My coach, John, pushes off the metal wall. "Good, but you're still throwing with your arm. Your power and consistency are going to come from your legs. How's the arm?"

Tired. Beth must hate this place. A warehouse full of guys hitting balls into nets and pitching into bags. Part of me is disappointed. She hasn't stood once to watch. "I can throw a couple more if you want."

"Have you been resting your arm like we've discussed?"

"Yes, sir." Not as much as I should. I can pinpoint the exact location of my rotator cuff: approximately two inches down from the top of my shoulder and, right now, it aches.

"Let's call it a night."

I roll the ball over my fingers. Beth isn't the only issue that's plagued me this practice and no matter how I try to ignore the thoughts, they keep returning. "Can I ask you something?"

"Shoot."

"If you had to choose between playing college ball and playing pro out of high school, what would you choose?"

John scratches his cheek as he stares at me with a mix of wonder and confusion. "Do you want to go to college?"

I don't know. "If you had the choice, what would you have done?"

"I didn't have that choice. College ball was my only option."

"But if you did?"

"I would have gone pro."

I slam the ball into my glove. Exactly. Everyone with their

college talk and writing competitions is screwing me up. "Thanks."

"The question isn't what I would have done. The question is what do you want to do?"

BETH

ISAIAH WRAPS HIS ARM tightly around my waist and heaves me out the window. Mom's hollow blue eyes have a haunting hurt as she stares at me one last time before slamming the glass pane shut and placing the cardboard back over the window.

"No!" I've left her behind. Again.

His grip becomes steel and the more I try to scramble back to the window, back to Mom's apartment, the more he pulls me away. My heart—it's literally breaking. It has to be, because the pain in my chest slices as if glass is ripping through it.

My legs tangle with Isaiah's. He keeps a firm hold on my hip bones and forces weightlessness by lifting me and moving me in the opposite direction of my mom. I struggle back to earth, kicking his shins, knocking my knees against his. "Isaiah, Trent's in there. He's going to kill her."

"Let's go." His growl rumbles against my ear.

"Did you hear me?" He couldn't have. Isaiah would never leave me to die, so he could never leave my mom. The one person I need.

"Yes." He presses against me and my smaller body yields

to his. *No.* My elbows bend back and with open palms I shove at his chest. My heart convulses with the smack of my hands against his body. I hit him—my best friend.

I'll do it again if he doesn't let me go. "I hate you!"

"Good," he says. His nostrils flare as he lightly shakes my hips. "Because I won't feel bad when I toss you over my shoulder and throw you in the damned car."

My palms, still stinging from hitting him, rest on his chest. His heart beats wildly, matching the crazy glare in his eyes. Isaiah means what he says.

So do I. "I'm not leaving without her."

"Get in the car before I force you into it."

His hands tighten. A warning. A threat. My chest constricts, making it impossible to breathe. Impossible to think. "He hits her."

I say it like it's a secret. Because it is. My secret. The secret I hide from everyone. The secret that leads to my worst secret: he hits me. Isaiah knows this already, but it's different. I'm saying it out loud. I'm making it real. And I'm asking him to save me. I'm asking him to save her.

Isaiah presses his face unimaginably close to mine. "He will never touch you again."

My throat swells and my voice comes out small. "I'll let him if it saves her."

A visible shiver runs through his body and his hands release my waist. Becoming a brick wall, Isaiah plants his feet on the ground and crosses his arms over his chest, practically daring me to move past him.

I step to the left. Isaiah steps with me. I step to the right. He mirrors the movement. "The car, Beth. Now."

"Get out of my way!" He doesn't and I feel like a cat trapped in a box. I claw at his chest. Push. Hit. Scream. Yell. Curse. Until my hands pound against him again and again and again.

Frustrated. Angry. Betrayed.

His arms weave through my attack, placing warm palms against my face. He strokes away the wetness on my cheeks. A wetness I don't understand. I smack his arms off me. "If you were my friend...if you cared, you'd help me!"

"Goddamn it, Beth, I'm doing this because I love you!"

My heart beats once and stalls as the world becomes horrifyingly still. I see it, in his eyes—the sincerity. I shake my head. "As a friend," I whisper. "You love me as a friend."

We stare at each other. Our chests rising and falling rapidly. "Say it, Isaiah. Tell me you love me as a friend." He's silent and my mind feels like it's on the verge of fracturing. "Say it!"

I don't want to deal with this. I don't have time for this. I step around him. "I'm getting her."

"Fuck this," he hisses as he bends. His shoulder makes contact with my waist and in seconds my head dangles over his back, my feet kicking him. I scream and watch through blurred vision as he creates more distance between me and Mom.

A car door clicks open. Isaiah slides my body from over his shoulder, covers my head, and uses his strength and size to push me into the backseat while keeping me from bolting out of it. The door slams shut and Isaiah has a death grip on my wrist. My head snaps to the left. The other door. It's locked. I pull at my wrist to gain freedom, to open the other door, but Isaiah retains his hold.

The car whips into Reverse and the engine whines when it accelerates.

"What the fuck were you thinking, Beth?" My eyes widen. Noah leans against the passenger door, one hand on the wheel. He doesn't even wait for an answer. "Isaiah said you'd come back for your mom, but I thought maybe you'd have enough sense to stay away. Jesus, at least you're predictable. Did you think we wouldn't remember that you'd check the damn bar before you checked out the apartment? Isaiah, remind me to pay Denny extra for calling us so damned fast."

Denny. Traitorous asshole. He told Noah and Isaiah I came for Mom.

"How did you get to Louisville?" Isaiah asks in an eerily calm voice.

"Fuck you." He told me he loved me. A cold sweat breaks out on my skin and my body begins to tremble. My best friend told me he loved me. And my mom. He forced me to leave my mom.

"Did you convince that Ryan bastard who's been messing with you to bring you?"

I glance at Isaiah and he swears. I yank at his hold on my wrist. "Get off of me."

Anger blazes from Isaiah's dark eyes and if the anger wasn't coming from him, it would frighten me. He has the calm anger. The controlled anger. The type that breaks if pressed too hard for too long. "Not until I know you're done thinking like an idiot and doing stupid things. You could have gotten yourself killed. Trent's been bragging at the bar for weeks on how he'll tear you limb from limb if he sees you again. He blames you for the cops coming to his apartment the week after you went to Groveton. He forgets though, that he has enemies everywhere."

I hear the snap inside my head and my entire body

flinches. I've talked to Isaiah every night and he never mentioned this piece of local gossip. Gossip that would have led me to act faster. If Trent blames me, then he'll blame Mom, and he already loves hitting her for no reason. Isaiah took me away from Mom and left her there with that asshole.

Isaiah's hand still holds my wrist and I don't want a backstabbing Judas touching me. Pulling my foot off the floorboard, I kick at him, again and again. "Let. Go. Of. Me!"

He releases my arm to shove my foot off him. "What is wrong with you?"

"You left her there to die!"

Isaiah punches the back of Noah's chair and collapses into the seat. His head falls back and he places his thumb and forefinger over his closed eyes.

The flat and bitter notes of a Nine Inch Nails song play on the radio and I sink into my corner of the car, pulling my legs into my chest. My heart aches with the lyrics. It's a phrase embedded in my soul, a lyric that talks about people you love and how in the end...they go away.

Isaiah took me away from Mom; he won't help me save her...he told me that he loves me. What used to be my best, strongest relationship has become a leaf withering and dying on a decaying vine.

I guess everything in life really does end.

RYAN

TEN MINUTES AGO, I left practice and found her gone. While I stood here losing my mind, deciding what to do, Beth was out having fun with her friends. I panicked, wondering if I should call Scott, the police, my dad. I imagined Scott's grief and thought about how angry my father would be when he learned I lost the niece of our town hero.

Mostly, I worried about Beth. Terrified someone took her. Praying she wasn't hurt or scared. Now I feel like a fool.

A few minutes ago, they pulled in and now Beth argues with the overrated tattooed punk I've seen before. I don't dare move a muscle, because I'm terrified I'll rip every single black hair out of Beth's head. Planting myself firmly next to my Jeep, I watch as Beth and her punked-out friend continue their heated discussion.

Beth played me like I've never been played before. I made a terrible mistake. I tried to like her. Screw Beth. Let her tank her life. She agreed to go to the party with me Friday. I won the dare. Deal done.

Beth bolts from the shitty car.

"Beth!" Tattoo Guy snags her by her belt loop. "You're not leaving. Not like this."

I flinch, but force myself to stay still. She wants this guy. She left me to be with him.

"Then keep the promise you made to me, Isaiah. Take me. Tonight." Her eyes search him and the desperation clawing at her face makes watching the scene uncomfortable. Whatever answer she's looking for, he doesn't have. He turns his head away with his eyes cast down. The other guy closes his door to the car and slowly approaches them, yet keeps his distance.

Great, I'm back to the odds of two against one. That is, if I cared enough to step in. Which I don't.

Isaiah glances at the other guy. "You always said you wanted a home and now you've got one."

Beth blinks. "Not this home."

I straighten. The attitude that makes her larger than life evaporates. She's small. Very small. Especially when standing in front of two menacing guys. Not only does she appear small, but she seems very...lost.

"Wait until you graduate. Just a couple more months. Noah and I talked and..."

With the name Noah, Beth's head jerks and anger blazes from her blue eyes. "You promised."

"Beth." The other guy, who I'm guessing must be Noah, uses a calm tone that even I know will send her over the edge. "You belong in Groveton."

In a flash of black, Beth races over to Noah. Her hand darts out, and she strikes him across the face. The sound echoes against the walls of the warehouse. Beth's chest heaves as she gasps for air. "Fuck you."

I push off the Jeep. What the hell? Noah gingerly touches his cheek, then inclines his head as if to release tension. "I was starting to feel left out after your little show back at the apartment complex."

"This is your fault!" she screams. "You and Echo and your new life. You turned Isaiah against me because you're too scared to be real. You want to be fake. Just like your girl."

Tattoo Guy—Isaiah—places his hand on Beth's arm and yanks her away from Noah. Hell no. Punk or no punk, a girl is in serious trouble if she hits a guy, and a guy should never touch a girl. My fingers tighten into a ball as I stalk over. "Get away from her."

"Groveton," Isaiah says as he ignores me. "With your uncle. That is exactly where you need to be." He points south, away from Louisville, toward home. "That world can give you what I can't. Not now. Just wait until graduation."

"If you meant what you said," she says in a low growl, "you'll keep your promise now."

A dark shadow seems to encompass the guy and I quicken my pace. "I said get away from her." My heart pounds in my chest. Two against one. The odds are bad, but I'll take them.

"Don't you dare throw that in my face," Isaiah says to her, then rips his stare from Beth to focus on me. "This doesn't involve you, man, so fuck off."

"The hell it doesn't. She came here with me and she's going home with me. Anything that happens to her in between *is* my business."

He angles his body toward me. "You say that like she's yours."

"Isaiah," Beth whispers. "Don't."

With only two feet between us, I take another step with

every muscle prepared for a fight. "She became mine the moment you laid a hand on her."

He closes the gap and we're standing toe-to-toe. His face inches from mine. Anger pulsates from his body. "She's not yours. She's mine and I don't like how you treat her."

A petite arm slides between our bodies. "Isaiah," says Beth. "Let it go."

"How I treat her?" Is this guy high? "She doesn't seem to want you."

"Ryan, stop, please." I've never heard Beth plead before and I want to look at her and confirm those words actually fell out of her mouth, but I don't dare. I keep solid eye contact with the asshole in front of me.

An insane smile tugs at his lips. "You think she wants you? Is that what you think? That you're some type of real man because you torture her at school? Because you spill her secrets? Because you humiliate her? You think she wants a guy that makes her cry?"

"Isaiah!" yells Beth.

His arm snaps back and so does mine. A large figure surges from my left and instead of the hit I'm prepared to take as I throw, Noah pushes Isaiah into a car. "Back off, bro."

"How could you!" I expect to see Beth's frigid, accusing stare in my direction. Instead, it's fixed on Isaiah. Her entire body shakes and she rubs her left arm with her right hand. A continuous motion over and over again. "How could you tell him that?"

Isaiah blinks and the anger drains out of him. "Beth..."

She rushes to the Jeep. "Let's go."

She doesn't have to tell me twice. I shove the keys in the ignition before I shut the door and roar out of the parking lot. Hitting the freeway, I click on my seat belt as Beth rests her head against the passenger window.

I search for the anger I felt earlier and try to find a way to blame her. She was the one that left. She was the one that spent time with those two guys. But the only thought turning in my brain is the accusation Isaiah spat at me: I make her cry.

BETH

LIVING IS LIKE BEING CHAINED at the bottom of a shallow pond with my eyes open and no air. I can see distorted images of happiness and light, even hear muffled laughter, but everything is out of my reach as I lie in suffocating agony. If death is the opposite of living, then I hope death is like floating.

I've never fought with Isaiah and Noah like that. I never thought Isaiah would betray me, but he has. I trusted my best friend with secrets—secrets I've never told another living soul. He knows about my father, he knows about my mother, he knows how many times a man has slapped a hand across my face...he knows that Ryan, the way he offers friendship when I know he's only playing me, hurts.

Resting my forehead against the glass of the passenger-side window, I watch the multiple white lines in the middle of the road speed by. On the two-lane road leading to my uncle's house, Ryan passes a tractor trailer, easily doing sixty in a forty-five. I sort of wish I had the courage to open the door and fall out.

It would hurt, but then the pain would be over when I

died. All the pain. The indescribable ache in my chest, the heaviness in my head, the hard lump in my throat—it would all be gone.

We've ridden in silence. I'm not sure if it's been an uncomfortable silence as I am on the verge of numb. I'm striving for numb. I crave numb. I want to be high.

The Jeep veers to the left and we begin the trip down the long driveway. My stomach growls. We never ate.

When he reaches the house, Ryan places the Jeep in Park and immediately turns off the engine. I hate the country. With no lights, the woods and fields become the playground of my nightmares. My skin pricks at the thought of the devil waiting in the darkness to snatch me up and expel me into nothingness.

There are so many things Ryan can do. He can yell. He can go inside and tell Scott everything. The latter would make him the upstanding kid that Scott wants me to be. It would also crush the remains of my life. Scott will send Mom to jail.

And me? I'll want to die.

Four hours ago, pride would have never let me say the words, but there's nothing left inside me. "I'm sorry."

Frogs croak near the creek that borders Scott's farm. Ryan says nothing back and I don't blame him. There really is nothing for him to say to a girl like me.

He examines the keys in his hands. "You played me for a ride into Louisville."

"Yes." And if my plan had worked, I would be gone, and my uncle would have blamed him.

"You planned to meet with that guy instead of spending time with me."

"Yes." He deserves honesty and that is as honest an answer as I can give him.

He twirls the keys around his finger. "From the moment you walked into Taco Bell, you were nothing more than a dare. Chris and Logan dared me to get your phone number and then I was dared to take you on a date."

The words sting, but I struggle to keep the pain from surfacing. What more should I expect? He's everything that's right with the world. I'm everything wrong. Guys like him don't go for girls like me.

"I almost got into a fight for you."

"I know." And I say those rare words again: "I'm sorry."

Ryan sticks the key into the ignition and starts the engine. "You owe me. I'll pick you up at seven on Friday. No games this time. A simple night. We go to the party. We hang for an hour. I win my dare, then I take you home. You go back to ignoring me. I'll ignore you."

"Fine." I should be happy, but I'm not. This is what I thought I wanted. Behind the numbness is an ache waiting to torture me. I open the door to the Jeep and close it without looking back.

RYAN

STATE LAW KEEPS ME FROM pitching more than fifteen innings a week. I'm only brought in on Thursday games if our other two pitchers dig us a hole. Three innings ago, when Coach put me in, we were so far deep we couldn't see daylight. Not that the rain helps.

It's rained for two weeks. Two weeks' worth of games have been called. Two weeks' worth of parties have been canceled. Two weeks of me and Beth ignoring each other.

Everyone is anticipating that the rain will end tonight and the field party will finally take place tomorrow. I'm ready too—eager to win the dare and have Beth officially out of my life.

Bottom of the seventh with the score tied, I need to hold this last batter to send the game into extra innings. Light rain cools the heat on the back of my neck. Pooled droplets drip from the brim of my hat. The ball's slick. So is my hand. I hate playing in the rain, but guys in the majors do it all the time.

The intensity of the rain increases. I can barely read Logan's signal. Out of habit, I peek at the runner on first, but I can't see a damn thing. I wind back and the game-changing sound of nature intervenes: thunder and lightning.

"Off the field!" the umpire shouts.

My cleats sink in the mud as I walk to the dugout. This is the third rain delay of the game. There won't be another. The game is done.

"Great job, guys." Coach claps each one of us on our soggy backs as we enter. "Drive home safely. Severe weather is moving through."

Rain beats against the roof. I don't see the point of a roof if everything underneath it is wet. The seats. The equipment. Our bags. I quickly change shoes, tying my Nikes harder and faster than normal.

Knowing me better than anyone else, Chris wedges his large body onto the bench beside me. "We didn't lose."

Rain cancellations don't count. "We didn't win either."

"You would have pulled us out."

"Maybe." I stand and sling my bag over my shoulder. "But I'll never know."

The rest of the team chatters, changes shoes, and waits in the dugout for the worst of the rain to end. I'm not in the mood for company and I'm already wet. The rain hammers my back as I head to the parking lot.

"Hey!" Chris runs to catch me. "What's your deal, dawg?"

"Nothing."

"Don't give me that shit," he yells over the rain. "You've been a walking mood for two weeks."

I open the door to my Jeep and toss my bag into the back. Beth. That's what happened, but I can't tell Chris that. I'm ending my losing streak tomorrow when the rain moves out and Beth comes with me to the party.

"Maybe he'll tell me." Standing next to Chris, Lacy looks like a drowned rat with her hair plastered to her face. When the rain began an hour ago, she sought shelter in Chris's car. "Take me home, Ryan."

The last thing I want is to be trapped in a car with her. "I'm not your boyfriend."

"No," she yells as another clap of thunder vibrates in the sky. "You're my friend."

Lacy kisses Chris's cheek and runs to the passenger side. I glance at Chris and he nods. "She doesn't want to be mad at you anymore."

I hop into the Jeep and start it up. In Lacy–like style, she goes to work turning on the heat and switching the radio to her favorite country station before lowering the sound. "Did you and Beth have a fight?"

The windshield wipers whine at a fast rate as I pull out of the parking lot. I wonder what Lacy knows. I didn't tell anyone that Beth and I went into Louisville. "Is that what she said?"

"No. I finally scored her home number the other week and her uncle told me you guys were out."

I calculate how this affects the dare. "Did you tell Chris?"

"It's not my business to tell. Did you take her into Louis-ville because of the dare?"

"Yes."

"So the dare's done. That's why you've been ignoring her?"

Silence. Why is Lacy making me feel like a dick? Beth's the one that screwed me over. She owes me this. "She treats you like crap, Lace. Why do you care?"

Lacy doesn't live far from the community ballpark. I ease

into her drive and watch the hanging ferns on the front porch blowing in the wind.

"She was my friend."

"Was! She was..."

Lacy holds both her hands out. "Stop. Listen to me. I'm not you. I've never been you. You walk into any situation and it's automatically perfect. I'm not perfect. I never have been."

What is she talking about? If Lace only knew how broken my family is; how since Mark left we're slowing dying. "I'm not perfect."

"Will you shut up?! God, I can't get you guys to say crap half the time and then anytime I try to actually SAY something worth saying, one of you interrupts me. So shut up!"

I gesture with my hand for her to continue.

"No one liked me, Ryan. Daddy moved us to Groveton when I was four and I knew then nobody liked me. My mom tried playdate after playdate and put me in preschool and no matter what, I was considered the outsider. I'm not you. I'm not Logan. I'm not Chris. I can't trace my roots to the founding fathers. I can't eat Sunday chicken with my grandma after church because she doesn't live on the next property over, but three states away."

I rub the back of my head, unsure if I should speak and if I do, what to say. Lacy never seemed to care what people thought of her. "We never treated you different."

She sighs heavily. "Why do you think I've hung out with you since sixth grade? Do you think I love baseball that much?"

I chuckle. "Don't let Chris hear you say you aren't a die-hard fan."

"I love him," she says, and I understand that means that

she also loves anything he loves. "Anyway, the whole point is, Beth liked me. When Gwen was mean to me..."

My mouth opens to protest. She points at me and narrows her eyes. "Don't say a word. One, I told you to shut up. Two, this is my monologue and not yours. Three, she's a bitch. As I was saying, when Gwen played to her true self and dropped the I'm-pretending-to-be-perfect-so-the-whole-world-will-love-me act, she made my life hell. I was labeled weird before I entered kindergarten, yet Beth liked me.

"When Gwen made me cry, Beth held my hand and told me that she loved me. When Gwen's friends told me I couldn't play on the swings, Beth pushed them off and told me the swings were mine. Beth taught me what it meant to have friends. I don't know what the hell happened to her between third grade and now, but I owe her. Here's the thing—I love you and I love her, but I swear to God I'll kick your ass if you hurt her."

Lacy has thrown out too much to process, so I focus on what I know. "You'll kick my ass?"

She cracks a smile. "Okay, maybe not, but I will be pissed off and I don't like being pissed off at you."

I don't like her being pissed off at me either. "She's coming with me to the party."

Disappointment clouds her face. "Dare or date?"

"Dare." I don't lie to friends. "But Beth knows it."

"If she knows, doesn't that break the rules?"

I shrug. "We don't have a rule book."

The porch light flips on and the front door opens. Through the pouring rain, I barely see Lacy's mom. I wave at her. A second later, she waves back.

"She thinks all Chris and I do is make out in cars." Lacy's

hand flutters away any further discussion about her and Chris making out in cars, which is fine by me.

I'd rather think about Beth. Who is she? The girl Lacy swears is a true friend? The girl with blond hair who loved ribbons and fancy dresses? The girl who crawls underneath my skin and stays? The girl strong enough to tell me what she really thinks of me? The girl who looks so small and defenseless at times that I wonder if she can survive in the world on her own? Lacy may hate me for these words, but they have to be said. "Maybe Beth isn't who you think she is."

"Funny," Lacy says. "I was about to say the same thing to you."

BETH

RYAN SWITCHES GEARS when the pavement ends and the Jeep's wheels hit gravel. The wind whips my hair into my face and neck, stinging me like the tiny tentacles of a jellyfish. He turns on the headlights when the sun sets lower in the west, causing the woods surrounding us to fall into shadows.

Besides the forced happy hellos we exchanged under my aunt's watchful eye, Ryan and I have said nothing to each other since he picked me up. The things he uttered to me two weeks ago still hurt—I was nothing more than a dare.

The offers of friendship, the smiles, the nice words—all games. Deep down I always knew it, but part of me hoped for more. I allowed hope. Stupid Beth making another stupid mistake. Story of my life.

"You know, it's rude to text while you're out with someone else." Ryan rests one hand on top of the steering wheel and leans cockily toward the door. "Especially when I saved you."

I ignore Ryan and stare at my cell. Owing him, I agreed to spend one hour with him at the party. I never agreed to conversation.

The constant dipping and bobbing in his Jeep makes reading Isaiah's texts nearly impossible. It's the first time I've had the courage to open them. Every message says the same thing: I'm sorry.

So am I. I'm sorry I trusted him. I'm sorry he betrayed me. I'm sorry I thought I could read his texts without my heart throbbing as if a swarm of bees attacked it. I want the heaviness to go away. I want the hurt to go away. How can I forgive him for telling Ryan my secret? How can I forgive him for forcing me to leave my mom?

And even worse, how can I talk to him now that I know he loves me and I know, beyond words, that I don't feel the same way? My throat tightens. Isaiah's my safe. He always has been. He's that place where I fall when the world tumbles into chaos. There were times I thought maybe we could be more, but then...I'd freeze up entirely. Isaiah and I were meant to be friends and now I'm losing my only friend.

The phone vibrates in my hands. It's as if he senses I'm finally on the other side. Call me. Text me. Please.

I toss the cell onto the floorboard of Ryan's Jeep. Texting Isaiah back will only increase the pain—for both of us.

Ryan concentrates on the road, looking deep in thought. I wish I had his life. No pain. No problems. Only lightness and freedom.

"You okay?" Ryan catches me staring. I remind myself that the sincerity melting in his brown eyes isn't real. Jocks are good at pretending. His hair sticks out behind the baseball cap he wears backward. He shifts gears again and the muscles in his arms ripple with the motion. It's kind of sexy. Not kind of—Ryan is sexy.

"Why are we on a dirt road? Did we officially reach the end of civilization?"

"It's a gravel road," says Ryan. "This is the way to my house."

His house. Please. That bastard Luke from my old school "showed" me his house too. "I'm not fucking you."

"And you talk so pretty. You must have had all the guys dangling from your fingertips in Louisville." He flexes his fingers and regrips the steering wheel before speaking matter-of-factly. "This is the fastest way to the party."

Ryan hates me and I don't blame him. I hate me. What I hate more in this moment is that part of me likes Ryan. He stood up for me like the prince does for the princess in the fairy tales Scott used to read to me as a child. I'm not a princess, but Ryan is a knight. He just belongs to someone else.

"Are you sure you're okay? You look pale."

"I'm fine." I hate how sharp the words come out. Fabulous. I yelled at him. Now I can feel like crap for that too.

Ryan breezes past what I assume is his house, a large one-story with a massive garage next to it, and switches gears again when we hit the grass. The Jeep jolts forward, tossing me in the seat like I'm on a roller coaster. I grab hold of the passenger grip on the ceiling and Ryan laughs. A crazy smile brightens his face and once again, I find myself drawn in.

No longer leaning away from me, Ryan sits straight, one hand on the steering wheel, another shifting gears as we hurtle down a hill to a creek. The Jeep accelerates as if it were a snowball on the verge of an avalanche. I can see the possibilities. The crashing. The water. The jostling. The dirt. My heart pumps faster in my chest and for the first time in weeks I feel *alive*.

The engine roars and he presses harder on the gas. The Jeep hits the rocks. Ryan and I both whoop and yell as water sprays the truck and smashes onto the windshield, making us blind. He pushes the Jeep forward, faster, past the creek, over the rocks. Daring to continue even when I have no idea what's on the other side.

The windshield wipers spring to life, clearing our view, and Ryan jerks the wheel to the right to miss a sprawling tree. He enters a clearing and kills the engine. I hear laughter and suck in a breath when I realize it's mine...and his. Together. It sounds nice. Kind of like music.

Ryan has that smile again. The genuine one that makes my stomach flip. He had it at Taco Bell. He had it when Scott introduced us. He does it with such ease and for a second I believe his smile is for me.

"You're smiling," he says.

I absently touch my face as if I'm surprised by the news.

"You should do that more. It's pretty." He pauses. "You're pretty."

My heart does this strange fluttering. Like it's stopping and starting at the same time. Heat creeps up my neck and flushes my face. What the hell? I'm blushing again?

"I'm sorry." Ryan keeps the enduring smile, but it turns a little repentant and his eyes cast down in a shy way.

"No, it was fun." The most fun I've had in weeks. The most fun I've had sober in...my mind ticks back and I come up empty. Life sucks sober.

"Yeah." His eyes become distant and the grin stays on his face, but I can tell it's a little forced. He blinks and the smile becomes natural again. "Yeah. The creek. I should have told you that was coming. Or slowed down."

Why I can't hold eye contact with him for longer than a second, I don't know. The uncharacteristic bashfulness causes me to feel inadequate and a little...girly? I lace my hands together and focus on them. "Really. It's okay. I had fun."

"Beth?" He hesitates. "Can we start over?"

I eye him—head to toe. No one's offered me a do-over before. I guess no one thought I was worth it. A strange tugging inside me lifts my lips and causes a floating sensation for about three seconds. Well aware that everything in life is short-lived, I feel the smile drop and the heaviness return. Still, I accept the offer. "Sure."

The sound of a guy shouting catches our attention. Farther into the clearing is a circle of trucks with headlights on and a bonfire in the middle. Kids from school are everywhere. What am I doing here?

"You ready?" he asks.

No, but I screwed everything up when I tried to run away. "I guess."

While I'm not a party virgin, a party in the woods with a bonfire is a first for me. A group dances in front of a large rusty Jeep. Others hang near the bonfire or on the tailgates of trucks. The whole setup has a *Lord of the Flies* quality. At least the movie version of the book.

Ryan and I wade through the knee-deep grass and it crunches beneath my wannabe Chuck Taylors. Some of the longer blades swat at me, slashing at the bare skin exposed by the rips in my jeans. I hate the country.

The closer we get to the party, the slower I walk and Ryan matches my pace. With each step, he bridges the distance between us and a couple of times his fingers skim against mine. Butterflies flutter through my blood and the stupid little girl part of me wants him to touch me.

The other part would slug him if he did.

"Parties make you uncomfortable?" he asks.

"When they make me feel like Daniel stepping into the lion's den."

I try to suck in my smile when I hear the surprise in his voice. "You know the story?"

Thanks to my short stint in VBS with Lacy, I can recite the books of the Bible, New and Old Testament, and a few other random verses. "Even the devil knows who God is."

"You're not the devil, Beth."

"Are you sure?"

That sweet smile graces his lips. "No."

I laugh. It's a good laugh. The type that digs deep down into my toes and tickles my insides. What feels even better is the sound of him laughing right along with me.

"Come on. I promise they won't eat you. Half the girls here claim they're vegetarians and I can take the guys." He does the one thing I hoped for and dreaded: his hand tangles with mine and he tugs gently for me to follow.

I like the touch of his hand. It's warm. Strong. And I let the part of me that loved ribbons live for a few seconds and entwine my fingers with his. If I learned one thing from Vacation Bible School, it was that resurrection of the dead is possible.

Ryan walks toward a truck where Chris and Logan sit on the tailgate. They laugh loudly, then stop when they see me. Tucked between Chris's legs, Lacy offers me a friendly smile.

"Did the mud call to you again, Ryan?" asks Lacy.

Ryan chuckles. "Yeah."

Mud? How did Lacy know... I glance down at my outfit. Mud—everywhere. Just great.

"Hell," says Chris. "You actually convinced her to show. Did you give him your phone number too?"

I blink. "What?"

"You're holding his damn hand."

Right. I am. Stupid me. The bet. First the phone number. Then the date. The Jeep ride disoriented me into momentary forgetfulness. Hurt pricks at my heart and I shove the little girl with ribbons into the dark recesses of my mind. Some things should never be reborn. I break free from his hand. So much for Ryan's offer of starting over.

"Don't let him snow you," Chris says while running a finger down Lacy's arm. "Ryan's a charmer."

Noah touches Echo like that. It's obvious from school that Chris is in love with Lacy. Some guys touch girls they love. Others touch girls they use. The worst touch girls they hurt. I stare at Chris and consider telling him to go fuck himself. Yet I can't find the anger. I'm the moron that walked into this situation.

"Don't let Chris get to you," Ryan retorts. "He's pissed because crap comes out of both ends."

Chris gives a hearty laugh. Ryan slings an arm around my shoulder and leads me from the group. Um—no. I may have fallen for the hand-holding before, but I'm not falling for anything else. "Get your arm off of me before I rip it off and beat the shit out of you with it."

We're heading for the bonfire. I feel small underneath his massive arm, like a girl, and such vulnerability makes me uncomfortable. Instead of letting go, Ryan effortlessly tucks me under his shoulder. "When you kiss guys, do they drop dead from the venom that spews out of your mouth?"

"I wish, because I would have kissed you days ago. I'm not kidding, get the hell off."

"No."

No? "Do you have a death wish?"

Ryan strides past the bonfire, and panic sweeps through me when he guides me into the thick crowd of people dancing. "You owe me one hour. Remember?"

Rap pounds so loudly from a truck that the ground beneath us vibrates. Around us people dance. Shimmy. Shake. Laugh. They move in hypnotic rhythms. Skin against skin. Body against body.

My stomach heaves and I'm overwhelmed with the urge to vomit. "Screw you. I'm not doing this."

Ryan bolts in front of me, stopping my retreat. "How about a deal? One dance and your debt is paid."

"I don't dance." True—I don't. Truer? I've never danced with a guy.

He raises a skeptical eyebrow. "You don't dance?"

"No."

The firelight flickers against Ryan's tan, giving his face a beautiful bronze glow. Gold shines in his hair. He's gorgeous. Honestly he is, and he wants me to dance. Could this day get any worse?

Ryan steps closer and flashes an all-knowing smile that makes him adorable and me weak. I hate him and I hate myself for wanting him to touch me again.

The music changes from superfast to a bit slower. Its strong beat mimics the frantic pounding in my chest. Ryan rests a hand on my hip and his heat seeps into my skin and creeps into my bloodstream. He lowers his lips to my ear and his breath tickles the nape of my neck. "Dance with me, Beth."

"No." I'm definitely learning impaired. I whispered the reply. I might as well have screamed yes. *This is a mistake, Beth. A huge, glaring mistake. Just run!*

Ryan places his other hand on the small of my back and molds his strong body to mine. I inhale and welcome the scent of warm earth and summer rain. Ryan smells...delicious.

"This works better if you touch me," he says.

I loosely lay my hands on his shoulders. Sort of like what I saw Echo do once when Noah swept her off the bed to dance. My skin tingles. Touching Ryan, oh God, it's too much...too intimate. "I'm only doing this because I owe you."

"That's okay." On rhythm, Ryan moves his hips from side to side. His hand slides an inch lower and the gentle pressure he exerts on my thigh stirs my body to sway in time with his. Our feet never leave the ground, but, I swear, I'm flying.

Ryan whispers to me again, "I'm dancing with you because I love the look on your face."

Figures. "Love watching me make a fool out of myself?"

"No. I love seeing the girl Scott and Lacy say you can be." He stares at me as if he's seeing beyond my skin and my heart pounds out of my chest so violently that he has to feel it. My nerve endings become raw. Somehow, Ryan's seeing me and I'm exposed—as if I'm standing naked in front of a large open window. My hands slip from his neck, but as I try to step back, he clutches my waist, rejecting my escape.

"Ryan! I wondered when you'd get here." The sound of an all-too-familiar voice creates the same electric shock as when I stuck my finger into a wall socket when I was four. My body seizes, then moves in warp drive away from Ryan.

Gwen wears a red sundress with printed white flowers.

Her lip curls at my wannabe Chuck Taylors, worn jeans, and black T-shirt. She links her arm with Ryan's. "You wouldn't mind if I steal Ryan for a moment, would you? There are some things we need to discuss."

They look nice together. Well matched. Like a couple should. "He's yours."

RYAN

SECONDS AGO, BETH AND I shared something...a moment, a connection. I saw it in her eyes. Something real. Now it's gone. Beth turns from me and heads in the direction of Lacy, Chris, and Logan. "Beth. Wait."

She faces me again, but walks backward—away from me. "Don't worry," she says with a hint of bite. "I'm not disappearing."

"Let her go," says Gwen. "You can chat with her later."

I let Beth go, but only because I remember how persistent Gwen can be. She'll follow me until she completes her mission. "What?"

"You don't have to be snippy," she chides.

"I'm not." Near the tree line, I notice Tim Richardson and Sarah Janes. Sarah sways and laughs a little too loud.

"Yes, you are."

Useless conversations. That's another reason we broke up. "Is Sarah wasted?"

Gwen glances over her shoulder at Sarah and refocuses on me. "Yeah. She was trashed before we arrived. So, I was thinking, we should walk onto the football field together for homecoming. The crowd likes couples."

"We're not a couple." Tim places a hand on Sarah's ass and she stops laughing. "Are Sarah and Tim an item?"

"No. She thinks he's dirt, but she's drunk and, well, he's Tim. Back to me and you. We were a couple and maybe we should try it again. You know, when you're done experimenting with Beth. I mean, you don't have to go to all of your practices, do you? Ryan...Ryan? Why do you keep staring over my shoulder?"

Sarah puts her hands on Tim's chest and pushes him. He doesn't move, but I do. "Excuse me," I mumble to Gwen.

She blocks my path and I halt, irritated she's still here. "What?"

"Did you hear what I said?"

Something about homecoming and Beth. "Can we talk about this later?" Sarah pushes Tim again. "Your friend needs help."

Gwen steps to the side and I advance to the tree line. Tim becomes touchier and Sarah keeps smacking him.

"Hey, Tim," I say. "I think Sarah wants to head back to the party."

"No, we're fine," Tim responds.

Sarah swats his hands away. "Get off of me."

"Tim," I say in a low tone. I'll back up my words with action and he knows it.

Tim releases Sarah and his chest puffs up as he watches her stumble back to the party. I ready myself by widening my stance. Tim owns a reputation for his dedication to the football team and his anger when he's drunk. "What's your problem, Ryan?"

"Don't have one as long as you give Sarah her space."

He sloppily points at me, then sways. "You made her think she wanted space."

"Come on, Tim. Let's go back to the party."

Tim rolls his shoulders back. He's looking for a fight. I'm not.

"You know what I think?" he asks.

"I think we should head back."

"I think you've got a problem with girls."

My back straightens. "What did you say?"

His lips turn up into a smirk. "Yeah," he says. "You have a problem with girls. You dumped Gwen and she's hot. You gay, man?"

Rage ignites inside me and as my muscles tighten to rush forward, delicate fingers wrap around my arm. "He's not worth it," Beth says in a smooth voice.

Chris and Logan slide in between me and Tim, a barrier of skin, muscle, and bone between me and the guy I want to pound.

Tim continues to taunt me. "Real men aren't saved by girls."

"You're drunk," Logan announces to him in a bored voice.

From the other side of Logan, Tim holds out his hands. "Come and get me, Ryan. Prove that you're a man."

My fists curl and I step closer. "I'm game, Tim. Let's do this."

Chris pushes against my chest, but the pressure does nearly nothing to hold me back. He yells at Beth, "Get him out of here!"

Her fingers intertwine with mine and that soft, feminine voice breaks through the anger. "Let's go."

My eyes flick over to her. "Ryan," she says. "Please."

Her one *please* breaks through the chaos disorienting my brain long enough to propel me in the opposite direction of Tim. I tighten my grip on Beth's hand and lead her back to my Jeep, but not before snagging a six-pack of beer from a cooler.

Her fingers still clutch mine as we walk through the tall grass without saying a word. I release her when we reach the Jeep and we both hop in. My heart bleeds and anger courses in my veins. I turn on the engine and peel out of the clearing.

My brother left.

My brother is gay and he left and he's never coming back. My father acts as if he never existed. My mother is miserable. My parents—people who once loved each other—hate each other.

Driving alongside the creek, I wait for a shallow part before crossing. I've tortured Beth enough. With this Jeep. With my presence. Isaiah said I made her cry. My fingers tighten on the wheel. Beth's right—I'm a jerk.

I'll take her home, then ride to the back field of my house. And drink. By myself. Drinking may not undo history, but it will cause me to forget for a few hours.

I jerk the wheel to the left when the rushing of the creek slows to a trickle. Water barely laps the tires as I cross, but the moment I hit the other side, I know I'm screwed. Mud.

Too much mud. Deep mud. I press on the gas and pull the wheel to the right to try to force the front tires on solid ground before the back ones sink, but it's too late. The back tires whine and halt all forward progress.

"Shit!" I slam my hand on the steering wheel. Knowing that fighting will drag us deeper, I cut the engine. I'm stuck.

I yank the hat from my head and throw it to the floorboard. That sums everything up—I'm in deep and I'm stuck.

My leg sinks a foot into the mud. Beth will be full of colorful words when I tell her we're going to have to walk. The mud acts like slow-drying concrete, making each step nearly impossible. My jeans rub and slosh in the filth. I'm a complete mess, but I don't have to let Beth get this dirty.

I haven't been much of a gentleman to her. In fact, I've been the opposite. Not that her shining personality has made it easy. I open her door and hold out my arms. "Come here."

Her forehead furrows. "What?"

"I'm going to carry you out of the mud."

She lifts an incredulous eyebrow. "The show's over, Bat Boy. You don't have to be nice to me anymore."

Not in the mood for her mouth or an argument, I slip my arms underneath her knees and lift her out of the seat. She won't be bitching me out the entire walk home because I ruined her shoes.

"Wait!" Beth wiggles in my arms and reaches for the Jeep. Can't she permit me one nice act? "Dammit, Beth, let me help you."

Ignoring me, Beth leans into the passenger side. The back of her shirt hitches up, exposing her smooth skin and Chinese symbols tattooed along her spine. My eyes follow the path of the symbols until they disappear into her jeans. Way too quickly for me, she leans back into my arms, two six-packs of beer cradled against her chest.

My eyes flicker from the beer to Beth. She shrugs. "Six wasn't enough."

For me, it's plenty. I don't want a drinking partner tonight and if I did, it wouldn't be her. I kick the door shut and wade out of the mud. Beth's light. Weighs one hundred; maybe one-o-five wet.

"You're obsessed with touching me," she says.

I jostle Beth to shut her up. The beer cans clank together as she juggles them to prevent them from falling out of her lap. "Readjusting" Beth did shut her up, but it positioned her head closer to mine. I stare straight ahead and try not to focus on the sweet scent of roses drifting from her hair.

"You are obsessed with touching me. You could have put me down forever ago."

Withdrawn into my own head, I hadn't noticed that we'd entered her uncle's woods. "Sorry."

I place Beth on her feet, snatch both six-packs from her hands, and stalk in the direction of her house. Scott all but bought billboard signs announcing that alcohol was off-limits for Beth.

Lucky for her, I drove along the creek toward Scott's property. Otherwise, it could have been one hell of a walk—for her. Something tells me she's not the outdoorsy type.

She stays a few steps behind and I appreciate the silence. Fall crickets chirp and a slight breeze rustles through the leaves on the trees. Right over the next hill is Scott's pasture and his back barn. A twig snaps behind me as Beth rushes to my side. "Where are we going?"

"I'm taking you home."

A light grip pulls on my biceps. "The hell you are."

I stop, not because Beth's touch halts me, but because I find her attempt to physically stop me amusing. "You've fulfilled your obligation. You came to the party, now I'm taking you home. We're done. I don't have to look at you. You don't have to look at me."

Beth bites her lower lip. "I thought we were starting over."

What the hell? Isn't this what she wanted—to be left alone? "You hate me."

Beth says nothing, neither confirming nor denying what I said, and the thought that my words are true causes my heart to clench. Screw it. I don't have to understand her. I don't need her. I turn my back to her and push forward—through the tall grass of the pasture, toward the red barn.

"Have you ever drank alone?" she asks.

I freeze. When I don't answer, she continues, "It sucks. I did it once—when I was fourteen. It makes you feel worse. Alone. My friend..." She falters. "My best friend and I agreed that we'd never drink alone again. We promised we'd have each other's backs."

It's weird to hear Beth talk so openly and part of me wishes she'd go back to being foulmouthed and rude. She seems less human then. "Is there a reason why you're telling me this?"

The grass rustles as she fidgets. "Six of those beers are mine and I have a little more than four hours to curfew. I guess I'm saying we could call a truce for tonight and neither one of us have to be alone."

"Your uncle Scott would crucify me."

"What he doesn't know won't hurt him."

I glance over my shoulder and watch as she weaves through the flowing grains to reach me. "I swear I have more to lose than you do. He won't know."

Mud spots her face, cakes in her hair, and stains her clothes. Half of that mud Beth gained on our trip in. I should have told her what she looked like before we went to the party, but Beth was laughing. Smiling. I selfishly held on to the moment.

On top of that, Isaiah said I made her cry. I assess the small beauty in front of me. There's more to her, I know there is. I saw it in her eyes when she laughed with me in the Jeep. Felt it in her touch as we danced.

I must be losing my mind. "One beer."

BETH

STRAW IS SOFT TO LIE ON.

Sort of scratchy.

Comfortable.

Great for weightlessness.

It smells musty and dusty and dirty. The corners of my lips flinch in a moment of joy. Musty. Dusty. And dirty. Those words flow well together. Staring at the shadows from the light created by the camping lantern Ryan found in the corner of Scott's barn, I inhale deeply. I'm finally high.

Not pot high. Ryan's too straitlaced for that. Airy in alcohol would be a better description.

Three beers. Isaiah would laugh his ass off. Three beers and I'm floating. Guess that's what happens when you stay sober for a couple of weeks in a row.

Isaiah.

My chest aches.

"My best friend is pissed at me and I'm pissed at him." I'm the first to break the silence beyond the crack and hiss of beer cans popping open and the rustle and cooing of birds in the rafters. "My only friend."

In slow motion, Ryan rolls his head to look at me. He sits on the ground with his torso sloppily supported by a stack of baled hay. A glaze covers his light brown eyes. I give him major props. At six beers, the boy has drunk me under the table. Correction—under bales of hay. "Which one?"

"Isaiah," I say and my heart twists. "He's the guy with the tattoos."

"Is the other one your boyfriend?"

I mean to chuckle. Instead, it comes out more of a snort and a hiccup. Ryan laughs at me, but I'm so weightless I don't care. "Noah? No, he's helplessly in love with some insane chick. Besides, Noah and I aren't friends. We're more like siblings."

"Really?" The disbelief oozes from Ryan. "You don't resemble each other."

I wave my hand frantically in the air. "No. We're not related. Noah can't stand me, but he loves me. Takes up for me. Like siblings."

Love. I purposely knock the back of my head against the ground in frustration. Isaiah said he loved me. I search the cobwebbed corridors of my emotions and try to imagine loving him back. All I find is a hollow emptiness. Is that what love is? Emptiness?

Ryan narrows his eyes for a deep-in-thought expression, but six beers in an hour tells me he probably spaced out. "So you don't have a boyfriend?"

"Nope."

Ryan cracks open another beer. I start to protest as he has infiltrated my stash, but decide against it. I want weightless, not puking. I have to return to Scott's in three hours and coherency will be required.

"Why is Isaiah mad at you?" he asks.

"He loves me," I say without thinking, and immediately regret it. "And other things."

"Do you love him back?" That's the fastest Ryan has responded since his second beer.

I sigh heavily. Do I? "I'd throw myself in front of a bus to push him out of the way." If it would save him. If it would make him happy. That's love, right?

"I'd do that for most people, but it doesn't mean that I love them."

"Oh." Oh. Then I have no idea what love is.

"What other things?" he prods.

Other things? Oh yeah, Ryan asked why Isaiah is mad at me. I shake my head back and forth, causing the straw to crackle. "You wouldn't understand. My problems..." My mom. "My family isn't perfect. We have problems."

Ryan chuckles and sips his beer.

I rise on my elbows. "What's so damn funny?"

Ryan tilts back the beer and I watch his throat move as he swallows. He crushes the empty can in his hand. "Perfect. Family. Problems. Gay brothers."

We're obviously not talking about me and Isaiah anymore. "You're drunk."

"Good." Even inebriated, the ache I saw earlier while he was carrying me out of the Jeep darkens his eyes.

"Is that why you got defensive with the football asshole?" I ask. "Because you have a gay brother?"

Ryan tosses the can near the other empty ones and rubs his eyes. "Yes. And if you don't mind, I'd prefer not to talk about it. Or talk at all."

"Fine." I can do silence. My arms fall over my head as I plop back onto the straw. Isaiah would let me talk. I could rattle on about anything…ribbons and dresses, and he'd placate me when I questioned whether I was too harsh with Noah. Sometimes I think about what life would be like if I gave Echo a break. I mean, she does make Noah happy and Isaiah likes her. Sometimes she's cool.

"You're talking," says Ryan. "In fact, you've been talking since you finished your first beer."

I blink and close my mouth, not having realized that I had verbalized a thing.

A black bird flaps its wings overhead, creating a shadow on the ceiling. Images of a deadly archangel coming to destroy us all enter my mind. The bird grows more agitated and the other birds fly to a beam on the opposite side of the barn. He takes off into the air and smacks the wall, dips down, flies across the barn, and rams into the opposite wall. My heart thunders with every hit. I watch with wide eyes and shaking hands. "We have to help him."

I jump up and stumble toward the barn door. Struggling for balance, I force one of the doors open with a loud creak. I lean against the frame and wait for the bird that's damaging itself over and over again to escape. "Go! Get out of here!"

"Shut the door," Ryan says. "Birds are stupid. If you want it out, you're going to have to trap it and drag it out."

I gesture wildly into the open night. "But the door is open!"

"And the bird's so panicked that it'll never see the opening. All you're doing is inviting your uncle to come in here and find us. Unless you're ready to go home, close the door."

The bird smacks itself into the wall again and flutters to a nearby beam. He ruffles his feathers over and over again, then finally draws in his wings to rest. My stomach rolls in torture. Why can't the bird see the way out?

"Who's Echo?" asks Ryan.

"But the bird..." I say, ignoring his question.

"Doesn't understand you're trying to help. If anything, it sees you as a threat. Now, tell me, who's Echo?"

I take a deep breath and close the door. I want the bird to find freedom, but I'm not ready to go back to Scott's. Thanks to my impaired state, I half walk, half trip back to my bed of straw. Damn bird. Why can't something be easy? "Noah's girlfriend."

"That's a screwed-up name," he says.

I giggle. "She's a screwed-up girl." I stop giggling and remember how Noah looked at her: as if she were the only person on the planet, the only person that mattered. "But Noah loves her."

That must be love: when everything else in the world could implode and you wouldn't care as long as you had that one person standing beside you. Isaiah has it all wrong. For many reasons. He doesn't love me. He can't. For starters, he doesn't look at me like Noah does Echo. Besides, I'm not worthy of that type of love.

The bird hides its head under its wing. I understand that feeling of wishing the world would go away. If I had wings, I'd hide underneath them too.

"It's just a bird, Beth. It'll find its way out eventually."

Something deep and dark and heavy inside me tells me it won't. The poor bird will die in this damn barn and will never see blue sky again.

Straw rustles and Ryan drops beside me, stirring dust into the air. He clumsily rolls onto his side to face me. His warm body touches mine and his eyes have a strange intensity. "Don't do that."

My heart trips over itself. Ryan kept his hat off and I like it more than I should. His hair kicks out crazily in the back and it gives a boyish charm to a face that belongs to a man.

"Do what?" I ask, ashamed that my voice comes out a little breathless.

His eyebrows inch closer together and he moves his hand near my face. He stops and so does my breathing. Ryan stares at my lips and then caresses my cheek.

"You do that a lot." His finger slides steadily to the tip of my mouth. My skin tingles under his touch. "Look sad. I hate it. Your mouth turns down. Your cheeks lose all color. You lose everything about you that makes you...you."

I lick my lips and I swear he watches. His finger pauses before tracing another teasing path across my cheek. My pulse quickens and heat spreads through my body. His touch—oh God—feels good. And I want good. So much.

But I don't want him. At least, I don't think so. "Are you stalking me?"

His lips burst into a bright smile and he withdraws his hand. "Welcome back."

"What is that supposed to mean?"

Ryan does it again—his smile. The one that makes my stomach flip.

"I like you," he says.

I raise an eyebrow. He must have snorted some crack earlier, or maybe he's doing that steroid crap. What do they call it? Juicing. Yeah. The kid is definitely juicing. And drunk. "You like me?"

He shakes his head and it's a strange clumsy mix of yes

and no at the same time. Ryan is sloshed. "I don't know. The way you talk. The way you act. I know what I'm going to get from you, but then I don't. I mean, you're unpredictable, yet I know whatever reaction you're going to give me is real, you know?"

Officially cutting him off, I slide the few remaining beers from him and conceal them in the hay while trying to keep his eyes on me. His declaration of "like" has placed him in the category of beyond intoxicated and there's no way I can lug him home. "You mean you like knowing that our conversations will end with me telling you to go fuck yourself?"

He laughs. "Exactly."

"You're weird."

"So are you."

He has me there.

"Is there anything you don't pierce?" Ryan stares at my belly button. My shirt must have ridden up, exposing the red jewel dangling on my stomach. On my sixteenth birthday, Isaiah paid for my belly button piercing. At seventeen he paid for the tattoo. Both times he came up with the "consent." Isaiah is crafty like that.

"Maybe. Maybe not."

Ryan's eyes flash to mine and I see he understands the innuendo. I laugh when his cheeks turn red. "What are you, Ryan?"

"Did you just ask *what* I am?"

I nod. "Why would a jock be holed up with me in a barn, drinking beer, when he could be screwing half the female population at school? You aren't fitting the profile."

His eyes search my face and he ignores my question. "What's your tattoo mean?"

"It's a reminder." It means freedom. Something I'll never have. My destiny was built for me before I sucked in my first breath.

"You're doing it again," says Ryan. And he touches me again. This time on my stomach, yet his eyes hold mine. His finger lightly explores the edges of the jeweled ring. Tickling me. Entrancing me. Taking my haze higher. And that's exactly where I want to go—higher.

"What would you say, Ryan, if I said I didn't want to be alone?"

His fingers slip to my side and his warm palm clings to the curve of my waist, inching me and my body slowly toward heaven. "I'd say I don't want to be alone either."

RYAN

THE LANTERN LIGHT FLICKERS, creating shadows over Beth's face. There's no mistaking the suggestion in her smoky-blue eyes or the invitation of her fingertips as they trace the curve of my biceps. With her black hair sprawled out against the golden hay, she reminds me of a modern-day version of Snow White—lips as red as roses, skin as white as snow.

Would a kiss bring Beth to life? Tonight she's shown me brief flashes of the girl hidden behind the facade. Maybe I can draw her out more. Maybe if I kiss her...no, not kiss. I'm no prince and this isn't a fairy tale.

Attempting to find sanity, I rub my head.

"You okay?" she asks.

"Yes." No. The thoughts in my brain crest and dip like waves in the ocean. Each thought harder to hold on to than the one before.

"It's all right." Beth's voice becomes smooth, as if she's casting a spell. "You're thinking too much. Just relax."

"We should talk," I say in a rush before the thought drifts away, but my hand draws another lazy circle on her stomach. Her muscles come alive under my touch, a shudder of pleasure, and I crave to please her.

"No, we shouldn't," she answers. "Talking is overrated."

And I nod in agreement, but the thought floats back to the surface: we should talk. I've fought it all night; hell, I've fought it since I met her, but I like it when Beth talks because she becomes real—she becomes more. I like more. I like her.

What I really like is how her smooth skin glows in the lantern light, how soft it feels against my fingers. Beth licks her lips again and my head tilts in expectation. Her mouth glistens now and I memorize the perfect shape while imagining her lips brushing against mine.

The hay rustles beneath Beth as she lifts her head. My senses are flooded with the scent of roses.

"Kiss me," she says.

Just one kiss and her black spell, the one that she's woven, the one that's constantly weighing her down, will be broken.

BETH

MY TANK RIDES UP FARTHER when Ryan strokes the bare flesh of my stomach. He angles closer to me and I'm immediately overwhelmed by the size of his body. My blood tingles with excitement. "You're soft," he whispers.

I knot my fingers in his hair, guiding his head to mine. "You talk too much."

"I do," he agrees and his lips finally meet mine.

It's an innocent kiss at first. Soft lips meeting; a gentle pressure that creates a slow burn. The type of kiss you give to someone that means something. This isn't the type of kiss to be wasted on me. But still, I prolong it by taking his lower lip into mine and I touch his smooth face.

For this one second, I'll feel. I'll let myself pretend that Ryan cares for me. That I'm the girl worthy of this type of kiss, and right as I sense the emotion becoming stronger, gaining traction, I break away.

Ryan swallows and stares down at me. I press my lips to his innocently one last time, then slide my tongue between his lips. Sparks sizzle in the air as we immediately part our mouths, hungry for more. It's a lightning storm of fiery kisses

and sounds of bliss. Each of us feeds off the other, only building a greater storm—a thunderhead on the verge of explosion.

My hands roam over his back, clawing for the hem of his
shirt, eager to explore the glorious muscles underneath.
Ryan follows my lead and picks up the pace. Cooler air pricks
at my back as he sweeps an arm beneath me and pulls my
tank over my head.

Ryan pauses for a second. His hesitant eyes meet mine
and I quickly reclaim his lips. He responds, but barely. He's
thinking again and if he follows his thoughts, then I'll lose
my chance at higher.

I trail my hand down his spine—a light touch, a dance that
crosses to the side of his waist, over his hip, and right as my
fingers circle lower, Ryan moans and rejoins the game. My
mouth slants up under his kiss.

I love the sound of his moan. I love how his hands memorize the small of my back and dare lower to my thighs. I
love how we've both moved beyond coherent thought. I love
floating.

We roll and I help Ryan lose his shirt. In seconds, our legs
tangle. My hands curl into his muscles as Ryan generously
trails hot kisses along the nape of my neck. He grows bold,
inching my bra strap off my shoulder. I reward bold.

We lose control—quickly, so fast we've broken beyond
floating to flying. I inhale and all I smell is Ryan: the sweet
scent of summer rain. I'm so giddy I could almost laugh—
I'm finally high. Higher than I've ever been without drugs,
higher than I've ever been with another guy, higher than...

Ryan's hand slides to cradle my face, his warm palm
touching my cheek. His head follows and we both gasp for

air as he rests his forehead against mine. He's pausing and I don't like pausing. Pausing means thinking.

"You're beautiful," he says. His hands still explore; his lips still exert gentle pressure against my skin. Maybe he's not pausing. Maybe he's...what? What is he doing? His body says one thing, but his mouth says another.

"No talking." I don't want talking. I want higher. I want further.

Ryan brushes the hair away from my face and my heart flutters. "I like you," he says in my ear. "I like *you*, Beth."

All movement stops as the corners of my lips tug up for a shy smile. He likes me. He likes me and I like him and... All the air rushes out of my body, leaving my lungs in a painful struggle for air. My fingers curl into fists and I push at Ryan's chest. "Let me go."

Instead, his hold on me tightens. His eyes clear of their haze and dart over my face, searching for the problem. "What's wrong?"

"Let me go!" I scream and he immediately releases me. On my hands and knees, I wrestle away from him...away from me...just away. I'm stupid. So stupid. Ryan doesn't like me. He doesn't. How could I let my emotions get involved? Why couldn't I just use him for higher?

I grab my shirt and bolt for the door. From behind me, I hear the hay crunch as Ryan battles his impaired state to stand. "Beth—wait! I'm sorry! Please."

At the door, I hesitate. The other guys, the ones I've used to feel something physical, they've never apologized. They've never asked me to stay. I risk a glance over my shoulder and my stomach twists when I see the agony etched on his face.

Ryan holds a hand out to me. "Please. Talk to me."

Talking—it's what got me into this situation. It's what turned what should have been nothing into something. Part of me begs to stay—to talk. Instead, I flee into the dark night. Staying will hurt and running is my only option.

RYAN

WE WON TODAY and I have no idea how. Throughout the game, the sun hurt my eyes. My head pounded in an annoying painful rhythm. Twice, I puked between innings. Playing with a hangover took hell to another level. Even now, I fight the urge to pull the Jeep over on the side of the road, let my head hit the steering wheel, and rest, but I can't.

I like her. I really like Beth. The moment she smiled at me in the Jeep after we drove through the creek, I knew. Yeah, she's hard-core, but at the same time, she's not. Last night, her walls cracked.

Holding her while we danced, I saw her—the beautiful girl who loved ribbons. When she entwined her fingers with mine to stop me from fighting Tim, I saw the girl who protected Lacy in elementary school. In the barn, I listened to her ramble about her life: Isaiah, Noah, Echo, and beaches. By listening, I found a person loyal to those she loves. It was the first unedited glimpse into a girl that holds everything inside.

I'm falling for her. Hard. And I messed everything up the moment I touched her. How could I be so stupid?

The evening sunlight filters through the thick trees lining Scott Risk's long driveway. I replay the words I'll say when Scott answers his door. I don't have much of an excuse to see Beth. The truth won't help: Hi. I took your niece out last night, got drunk, made out with her until she bolted from the barn, and I'd appreciate the opportunity to apologize to her and convince her to give me a shot.

Yeah. I see that conversation going well.

Bent forward with her head in her hands, Beth sits on the front porch stairs. My stomach drops to the floorboard of the Jeep. I did this to her. Beth peeks at me through her hair as I park in front of the garage. She straightens and wraps her arms around her stomach.

"Hey," I say as I approach. "How do you feel?"

"Like shit." She's barefoot and wears a deep purple cotton shirt that hugs her waist and a pair of overly ripped jeans. Her shirt slips off her shoulder, exposing her black bra strap. I force my eyes to glance away. I became way too familiar with that tantalizing bra last night.

I stop at the foot of the stairs and shove my hands into my pockets. Does she feel like shit because she's also hungover, or because she regrets making out with me? "My head's hammered all day."

Beth slowly sucks in air and releases it, blowing a few strands of her hair from her face. "What do you want?"

"You left in a rush last night." Images of our night together flash in my mind. Her hands tugging off my shirt, hot on my skin, messing through my hair. I remember my lips on her neck and the sweet taste of her skin. The curve of her body against my hands. Her fingernails teasing my back. "I wanted to make sure you're okay."

"I'm fine," she says.

Beth retreats behind her brick wall. Closed off. Emotions cemented in. I stare at her. She stares at me. I have no idea what to say. Last night, we weren't really on a date. It was an agreement. She wasn't my girlfriend who I slowly worked through the bases with. She wasn't a girl I took to dinner a couple of times and kissed a little too much for too long. With Beth, I crossed lines a real man wouldn't cross. "I'm sorry."

"For what?"

Her glare makes me feel like I'm standing in front of a firing squad, awaiting my sentence. "For..." What am I sorry for? Taking off her shirt? Kissing her until I thought I was going to lose my mind? Touching her? Feeling her? Of all the things I may be sorry for in my life, I'm honestly not sorry for any of that. "For taking advantage of you."

The right corner of her mouth struggles up, then down, then slowly back up. "We didn't have sex last night."

Heat runs up my neck and I focus on my shoes. "I know."

Part of me is thankful she left when she did. The moment my lips found her body, we quickly became an erupting volcano. Hot and fast. Very fast. Fast enough that I would have given her my virginity.

"Then what are you apologizing for?"

I gather my courage and face her. "You left. In a hurry. And what I did... We were drunk. I don't get drunk and I don't take advantage of girls. You left upset. I crossed lines, and the way you left... I'm sorry."

Beth clears her throat. "Ryan." She stretches out my name, as if giving herself time to think. "I was the one who took advantage of you."

I still. "No, you didn't. Girls don't take advantage of guys. Guys take advantage of girls."

Her lips bunch and twist to the side as she shakes her head. "Nope. I distinctly remember telling you I didn't want to be alone."

"And that's the moment I should have walked away."

"I didn't want you to."

"But I should have. It's what an honorable guy does. Especially for a girl he likes."

Beth points a finger. "See, that's where you're confused. You don't like me."

Why is she making this apology complicated? Why does she make everything complicated? "Yes, I do."

"No, you don't. You're telling yourself you like me."

She drives me insane by finding a way to slink underneath my skin. "That makes no sense."

"You feel guilty for hooking up with me so you're trying to make yourself feel better by convincing yourself that you like me, when you don't."

"Wha..." The more she talks, the more my mind becomes a cluttered mess. "I like you. I. Like. You. I'll admit, you're annoying. Sometimes you agitate me to the brink of insanity, but you can throw it back at me like no one else. When you laugh, I want to laugh. When you smile, I want to smile. Hell, I want to be the one to make you smile. And you're pretty. No, you're sexy, and last night was..."

"Stop." Beth holds out her hand. "You're a good guy and you don't want to think you could have done something not good, okay? What we did wasn't bad. It wasn't wholesome, but it wasn't bad. Don't read anything more into it."

Beth's beautiful blue eyes are pleading with me. Pleading!

She wants me to agree with her. "If you really feel that way, then why did you bolt last night?"

The front door opens and, with narrowed eyes, Scott glares at me from the other side of the storm door. Beth glances at him over her shoulder and holds his gaze. He walks away, leaving the front door open. A knot forms between my shoulder blades. Not good.

"You should go," says Beth.

Probably, but I can't. Not with Beth telling me that I don't like her. Not when she honestly believes it. "Go out with me again—a real date this time."

"What?"

I climb the three steps and sit next to her. We were so close last night. Skin against skin. She's inches from me, but it feels like miles. My hand becomes heavy with the need to touch her, comfort her. I raise it. Put it down. Come on, I had no problems touching her last night. I raise it again and place my hand over hers.

Under my fingers, Beth stiffens. My heart beats once against my chest, creating an ache. I don't want her to hate my touch. "We've started everything ass backward. I like you. Let's see what happens."

"Date you?" she asks.

"Date me."

"Like friends—" Beth scrunches her face in disgust "—with benefits?"

I can almost feel her body under mine again and I shake away the memory. I'm not going to prove to her I like her if we have a repeat performance of last night. "No. Friends who go out together. I pay. You smile. Sometimes we kiss."

She raises a skeptical eyebrow on the word *kiss* and I immediately backtrack. "But we date first—for a while. Friends who like each other and want to date."

"I never said I liked you."

I chuckle and a warm tingle enters my blood when she gives that small, peaceful smile. "You haven't said you hate me."

"Friends who date," she says as if she's trying to find the hidden meaning in the phrase.

"Friends who date," I repeat and squeeze her fingers.

Beth tenses and withdraws her hand. "No." She pads down the stairs on bare feet. "No. This isn't the way things work. Guys like you don't date girls like me. What angle are you playing? Is this about the dare?"

Her words cause me to flinch, but they aren't a surprise. Last night, I pushed her too far. I showed her no respect. She has no reason to believe me, yet I want her to. "No. The dare is done."

"Because you won last night?"

No, I didn't. The dare required that Beth and I stay at the party for an hour. We barely lasted fifteen minutes. "It's over, Beth. I don't play people I care about."

Myriad emotions cross her face, as if she's wrestling with God and the devil. "You could be playing me. If this is the dare, just tell me."

"I did tell you. The dare is over." I told Lacy that no one gets hurt on my dares. Especially in this one. How could I be so blind? I thought Beth walked away from the trust fall because she wanted to hurt me. I thought she wanted to watch my team lose. Wrong. Beth didn't jump because she doesn't trust and, because of this dare, I've ruined any trust she could have had in me.

"Did you win then?" Beth stubbornly holds on to the dare. "Were you dared to make out with me?" The hurt gives way to panic. "You fucking asshole, you did play me, didn't you? Does everyone at school already know? Are you here for bonus points? Try to fuck the girl, tell your friends, then convince her you want more?"

"No!" I shout, then remind myself to rein it in. I created her doubt when I accepted the dare. "No. What happened between us last night wasn't about any dare. I didn't plan it and I would never tell anyone."

"So, I'm a secret. We'll date in private, but not in public. No thanks."

Damn. I can't win. I rub my hand over my head. "I want to be with you. Here. At school. Wherever. I didn't play you. Just trust me."

Beth angles her body away from me. *Trust* must be the ugliest word in her vocabulary. Desperate to make everything right, I blurt out, "Ask me for anything and I'll do it. Trust me with something. I'll prove to you I'm worth trusting."

She assesses me: Nikes first, blue jeans, Reds T-shirt, then my face. "Will you take me into Louisville again?"

The nausea I fought all afternoon returns. Anything but that. "Beth..."

"I won't disappear again. I need you to drop me off someplace and I swear I'll be at the same exact spot you left me at the exact time you tell me to show. You're asking me to trust you, well...you're going to have to trust me first."

It doesn't seem fair, but fair went out the window the moment I touched her last night. It possibly went out the window the moment I accepted the dare at Taco Bell. "I did trust you." My mouth shuts and everything inside me hardens.

The words taste bitter on my tongue. "I told you about my brother."

Beth bites her lower lip. "It's a secret?"

I nod. I really don't want to discuss Mark.

Worry lines clutter her forehead. "Drunken admissions don't equate to trust."

I sigh heavily. She's right. "Fine. I have a game two weeks from Saturday in Louisville, but you're sitting through it. I'm not budging on that requirement. Take it or leave it."

Beth's face explodes into this radiant smile and her blue eyes shine like the sun. My insides melt. This moment is special and I don't want to let it go. I'm the one that put that look there. "Really?" she asks.

Do I want her to come to my game? Do I want the opportunity for her to see that I'm more than some stupid jock? "Yes. Don't play me, Beth." Because I'm falling for you, more than I should, and if you betray me again, it will hurt like hell.

The smile fades and she solemnly answers, "I won't. When we go into Louisville, I just need an hour to myself."

An hour. To do what? See Isaiah? I guess she could. I only asked her to date me. She'd probably bolt if I said the word *relationship,* even though I have no interest in seeing anyone else. I went too fast with her last night. This time, I'll go slow. "I'll give you an hour alone in Louisville. Then we're going on a real date, even if it kills us."

Beth rejoins me on the steps. Her knee rests against mine and we lapse into silence. Typically, silence with girls makes me uncomfortable, but this one doesn't bother me. She doesn't have anything to say. Neither do I. I'm not ready to leave and it appears she's not ready for me to go. Beth, out of anybody, would tell me what she really wanted or thought.

She finally breaks the silence. "How do I take my name off the homecoming list? Does it require a two-thirds vote of the student population or do I have to ask someone in the front office?"

Panic flickers through me. "Stay on the court."

"No. Way."

"Do it with me. I'll be right by your side the entire time." Putting her on the court was my way of pissing her off, but now I want her on it—with me.

"That's your world. Not mine."

But it could be her world if she tried. "Nothing will happen with homecoming for another month. How about this—if I can find a way to completely wow you by then, you agree to stay on the court and if I can't, then I'll help you remove your name."

Silence as she contemplates. "Are you asking me to dare you to wow me?"

Even I see the irony. "Guess I am."

"Should I remind you that you have a lousy track record with me in regards to dares?"

I sit up straighter. "I don't lose."

Scott knocks on the door and points at his eyes then points at me. He leaves again. Hell. "Did you come home drunk last night?" The last time Scott and I talked, we were on good terms. Something's changed.

"No, but you did leave this." Beth flips her hair over her shoulder and reveals a red-and-blue spot on her neck. Everything within me wants to disintegrate and hide beneath the porch. I gave her a hickey. I haven't done that to a girl since middle school.

"He hates me," I say.

Beth laughs. "Something like that."

BETH

I PUMP MY HANDS HARDER into his chest and ignore the world around me. My wrists hurt, but I must keep the heart going. I must. Twenty-seven, twenty-eight, twenty-nine, thirty.

"Breathe!" I yell.

Lacy tilts the head back and blows into the mouth. The chest moves up, then back down. Lacy begins to pull away.

"No, Lacy, check the vitals." She puts her ear near the mouth and nose. I wait. She places her fingers against the artery in the neck. I wait again. Lacy shakes her head. Nothing.

"Your turn," I tell her. I'm frightened that I won't be able to give the heart enough pressure if I go another round. Lacy scrambles toward his chest and I slide my body near the head. She counts out loud with each compression.

A long beeping noise comes from the team next to us. "Flat line," says Mr. Knox.

"Yes!" says Chris. "This is ours!"

Of our entire health class, it's down to me and Lacy against the combo of Ryan and Chris. With his hands clasped together, Ryan pumps his dummy's chest.

"Breathe!" says Lacy.

I blow air into the mouth, check vitals, and freeze. With my fingers against the neck, I feel something. It's faint, but there. Lacy gestures for me to pump, but I shake my head. Our dummy—he's alive!

The boys start compressions again and a wretched noise blares from their machine. Mr. Knox unplugs it. "You boys forgot to check vitals."

Chris swears and Ryan falls onto his ass. Suck it up, boys. Get used to losing.

Mr. Knox glances my way. "Congratulations, Lacy and Beth. You're the only two who kept your patient alive. Good call on the vitals, Beth."

Good call on the vitals. Mr. Knox walks away as if this isn't the most amazing moment of my life. I did something. I saved a life. Well, not really, but I saved the dummy. But I did something right. This unspeakable, overwhelming sense of... I don't know... I've not experienced it before...this feeling of...joy? Anyhow...it floods me. Every part of me.

I—Beth Risk—did something good.

Lacy points at Chris, then at Logan standing over his dead dummy. "We won." In her sitting position she moves her shoulders in a crazy little dance. "We won. We won. We won."

"Your girl is a sore winner." Logan edges closer to us.

"It's kinda hot though," says Chris. "Now that you experienced the rush, are you going to take on more dares from us, baby?"

Lacy laughs. "I didn't take the dare. Beth did."

Logan and Chris nod at me in appreciation. I shrug in return. For the past week, we've been feeling each other out. Lacy talks to me. Ryan talks to me. Sometimes, I talk back.

On Monday, I caved to their brow-beating and began sitting with them at lunch. When Ryan's feeling bold, he takes my hand. When I'm feeling bolder, I hold his hand back.

At the mention of the dare, I fish a black marker out of my pack. Ryan's last words before we started CPR were that Lacy and I couldn't hold out; that we were too weak to outlast the combination of him and Chris. I write the four most beautiful letters on my palm and turn it for Ryan to see: *can't*.

As he leans against the wall, that brilliant smile spreads across Ryan's face and he shakes his head. Warm fuzzies race through my bloodstream. I love that smile. Maybe a little too much.

"I'm not wowed," I say to him. It's been four days since our agreement and Ryan's done nothing to "wow" me.

His smile turns cocky and, I have to admit, I like that smile too. "I've got time."

From the opposite side of the island, Scott watches as I scoop another spoonful of Lucky Charms into my mouth. I talk through the crunches. "And then I felt a pulse and Lacy thought we should pump again and I shook my head no."

"Then what happened?" asks Scott.

I feel like I'm going to burst out of my skin. "We won. I mean, we saved the dummy and Mr. Knox said I did good." I did something right. I still can't get over it.

"That's fantastic. Isn't it, Allison?"

It's eight o'clock at night. Allison sits at the opposite end of the bar and doesn't bother glancing up from the latest toy Scott bought her last week: an e-reader. "Fantastic," she echoes in a voice that tells me she doesn't actually think so.

Shoving another spoonful of cereal into my mouth keeps

me from muttering my exact thoughts. I should have waited to tell Scott the story over breakfast, when it's just the two of us, but I was too excited.

"Is that what it's like to be a nurse?" I ask Scott. "To feel all powerful and in control." And to have someone tell me that I did good? My mind races with the possibilities. Maybe I could be a nurse. Blood doesn't bother me. Neither does puke. Too worked up to sit still, I drum my hands on the counter—I could really do this.

"You need to excel at science to be a nurse," says Allison in her bored voice. "And your grades on your last progress report suggest that might be a problem for you."

My face reddens as if she slapped me. I wish I could think of something wittier, but at times, the plain truth is good enough. "You really are a bitch."

"Stop it, Elisabeth," says Scott. "And, Allison, her grades are improving."

Well, screw me, Scott reprimanded the wench. Huh. Allison tears her eyes from the e-reader. I could bask in the glory of this moment, but I decided weeks ago that she's not worth my time. I turn to Scott. Daydreaming is over. I have real problems. "I need black hair dye."

"For what?" Scott asks.

Is he blind? I shake my hair and lower my head so he can see my roots. *My roots.* The blond pokes out from my jet-black hair like annoying rays of sun. I flip my hair back over my shoulder. "Will you buy me some?"

If I buy anything with the cash Isaiah gave me, Scott would be all over me like flies to crap. I'm not ready to tip my hand that I have cash. Besides, he's always wanting to *do* something for me—now he can.

"No," he says.

Um...did I misunderstand him? "No?"

"No."

"I'm not going to be a blonde."

"It's who you are. Why do you have to change something so beautiful?"

"So only blondes are beautiful?"

Scott closes his eyes. "I never said that."

"Then buy me the dye."

He reopens them and studies me during one of his patented long silences. "I'll buy you something that will match your original hair color."

"I don't want to be blond."

"Give me a good reason why not."

"I prefer black."

"Not good enough."

I purposefully gawk at Allison. "I hate blondes."

"Still not good enough."

I cross my arms over my chest and redirect my gaze to him. I can also do long silences.

"That's it, Elisabeth? You want to have black hair. Just because. You have no reason. You want what you want."

"Yeah." I don't like his tone or the way his blue eyes look right through me.

"When did you first dye it?" he asks.

"Eighth grade." My instincts yell at me to run.

"Why?"

My throat becomes tight and I glance away. "Because."

"Because why, Elisabeth?"

Because one of Mom's boyfriends thought I was her in the middle of the night.

"Tell me." Scott keeps staring right through me. "Tell me why you dyed your hair."

Isaiah knows. I told him once when I was too high to keep secrets. Mom's boyfriend stumbled out of our only bedroom in the middle of the night. He sat on the floor next to where I slept on the couch. He lifted my hand, kissed it, and called me my mother's name. He smacked me when I screamed and he smacked me again when he realized I wasn't my mother.

The memories rush forward and I can't shove them away. They need to go away. I need someone to ground me. I need someone to erase the bad memories. I haven't forgiven Isaiah yet for betraying me. I haven't talked to him in weeks and I'm not sure I'm ready to.

Even if there wasn't our recent past between us, I'm not sure that I'd want Isaiah. For some reason, I crave someone else...and that scares me, and being scared only gives power to the memories.

In my head, I can hear the bastard's voice. I can feel the bastard's touch. My fingers claw at my head. *Get out, get out, get out!* I stand so abruptly the stool wobbles, then crashes to the floor. "Fuck you, Scott. I'll buy the dye myself."

RYAN

...and George looked at the girl with new eyes. No—not with new eyes, but maybe with eyes he had possessed in another life. With eyes that belonged not to his head, but to his heart.

Her smile caressed him as if her fingers had slid up his arm. She constantly amazed him—a human willingly befriending a zombie. The opposite of him somehow gave this horrifying new life meaning. But what really amazed George was that she granted him the grace of a second chance.

PLEASED WITH MYSELF, I lean back in the chair and fold my hands over my stomach. Turns out George's life was more confusing than he could have imagined. First he wakes up a zombie. Then he discovers that the other zombies expect him to be a leader, and then he shocks himself by loving his newfound power.

And then comes the girl.

Girls always complicate things. My lips turn up as I think of Beth. Yeah, they do, but in a good way.

My phone vibrates and I glance at the caller ID. It's an unknown number so I let it go to voice mail. Seconds later the phone chimes, telling me I have a text. I grab the phone and smile: Friends, right?—Beth

Me: Yes

"Then let me in." Beth's sexy voice drifts from the other side of my open window.

I check the clock—eleven. Mom and Dad would be in bed. To be safe, I lock the door to my bedroom before I raise the pane and pop the screen out. "What are you doing here?"

Beth swings one leg into my room, followed by the other, with such ease that I believe she's done this before. "I got bored."

"You could have called." Popping the screen in isn't nearly as easy as popping it out.

"I did." Beth assesses my room. She picks up a baseball on my dresser, tosses it into the air, and barely makes the catch. "You didn't answer."

"You called thirty seconds ago."

She drops the ball back onto my dresser. "But I did call."

The reality of the moment smacks me when she leans over and taps the lava lamp that stopped working a year ago. Her smooth skin and tattoo peek out when her top rides up. I inhale and focus on anything but touching her. "Does your uncle know you're here?"

"No." Beth walks over to the computer. "What are you working on?"

"A creative writing assignment."

She pinches her lips as her head falls back. "Damn. Do we have one? When is it due? Ah hell, Scott is going to rip me on this. And here I thought I was finally keeping up."

Crap. Until now, I didn't have to tell anyone. "No, it's not a class assignment. It's something...extra...yeah. Something Mrs. Rowe asked me to do."

Beth's shoulders relax like she received a pardon from a death sentence. "Can I read it?"

Besides my teacher, no one's asked to read my stuff before and I pause...long enough that Beth raises her eyebrows. If anyone's going to read this, I'd prefer it to be her. Something tells me she'd understand. "Sure."

"Print it out for me." Beth plops on my bed and curls up around the pillows.

Her blue eyes survey me as she teases me with a slumberous look. My jeans get tight and I want to join her on the bed, badly, but I'll show restraint even though she's going to kill me in the process. "Plan on staying for a while?"

"Did you have other plans?"

No. "I'm going to sleep soon. We do have school tomorrow."

"I've shared a bed way smaller than this for the past two years. Trust me, I'm the queen of not touching if that's what you're concerned about. Go on, print it out."

"Not touching and sharing with who?"

Beth chuckles and shakes her head at the same time. "Jealous much? I think you were printing something out for me."

Just go with it, Ryan. Like other predators, Beth can smell fear. Without another word, I print out the pages and she snatches them from my hand. I stare at her. She stares at me. "I'm not going to read it with you watching me. That's weird."

"You're in my room, Beth. You walked a half mile to get here. On a Wednesday. In the middle of the night. Uninvited." I should define for her what weird is.

"Do you want me to go?"

"No." I don't. Somehow nothing has ever felt more right.

That evil smile slips onto her face. "Am I the first girl to be in your bed?"

Yes. I take a deep breath and return to the computer. I've dated girls. Been exclusive with a few and I've been respectful enough to proceed slowly to each base. There are some bases I have yet to reach. A girl in my bed being one of them. If she's determined to be here, I'm determined to be okay with it and not let the nerves show. I guess my zombie found a girl he likes and wants to throttle at the same time.

"This is good, Ryan." Beth's distant voice snaps me out of the story and my hands stop tapping on the keyboard.

"Thanks," I say. Beth lies on her stomach, propped up on her elbows. Her cleavage is beautifully exposed. My eyes avert to the floor.

"No, really. It's good. Like this could be in a bookstore good. I totally get this guy."

Yeah, so do I. "I finaled in a state writing competition." The words come out naturally, as if I normally tell the world this sort of thing.

Beth flips through the pages. "I can see why. Whoever judged the winner must have been on meth not to choose you."

I glance around the room, waiting for the lightning to hit. Did she pay me a compliment? "The winner hasn't been announced. There's another round of competition in a couple of weeks."

"Oh," she says. "Then I'm sure you'll win."

My stomach hollows out as I turn off my computer. Yeah,

I'm writing the short story, but I still haven't signed up for the competition. How can I? I've got games that day and Dad...

My thoughts trail off. I'm bowing out of a competition—an event I could win. Would the rush of winning the writing competition be the same as winning a baseball game or a dare? Guess I'll never know.

When I turn back, Beth is stretched out on her back with her head against the pillows. She's kicked her shoes off and folded her hands on her stomach. The belly button ring sparkles in the light. She stacked my story neatly on the bedside table.

We're dating. Friends who are dating and who will eventually kiss. Four days could be considered *eventually*...yeah, I'm not stupid enough to believe that.

"I'm going to bed," I say, giving her the opportunity to leave.

"Do you normally sleep in all your clothes?" she asks.

No. I usually take off my shirt. "This is safer."

"Okay."

Okay. I flip off the light and climb into bed. Taking a cue from Beth, I stay on top of the covers. The heat from her body warms mine. She's right. She can lie in bed without touching. I inhale and her sweet scent envelops me.

Last year, our science teacher dispelled the myth that sex crosses the minds of guys every seven seconds. I'm going to have to disagree with him on that. My fingers itch with the need to caress Beth's soft skin. I want my lips whispering against hers.

"So, I have this friend," she says into the darkness. "Isaiah. You've met him."

"Yeah." My muscles tense and the images of her body moving against mine disappear. I understand that dating means I'm leaving open the possibility that she can see other guys, but I'm not fond of her discussing said guys while she's lying in my bed.

"He betrayed me and I don't know what to do. In Louisville, he was the only friend I had and when I came here he bought me my phone. We talked every night or texted or both and he still calls every day and texts me a million times. I refuse to answer him and I think our friendship is over and then I talked to Scott tonight and the conversation didn't go as I planned and I don't know...."

My skin prickles. It's more than Beth being so close to me. It's more than the need and attraction raging in my body. Beth is on the verge of telling me something. On the verge of stepping outside her wall. I urge her on. "You don't know what?"

"Everything was so much easier in Louisville," she says softly. The sadness in her voice is hard to miss. "I miss easy."

"After my game, I'll drop you off." I hate the thought of it, but I'm determined to win her over. "Then afterward, we'll go to dinner and then maybe a movie. What do you think?"

I hear her swallow. "I think I'd like that."

I inhale. The clean, full intake of air feels as if it's the first breath I've taken in days.

"Sometimes," she says, then pauses. It's a heavy pause and her struggle for words makes me want to comfort her. "Sometimes I just want..."

What does she want? I know what I want: for her to trust me, for her to feel what I feel. But what I really want right now is for her to be okay. I extend my arm across the bed in

Beth's direction, careful not to touch her. "I'm here if you need me."

One heartbeat. Another. Beth stays so perfectly still in the darkness that part of me wonders if this entire evening was a dream.

Her body scratches against the comforter as she moves. One inch in my direction. A hesitation. Then another inch. My blood tingles with anticipation. This moment is huge— no doubt. I'm asking her to lean on me and Beth is actually considering it.

Come on, Beth, you can trust me. Finally, in a swift movement, she lays her head on my chest and curls the rest of her body around me. Need slams into me and if her hand shifts down three inches, she'll know. I want to touch her, but do I dare? Her breath tickles my chest as she whispers, "I like you, Ryan."

I close my eyes and celebrate the words. She likes me. "I like you too." A lot.

I want her, but I refuse to let my lower body make the decisions. Slowly, purposefully, I wrap one arm around her and lay my other hand on my stomach right next to hers. This is my best attempt at friends-who-date touching.

Parts of me want to caress the warm blush that appears on her beautiful skin when I look at her with desire. Those same parts imagine me placing a hand on her chin and tilting her head up so I can kiss her. Those parts are currently trying to talk "logic" to my brain. Kissing could be good. I loved kissing her full lips and I loved her soft moans. I could kiss her until she forgets Isaiah. I could kiss her until I forget that I'm a virgin. My grip on her shoulder tightens. She's killing me. I'm killing myself. "Sandy Koufax was left-handed like you. He was the youngest pitcher inducted into the Baseball Hall of Fame."

"That's possibly the most screwed-up thing I've ever heard you say," she mumbles.

True, but it keeps my mind off kissing her. "I'm not the one that talks in code."

"You have me there."

Beth's body relaxes and molds into mine. The silence stretches from seconds to minutes to longer and I wonder if she fell asleep. Part of me wishes I could sleep. Then I wouldn't fantasize about touching her or kissing her or touching her some more. But then I also want to stay awake. I like this—holding her.

"Ryan?" she whispers.

"Yeah?" I whisper back.

"Can I stay? I set your alarm for four so I'll be back before Scott misses me."

I absently rub my hand up and down her back and she shifts closer to me. "Yeah."

Beth nuzzles her head against my chest like a cat curling into a ball for sleep. Her arm presses into me and I let myself cheat for one second when I bunch her hair in my hand and kiss the top of her head. I could tell myself that friends who date do this, but it's way too late and I'm way too tired for lying.

BETH

THIRTY MINUTES OF OBSERVING Ryan squirm on the couch across from Scott was enough to atone for allowing Ryan to drag me to the marathon game at the ballpark. Scott finally let me go with Ryan only after he threatened to kill Ryan if he returned me with any marks on my body.

I'm not sure if I'll ever admit it to Ryan, but this has been my best Saturday since being sentenced to hell. On the drive into Louisville, Ryan explained baseball. Most of it I knew, but Ryan somehow made it interesting. The sport came alive when he described a game that's more than a bat and a ball and some bases. He said it involved teamwork and trust.

As I sit on the bleachers and watch the game, I appreciate the gracefulness of his team's movements. A network of signals and glances and unsaid understandings.

What I really find amazing is Ryan. The raw intensity in the way he moves. The strength of his broad shoulders and the power that explodes from his body when he throws the ball. Ryan is a force all his own. A force that pulls me in. An attraction that curls warmth into my body. He possesses a simple touch that's strong enough to hold me together yet soft enough to make me shiver.

We're friends. Just friends. I sigh. Even as a friend, he deserves better than me. He seems hell-bent on liking me. Hell-bent on dating me. Why? What does he gain by being with a girl that everyone else has thrown away?

Chris pops a ball into left field and the other team catches it for the third out. Ryan stands in the dugout and winks at me before taking the field. My answering smile forms in spite of myself. *You're setting yourself up for a world of hurt, Beth.* Like when I set myself up with Luke at fifteen. Luke called me pretty. Luke said all the right words. Then again, Luke never brought me to a place as public as this.

Maybe Scott is right. I have a clean slate. Maybe I should take advantage of it. Maybe I should enjoy the ride while it lasts. After all, I'll be leaving with Mom soon. Each day that she remains with Trent is one day closer to her death. Today, after the game, Mom and I will work out a plan to leave, but until then, maybe I should enjoy what's in front of me.

Ryan likes me or at least he thinks he does. Why am I in such a rush to move on to the next guy who'll treat me like Luke did or the way Trent treats Mom?

I can be the girl who shows Ryan a few things. The girl who doesn't laugh when he blushes. I can be the girl who, in the future, when he's been married to the good girl and has three babies clinging to his leg, he can remember and smile at the memories. Then he'll look at his wife and be grateful I left when I did. Grateful he didn't end up with me.

"Are you Ryan's girlfriend?" A tall guy plops next to me on the bleachers and watches as Ryan throws the ball. This dude is close. Super close. Not touching close, but he has broken the unspoken barrier of how close complete strangers should be to each other.

The skin on my arm prickles. "And you are?"

He turns his head and gives me a smile that reminds me of Ryan's. In fact, he looks a lot like Ryan, just a little older. "Mark. I'm his older brother."

Hello. Could this be the brother Ryan was all torn up over in the barn? But curiosity gives way to nerves. I've never met a guy's family and I don't know a thing about etiquette. "Nice to meet you." There, isn't that what proper girls say?

"Are you sure? I've seen worms on hooks happier than you."

My lips twist up. "I'm Beth and we're just friends." Friends who are dating, but I don't need to broadcast my insecurities.

"Huh," he drawls. "Ryan doesn't bring friends to games. He calls people distractions."

Not sure how to respond, I focus on the game. Mark lowers his voice. "Am I making you uncomfortable?"

I might as well be honest. It's not like I could pass as respectable for long. "Guys who invade my personal space generally make me uncomfortable, but I don't blame you. Ryan has space issues too. Must be genetic."

Mark laughs and it's a boisterous laughter that causes people to stare—even Ryan from the mound. Ryan's eyes flicker between his brother and me. A shadow crosses his face as he focuses on Mark. Not liking the hurt he's wearing, I give him a halfhearted wave and he gives me his heart-stopping smile in return. Heat creeps along the back of my neck and marks my face.

"Yeah," says Mark. "You two are just friends."

"I didn't ask for your opinion," I mutter.

Mark laughs again, but not as loudly. "My mother must hate you."

I should be insulted, but I'm not. If she ever met me, she probably would. "Don't know."

"That's okay. I like you."

"You don't know me."

Mark gestures to the scoreboard. "We've got a few more innings to rectify that. So, tell me, how did you meet my brother?"

RYAN

UNLACING MY CLEATS, I stare at the bleachers. Mark is here and he's talking to Beth. Actually, he's laughing with Beth. Jealousy lurches inside me and I'm pissed at both of them. I've texted and called Mark for months and I got shit. Beth smiles once and he's rattling like he's on a talk show. And to top it all off, Mark's talked to her for a whole twenty minutes and Beth's already laughing. It took me weeks to get her to laugh with me.

I slam my cleat against the bench to knock the dirt off. Mark is my brother, therefore he wouldn't steal my girl. Not to mention that he likes men. Several of the guys glance at me when I hammer my cleat against the bench again. Logan raises a brow. I shake my head to stop him from speaking to me.

Resting my arms on my knees, I try to suck it up. Beth's not really my girl. We're just friends who date because I screwed everything up with her from the beginning.

"Ryan?" Coach waves me over to him. I shove my feet into my Nikes and toss my bag over my shoulder. He probably has plenty to say to me. I pulled the game out, but I cost us two runs in the last inning. Mark and Beth's friendly interaction distracted me.

"Yes, sir."

Coach nods to a man in his thirties and a woman standing next to him. They're dressed in Sunday casual—jeans and nice shirts. "I'd like you to meet Pete Carson and his wife, Vickie."

I shake the extended hands—Mr. Carson first, then his wife. "Nice to meet you."

"Pete is a scout with the University of Louisville."

I glance at Coach and try to keep the surprise off my face. He knows how Dad and I feel about playing pro ball after I graduate. Mr. Carson clears his throat. "Ryan, I've been scouting for the early draft and your name is the one on everyone's lips. I was wondering if you've given any thought to our school."

"No, sir. I plan on joining the pro draft after graduation."

"That would be a waste." The words rush out of his wife's mouth. The three of us look at her and she laughs nervously. "Sorry, but it's the truth. I should introduce myself appropriately—I'm Dr. Carson, dean of the English Department at Spalding University."

"Uh-huh." A very un-grammatically-correct response. Why do I feel cornered?

"Mrs. Rowe, your English teacher, is a good friend of mine. She's shown me some of your writing. You're very talented. Both on the field and off. Spalding University offers a wonderful course study in Creative Writing and many of our students go on to pursue their master's in Fine Arts...."

Mr. Carson puts his hand on his wife's arm. "You're recruiting him. I thought I won the coin toss."

"You weren't talking fast enough." She pats the hand he just placed on her. "Spalding has a baseball team too."

I fake laugh because everyone else does, but my uneasiness builds. Standing here listening to them makes me feel like I'm betraying my father.

Mr. Carson lets go of his wife. "Spalding is a Division Three school. The University of Louisville is Division One. Several of our players went on to be drafted into the pros. You have talent that can't be taught, but you've got some tells on your pitches and some issues with your placement. My coaches can work with you and take your pitches to another level. We'll prepare you for the pros, plus you'll be walking away with a degree."

"Are you offering me a scholarship?"

"Spalding will," says Mrs. Carson. She smiles unrepentantly when her husband grimaces.

Mr. Carson exchanges a wary look with Coach. "I need to know if you're interested. I have room for a pitcher on my team and I'm looking to offer a scholarship to someone during the early signing period in November."

November, which means if I want to go to college, I have a little more than a month to decide. No pressure. Mr. and Mrs. Carson describe college life while I pretend to listen. What will Dad say if he finds out? They both hand me cards, to Mr. Carson's dismay, and say their goodbyes, leaving me and Coach alone.

I wait for the Carsons to be out of earshot before I ask the question bugging me. "Have you been talking to Mrs. Rowe?"

"We talked last month. I think it's in your best interests to explore all of your options."

"You don't think I can make pros?" This is the man who has encouraged me almost as much as my dad.

"No," he says slowly. "I believe you can, but I also know that your father isn't presenting you with everything on the table. Your father's a good man, but I consider you one of my own sons and I wouldn't be helping you if I didn't make that introduction."

My world tips. Coach and Dad have always seen eye to eye. Why the change? "I'm not doing the writing competition."

"Ryan," Coach says with an exasperated sigh. "We'll discuss this later. You have company." His gaze wanders over my shoulder and dread settles in my gut.

Mark waits for me at the bottom of the bleachers while Beth remains in her seat at the top. I make a sweep of the area to be sure no one from town is around to see this reunion.

"Hey," Mark says. "You played a hell of a game."

I inhale deeply, attempting to find a center. Mark left. Dad looked him straight in the eye and asked him to choose. My brother didn't choose me. I asked him to stay and fight and he didn't. I asked him to come home and he didn't. And now he thinks he can show up here and everything will be fine. Guess what? It's not fine. "What are you doing here?"

Mark plays linebacker for the University of Kentucky. In his freshman year, he gained twenty-five pounds of muscle. He's a big son-of-a-bitch. "I want to talk, Ry."

"I think your silence since this summer said everything." I walk past him and gesture for Beth to come off the bleachers.

"I wanted to contact you, but each time I tried I couldn't. I kept thinking about Mom and Dad and I needed space."

Space. Why didn't he just knee me in the groin? I throw out my arms. "You got what you wanted, didn't you?"

"It doesn't have to be this way," Mark says loud enough for the few remaining spectators to hear.

"Yeah." I keep walking. "It does."

In lethargic steady strides, Beth's feet plunk against the metal of the bleachers as she wanders down. "What are you doing?"

"We need to go. You need an hour, remember? And then we're going out to dinner."

"We have time. Go talk to your brother."

"It's fine, Beth." Mark responds for me in a tone that indicates an apology. "I'm glad I got a chance to meet you. Don't let Groveton smother you to death."

She gives him one of her rare genuine smiles and I want to hit something—hard. "Good luck with your game next week."

Mark shoves his hands into his jeans as he leaves. "You know where to find me when you're ready, Ry."

Beth watches him until he's out of sight. "What the fuck is wrong with you?"

"You wouldn't understand." I stalk off to the parking lot and toss my stuff into the Jeep. Beth slams her passenger door shut and I answer her anger by slamming my own. "Tell me where I'm supposed to be taking you."

"The strip mall a half mile before your pitching facility."

My head jerks. That place is a step above ghetto. "I'm not leaving you there."

"I didn't ask for your approval. You made a deal with me. It's your decision if you want to keep it." Her frozen blue eyes pierce into me.

I yank hard on the bill of my hat and peel out onto the main road. She's angry. I'm angry. We stay silent as I drive the thirty minutes to the other side of town. There's enough electricity in the air to propel the car without gas. One word from either of us could cause an explosion.

Beth obviously likes playing with fire. "Is your brother one of those guys that can be awesome to strangers, then turn into a complete dick in private? Did he piss in your Cheerios every morning before you went to school?"

"No," I grit out. "He was a great brother."

"Then what is wrong with you? He said you guys haven't talked in three months and that he was here to see you. What's so damned important that you couldn't take three seconds out of your day to say hi?"

I turn on the radio. She turns it off. I pound my hand against the wheel. "I thought you were in a hurry for your one hour of freedom in Louisville."

"Waiting fifteen minutes so you can talk to your brother isn't going to ruin my one hour. Let's try this again. What's going on?"

"He's gay."

Beth blinks. "You already told me that. Catch me up on the you being an asshole part."

I am not an asshole. The whole reason for this day was for her to see that I'm not an asshole. "He left, okay? He left and he's made it clear he's not coming back."

She angles her body toward me. "Tell me that's a self-imposed decision Mark made."

Beth doesn't tell me squat about her family, yet she expects perfection from mine. "My dad threw him out and Mark didn't even try to see what would happen if he attempted to stay. Are you happy now?"

"No. So your dad's a homophobic bastard. What's your excuse?"

The anger bursts out of me. "What did you expect me to do? Go against my dad? He told me and Mom that we weren't allowed to talk to him anymore. He's my dad, Beth. What would you have done?"

I don't bother telling her that I tried reaching out to him or that Mark didn't respond to me...until now. Now when it's too late.

"Grown a pair of balls, that's what I would have done. God, Ryan, you *are* an asshole. Your brother is gay and you toss him out of your life because you're too much of a pansy to stand up to your father."

I pull into the strip mall and park in the back of the lot. This place is a shithole. Down by the Laundromat, a guy in a wife-beater screams at a girl with bleached-blond hair holding a diaper-clad baby on her hip. Guys my age smoke cigarettes while purposely skateboarding into girls coming in and out of the stores. Someone needs to teach them respect.

Beth hops out of the Jeep. Her hair blows in the breeze behind her as she strides toward the shopping center. Why is this girl always walking away from me? I jump out after her, catch her hand, and turn her to face me. I thought I pissed Beth off by nominating her to homecoming court. The fire blazing out of her eyes tells me this anger is on a completely different level. She needs to hear me out and understand my dad—to understand my family. "Mark abandoned us."

"Bullshit. You abandoned him." She rams a finger into my chest. "You and me. We're a mistake. You're a leaver. My father left me, Saint Scott left me, and I will never be left again."

Yet Beth is the one who leaves. She retreats to the shopping plaza and disappears into the grocery store. She told me on the way into Louisville to drop her off and come back for her later. I never intended to let Beth walk away, but her words rock me. Is she right? Did I abandon Mark?

BETH

I CUT IN THE SUPERMARKET, duck back out, and beeline it for the Last Stop, avoiding the group of skateboarders. I'm careful, guarding Echo's money that burns the back pocket of my jeans. More pickpockets hang here than people with high school diplomas.

Denny slaps his hand on the counter when I step into the bar. "Get out, kid."

Pool balls click against each other as a guy in jeans and a leather vest plays solo. Two older men in blue factory uniforms slouch over beers at the bar. My heart drains of any shred of hope I had gained in Groveton when I see the blond-haired mess at the table in the corner. Holding myself proud, I glide to the bar. "Whatever Isaiah is paying you, I'll pay you double to keep your mouth shut."

He chuckles darkly. "That's the same offer he gave me concerning you. Go play with your boyfriend and stay out of my bar."

"Isaiah isn't my boyfriend."

Wearing a smart-ass smile, Denny grabs a wet shot glass

out of a tub and dries it with a towel. "Have you told him that?"

When I say nothing back, Denny gestures to Mom. "She's been crying today. Trent was arrested by the cops last night for drunk driving and they impounded her car. Get her out and spend some time with her."

Yay and damn. Without Isaiah on board, I need a car and Mom's piece of crap is our only way out of Louisville. On the rare good side, I don't have to worry about Trent beating the shit out of either one of us today.

"Next time you come into my bar, I'm calling Isaiah to drag you back out," Denny says. "Even if she's crying."

Next to a half-empty bottle of tequila, Mom's head lies in her folded arms. She's thinner. The rush of emotions creates a light-headed sensation. This poor, pathetic creature is my mom and I've completely failed her. "Let's go, Mom."

She doesn't stir. I sweep the hair from her face. Several of the strands fall to the floor and stick to my hand. God, has she eaten at all? Yellow-and-brown patches litter the left side of her face. On her right wrist, Mom wears a black brace. I nudge her with a tender touch. "Mom, it's Elisabeth."

Her eyelids flutter open and her hollow blue eyes have a sunken quality. "Baby?"

"It's me. Let's go home."

Mom reaches out as if I'm a ghost. Her fingertips barely brush my leg before her arm drops to her side. "Are you a dream?"

"When was the last time you ate?"

With her head still on her arms, she surveys me. "You used to buy food for me and make it, didn't you? Ham and cheese on white with mustard tucked in the fridge. That was you."

My insides wither like a plant without water. Who did she think took care of her? I close my eyes and search for my perspective. Being at Scott's has made me soft. I need to be more aware for both me and Mom. "Let's go."

I place an arm around her shoulder blades and yank at her body. "Come on. You need to stand. I can't drag you home."

"I hate it when you yell, Elisabeth."

"I didn't yell." But I'm being a bitch. Like most toddlers, Mom obeys a strong reprimand. Also like most toddlers, she often obeys the wrong person.

"Yes, you did," she mutters. "You're always angry."

Even with me holding her up, she still sways from side to side. The door to the back room is shut. Hell. This means we'll have to go out the front. Baby steps are a struggle for her and I calculate how long it will take me to get her home at this rate. So many things to do before I meet Ryan—grocery shop, figure out how to get the car out of impound, and nail down the date to leave.

Mom stumbles when we meet daylight. She tries to shield her eyes, but it affects her already-fragile balance and I have to use both of my hands to keep her upright. She's right. I am always angry, because right now a volcano is stewing inside of me. "What else are you taking?"

"Nothing," she says too quickly.

Right. Nothing. "That bottle of tequila wasn't empty. Are you becoming a lightweight?"

She says nothing and I let it go, reminding myself that there are things better left unknown. I drag her forward and occasionally she lifts her feet to help with the progression on the sidewalk. Several guys I used to go to school with fly past on skateboards. Two whistle at me and ask if I'm back to stay. The other...

He flips up his skateboard and takes a ten-dollar bill from his pocket. "Run out of money again, Sky? I'll take a blow right now."

Shame heats my face, but I force myself to stand taller as I haul my mother toward her home. "Fuck you."

"I've missed seeing you around, Beth, but your mom's more fun without you babysitting." He drops the board and rolls away. Yes, being at Scott's has softened me and it makes this experience a million times worse. I wish Scott would have left me alone.

"We'll move to Florida." We slowly pass the pawnshop. "White sandy beaches. Warm air. The sound of water lapping against the shore." My mom's not a whore. She's not. Please God, please let her not be. "We'll sober you up and we'll get jobs...." Doing? "Something." Because Scott has custody of me we'll have to be careful. I'll be labeled a runaway. "We'll go to the ocean. Give me a date and we'll leave."

"I have to bail Trent out first," Mom whispers. "Then unpound the car."

"Fuck Trent. Let him rot in jail."

"I can't." Mom pulls on my hair to stay upright and the pain makes me want to scream. Instead, I bite my lip. Screaming will draw more attention to us.

We reach the end of the sidewalk. Mom falls forward when she misses the step, and collapses onto the pavement. "Come on, Mom!" I want nothing more than to sit on the ground and cry, but I can't. Not with people watching. Not with Mom right here. "Get up!"

"I've got her." The deep, smooth voice causes my heart to

still and my lungs to freeze. Isaiah effortlessly scoops my mother into his arms. Without waiting for me, he heads right for Mom's apartment building.

Isaiah.

I blink.

My best friend.

My heart beats twice and both beats hurt.

Mom slips in and out of coherence as Isaiah carries her. When we reach her door, I slide the string of keys I used to wear as a necklace in elementary school from around Mom's neck.

I briefly catch Isaiah's gaze and I cower from the pain in his eyes. He wears his uniform shirt for the garage he works at. Grease and oil stain the blue material. Every day for three weeks, Isaiah has texted and called and I haven't answered him. I bury the guilt. He's the one that betrayed me and there's nothing I can do about not responding to him now.

A horrible rancid odor slaps me when I open the door. I'm dizzy with dread. I don't want to know. I just don't. We're going to Florida. We're running away.

Isaiah follows me in and swears. At the smell, the damage, or the trash, I don't know. Nothing has changed from the last time I was here, except the refrigerator door hangs wide-open.

"Did you forget to pay the cleaning lady?" Isaiah asks.

I half smile at his attempt to defuse the situation. He knows I hate for anyone else to see how Mom lives. "She only accepted cash and Mom was insistent that we use the credit cards for the frequent flyer miles."

I step over trash and broken pieces of furniture and lead Isaiah to Mom's bedroom. He gently lays her on the bed.

This isn't the first time he's helped me with Mom. When we were fourteen, Isaiah helped me pick her up from the bar. He's used to the cracks in the wall, the worn green carpeting, and the picture of me and her taped over her broken mirror.

"Give me a few minutes," I say. "Then I'll go grocery shopping."

He gruffly nods. "I'll wait in the living room."

I remove Mom's shoes from her feet and sit on the bed next to her. "Wake up, Mom. Tell me what happened to your hand." As if I don't already know.

Her eyes barely open and she curls into the fetal position. "Trent and I had a fight. He didn't mean it."

He never does. "The faster we get away from him the better."

"He loves me."

"No. He doesn't."

"Yes, he does. You two just don't know each other real well."

"I know enough." I know he wears a ring that hurt like hell when he punched me in the face. "You're leaving with me, right? Because if not, I can't take care of you."

I want her to say yes and say it quickly. The pause feels like someone ripping my intestines through my belly button. Finally, she speaks. "You don't understand. You're a gypsy."

And she's high. "Are you going to leave with me?"

"Yeah, baby," she mumbles. "I'll go with you."

"How much do we need to get the car out of impoundment?"

"I need five hundred to get Trent out of jail."

Trent can die in jail. "The car. How much to get the car

out? I can't find regular rides into Louisville and I can't take care of you if we don't leave town."

She shrugs. "Couple hundred."

Mom begins to sing an old song Grandpa used to sing before he drank himself to sleep. I rub my forehead. We need that damn car and I need a damn plan. Mom and I should have been gone weeks ago, but Isaiah ruined that. My windows of opportunity keep closing and I'm not sure how much longer Mom will last on her own.

I pull out Echo's cash and place half of it on Mom's bedside table. She stops singing and stares at the cash.

"Listen to me, Mom. You need to sober up and get the car out of the impound lot. I also want you to pay the phone bill. We'll be leaving soon. Do you understand?"

Mom keeps her eyes on the money. "Did Scott give you that?"

"Mom!" I yell and she flinches. "Repeat what you need to do."

Mom produces an old stuffed animal of mine from under her pillow. "I sleep with this when I miss you."

I slept with that stuffed animal every night until I turned thirteen. It's the only thing my father ever gave to me. The fact that she kept it rips me into pieces. I can't focus on that now. I need Mom to remember what she needs to do. Her life depends on it. "Repeat what I said."

"Get the car. Pay the phone bill."

I stand and Mom grabs my hand. "Don't leave me alone again. I don't want to be alone."

The request feeds on my guilt. We all have our fears. Those things that exist in the dark corners of our mind that terrify us beyond belief. This is hers. My fear? It's leaving her.

"I need to buy you food. I'll make some sandwiches and put them in the fridge."

"Stay," she says. "Stay until I fall asleep."

How many nights as a child did I beg her to stay with me? I lie on the bed next to her, run my fingers through her hair, and continue the song where she left off. It's her favorite verse. One that talks about birds, freedom, and change.

I slice the last sandwich in half and place the full plate in the fridge, along with the remains of the ham and cheese Isaiah bought while I sang Mom to sleep. Isaiah busies himself by putting the boxes of cereal and crackers in the pantry. He bought food Mom can easily fix for herself.

"Haven't you punished me long enough?" Isaiah asks.

The chains that permanently weigh me down become heavier. "Are you going to sling me over your shoulder and force me to leave again?"

"No," he says. "Everyone knows Trent's in jail. The worst thing that's going to happen to you here..." He glances over at the closed door of my old bedroom. "Maybe I should toss you over my shoulder again. This place is no good for you, Beth."

"I know." And that is exactly why I want to leave...with my mom. A small part of me is curious as to what Isaiah knows that I don't. I could open the door to my old room and find out, but I shake away the thought. I don't want to know. I really, really don't.

"You should go back to work," I say. He changed from his work clothes to his favorite black T-shirt and jeans, which means he intends to stick around. I don't want to be responsible for him losing a job he loves. The garage he works for is across the street from the strip mall, which explains why he reached me so quickly.

"I got off an hour ago. I stuck around to bullshit and to tinker with a newer Mustang someone brought in. She's real pretty. I think even you would like her."

I've missed this. Isaiah telling me about his day and his excited tone when he talks about cars. With his gray eyes, Isaiah looks me over. I've missed him. His voice. The tattoos covering his arms. His constant, steady presence. The last is what I miss the most. Isaiah is that one relationship I've never had to question. The one relationship where I don't wonder if it'll change when I wake in the morning.

I take the two steps and wrap my arms around his chest. One arm at a time, Isaiah embraces me. I love the sound of his heart. So steady. So strong. For a brief few seconds, the chains lift. "I've missed you," I say.

"I've missed you too." Isaiah rests his head against the top of mine. One hand reaches up and cups the back of my head. His fingers graze my cheek and my spine straightens. We've touched many times over the past four years. All those times we touched we were high. Since my arrest, Isaiah has touched me way too much sober.

One night last year, we pushed too far when we were high. Sort of like me and Ryan. Unlike me and Ryan, Isaiah and I pretended it never happened. If it weren't for Ryan, I probably would have forced amnesia on our night together in the barn.

And then I remember...Isaiah told me that he loved me.

"When we graduate, Beth, I promise I'll take you away from here."

"Okay," I say, knowing I'll be long gone before graduation.

I slip out of his grasp and wonder if I misunderstood Isaiah. Maybe he didn't tell me he loved me. Maybe he did and once again we're ignoring things. "Denny call you again?"

"Yeah, and he'll keep calling me. Do all of us a favor and just call me first. If you have to see your mom, let me be by your side when you do it. I'll kill Trent if he touches you again and I'd rather not go to jail."

"Sure." Even though I won't call. The next time I come into Louisville, it'll be to collect Mom and leave town for good.

"Rico's throwing a party tonight," Isaiah continues. "Noah's going to be there. I promise the two of us will have you back at your uncle's before you can be missed."

A sinking hollowness dwells in my soul. I hit Noah. "Is he mad at me?"

Isaiah shakes his head. "Mad at himself. Same way I am. We should have approached everything different with you, but we arrived right after Trent. Noah and I were terrified Trent was going to hurt you again."

I pull out my cell and check the time. I have five minutes to get back to Ryan. Running a hand through my hair, I consider my options. I want to see Noah and I want to spend time with Isaiah. I'd like to push Ryan in front of a bus for what he did to his brother. My heart trips over itself. What I really crave is for Ryan to give me his gorgeous smile and tell me he made a terrible mistake.

What is wrong with me?

I bite my bottom lip and face Isaiah. "I need to talk to Ryan first."

RYAN

BETH WALKS OUT OF THE shabby apartment complex, Isaiah on her heels. The same mantra circles in my brain: I'm not losing Beth. I'm not giving up on us.

I could have approached her earlier, but I decided to respect Beth and stick to our original plan: go shower and change at the pitching facility, then pick her up an hour later. I modified one part of her request—I'm picking her up where I last saw her. An hour ago, I watched as Beth followed Isaiah into this building with a grown woman passed out in his arms.

Giving Beth her space—knowing she was with him and not me—was one of the hardest damn things I've ever done. But I'm going to keep Beth. Regardless of the words I say to her, she *is* my girl.

Beth stops when she sees me leaning against the passenger door of my Jeep. Her eyes widen and her face pales. "What are you doing here?"

"We have dinner plans."

She blinks and Isaiah stiffens behind her. He may be looking for a fight, but I'm not. "Can we talk for a second, Beth?" I stare at Isaiah. "Alone."

"I go only if she tells me to go." Isaiah has a cool demeanor, almost friendly, but all of it is forced.

"Isaiah," says Beth, "I need to talk to him."

From behind her, Isaiah places a hand on her shoulder, kisses the top of her head, and stares straight at me. Bile rises in my throat. The only thing keeping me from punching him is Beth's expression. Her striking eyes become too large for her face. Good girl. I like that she didn't expect a move like that from him.

Isaiah hops in an old Mustang and glares at me as he starts the engine. It turns over immediately with an angry rumble. He backs out and leaves the lot.

Beth kneads her fists against her eyes. A million questions float in my brain, but right now I'm only interested in salvaging us. "I'm sorry."

She slowly lowers her hands. "For what?"

That this run-down shithole is her previous life. That she doesn't trust me enough to let me help her with her problems. That I've been stupid enough to think she was nothing more than a spoiled brat who freeloaded off her uncle. For being the ass she told me I was weeks ago.

"Mark was my best friend," I tell her. "When he left, I felt like he took part of me with him. When my dad threw him out, I couldn't understand why he wouldn't stay and fight— if not for him, then for me."

I've never told anyone that before. Not even Chris or Logan. Beth's the first person to ever call me out on something so major—so personal. I deserve whatever wrath will come next.

With a weighty sigh, Beth deflates to the crumbling parking curb. "I get it." She looks small and lost again and my heart rips from my chest.

I sit on the curb and everything in my world becomes right when she rests her head on my shoulder. Wrapping an arm around her, I briefly close my eyes as she inches her warm body next to mine. This is where Beth belongs—tucked in close to me.

"You were still an asshole to Mark," she says.

"Yeah." The regret eats at my stomach. "But what do I do? It's him or my dad. The two of them have drawn battle lines. I'm supposed to choose one or the other, but I need them both."

Silence. A balmy breeze dances across the parking lot.

"She's my mom," Beth says with the same heaviness I'd heard in Scott's voice when he talked about Beth as a child. "In case you were wondering."

"I was." But I wasn't ready to push her. My fingers lightly trace her arm and I swear she presses closer to me. I'd love to kiss her right now. Not the type of kiss that makes her body come alive. The type of kiss that shows her how much I care—the type that involves my soul.

Beth lifts her head and I drop my arm. She needs her space and I need to learn how to give it.

"We suck at dating," she says.

I chuckle. We do suck at it. Hoping for a perfect moment, I was going to wait until after dinner to give her what I've brought with me, but the one thing I'm learning with Beth is that perfection will never happen. I shove my hand into my pocket, pull out the thin satin strip of material, and dangle it in front of her. "This is my gift to you. This is my wow."

Beth blinks once and her head slowly inclines to the left

as she stares at the ribbon. How do guys do it? How do they give gifts to the girls they have feelings for and stay sane? I want her to be wowed so she'll stay on homecoming court, but more...I want this gift to prove that I know her and that I see beyond black hair and nose rings and cut-up jeans. I see her as she really is—I see Beth.

"You bought me a ribbon," she whispers. "How did you know?"

My mouth is dry. "I saw a picture of you when you were young in Scott's office and you talked about it...in the barn."

Her words were hypnotic. "Ribbons," she said in a whimsical voice. "I still love ribbons."

In a dawdling, methodical movement, Beth holds out her wrist. "Put it on me."

"I'm a guy. I don't know how to put ribbons in a girl's hair."

Beth's lips break into a smile that's part wicked and part laughter. "Tie it on my wrist. I'm not sure if you noticed, but I'm not exactly the hair-ribbon kind of girl anymore."

As I wrap the long strip of material around her wrist and do my best to tie an acceptable knot, I suck up the courage to ask, "Are you wowed?"

Her pause is debilitating. "Yes," she says a little breathlessly. "I'm wowed."

Beth offers me a rare gift: blue eyes so soft I'm reminded of the ocean, a smile so peaceful I think of heaven.

"Let's go to dinner," I say.

Beth's expression grows too innocent. She bites her lower lip and my eyes narrow on those lips. I ache to taste them again. In the back of my mind, red flags rise, but I don't care. I'd do anything to keep her looking at me like that forever.

"Actually," she says, "I have another idea."

★ ★ ★

Two blocks from the strip mall, we enter well-defined gang territory. I've heard rumors about the south side of the city, but never believed them. I thought they were urban legends created by girls at sleepovers. I've been on the main roads of this area a hundred times with my friends. I ate at the fast-food restaurants and shared sit-down meals with my parents. I never knew that behind the bright colors and manicured landscaping of the main strip sat tiny boxed houses and freeway overpasses littered with graffiti.

On the front stoop, Isaiah laughs with two Latino guys, then nods to my Jeep parked on the street behind his Mustang. They stop laughing. I agree. I'm not seeing an ounce of humor in this scenario. "This place is no good."

"They're my friends," Beth says. "Scott ripped me away and I never got a chance to say goodbye. You can stay in the car. Just give me twenty minutes, thirty tops. And then we'll go out. I swear."

No way in hell is she going in there alone. I register the threat level of the neighborhood and the guys on the porch. "I can't protect you here."

"I'm not asking you to. You said you'd wait—"

I cut her off. "When you said you wanted to stop by and say goodbye to some friends. That guy is wearing gang colors."

She hits the back of her head against the seat. "Ryan. I'm probably never going to see any of them again. Will you please just let me say goodbye?"

Those words, *never going to see again* and *goodbye,* are the only reasons I'm saying this. "Then I'm going in with you."

"Fine." She hops out and I follow. She can live under whatever delusion she wants, but she's no safer here than I am and

I'll go down swinging before anyone hurts her. We reach the front stoop and I see that Isaiah has disappeared. Is it too much to hope that he's called it a night? The inside of the house is smaller than I expected, and I expected cramped.

The kitchen and living room are really one room put together and separated by the angle of furniture. Teenagers sit everywhere—on the furniture, on the floor. Others lean against walls. A haze of smoke lingers in the room. Cigarette smoke. Other types of smoke.

I draw the stares of most everyone, but they continue their conversations. The guys size me up. The girls' eyes wander to my chest. Some outright gawk lower. Beth entwines her hand with mine, then caresses her soft fingers against my cheek, enticing me to drop my head to hers.

"Stay close to me," she whispers. "Don't talk and don't stare. Things will be better in the backyard."

For days, I've dreamed of Beth being this close to me again, but right now I can only focus on the multiple sets of eyes watching our every movement. Beth turns, holds tighter to my fingers, and leads me through the living room and out the back door of the kitchen.

Several strings of Christmas lights hang between three trees scattered in the narrow yard. A patch of grass grows in the far corner. The rest of it is a mix of weeds and dirt. In the middle of a ring of worn lawn chairs, Isaiah talks to Noah, a redheaded girl tucked close to Noah, and one of the Latino guys from the stoop.

Noah breaks from the group when he sees Beth. She releases me and falls into his waiting arms. They whisper to one another. I don't like how he holds on to her and don't like how long he's holding. That doesn't look like brotherly love to me. I stare at his girl. Why is she so damned happy to see her guy hugging someone else?

When he lets her go, Noah extends his hand to me. "S'up."

I take his hand and squeeze extra tight. "Nothing. You?"

The moment I squeeze, Noah grins and squeezes back. "Chill, bro. Beth says you're good, so that makes us good."

Beth hugs the Latino guy and laughs as he playfully talks in Spanish. "That's Rico," says Noah. "Relax. We've got your back."

"It's Beth I'm worried about. She shouldn't be here."

Noah loses the easygoing front. "No, she shouldn't."

Beth glances over her shoulder and flashes me that joyous smile—the one I've only seen a handful of times.

"Is she wearing a ribbon?" Noah asks in clear disbelief.

Feeling proud, I answer, "I gave it to her."

"Fucking wonderful," Noah mumbles as he eyes Isaiah. "Don't stay long."

Noah returns to the group and pulls his girl onto a hammock strung along two posts in the ground. The hammock swings gently back and forth as they lie together. Propped up on an elbow, Noah focuses on her. "Echo, that's Ryan. Ryan, this is my girl."

Message received. Screw with his girl and he'll screw with me. "Nice to meet you."

Echo sits up, but Noah snakes an arm around her waist and drags her back down.

"Beth brought a guy who has manners," Echo teases him. "See, it's not so hard."

Noah pushes her hair over her shoulder, then runs a finger along her arm. "I've got manners, baby."

"No." She swats at his hand and laughs. "You don't."

Disgust weaves through me as I register what I'm seeing. Scars cover Echo's arms. I rub a hand over my face. What the hell happened to her? Noah continues to tease Echo and she continues to laugh, yet his tone as he addresses me is a menacing threat. "Stare any longer, Ryan, and I'll kick your ass."

"Noah," Echo reprimands. "Don't."

Beth returns to me. "What did I say about staring?"

"I apologize," I say directly to Echo.

Echo smiles. "See? Manners."

"Come on," says Beth. "Let's get you a beer before you give them a good reason to kick your ass."

BETH

I MISS LAUGHING.

Most days I can find something amusing to make my lips flinch up. Sometimes it will be funny enough to make me chuckle. But I miss laughing. Really laughing. Laughing to the point that my insides hurt, my chest aches, my face is exhausted from holding the smile.

For effect, Rico stands in the middle of the circle of lawn chairs and in slow motion reenacts how Isaiah and I kept him from being busted for underage drinking this summer by distracting a pair of cops with a very bad mime routine.

"I'm hiding in the bushes and if the police step back, they'd be on top of me. Beth's just standing there," Rico chokes out between laughs. "Her arm stiff at the shoulder and her forearm dangling back and forth like a pendulum. The cop asked if she needed medical help. He thought she was having a seizure."

Everyone, including me, bursts into laugher. Rico composes himself to spit out the rest. "And she breaks her self-imposed silence and says, 'I'm a mime, you moron. Why do you think I've been doing all these retarded moves?'"

Everyone laughs harder and as our group gasps for air Rico glances at Ryan. *"Incluso el nino blanco se esta riendo."*

I'm not fluent in Spanish, but I know enough to pick out the words *white boy* and *laughter*. My heart shivers when I catch Ryan at the tail end of a chuckle. He's always cute, but he's breathtaking when he laughs.

Rico lifts his beer to his lips, then tosses it across the yard. "I'm out."

Isaiah tips the cooler. "We're all out, man."

"Isaiah, help me snag some of Antonio's stash, then we'll hit the *mota*."

Mota. Weed. The layer between my skin and muscles itches. I want a hit. More like I crave a hit—the smell surrounding me, the smoke burning my lungs, the feeling of freedom and floating. Oh God, I want more than anything to float.

Isaiah stands and Rico kicks my foot as he passes. "You're in, right, Beth?"

It kills me to shake my head. "Curfew."

I peek at Ryan. Does he know what *mota* is? The smile falls from my lips as I flip through the stories we've told. Oh crap, I feel sick. The drinking. The drugs. The parties. He heard it all. My stomach sways. He knows what I am.

"Beth," says Isaiah. He waits until I look at him. "The stuff is mild. You'll be sober by curfew."

"Isaiah," Noah warns.

Isaiah would never steer me wrong. If he says I'll be sober in an hour, then I will be. He knows how much I long for weightlessness. A loud crashing noise comes from the house. I know these people. Ryan doesn't. I can't leave him defenseless. "No, I'm good."

"Suit yourself." Rico heads into the house. Isaiah stares at me and I don't understand the gleam in his eye. Abruptly, he follows Rico.

In the hammock, Noah begins to kiss Echo. The two of them will be lost in their own world for the rest of the night and Isaiah will easily be gone ten minutes. The night has been fun, but it's also made me the rope in a strange invisible tug-of-war. Ryan sat on one side of me. Isaiah the other. It felt weird to be next to both my best friend and the guy I really like.

Why can't Isaiah see that we're just friends? Friends only. I need to talk to him before I leave. I need to straighten this whole mess out. Honestly, I just need to hear him say that he didn't mean it and that he's still my best friend.

Ryan stands, stretches, and walks over to the tree on the opposite side of the yard. I glance over my shoulder at the house. I've been careful not to rub Ryan in Isaiah's face, but I need to make sure Ryan's okay too. Yeah, Isaiah will be gone for a while. Rico's a slow tripper.

I follow after Ryan. "You don't have to move for Noah and Echo's sake."

Hundreds of Christmas lights hang from the tree. His sun-kissed skin is beautiful under their glow. "I didn't move because of them."

I raise an eyebrow. "Then why did you?"

Ryan inclines his head and his eyes roam my body as if savoring the sight. "You're beautiful when you laugh."

Warmth blazes on my cheeks and I break eye contact. Ryan reaches out and touches me. His fingers linger on my neckline and the whisper of his caress on my skin heats my blood.

"You should laugh more," he says.

I swallow. "Life hasn't given me much to laugh about."

"I could change that." Ryan invades my personal space and every part of him connects with a part of me.

I inhale and smell the delicious scent of earth after the rain. "You smell good," I say.

His hand glides along the curve of my spine and into my hair. Chills energize my body. "So do you. You always smell like roses."

I giggle at the thought of me smelling sweet and bite my lip to stop the girlish reaction. "No one's ever said that to me before."

Ryan's lips form that glorious smile with dimples and my blood tingles straight to my toes. This smile is for me and me alone.

"There are lots of things I want to say to you, Beth, and I want to be the first to say them to you."

Intense hunger glazes his eyes. I've seen the same look on other guys, but on Ryan it's different. That stare has more depth—more meaning—as if he's seeing inside me.

"I want to kiss you," he murmurs. "Do you want to kiss me?"

My heart beats faster. Oh, Ryan can kiss. I've stayed awake at night and replayed his lips against mine. His kisses are strong like him, possessive and demanding. Ryan said beautiful things to me in the barn and he touched me in ways I only dreamed someone could touch me. My fingers burrow into his thick hair. "Yes."

Ryan lowers his head and I close my eyes. The anticipation of this moment creates an energy that sizzles in the autumn air. I'm going to do it. I'm going to kiss Ryan—sober.

"Fuck, Beth." From behind me, Isaiah spits out the words. I whirl around and barely catch sight of him bolting out the back gate into the alley. Noah falls out of the hammock and heads after him. I need to go after Isaiah, not Noah. I take several steps, but laughter from the house stops me. I can't leave Ryan. "Noah!"

"Go home, Beth," he says as he strides toward the alley. "Back to Groveton and don't come back."

That's the deal we made. When we hugged and apologized to each other, Noah promised to let me stay and enjoy my evening if, when it was over, I left and never looked back. It wasn't a hard promise to make. In a few weeks, I'll be gone for good. "I can't leave knowing he's upset." Because after tonight, I may never see him again.

"Just go," says Noah.

"No!" I grab Noah and fling myself in front of him. "He's mad at me. I know he gets upset when I make out with guys, but Ryan isn't some random guy. I have to explain that to him." I have to explain to Isaiah that he is not in love with me. "But I can't go after Isaiah and leave Ryan here. You know what will happen if some of Rico's friends see Ryan without you or me."

Noah rubs his eyes. Yes, he does know. Ryan isn't a part of our circle and is fair game for a good beating. Noah gestures for me to go after Isaiah. "Fifteen minutes, Beth. I mean it. You need to go back to Groveton and finish out your life there."

I turn and flinch to find Ryan standing close with his hands shoved into his pockets. Hurt wounds the brown eyes that glowed with promise moments before.

"Ryan," I stutter out. "He's my best friend and he's upset and..."

"Go after him." Ryan crosses his arms over his chest. "But don't string me along if it's him you want."

"What?" I shake my head. Ryan misunderstands. "Isaiah and I...we're not like that."

But I'm not going to waste time standing here arguing with Ryan over stupid jealousy issues when my best friend is upset. I push past Noah and run into the alley. A few steps into the darkness, strong hands grab my arms.

I suck in air to scream and I'm silenced by a familiar deep voice. "You've changed." As if to prove his point, Isaiah shoves my wrist in front of my face and shows me Ryan's pink ribbon.

"So have you. The Isaiah I knew would have run away with me and Mom when I asked. You left my mom with Trent and he broke her wrist! It's like I don't even know you anymore. You used to take care of me!" My pulse thuds in my ears as I shove away from Isaiah.

The streetlamp attached to an aging utility pole flickers on and off. With each flash of light, a mix of anger and sadness crosses Isaiah's face. "You used to let me take care of you. Now you've got some asshole jock doing your bidding."

White-hot anger flashes through me. "Leave Ryan out of this. You're the one PMS-ing like a girl. First you want to run away with me. Then you don't want anything to do with me. Then you want to run away with me after graduation. Then you keep telling me to live my life in Groveton. Then you go and tell me that you love me when we both know you don't."

My heart jumps out of my chest when he punches his curled fists into the chain-link fence behind him. The metal of the fence vibrates. "Dammit, Beth."

Isaiah clutches the fence and he bends over as if he's ready to vomit. Not once in four years have I seen him this emotional. My hands shake with adrenaline. "I don't understand."

Isaiah swears softly under his breath. "I am in love with you."

Ice freezes my muscles. He said it—again. "No, you aren't."

Isaiah spins and cups my face with his hands. I don't feel warmth. I only feel cold. Cold and confused. He lowers his head so that his face is close to mine. "I've been in love with you since I was fifteen. I wasn't man enough to tell you, so Luke swooped in. You were so hurt after he used you that I swore to protect you until you could listen to what I had to say. I'm in love with you."

My lungs tighten. God, I can't breathe. Help me breathe. "You're my best friend."

"And you're mine. I want more from you and I'm begging you to please give me more."

My throat becomes raw and slowly swells. "But you're my best friend."

His fingers gently move against my cheek. "You want to leave, I'll go. I'll take you now. We'll get in my car, find your mom, and we'll never look back. Your terms. Not mine. Whatever you want. Whatever you need. Just say the words. Please say them."

I love him.

Those words. My hand presses against his chest. His heart continues in the same steady beat I've come to depend upon. Isaiah is my rock. The string that holds me together when I'm ready to fall apart. He's the anchor that keeps me from floating away when I go too far. His heart has been the one constant rhythm in my life and I don't want to let it go. "I love you."

Isaiah tucks his chin toward his chest and I force air into my lungs when he clears his throat. "You've got to mean it."

I try to physically shake the tears forming, but his hold on my face makes it impossible. We haven't talked for weeks, but I knew, in the deep recesses of my mind, that our separation was temporary. This somehow feels too real and that means this goodbye could be concrete. I can't lose him. I can't. "I mean it. I love you."

Like a friend. Like my best friend. Before Groveton, I never understood love and now...I still don't understand it. But I know that it's not emptiness, I know it's not letting a guy use me, I know there are different types and what I feel for Isaiah...it's not how I feel when I'm with Ryan.

Isaiah rests his forehead on mine. "Like you love him. Tell me you love me as much as you love him."

Ryan. Am I in love with him? The thought causes panic. Just the sound of his name causes my heart to trip over itself. I love the way Ryan makes me feel. I love his words. I love his hands on my body. I love the way his gaze causes me to blush.

But I have to leave Ryan soon in order to protect my mom. If I say the right words, Isaiah will go with me. "Isaiah, I..."

Once upon a time, I wondered if I was falling in love with Isaiah. Echo had hugged him and he happily hugged her back. The pain and jealousy that shot through my body surprised even me. But I wasn't falling for him. I was scared of Echo. Scared of the changes she was bringing to our lives. Changes that would have happened even if she had never existed.

I stare into his gray eyes. Isaiah's wrong; he doesn't love

me. Not in the way he thinks. The truth is there—in his eyes. He doesn't look at me the way Noah does Echo or how Chris does Lacy. He doesn't look at me the way Ryan does....

"I love you..."

I love Isaiah's safety and I love his calm. I love his voice and his laughter. I love his constant, steady presence. But if the world were coming to an end, he's not the person I'd want at my side. I love him. I love him so much that I know he deserves to have a girl who falls apart at his touch. He deserves to have a girl whose heart stops working every time he glances at her. He deserves someone who is "in" love with him.

"...as a friend. The same way that you love me."

Isaiah shakes his head, as if doing that will make my words less true. "You're wrong."

He presses his lips against my forehead. My lower lip trembles as I ball the material of his shirt into my hand. I'm losing him. I'm losing my best friend.

"I'm not," I say. "And someday you're going to figure it out."

"If you change your mind..." There's a heaviness in his voice, and a part of me dies at the thought of him in so much pain. He touches his lips to my forehead once more, the caress lasting longer, the pressure more intense. Isaiah walks away from me and fades into the darkness.

"I won't," I whisper as I close my eyes and wish that one day, he'll change his.

RYAN

BETH ASKED FOR TIME. How long does she need? A day? A week? Hours? Any amount is too long when the girl I'm falling for had tears in her eyes. Any amount is too long when I wonder if she cares for me. I won't see her until Tuesday. Tomorrow is parent–teacher conferences. Today is Sunday and my parents are hosting a barbecue for the mayor, the town council, and a few other friends of our family. I'm dressed up and playing the perfect part.

Perfect.

It's what Lacy called me when she explained why she would never fit into Groveton.

Perfect.

It's what Beth spat at me when she refused the trust fall.

Perfect.

It's the word Gwen just used when discussing how she wants the two of us to walk onto the football field together for homecoming.

Perfect.

Looking out on our back patio, I see nothing but boring perfection. The grass trimmed perfectly to three inches.

The shrubs perfectly edged in the shape of round balls. The pots of fall chrysanthemums lining the edging of the patio perfectly placed one foot apart. Perfect people who grew up in this town and perfectly filled their parents' shoes.

At the other end of the table, my mother inclines her head toward Gwen. I take the nonverbal cue and turn my attention to my "dinner partner." Gwen gives me a smile that's one more perfect thing in the backyard. "Wouldn't that be awesome, Ryan?"

No, walking onto the field with her on my arm at homecoming wouldn't be awesome. I want to share that moment with Beth. "I'm not sure we get to decide who we walk with."

Gwen ignores my comment. "Could you pour me some more water?"

I reach for the pitcher in front of me and do as she asks. This is my obligation to my parents. My job is to fill Gwen's drink when it's empty, remove her dishes when she's done, and to entertain her. Déjà vu sets in and my head swims with a sinking revelation. This same exact moment is how Gwen and I started dating.

Gwen's mother sips her wine. Her face is tighter than it was last fall. "We need to make a decision regarding Allison Risk and the event committee at church."

Mom fidgets with her pearl necklace. She hates uncomfortable decisions. "Allison is a sweet young woman."

"Are you in favor of her joining, Miriam?" Gwen's mother asks.

Uncharacteristically, my mother pours wine into her empty water glass. "I don't know. The Risks were dreadful people. Do you remember Scott's parents? The man was a mean drunk and the woman wasn't much better."

"But Scott's not his parents," I say and everyone at the table glances at me. My mother shoots me a warning glare, but my father puts a hand on my mother's arm to back her off. Mom removes her arm from under his touch. I continue, "He became the best baseball player the Yankees have seen in twenty years. Why should his wife be punished for his parents' mistakes?"

Dad's eyes narrow on the last sentence. His own private warning to me that I may have gone too far.

"I have to be honest," says Gwen's mother. "I am fond of Allison, but it's the niece I'm concerned with."

"How so?" asks my mother as I stiffen. "Have you heard anything about her?"

"I've heard she smokes, was disrespectful to a teacher, and swears. All traits we cannot condone, and putting Allison on the committee will reflect upon our church. Which is so sad, since Allison is a dear and the niece is..." Gwen's mother flitters her fingers in the air. "Savage. It's obvious that the girl didn't go with Scott like we hoped after the incident with her father."

My mind awakens. The people at this table know what happened to Beth. I'm torn in two. Part of me wants to defend Beth. The other half wants to know what happened to her as a child. If I speak now, I'll lose my opportunity to learn the truth.

"Liza," Gwen's father interjects, "I won't stand for that child to be gossiped about."

Red in the cheeks, Mrs. Gardner forces a smile on her face. "I'm not gossiping and she's hardly a child anymore. The event committee is an offshoot of a bigger issue. I'm concerned with the girl's influence. I'm scared everyone will be so wrapped up in who her uncle is that they won't see the threat in front of them. Do you want your daughter swearing and smoking and talking back to teachers?"

"I hardly think that's going to happen," Mr. Gardner replies.

"Why not?" she argues. "The senior class already nominated Beth for homecoming court and Ryan is dating her."

I become rock. This isn't how I wanted my parents to find out.

"What?" My mother's fast and irritated question silences the group. My eyes flash to Gwen. Wide-eyed and pale, Gwen sits perfectly still and stares at the remains of her chicken cordon bleu.

Her mother poorly hides her smugness behind her wineglass. "I'm sorry, Miriam, I assumed that Ryan told you." She places a hand over Gwen's. "I apologize to you too, sweetheart. I didn't know that what you told me was a secret."

Mom places her napkin on the table. "Who's ready for dessert?"

I stand, needing to get the hell out of here. "I'll get it."

Mom deflates in her chair with a nod. What I don't expect is Gwen hopping up and volunteering, "And I'll help."

Unable to look at her, I pivot and head for the kitchen. The rapid click of Gwen's heels informs me she's right behind me.

"Ryan," she says the moment the door is closed to any eavesdropping ears. "Ryan, I'm sorry. I had no idea my mom would humiliate you like that. But it's not my fault. How was I to know that you were keeping Beth a secret?"

"I'm not," I snap. Gwen looks like a stranger to me in this kitchen. Maybe it's because I'm still not used to the gray walls or the granite counters or the mahogany cupboards. Or maybe it's because I never really knew her to begin with.

She crosses her arms over her chest and her red sundress swirls with the motion. "Could have fooled me. I mean, come on, Ryan, your parents will hate her—and for good reason."

"You don't know Beth." The irony of this conversation is not lost on me. Lacy once said those same words to me.

Gwen loses the perfect glow about her and does a very uncharacteristic thing—she sags against the counter. "I know more than you think. I'd bet I know more than you." She pauses and nervously fidgets with her hands. What the hell? Gwen is never nervous.

And that's when I notice the bare spot on her finger. Mike's ring is gone.

"I love you. In fact, I've always loved you." Gwen stares at the gray tiled floor. "And for some stupid reason you care about *her*. I think you were right in the dugout—I wasn't clear on what I needed from you. Maybe the reason we aren't together now is because I didn't try hard enough."

My forehead furrows. If she had said those words six months ago... I shake my head. It wouldn't have mattered. What I feel for Beth is a hundred times stronger than what I ever felt for Gwen. "We would never have worked."

Gwen straightens and lifts her chin. "You're seeing everything all wrong. Me. Beth. Everything. I think you're aware that you and Beth don't belong together and that's the reason you never told your parents. But don't worry, Ryan. I know what I did wrong and I don't make the same mistakes twice."

In one graceful movement, Gwen swoops the cake off the counter and ushers it out the kitchen door. I inhale and let my head fall back. I don't know what the hell just happened, but every cell in my body screams it's bad and I'm going to hate the consequences.

My grandmother left my mother her pendulum clock. It hangs on the wall behind Mom. With each swing, the clock ticks. It's nine o'clock at night. The last of the guests left an hour ago. I should be wondering why my parents called me in here, especially since they're voluntarily in the same room. Instead, I'm wondering what Beth is thinking.

Mom sits across from me at our kitchen table while Dad leans against the door frame leading to the formal dining room. The temperature, like always, is frigid.

"Mrs. Rowe is under the impression you're still participating in the writing competition," says Dad.

I glance up at him. "I'm considering it."

"There's nothing to consider. You're playing Eastwick that weekend and that game will decide rankings going into the spring season."

Eastwick is the only team that beat us during regular season play last spring. "We're playing Northside that Monday and they're undefeated this year. Coach may want me to pitch that game."

"Maybe," says Dad. "But you'll still be able to play a couple of innings on Monday. They'll need you to close the game out."

Mom takes off her pearl necklace. "I talked to Mrs. Rowe last week. She said that Ryan has a rare talent."

"He does," says Dad. "Baseball."

"No," bites out Mom. "Writing."

Dad rubs his eyes. "Explain to your mother you're not interested in the writing."

"Ryan, tell your father what Mrs. Rowe told me. Tell him how much you enjoy her class."

My shoulders curl in with the anger. I hate their constant fighting. I hate that I've caused them to fight more. I hate that they're fighting over me. But what I hate more is the feeling that everyone else is controlling my choices. "I love baseball."

Dad releases a sigh of relief.

"And I love writing. I want to go to the competition."

Dad swears under his breath and heads for the fridge. I turn in my chair to face him. "You've never let me walk away from a competition before and I don't like the feeling of giving up. I'll miss one game. And this is recreational league play. It would be different if this was spring season."

Dad pops open a bottle of beer and takes a swig. "What happens if you win the writing competition? Are you going to give up pitching against the best team in the state for a piece of paper that says congratulations?"

"I want to know if I'm any good."

"Jesus, Ryan. Why? What difference would it make?"

"I've been offered the chance at a college scholarship— to play ball."

Dad stares at me and the dishwasher enters the rinse cycle. "Have you been talking to college scouts behind my back?"

Yes. No. "The recruiter made sense. He said their pitch coach can help me with my placement issues and teach me to break the tell on my pitches. They'll pay for me to go to school and I can get free coaching. I can train with them for four years and then go for the pros."

Beer sloshes from the bottle when Dad throws out his

arms. "What happens if you get injured? What happens if instead of improving, you lose your edge? You're a pitcher. There is no better time for you to go after your dreams than now."

"What if..."

He stalks across the kitchen and slams the beer down in front of me. "Do I need to remind you how much money we've pumped into you? Do you think the coaching we've paid for over the years is cheap? Do you think the equipment, the Jeep we bought you were free?"

My gut aches as if he punched me. "No. I don't think they were free. I've offered to get a job."

"I'm not looking for you to get a job, Ryan. I'm looking for you to do something with your talent. I'm looking for you to make a name for this family. I want to know that the years your mother and I have sacrificed financially, emotionally, with our time are not in vain."

Mom calmly folds her hands on the table. "He does have talent, Andrew. You're angry he doesn't want what you want. You're angry he's choosing something different."

"Baseball is what he wants!" Dad's knuckles turn white as he grips the back of the chair.

"You have no idea what anyone in this family wants."

His voice shakes as he talks. "What do you want, Miriam? What will finally make you happy? You always wanted me to run for mayor and I've agreed to it. You wanted me to expand the business and I am. I have done everything to make you happy. Just tell me what you want."

"I want my family back!" Mom screams. Over the past months, my mother has been sarcastic and rude to my father. But in seventeen years, I've never known her to scream.

The shock wears off Dad's face. "You can't have it all! Do you want your friends to know that your son is gay? Do you want your church to know your son is gay?"

"But we could talk to Mark. Maybe if he agreed to keep it a secret—"

"No!" my father roars.

I lean back in my chair, disgusted with them. Disgusted with myself. Since Mark walked away, I've been so obsessed with the fact that he left that I never really listened to what my parents were saying. It makes me realize that I probably never really listened to Mark either. No wonder he left. How could anyone live with so much hate?

A sickening nausea strikes and I grow dizzy. Does Mark believe I feel the same way as my parents?

Dad rams the chair into the table, then stalks away. "Mark made his choice. You wanted to talk to Ryan tonight—talk to him. I'll be in my office."

Mom stands. "He should hear it from you."

In the door frame, he pauses and looks back at me. "I'll be running for my party's nomination for mayor in the spring. Your mother and I don't want you dating Beth Risk. Be her friend at school, but we can't risk the bad publicity if she's trouble. Do you understand?"

My mind races to process. Dad's running for mayor. Mom wants Mark back in the house. I've let down my brother. They both want me to dump Beth. "You said that you never wanted to be mayor."

But Mom has wanted him to. Her dad was mayor. Her grandfather was mayor. It's a tradition she's always craved to continue.

Neither Mom nor Dad will look at me or at each other, and

neither appears to want to discuss his nomination. "About Beth..." I say.

Dad cuts me off. "The girl is off-limits."

"You should date Gwen again," Mom says. "Her father is going to back your father."

The seat jerks under me when I stand and my sudden movement causes Mom to flinch. I stare at them both, waiting for one of them to make sense of anything they've said. When they remain silent, I finally understand why Mark left.

BETH

I DON'T OWN A JACKET. Never have. I always told Isaiah and Noah my body temperature runs hot when actually it runs low. In Kentucky, autumn weather can be a bitch. Hot in the afternoons. Cold at night. This morning, the slick dew covering Ryan's pasture permeates past my worn shoes to my socks. Few things suck more than cold, wet feet.

I stop in my tracks. Losing my best friend sucks. I let myself feel the ache, then continue forward. One day Isaiah will realize that we're just friends. One day he'll find me—even if I'm at the ocean. Friendships like ours are too strong to die.

Today is parent–teacher conferences and I can't think of a better way to spend a day free from school than with Ryan. Actually, I can't think of a better way to spend any day. My time with Ryan is dwindling and I want to make the most of every moment with him.

Thump. I first heard that sound when I came out of the woods. Every few seconds, the sound repeats. Thump. Instead of heading straight for Ryan's house, I decided to follow the thumps and I'm glad I did when I see beautiful, glistening, sun-kissed skin. Wearing only a pair of nylon athletic pants, Ryan winds back then hurls a ball toward a painted target on a piece of plywood. Thump. The ball hits square in the middle.

"And you wonder why people think jocks are stupid," I say. Ryan whirls around with wide eyes and I continue, "It's fifty degrees outside and you aren't wearing a shirt."

A cold breeze blows through the open pasture, causing goose bumps to prick my arms. Okay, possibly not the smartest opening line since rubbing my arms would be the definition of both hypocrisy and irony.

Ryan grabs his shirt off the ground and walks over to me. The early morning rays highlight the curves of the muscles in his abdomen. My heart flutters like a bird shaking water from its wings. God, he's gorgeous. Sexy. A vision. Too perfect for someone like me.

"I'm cooling down," Ryan says. Caught up in staring at his body, I have to pause to remember what I last said. Ryan gives me a cocky smile and to my mortification, I blush. What is with me and all this blushing?

Ryan caresses my burning cheeks, and my heart trembles again.

"I love it when you do that," he says.

Pull it together, Beth. This is not why you're here. Ryan has dealt with enough of my crap over the past two months and for some reason he insists on looking at me like I'm the princess to his prince. He is a prince. I'm not a princess, but I can help with his happily-ever-after before I leave his life for good.

Ryan withdraws his hand, but remains annoyingly close— with his shirt still off.

"Don't you ever get tired of baseball?" I ask.

"No." Ryan finally pulls his shirt over his head. "I wake up every morning at six, run two miles, then pitch. There's not a morning it gets old."

His routine fits him. Perfectly. But then I think of him at his computer. His fingers flying over the keyboard. His eyes seeing a world beyond the one his body belongs to. "Do you write every night?"

Ryan combs his fingers through my hair and my roots flip over. What normally is a motion that sends tingles down my spine instead brings a sense of dread. His eyes narrow at the roots and I know what he sees: a half inch of golden-blond hair.

He tears his eyes away and does a good job of pretending the malformation doesn't exist. "With that short story due? Yeah, I write every night." Ryan shrugs and stares at the ground. "And I think I might keep it up when the story is done. I don't know, maybe start another."

Good. It's the image I'll take with me when I go: Ryan pitching balls in the morning and lost in his beautifully written words at night. I kick at the ground. "Do you have plans for today?"

"I do if they include you."

I try to hide my smile, but I can't. "Get cleaned up and pick me up in an hour."

Tickling my skin, Ryan's fingers graze the pink ribbon still tied to my wrist. "Yes, ma'am."

RYAN

"YOU'RE A WUSS." My little black-haired threat flips through the University of Kentucky student directory. "You can move a car across a pasture, but you can't see your own brother."

"That's different," I say. "I moved the car on a dare."

Outside the guys' athletic dorms, I attempt to stand in front of Beth as she searches for my brother's room number. Beth wears a cotton T-shirt that hugs her slim form and ends a half inch short of her low-rise jeans. With her smooth skin tempting me in very right, yet wrong, places, I would bet my Jeep that the outfit doesn't have Scott's seal of approval. Don't get me wrong, I love it, and so does every guy walking in and out of the dorms. She's my girl and I prefer to be the only one looking at her.

My girl. We're not official—not yet—but Beth said four critical words when she climbed into my Jeep this morning: "I let Isaiah go." Which means she's with me and not him. Later today, I'm asking Beth to make us exclusive.

Beth stabs her finger into the book. "Jackpot." She scribbles the room number onto the palm of her hand. "I double dog dare you to talk to your brother."

"Do you know nothing about dares?" I ask while giving the evil eye to some guy who stares at the contours of Beth's waist. "You can't double dog dare unless I turn down the initial dare."

She arches a brow. "Are we really going to talk semantics?"

I place a hand on her hip and back her against the wall. "That's a big word, Beth. Maybe you should explain it."

A wicked smile touches her lips and raw hunger settles in her eyes, but instead of melting into me as I am into her, Beth pushes me away and ducks underneath my arm. A guy walks out of the building and Beth catches the door before it has a chance to lock behind him. "It means you're an idiot if you think I'm going to let you talk your way out of this."

She gestures for me to enter the lobby and I do. "I wasn't going to talk. I was going to kiss my way out of it. Do you have any idea how long it's been since we kissed?"

"If you talk to your brother, we'll kiss. A lot."

"How about we skip this and move straight on to kissing?"

She ignores me and studies the large map of the dorm layout on the wall. "I officially dare you to talk to your brother."

I cross my arms over my chest as my back straightens. Beth officially threw down the gauntlet. "Fine. What do I get if I win?"

Her raven hair cascades like a waterfall as she inclines her head toward me. A sexy glint lights her eyes. "What do you want?"

You. But that isn't what I permit to come out of my mouth. "I want you to spend the rest of the day with me. No cell phones. No friends. Nothing but me and you."

"Deal."

★ ★ ★

Beth expertly manipulates our way past the RA guarding the entrance to Mark's floor. I'd call him an idiot, but I'm well aware that she used the same manipulation skills to convince me to drive to Lexington. To my horror, Beth knocks on my brother's door without asking if I'm ready. Any hope Mark would be in class ends when the doorknob jiggles and Mark's large, looming figure stands in the door frame.

Beth flashes a wicked smile. "S'up, Mark. How was the game against Florida?"

He hesitantly grins as his eyes flicker between me and Beth. "I sacked the quarterback twice. Don't you watch the news?"

She shrugs. "No. I'm pretending to care about football in order to break the ice. I'll be in the lobby." Beth nonchalantly walks off the way we came. Even when the door at the end of the hallway shuts, I still watch. After dragging my ass here, I never thought she'd leave me to do this on my own.

Mark steps away from the door and forces cheerfulness. "Do you want to come in?"

"Yeah." I mimic his tone. Mark and I never forced anything before this summer.

Mark's dorm room is the same as it was last year. I can tell he has the same roommate by the posters of *Star Wars* hanging on the wall. "Where's Greg?"

"Class. Do you want something to drink?" He opens a small fridge. "Gatorade, water?"

My mouth tastes like the desert, but I don't want to prolong this. "I'm sorry."

Mark closes the fridge and sits on the bottom bunk. His fake smile vanishes and I shove my hands in my pockets.

The Band-Aid method sucked for both of us. I wish I could make our relationship strong again. Mark was the first person I told when I pitched a no-hitter, made my first all-star team, and kissed a girl. Now, I don't even know what words to stutter out next.

"How're Mom and Dad?" he asks.

How're Mom and Dad. I can answer that. I take a seat on the two-seater couch next to the bunks. "Okay. Dad's busy. He's expanding the construction business and he plans on running for mayor."

"Wow."

"Yeah." Wow.

"And Mom?"

"Wrapped up in her social clubs and events like normal. Lunches. Dinners. Teas." I pause, wondering if I should say what I'm about to. "She misses you."

Mark leans forward and holds his hands together between his bent knees. "Does Dad ever mention me?"

The hope fighting to surface on Mark's face makes looking at him painful. If I answer with a plain yes, I create false hope, or I could tell him the truth. None of the answers are ones I want to give. "Did you ever want to do anything besides football?"

Mark scrapes his knuckles against his jaw before snatching a book off his bed and tossing it to me. I catch it in midair. *Quality Lesson Plans for Secondary Physical Education?*

"I'm an education major."

"Since when?"

"Since..." Mark drums the fingers of his clasped hands once. "Always."

Faking interest in the pages, I flip through the book. "I thought you were pre-med."

"That's what Dad wanted me to major in. College for Dad was nothing more than a step toward the NFL. The pre-med was if I got injured. Mom wanted one of us to be a doctor. That was Dad's way of making her happy."

Mark's organized his desk the same as last year: laptop, iPod dock. After Mark's first college football game, Mom had someone take a family picture on the field. He's taped the photograph on the wall next to his practice schedule. Some things are the same. Others are not. "Do you hate football?"

"No. I love football and want to play. In fact, I want to become a high school football coach. Dad knew that. He didn't agree with me, but he knew it. I thought if I played along, that if I pretended that—" He cuts himself off.

I came here. I brought this up. I can finish the statement for him. "They'd accept who you are?"

Mark nods. "Yeah."

The two of us sit in silence. My stomach twists and turns like I'm on a boat on the verge of capsizing. My life was perfect and I enjoyed every second. Mark's two little words "I'm gay" tipped my world. Maybe I get why he left. Maybe I don't. Either way, anger still festers, and if I'm doing this, I'm doing this. "You left me."

"What did you want me to do?" Resentment thickens his tone. "I can't change who I am."

I need to move. Hit something. Throw something. I stand instead. "Not leave. You said you pretended before. Why couldn't you pretend again? Or you could have stayed and fought and, I don't know, convinced Mom and Dad to let you stay."

Mark calmly watches as I pace the length of the narrow room. He clears his throat. "Someday, you're going to see how Mom and Dad controlled and manipulated our lives. You're going to notice how they made us believe that their dreams were our dreams. They dictated our every breath. Think about it—do you have any idea who you are without them?"

Mom sat me next to Gwen last night and she specifically asked me to take care of Gwen's needs during the evening. Just like she asked me to take care of Gwen when I was fifteen. After that first dinner, Mom encouraged me to ask her out and I did.

But baseball is my choice. It always has been. Dad understands baseball. Because of that, he's managed every part of my baseball career: the coaches, the leagues. Hell, he even stands up to umps. He does it all for me.

Right?

Mom and Dad's concerns, all of their pushing, they do it because they love me. But they flat-out told me not to date Beth, regardless of my feelings for her, and they expect nothing less than compliance.

"You're going to wear a hole in my carpet," Mark says.

No, Mark's wrong. He has to be wrong. "I'm a good ballplayer." I am. The best.

"You are. Dad did that right. He didn't force us into a sport we had no talent in. He took his time and found the one sport each of us was good at. The question is—who are you playing for, Ry? You or Dad?"

Between the door and bunk beds, I freeze. "What is that supposed to mean?"

"Dad wants perfection. Scratch that. Dad wants perfection on the outside so everyone else can see it. Mom too. They couldn't care less if we're torn up on the inside as long as the rest of the world envies us."

Everyone in Groveton assumes Mom and Dad have the perfect marriage. The homecoming queen married the star quarterback. Behind closed doors, Mom and Dad hate each other. I thought they'd get over it. Now...

"I've learned a lot playing college ball," Mark says. "What you do in high school doesn't mean shit. You can be the best ballplayer in your high school. The best in the county or state, but when you get to college, you're going to meet fifty other guys who can brag the same thing. You'll meet guys better than you, stronger than you, faster than you, and then you're up against better teams. The world changes when you leave Groveton."

When I leave Groveton. Decisions need to be made before that can happen: pros, college, literary competitions, scholarships. "Why are you telling me this?"

"I wish someone would have told me, but I had to figure it out on my own. You're not alone, Ry."

"Yeah, I am." And my eyes burn. I close them quickly and suck in a breath. He left. And Mom and Dad's marriage is falling apart and everything I have ever known and loved is disintegrating into ashes.

"I never left you."

"But you didn't come home. You never answered my texts." The voice falling out of my mouth isn't my own. It's strained. Tight. On the verge of breaking.

"I'm sorry, but you have to understand, until Mom or Dad reach out to me, I can't go back. I'll admit, I left them. But I get it now. I should have tried harder when it came to you. I should have called. I should have visited. I messed up, but I swear, I never left you."

I pull off my cap and run my hand through my hair. He never left me. Beth's right—I left him. My throat thickens. "I've missed you." I shake my head, trying to find a way to say the next words. "I never cared that you're gay, but I cared that you...that you left."

"Yeah." His voice becomes gruff. "I know. It's okay, Ry. Me and you, we're okay."

He stands and the action takes me off guard. We're Stones and Stone men don't touch, but the moment he puts his hand on my arm, a tentative offer, I accept and allow him to pull me into his body. Our arms wind tight around each other for one brief second. I squint my eyes to combat the tears and when we release, we both retreat to opposite sides of the room.

"So." Mark clears his throat and claps his hands together. "Tell me about Beth."

BETH

I DID GOOD. ME, BETH RISK—I did a good deed. I would have made a great fucking Girl Scout and I so would have scored the Reunite Your Jock-Sorta-Boyfriend with His Jock-Gay-Brother badge. If they don't make those, they seriously should. Ryan will look back in twenty years and not think of the girl that left in the dead of night. Nope, he'll remember the girl that gave him back his brother.

I stare up at the gray clouds moving across the sky. Ryan and I lie on the banks of a large pond located on the back end of his father's property. Just like everything else about Ryan, this spot is perfect. This day is perfect.

Propped up on an elbow, Ryan tucks a stray hair behind my ear, causing a warming tickle to caress my neck. I'm going to enjoy myself today. I'm going to laugh. I'm going to smile. I'm going to drop the chains that drag me down. Ryan's a great guy and for some reason, he's really into me. Or better, he's really into the mirage he's created.

"You're beautiful," he says.

"So are you." He truly is. I reach up and take the baseball cap he's been wearing backward off his head. He's hot with his hat on. He's gorgeous with it off. His mop of sandy hair blows with the breeze.

When I release the cap from my grasp, Ryan twines his strong hand with mine. *Strong* is an understatement. This hand can make a ball fly faster than most cars will ever go. His hand on my skin can make warmth curl in very private areas of my body.

"So..." Ryan says as he glances away and attempts to look nonchalant. I know what's eating him. On the way back from Lexington, he gave me more of his zombie story to read. Waiting for my thoughts drives him insane. "I think George and Olivia will end up together."

Five minutes. He couldn't go five minutes outside his Jeep without asking. I try to keep from smiling, but I fail miserably. He catches it and his forehead furrows. "What?"

I shrug. "You're cute when you're anxious."

"I'm not anxious."

"I like it about you." I like everything about Ryan. "The story was fabulous. Really. I'm sucked in when I read it, but I have to disagree with you. George and Olivia will not end up together."

"Why not?"

"They live in two different worlds and they're sort of two different creatures. I mean—he's a zombie and she isn't."

"But he loves her," he says doggedly. "And she loves him."

"George is going to walk away from becoming the leader of his zombie friends for her?" I ask. "Come on, you have him wanting to be the leader so badly that he crossed his best friend for the title. And do you honestly believe Olivia is going to walk away from her family for him?"

"Her family sucks." Ryan grins as if he won.

My stomach hurts like someone stabbed me. "Yeah, but it's still her family. I don't think I could like her if she walked away. What does that say about a person?"

"I think it says she's willing to live her own life."

Overhead, honking Canadian geese fly in a V formation and head south for the winter. That'll be me soon, but will I feel as free as they look? "I think it says she's selfish. How can she walk away from her dad? He needs her."

"He uses her," says Ryan.

I shrug again, not a fan of conversations that go nowhere. Ryan loosens his grip on my hand and begins to trace the ribbon tied to my wrist. He's nervous and something deep within me nudges that it's not about the story. "What's going on?"

My anxiety level increases as Ryan continues to outline the ribbon.

"I want us to be permanent," he says. "I don't like the idea of you dating other guys."

Panic seizes my chest and I feel suddenly claustrophobic. I'm leaving. Soon. As soon as Mom gets the car out of impoundment. A clamminess invades my hands and I immediately roll away from Ryan. I need air. Lots and lots of air.

I stumble to the edge of the pond and catch myself before I plummet down the two-foot ledge into the water. Catfish swim near the surface. I can't get rid of the chains, no matter how hard I try. Today was supposed to be the one day I didn't feel like I was drowning.

"What's wrong?" Ryan asks from behind me.

"Nothing," I say.

"Beth." He stops, then starts again. "I really care for you and I was hoping you felt the same way."

A single drop of rain hits the pond and ripples break onto the smooth water. He can't have feelings for me. He can't. Liking me is one thing—feeling is another. It doesn't fit with the plan. No. This isn't how it was supposed to go.

I knead my hands against my eyes. *Fuck, Beth, how did you think this was going to go? You knew you were falling for him, but he wasn't supposed to fall for you.* His words make everything real. Too real. I spin around and spit out the accusation that has become my mantra. "Guys like you don't fall for girls like me."

"What? I can't fall for pretty girls with smart mouths?"

He doesn't get it. "I'm a whore."

Ryan's head flinches as if I slapped him. Pretending I don't care what he thinks about me, I jut out my chin. Fairy tales happen, just not to me. Time to tell the prince he rescued the wrong girl.

"Two years ago, the guy every girl dreamed about spent an entire summer making me feel special. A week before school started, he told me he loved me, and I gave him my virginity. When school began, he told his friends I was a slut."

Ryan reaches out and I lean away. Some pain isn't meant to be shared. I was the idiot who believed Luke. I was the one who honestly thought I was special enough to be loved.

"He took advantage of you." An undercurrent of anger surges in his voice. "That doesn't make you a whore, that makes him an asshole."

He's missing the point. "I drink. I smoke pot. Before I came to Groveton, I was high all the time. I am not the girl you want to be permanent with. You don't see me for who I am."

"I know you turned down the chance to smoke pot on Saturday. I know the rumors at school say you've turned down the guys who smoke that shit endlessly. I know that you walk a straighter line than most of the kids at school. This is a small town, Beth. You can't breathe without someone knowing. I don't know who you pretended to be in Louisville, but I see the girl you really are now."

The way he stares at me—it's as if he doesn't even see the outside anymore. His eyes pierce me as if he can see my soul and the thought terrifies me. He can't fall for me. He can't. "Do you think you're the only guy I've made out with because I wanted to *feel* something?"

"I was different," he says with confidence.

I swallow, look away, and lie, "No, you weren't."

Ryan steps toward me and I step back. He's not reacting like he should. Ryan should be disgusted by me. He should be walking away, not coming closer. Hope lights his face. "You are the one person who can have an entire conversation with someone and stare straight into their eyes and never blink. That is, unless you're lying. Look me in the eye and tell me the truth. You fell for me that night in the barn."

My eyes dart to his and I curse internally when he smiles. "That's why you bolted."

How can someone experience so much joy when I'm in so much agony? Doesn't he understand we aren't going to work?

"You felt something for me and you didn't want to. You wanted a mindless hookup, but it blew up in your face."

I can see the memory of the night playing in his eyes, and my chest aches. He's on the verge of figuring it out. His eyebrows shoot up. "You bolted when I whispered your name. You felt something for me right then, didn't you?"

My head shakes back and forth as I whisper, "No."

Relief softens his face and a hint of hope lifts his lips. "You're falling for me like I'm falling for you. That's why you're pushing me so hard."

"Leave me alone!" Filled with the need to flee, I turn. If I run fast enough, I can leave behind the awful memories of my past and Ryan's beautiful words can never wind their way into my soul. I step into air. My heart races to my throat as I fall forward. The pond. Terrified of the water, I scream. Strong arms weave around my waist and pull me to solid ground.

I lean my back into Ryan's chest and clutch his arms. My fingernails dig into his skin like hooks. If I fall in, I'm going to drown. The weights upon me are too heavy to stay afloat. My only option is to sink.

I suck in a few breaths and after I take one longer one, Ryan lowers his head to my ear. "Are you okay?"

"I'm fine."

"You're shaking. Fine doesn't mean you shake."

"I can't swim, but I'm fine now."

"You can't swim," he repeats.

"No." A drop of rain lands on my head and slithers down my scalp. "We should go." The day is ruined. "It's going to rain."

Ryan loosens his grip on me and within seconds, he sweeps me into the air and cradles me against his chest. My face is devastatingly close to his. I blink several times. "What are you doing?"

Instead of answering, he jumps into the pond.

Dizziness overcomes me and my blood pressure tanks. Water rises and smacks my face, my hair, my clothing. My arms strangle his neck. I'm going to drown. "Ryan!"

"I've got you," he says in a calm tone. "You're okay."

He wades deeper into the cold water. Gravity calls for me to slide out of his arms and become constrained by the water below. I'll suffocate with my eyes open. My hold on him tightens. "Take me back!"

Water penetrates my shoes, my jeans, the back of my shirt. It pours over my stomach and I grow heavier and heavier. Cold wetness teases my skin—calling out a hateful, mimicking laugh. I bury my head in the crook of his neck. I don't want to die. I don't.

He stops and whispers into my ear, "Look at me."

I don't have the strength to lift my head. Instead, I ease it to his shoulder and open my eyes.

"I'm going to teach you how to float."

I tighten my grip. "You're going to kill me."

"Trust me."

"I can't," I whisper. I trusted Scott, my mother, and my father. I trusted Luke, my aunt, and Isaiah. All people who left me. All people who faded into darkness. My heart has been ripped multiple times and each time I repaired it on my own. I know my limits and if someone rips me apart again, I'll never find the strength to pick up the pieces.

An intensity warms his brown eyes and he gently hugs my body to his. "You can."

I suck in a breath. Ryan's doing it. He's giving me the same look Chris gives Lacy. The same look Noah gives Echo. Maybe I can. My heart thunders as I reach up and grab the hair curling near the base of Ryan's neck. "Don't drop me."

"I won't." Ryan's voice is so soothing—so confident—I almost believe him. Maybe I can believe him. He won't drop me. He'll hold me. He swore it.

"It's time to let go," he says.

One breath. Another. He won't let me go. I loosen my grip and Ryan immediately lowers his arms. Water floods over my body and laps against his chest. My head snaps up and I kick and splash to stay above water. Panic commands my lungs. He's taller than me, which means I wouldn't be able to stand in the water. "Take me back."

Ryan lowers his forehead to mine. His warm breath fans over my face. "I will never let you go."

He won't let me go. He won't. "Okay."

Ryan skims his nose along my cheek and goose bumps rise on my neck. He pulls his head back. I fight the urge to cling to him. Ryan said he wouldn't drop me and he won't. He won't.

My hair becomes weightless in the water and licks my cheeks. Ryan's strong arms reaffirm his promise to me. "Tilt your head back," he says.

I inhale and do as he asks. Water enters my ears and my muscles flinch with fear. Ryan keeps his firm hold. "Spread your arms to your sides and arch your back. Let your legs float."

As I slowly follow instructions, Ryan steps from me. I jerk toward him. "Ryan!"

He shakes his head. "I'm not letting go. I'm giving you room. Keep your head tilted back."

Head tilted back. Arms and legs spread out. My pulse throbs in my ears. Ryan's voice is muffled, but I can read his lips. "Relax. Breathe."

Relax. Head tilted back. Arms and legs spread out. Breathe. I stare at the clouds overhead and the trees hanging over the pond. Relax. Head tilted back. Arms and legs spread out. Breathe.

A pair of birds circle in the sky. It's a playful dance. They spread their wings and let the gentle wind pull them up and over. Down and around. God, I wish I was free. I wish I was a bird floating in the breeze. I close my eyes and pretend I'm a bird. My muscles melt. The water makes a rhythmic swishing melody in my ears. Away and near. Away and near.

I'm a bird—floating on the breeze. A gentle nudge in the back of my mind whispers that I know this feeling. I've owned this feeling for years. This feeling of drifting, swaying, floating. I'm floating. Through the water I hear Ryan's sweet muffled voice: "You're doing it."

I open my eyes and see that glorious smile on his lips. The smile that is for me. Me alone. I go to smile back and I realize I already am. I'm smiling. My stomach clenches and the chains return. Oh God, no. I've fallen in love with him. I've done it. I've given him power over me.

RYAN

BETH IS A BEAUTIFUL FLOATING VISION. Her black hair drifts on the surface of the water and the peaceful smile I love graces her lips. Her eyes no longer have their glazed guard. They are as calm and deep as the ocean. For the first time ever, Beth is letting me see her soul and if I had any doubts before, they're gone. I'm in love with Beth Risk.

Beth blinks and the smile fades. Several raindrops plop into the pond and the sound of the incoming storm taps against the trees. Beth sinks and I catch her before her head goes under.

"Let me go!" Her grip isn't nearly as tight as I carry her onto the shore. The light rain becomes steady and quickly saturates my hair. I place Beth on her feet and my heart plummets. She's slammed shut her walls.

She pivots on her feet and darts toward Scott's tree line. Beth trusted me in the water. She cares for me. I know it. The promise I made to her is forever—I will not let her go. I chase after her and grab her by her waist before she steps into the woods. "Dammit, Beth! Stop running from me!"

My pulse hammers through my body. She's been running

from me from the moment I met her. No matter how hard I try to hold on to her, she finds a way to slip out of my grasp.

Not anymore. Not today.

Water streaks down her cheeks and her hair clings to her head. She shivers violently in the warm fall storm. I rub my hands up and down her arms.

"Let me go," she yells again over the rain.

"No." I move my hand to her cheek. Those eyes that looked so peaceful moments before are crazy with panic. I want her to trust me. I want her to feel what I'm feeling. "I'm in love with you."

"No! Please. Just don't!" Her lower lip trembles and she unsuccessfully smacks at the hand holding her waist.

"Tell me why you're fighting me. What are you scared of?"

Beth's fingernails dig into the skin of my arm. "I'm scared of nothing."

"I love you," I say again and Beth's panic rises in intensity. She pushes at my arms. The words scare her. She's scared of love. "I love you, Beth."

She raises her face and fire rages in her eyes. "Stop saying that!"

"Why?" Without meaning to, I shake her gently. I want her to say it back. "I'm in love with you. Tell me why I can't say it to you."

"Because you'll leave!" she screams.

Beth's chest heaves as if she ran a race. My hold on her tightens. Rain beats against the pond and the trees, creating a strange deafness from the world surrounding us.

"I couldn't." Never. Leaving her would be like tearing off my own arm. I've never been in love before. I thought I had been, but I wasn't. This overwhelming, encompassing feeling is love. It's not perfect and it's messy as hell. And it's exactly what I need.

She steps back and the pouring rain makes it impossible to keep my grip on her slick arms, but I do my best to hold on. My heart aches. Beth's doing it again. She's walking away. Desperation seizes my muscles. If she leaves, I'll lose her for good and I can't. Not when I just found her. "Don't walk away from me."

"I have a gypsy soul." Beth yanks her hands out of my grasp and stumbles backward. "We won't work."

Why is she always slipping through my fingers? "You're the one leaving me. Not the other way around."

She wraps her hands over her stomach as she continues to walk backward. "I'm sorry."

Anger erupts from deep inside and takes control. I don't lose and I won't lose her. Beth turns and runs for the forest. She's fast, but I'm faster. I grab Beth by the waist, yank her to face me, tunnel my fingers into her hair, and kiss her.

She tastes like fresh rain and smells like crushed roses. I don't care that she's not kissing back. I move my lips against hers and hug her body to mine. I love Beth and she needs to know that. Know it in her head. More importantly, know it in her heart.

Her fingers lightly tickle my neck as I taste her warm lips. She answers by hesitantly kissing my lower lip. Beth tilts her head and we both open our mouths. Her tongue meets mine and I swear the world explodes around us. Her hands tangle in my wet hair and she presses her body into me. She roams my back, and my fingers hungrily touch the soft contours of her waist, then drift lower, gliding along the curves of her thighs. I won't let her go. I won't. I love her.

Beth gasps for air as she pulls my head closer to her body. My lips trail kisses down her neck and I savor each delicious taste of her skin.

Her hands slide to my chest, curl into fists, and she pushes me away as she takes a step back. "I can't do this!" And she runs off into the rain.

I've stared at the computer since ten. At eleven, I'm still staring. The cursor blinks on and off. I've got no words. The decision has to be made. Do George the zombie and Olivia the human fall in love and stay together, or is Beth right? Am I forcing my characters into something so unrealistic that no reader would ever believe it?

My cell vibrates again. I glance at it in anticipation. Maybe it's Beth. I sink lower in my chair. It's Gwen. Again.

Gwen: why aren't you answering?

Because I'm not in love with you. She's not used to being denied. I'm not used to denying her and her constant barrage of texts and calls throughout the night shoves the knife further into my windpipe. I'm in love with a girl who doesn't love me back.

Part of me wants to answer Gwen and go back to my previous life. Nothing was complicated then. Nothing hurt too much or seemed confusing. Everything was planned. Perfect.

On the outside, that is. How did I miss that everything internal was a mess? My parents. Mark. Me and Gwen. Lacy. Is Chris a mess? Logan? How many more of us are faking the facade? How many more of us are pretending to be something we're not? Even better, how many of us will have the courage to be ourselves regardless of what others think?

I flip off my computer screen and the overhead light, yank off my shirt, and lie down in bed, even though I know sleep won't come. The problem with feeling too much is how the hurt consumes every part of me. A slow agonizing throb aches in my head.

Rain continues to beat against the roof. A storm front that was supposed to hit tomorrow flew into the area today and stalled out over town. Part of me doesn't want the storm to pass. This was our rain—mine and Beth's.

"Can I come in?"

I jerk up at the sweet sound of Beth's voice coming from the other side of my open window. My fingers fumble with the screen and it bangs against the house as it falls to the ground. I hold my hand out to her and help as she swings one drenched jean-clad leg over the frame, then the other.

The dim light from my alarm clock casts a strange blue shadow over Beth as she shakes uncontrollably next to the window. Her wet hair clings to her head and her clothes cleave to her body. Drops of rain slither down her face and her teeth chatter. "I hhaadd ttoo sseee youu."

"Here, use this to towel off." I drape a blanket around her shoulders, stare at her to convince myself she's really here, then rummage through my drawer. I pull out a T-shirt and a pair of cotton sweatpants and hand them to her. In one quick motion, I turn. "Change. I promise I won't look."

Though I want to. She's here and I'll do anything to keep her from running. Beth feels like this storm. Constant and persistent as a whole, but the more I get close and try to clutch the individual drops of rain, the more the water falls out of my hands.

I hear the sound of wet material stubbornly moving

against her skin and then the sound of cotton being tugged over her head. "Okay," she says in a small voice.

I suck in a breath and suppress the groan. She's absolutely killing me. My T-shirt ends at the middle of her bare thighs. "Are you going to put the pants on?"

Beth shrugs. "They'll just fall off."

She's right. I force my eyes to her face. "I'm glad you're here. I've been worried about you." About us.

Beth fidgets with the hem of my T-shirt. "I can't say it back."

And she crushes me into nothing.

"But I want to."

Hope. A single thread exists and it keeps Beth and me alive. "Because you want to love me or because you do?"

She straightens out the shirt and runs her fingers through her hair. "What if I do? Feel that way?"

I let her words sink in. Beth loves me. My heart settles and I swallow to find my bearings.

"Because if I do..." She stalls and I start to wonder if her trembling is from the cold or from her emotions. "And you..." Beth sucks in air, then lifts her head so that her eyes plead with mine. "I can't say it, but I...I want to be here...with you."

We're still on shaky ground—Beth and I. If I do the wrong thing, she'll bolt. The rain picks up and patters harder against the roof. My ribbon clings to her wrist. Beth doesn't believe in the unseen. She needs a physical reminder that I mean what I say.

My eyes dart around the room and discover the perfect object on my dresser. I brush past Beth, grab the clear bottle, and pour the scant remains of cologne out the window.

"What are you doing?" she asks as if I lost my mind. Who knows, I probably have.

I hold the bottle out into the rain and watch as the steady flow slowly fills it. When there is enough, enough that Beth can clearly see, I close the bottle and hand it to her.

She raises a skeptical eyebrow, but accepts the bottle.

"It's our rain, Beth."

Her head barely shakes to show her confusion while I rub the back of my neck and search for my courage. "I told you I loved you in this rain and when you doubt my words, I want you to look at this bottle."

Beth's forehead wrinkles and she stares at the gift I've given her. "I don't..." she starts. "I don't have anything to give you."

"You're here," I answer. "It's all I want."

Her fingers tighten around the bottle. "I still can't say it."

"I don't care."

Beth crawls onto my bed and I join her by lying like we did the first night she came to my room. If she needs space, I'll give her space. This time, Beth immediately places her head on me. The bare skin of my chest screams in protest of her cold, wet hair. I focus on not flinching or shivering. I won't give her a reason to turn away.

Her arm relaxes over my stomach and, in her hand, she clutches the bottle of rain.

"I'm scared," she says.

Are her running days over? Am I handing my heart to a girl who's going to break it? I choose not to think about it and instead wrap my arms tighter around Beth and bring her closer to me. "So am I. But we'll be okay. I promise."

"You could really hurt me if you wanted."

"But I won't."

"Say it again," she whispers, and there's heartfelt sincerity in her voice that tells me everything I want to hear. My heart explodes and a surging, powerful warmth rushes through my bloodstream. She loves me. I know she does.

"I love you." I kiss the top of her head, never feeling so complete in my life.

"Can I stay?" she asks.

"Yes."

She willingly molds her body to mine. We snuggle closer together and I shut my eyes, welcoming sleep. Beth's here and she's mine and I silently promise to never let go.

BETH

SITTING ON THE BED OF LOGAN'S TRUCK, Ryan keeps me tucked close between his legs and his hands rest on the sides of my hips. Ryan's sweatshirt wraps around me like a minidress and the heat from his body protects me from the chilly autumn Friday evening. He's enveloped me in a small, warm bubble. Wood in the bonfire crackles and snaps and creates a rich scent that relaxes me. I cuddle against him, and the deep rhythmic vibrations of his voice lull me into a sense of ease. Ryan has created the sensation of comforter-out-of-the-dryer warmth.

He runs his hand through my hair and whispers, "You're falling asleep. Do you want me to take you home?"

"I'm awake." I pretend that he will hold me forever. Today, I called Mom before gym. Like always, good news comes with bad. She got the car out of the impoundment lot, but she also bailed Trent out of jail and she was somehow shocked that jail hadn't changed his thunderstorm disposition. She asked me to come get her a week from Monday—after her social security check comes in. I have ten days left with Ryan.

Ryan kisses the top of my head and returns to the same

discussion he and his friends have had every day at lunch—baseball playoffs. Lacy sits next to me in the same exact position with Chris. She drinks from a longneck. "I'm happy you and Ryan are together. It's nice to be around someone else who never says the word *baseball*." Lacy takes another drink and shakes her head. "I take that back—not someone else. I'm glad it's you. I'm glad you're back."

She's buzzing. I'm not. It's strange to be at a party and not be blitzed. The past two weeks have been strange. Now that Ryan has done whatever popular people do to announce their commitments, his friends treat me like one of their own and I'm not sure how I feel about it. I mean—they're jocks. All the guys standing around or sitting on this truck are big, huge, can't-stop-talking-about-baseball jocks. None of them has made me feel inconsequential or like a freak. They're nothing like Luke and his friends, who drank every chance they got. Not one of these guys has touched alcohol tonight. Ryan and his friends have an early morning game and they want to be at one hundred percent.

Lacy holds out her hand and waves it until I take it. "I'm happy I have a best friend again."

"All right." Chris swings Lacy into his arms. "She's talking sentimental, which means it's time to dance." With her laughing uncontrollably, he carries her to the crowd dancing near the bonfire.

Ryan's lips graze my earlobe, sending seductive shivers through my body. "Walk with me?"

Anywhere. "Okay."

Ryan jumps off the bed of the truck and when I scoot to the end of the tailgate, he places his hands on my hips to help me down. I don't need the help. I'm perfectly capable of getting myself down, but I enjoy the feel of his hands on me. His warmth burns through my clothes and onto my skin.

He lifts me and my body slowly slides against his. I want to kiss him and from the hunger smoldering in his eyes, he feels the same way. He takes my hand in his and leads me away from the bonfire, away from other people, into the woods, and into a world of our own.

The moon creates a silvery glow and the babble of the creek gives the moment a mystical quality. The darkness isn't so frightening with Ryan. With him I can believe that I am a princess with a wreath of flowers and ribbons crowning my head and he is my prince sworn to protect me from the evils in the night.

Ryan releases my hand and turns his baseball cap to wear it backward, a sure sign he's going to kiss me. My insides flutter. The enduring cockiness that exudes from Ryan fades and he shoves his hands in his pockets while shifting. "I wasn't going to do the writing competition, but I am now. I talked to Coach today and told him I'm not playing next Saturday's game."

"Why wouldn't you have done the competition?" I'm confused. Ryan has a gift. Why wouldn't he use it?

"My dad, he didn't want..." Ryan shakes his head. "It's not important. You've opened my eyes to a lot of things and I wanted to let you know that you're a big part of this. A huge part." He shrugs and for the first time I see Ryan unsure of himself. It's an odd thing to watch from someone who is always nothing less than perfection.

"You'll be perfect." Some lives are blessed. His is. Mine isn't. I'm not sure how I helped, but at least he'll have another good memory of me. I have ten days to tuck in as many good memories as I can for the both of us. I don't want him to hate me forever. I want him to look back on our time together and smile.

Ryan sucks in a deep breath and his continued track down the path of uncomfortable makes me restless. "My parents are going to be out of town for a week starting tomorrow. They won't be back until next Sunday."

Awesome. "I get to use the front door?"

"Yeah. If you want. Don't get me wrong, I want you to come...I mean I want you to sleep with me...I mean." Ryan swears under his breath. "I want you at my house if you want to be there."

If it was anyone else stumbling through that awkwardness, I'd laugh, but it's Ryan, so I choke on the chuckles. "Are you asking me to have sex?"

His eyes widen. "No. I would never ask that. I mean, I would. Someday. Now if I could. But no. No. We'll wait. Ah hell, Beth, can I screw this up any more than I already have?"

I smile at the word *screw* and Ryan catches it. He says a word I thought only pops out of my mouth. Ryan's cheeks turn red and the blush on his face makes me blush. God, we're standing here acting like two virgins.

In fact, this whole week we've acted like virgins. We do this uncomfortable dance when I slip into his room and climb into his bed. He waits forever to kiss me, no matter how many signals I give. And when we do kiss—the fire between us is hotter than flames in hell. Then we reach certain points where neither one of us seem to want to cross the line. I'm used to guys pushing forward. I guess I could cross the lines, but the thought frightens me. Such a squeamish-little-girl feeling makes me want to slap myself. It's not like I've never seen a guy's penis before.

Ryan readjusts his hat and I tilt my head as I understand the agony marring his beautiful face. "You're a virgin," I say.

I curse internally when Ryan flips his hat back and yanks the bill hard over his face. *Go ahead, Beth, embarrass the boy a little more. Why don't you ask him if he has a small dick too?* Talk about screwing things up. This is not the memory I want Ryan to have of me, but the knowledge he's supplied will ensure I can give him something he'll never forget: his first time.

I close the distance between us. He's stiff when I wrap my arms around him and press my cheek against his chest. "I don't care. In fact, it makes you more perfect."

Ryan sighs loudly, but his body relaxes under my touch. His strong hands caress my back and weave through my hair. "I'm not perfect, Beth."

"Yes, you are."

"Ryan!" Chris yells close to the tree line. "Get your sorry ass over here. Logan took on a dare."

"Of course he did," mumbles Ryan. He keeps his arm around my shoulder and leads me back into the pasture.

Logan stands beside Chris and wears a crazy grin on his face. "Do you still have those bungee cords in your Jeep?"

"Yes," Ryan answers hesitantly.

An excited gleam that frightens even me sparkles in Logan's eyes. "Great. Let's go."

Chris and Logan head toward the parked cars. I nudge Ryan when he stays still. "Go."

He traces circles on my arm. "It'll only be a few minutes."

"It doesn't bother me if you want to hang with your friends."

The sincerity swims in his eyes. "But I'm leaving you alone."

"Not sure if you noticed, but sometimes I prefer to be alone."

Ryan flips his hat back around, leans down, and his kiss warms areas that sweatshirts can't touch. The second his lips leave mine, he pulls his baseball cap off and places it on top of my head. He laughs as the bill falls forward and covers my face. Not wanting him to take it back, I spin it and wear it backward. "You have a big head."

"Naw," he says. "You're just small."

With pride, I watch Ryan stride across the pasture. He's a natural athlete with his broad shoulders and strong arms. My heart dances. For the next ten days—he's mine.

"I can't believe you let Ryan put that hat on your head. He sweats in it." Gwen emerges from the darkness and I immediately think of my fear of demons waiting in the shadows, ready to grab me in the dead of night.

"It doesn't bother me."

"If I was you I'd want to hide my hair too," she says, standing unusually close to me.

I'm going soft if she thinks she's safe speaking to me that way. Allison would love this chick. They share the same awful taste in clothes. "I remember pushing you to the ground and making you cry in elementary school for fucking with Lacy."

"I remember you wearing the same damn dress with holes and those pathetic ribbons." She stares at my wrist, then at my jeans. "I see your tastes haven't changed."

"No," I say. "But Ryan's have."

Her face reddens and I smile. Damn, I really enjoy being me. I give her credit—Gwen quickly rejoins the game. "Look, I'm trying to be helpful. Rumor at school says Ryan is only with you over a dare. Ryan and his friends take dares very seriously and he'd string you along in order to win. Don't get me wrong, he's a good guy, but he's a guy, you know? I would hate to see you take a fall once the dare's complete."

My entire body tenses. It's the truth. He did ask me out on a dare, but I'm not a dare anymore. I'm not. "Wow, Gwen. Thanks for your concern. Is this where you ask me to braid your hair and then we'll giggle about getting to first base with a boy?"

Gwen twines her golden hair around a finger. I should bring her over to Scott as Exhibit B for why I hate blondes. "I'm trying to be your friend, Beth."

"If you wanted to be my friend, you wouldn't have tried to slip your tongue in Ryan's mouth last Tuesday when you cornered him after baseball practice."

Blood drains from her face and I darkly chuckle to rub in her embarrassment. She didn't think he would tell me. "Do I sound like a dare now?"

"Why haven't you dropped out of the homecoming court yet? They're going to take yearbook pictures next week, so this would be the time to leave."

"I'm not dropping out." I'll be leaving soon, but I won't drop out. Ryan wowed me and I lost the dare. I have ten days to keep my word to him.

Gwen eyes me coolly. "I thought you didn't want the nomination."

I shrug. "I changed my mind."

"You're not going to win," she says. "Some people don't like you."

My spine straightens. "Do I look like I give a fuck what people think of me?"

"You should," she says. "Because Ryan does. If you cared for him, you'd walk away."

Gwen doesn't wait for me to reply. She tosses that sickening yellow hair over her shoulder and struts away like she's queen. Unwanted demons race into my mind, taunting me with her words. I'm only a dare. Ryan doesn't love me. I'm no good for him.

Maybe she's right. Maybe she's wrong. None of it matters. I'm here for ten days and even if that wasn't the case, I have a bottle of rain to prove her wrong.

RYAN

CHRIS AND I BYPASS A WOMAN with three screaming children and an old guy guarding the shopping carts. It's Tuesday evening and at Chris's insistence, I drove the two of us into Louisville so we could shop at the Super Wal-Mart.

"Do you want to tell me why we're here?" I ask. We have a Wal-Mart near the freeway back in Groveton, but it's a much smaller version and thirty years older.

"We know the people who work at our Wal-Mart. More importantly, our parents know the people who work there." Chris swings to the right, away from the food section and toward the pharmacy.

"So?"

"You want to keep Beth a secret from your parents, right?"

I cringe when he says it that way, but in the end, it's the truth. I want Beth to be my girl in every aspect of my life, but I need to pick my battles. I'm going to nail the writing competition, make the decision regarding going pro or going to college, then own up to keeping Beth. "What does that have to do with Wal-Mart?"

Chris cuts into an aisle and waves his hand at the merchandise in front of him. "This."

Condoms. Everywhere. I scratch the back of my neck and try to think of anything to say, but there isn't a statement that could make this moment less uncomfortable.

"You need condoms," says Chris.

Chris and I engulf the entire cramped aisle in front of the pharmacy. The middle-aged woman with the three kids eyes us as she walks past. "I'm taking it slow with Beth."

"Slow wasn't the position I caught the two of you in yesterday. I'm happy you're happy, but none of us are going to be happy if little Ryans and Beths pop out of that girl."

Point taken. Sex may not be in the plan, but it's best to be prepared. "What do you use?"

He shrugs. "The normal shit. Are you going to do it? The writing competition?"

"Yeah." The normal shit. That narrows it down. I survey the assortment before me. Colored, ribbed, lubricated, and because this experience isn't God-awful enough—they have sizes.

"We need you against Eastwick," Chris says flatly. "We're a game behind Northside so we need two wins in order to move into first place. If we don't win against Eastwick on Saturday, then it doesn't matter if we win or lose against Northside on Monday."

"I can't play fully for both games anyhow. There's a state law about how many innings I can pitch, remember?" How the hell am I supposed to know what size I am? I don't go around staring at guys' dicks. I don't think I'm small and I sure as hell wouldn't buy small even if I was. A guy has to have some pride.

"But you could guarantee us the win on Saturday against Eastwick, then play the later innings against Northside. You've dug us out of a hole before in later innings and if we get low on Monday, you could dig us out. Get the glow-in-the-dark ones. I bet Beth's into freaky shit."

My stomach clenches. "Beth is not into freaky shit."

"I saw her tattoo. She's a freaky-shit kind of girl. Look, I get that you don't want to back out of a competition, even if it is writing, but I'm not going to lie. You're scaring the team. You're the leader, dawg, and what does it say when our leader walks from a game? The guys are starting to question if you're losing your edge."

I zero in on Chris. "What does that mean?"

Chris meets my glare and I discover he's one of the "guys." "I've never seen you walk from a dare in my life and you walked from the one with Beth. You just gave up."

"I didn't give up. I fell for her."

"Exactly. You could have bagged the dare by bringing her to the next party, but you threw down the white flag the moment you hooked up with her. She's got her hooks in you and I want to make sure she's worth it."

Not liking the tone or turn of this conversation, I fold my arms over my chest. "What are you trying to say?"

Chris's muscles ripple as he inches near me. "You've changed since she's come to Groveton and I'm not sure I like it. It was us and baseball—what you used to care about. Then she comes around and it's me, you, Beth, writing, and sometimes baseball. You never once talked about going to college and now you want to walk from the pros. Who the hell are you?"

Who the hell am I? Who the hell is the guy in front of me?

I step within swinging distance and, for the first time in my life, I'm willing to hit my best friend. "I'm the same damn guy who's led this team year after year and I'm the same damn guy who encouraged you to date our best friend. I can't help it you never looked close enough to see I could be more than a man with a ball and a bat."

We stare at each other. Unblinking. Unmoving. Until Chris flexes his fingers and gestures to a box of studded condoms. "That's some freaky shit too."

I pull on the bill of my hat. What the hell? Part of me wants to punch him. Part of me wants to ask what just happened between us. I go the easy route and let Chris off the hook. "Show me what you get."

What if she is into freaky shit? What if she wants ribbed? When do you need lubricated? I don't even want to think about the kind that says they'll make her tingle.

"Does she have a latex allergy? That could suck if she does. I've heard stories of girls puffing up like blowfish and having to be rushed to the emergency room."

My heart stops. "Really?"

"Naw, I'm messing with you, but I'd ask about the latex allergy before you put it on."

Two teenage girls walk down the aisle. One sips on a slushy and twirls her hair. They glance at each other and giggle. Heat rises on the back of my neck.

"I'm not you, Ry," Chris says after they round the corner. "I'm not going to college and I don't have the pros knocking on my door. Winning state this year, that's my dream, and I need you in order to complete it. Promise me that you won't let anything get in the way of that."

Since I was seven years old I've glanced to my right and

seen Chris backing me up between third and second. He saved plays I screwed up because of my pitch. My insides twist with the startling revelation—regardless of the path I choose, come graduation, Chris isn't going to be the guy on my right anymore. "You guys can take Eastwick without me and you know it. Northside is the team with the hitters. In the spring, we're going to state. The only game I'm missing is Saturday and I wouldn't walk away if I didn't believe that you guys have it covered."

Chris studies me and I silently urge him to be okay with this. He's my best friend and I need *us* to be okay. He offers me his hand and I exhale.

"Swear it, dawg."

I clasp it. "Sworn."

An easy grin spreads across his face. "Pick something out and let's get out of here."

I try one more time. "Tell me what you get."

Chris places his hands on his hips. "I've never bought condoms before. Lacy wants to wait until we graduate."

BETH

IT'S FRIDAY NIGHT and I inhale deeply before I knock. I have three days left until I leave. Ryan deserves better than me, but tonight I can pretend I'm good enough. The door opens and my heart starts, stops, and skips over itself when Ryan flashes that glorious smile with the right mixture of warmth and dimples.

"Hi," he says. His voice alone creates pleasing goose bumps on my arms.

"Hey." *I'm going to make love to you tonight.* Feeling shy, I glance away and I want to kick myself. Where's the girl who could frighten football players with one look?

"You're early." Ryan closes the door and I move straight for his bedroom. Twice, Ryan tried to convince me to hang in another room, but being anywhere else in his perfect house reminds me that I can never measure up.

"Scott and Allison went to bed early." I lean against the door frame to his room and try to calm the thousands of feathers swirling in my stomach. "Chris isn't stopping by, is he?"

"No. He knows I'm seeing you tonight and that I have to

be up early for my writing competition." Ryan cups my waist with his hand. His thumb sneaks underneath my shirt and draws circles onto my skin.

I notice a bundle of papers tied together with two pink ribbons on the middle of his bed. "What's that?"

Ryan places some space between us, but slides his fingers into mine. "A finished copy of 'George and Olivia.' It's yours. So are the ribbons."

"Cool." Because it is. Ryan will do well at so many things when he graduates.

"Take a look at the title page." Ryan releases me and I immediately miss his touch.

I plop on the bed, untie the bow, and blink—*Dedicated to the girl I love: Beth Risk*. My fingers skim the page as if caressing the words will make them more real. George was a short story for class. Olivia came to life because Ryan couldn't stop thinking about the story. He dedicated it to me because... because he actually loves me.

A twinge of pain flashes in my chest. I could be happy here in Groveton. Scott's not so bad. In fact, I kinda enjoy waking in the morning and telling him about school. I appreciate how Scott nods while I talk and when I stop, how he asks questions to show he heard what I said. I adore sitting in class next to Lacy and listening to her ramble about useless gossip. I love health class and despite what Allison said, I'm becoming fond of science. I like watching Logan, Chris, and Ryan one-up each other. I like...I like...

I run my hand over the paper again. I love Ryan. I'm in love with him. I love how he smiles. I love how he moves. I love his hands on my body and his lips on mine. I love how he laughs. I love how he makes me laugh. I love how he can smooth away the roughness and make me feel like someone worth loving. "It's perfect."

RYAN

IN THE MIDDLE OF MY BED, Beth touches the title page for a third time. She likes the gift. The queasy anxiety I've had all day fades. The mattress sinks when I sit beside her. Crimson stains her cheeks as I brush my fingers against her skin. It's hard to believe she's the same girl from Taco Bell. Beth was hard and shut down that night. The girl on my bed is open and soft.

The physical differences are obvious. I run my hand through the sleek, silky strands and she edges away. She hates what I see, but I don't. One inch of golden-blond stretches from her roots. The blond highlights the blackness of the rest of her hair. I love the black. I love the blond. I'd hate to see either one of them go. Somehow both suit her.

I take the manuscript from her and place it on the nightstand. Her hands shake and she bites her lower lip. She's nervous and I don't know why. "Are you okay?"

She nods but refuses eye contact. "I wish I was perfect for you."

"You are perfect for me."

Beth rests her hand on my inner thigh and her fingers

slowly trace the seam of my jeans. Fire races through me and flames lick areas very close to her fingers. Beth starts again. "No, I wish..." And stops.

Even though part of me wants nothing more than for her to keep touching me, I force my hand over hers. When Beth struggles with words it means she's on the verge of saying something worth hearing. Her emotions confuse her. Maybe tonight, she'll finally find the courage to say the words I'm longing to hear.

"I wish..." She sighs. "I wish I never had sex with Luke. I wish I could take back so many things, but I can't. I wish I could be someone worthy of you."

Beth is on my bed. Her body is close to mine and her fingers hold on to me, but something in her voice makes me feel like she's slipping away again.

"I'm not perfect," I tell her. "And you're exactly who I want you to be—you."

"I want you to be happy," she says and even though she's physically near me, I look into her eyes and see the glaze creating a wall.

Beth slides a leg over my body and straddles me. Her parts are right on top of mine and the fire within threatens to become an inferno. She knots her fingers in my hair, sending chills along my neck and down my spine. Her lips graze my earlobe, followed by a gentle tug with her teeth. Warm breath tickles my ear. "Let me make you happy."

My mind's a mess and a small voice yells at me that she's leaving. But she can't be. She's here, in front of me, driving me insane by pressing her body against me. My hands grasp her moving hips, physically keeping her near. She grabs hold of the hem of my shirt and I let her ease it over my head. Her fingernails whisper against the muscles of my abs and clear thought no longer exists as she explores downward.

We fall backward onto the bed and Beth continues to move with me. I moan when her hair brushes my chest and her lips kiss my neck. Against my skin, her mouth tilts into a smile. My hands wander underneath her shirt. Her body is burning hot under my touch and I want her skin brushing against mine. I yank her shirt over her head and kiss that blessed spot right between her breasts.

Beth gasps and I no longer want her to be in control. I want this. I want to be the one to make her happy. I want to make her feel good. Wrapping my arm around her stomach, I twist both of us and flip her onto her back on my bed. I love the feel of her underneath me.

She tangles her leg with mine and her fingers lace in my hair, tempting me down again. My hand glides along the curve of her waist and I want to touch places I know will make her move in rhythm with me. My fingers drift against her stomach and I hesitate when I come into contact with her belly button ring.

Our first night together in the barn creeps into the forefront of my brain. I asked her a question that night and she never answered. I slip off her even though her hands pressure me to stay. "What's your tattoo mean?"

BETH

WHAT DOES MY TATTOO MEAN? Five seconds ago my body was blazing and five words freeze me like an arctic wind. Ryan brushes my hair off my shoulder and tilts his head as he waits for an answer.

I keep eye contact as the devil inside me fights with my desire to tell Ryan something I've never told anyone before. "It means freedom."

Ryan readjusts so that his body touches mine. His abs ripple as he moves. Oh my God, he's incredible and I'm shirtless on his bed and he wants to have a conversation. Ryan can be so...so...frustrating.

"Why did you choose that tattoo?"

I glance away and blow out air through my lips. There are some secrets that are mine and mine alone. Why can't Ryan work with me? Why can't he let me give him this night? I lean up and kiss his lips. Ryan presses back, but he keeps the exchange short. I flop back on the bed. "You're straight, right?"

Ryan chuckles. "Very." And to prove his point he makes my toes curl when he skims a finger in the narrow valley between my breasts, down my stomach, and plays with the edge of my low-rise jeans. "I'm dying right now."

I refuse to give him the satisfaction of closing my eyes in pleasure. There should be another badge in that for me. "Then why are we talking?"

"What do you know about me?" he asks.

I shrug. "A lot."

"Tell me some of it."

Oookaaay. "You love baseball and writing. Your gay brother can kick most guys' asses."

Ryan laughs and I smile. I love his laughter. It reminds me of music.

An ache darkens his eyes and his hand stops flirting with the elastic of my underwear. "You know a lot more than that."

"I do." I link my fingers with his and wish I could take his pain. I know his parents hate each other and that this trip is an attempt to save their marriage. They won't divorce, but it's an attempt to rekindle the flame. I also know that watching his family fall apart is killing Ryan.

More importantly, beyond all the hurt that pricks at him, I know that I bring a smile to his face and I know that he loves me.

"I know very little about you and I want to know everything."

And we're done. "You know plenty." He knows enough. I roll away and reach for my shirt on the pillow beside him. Ryan snatches it and tosses it across the room. "You're not running from me anymore, Beth."

Hot anger courses through my bloodstream. "I'm not running. I thought we were going to enjoy each other tonight and obviously you're not up for it."

"Tell me about your dad." Ryan stays lazily stretched on the bed while I straighten my spine by his pillows. How can he be so arrogant as to think he deserves answers from me?

"That is none of your business." That's no one's business.

"Come on. Tell me something. Tell me about your mom." His voice becomes taunting and I curl my legs into my chest.

"Her name is Sky." There, I gave him something.

"You can do better." Anger creeps into his patient tone. "Tell me why Scott won't let you see her. Tell me something. Anything. You told me once that you aren't scared of anything. Right now I see a liar, because you're terrified."

My head snaps up. "Fuck you."

Ryan doesn't flinch. "Tell me why you're back in Groveton. Why aren't you still in Louisville with your mom?"

"I was arrested, all right?" My pulse thunders at every pressure point in my body. Will this be it? The final blow that pushes him from me? Three days. I have three days until I leave and this is not how tonight was supposed to go.

Not expecting that answer, Ryan's eyebrows furrow together. Nausea spins in my stomach. He's judging me. I know it. Ryan grabs hold of my ankle before I can step onto the floor. "You already know my opinion on running. What were you arrested for?"

Sweat breaks out on my skin. I can imagine the thoughts in his head and his impending judgment. "Does it matter?"

He loosens his grip as his fingers slowly slide up my leg and massage my calf through the material of my jeans. "I don't care who you were in Louisville because I'm in love with the girl you are now."

Love. That word from him makes my heart flutter and my head hurt. "Then why do you want to know?"

"Because I want you to trust me."

Blah. Trust. "I'm half-naked on your bed. We could be doing so many other things."

The right side of Ryan's mouth quirks up. "And if you tell me, maybe we'll get around to those things."

I pull my hair forward. What do I tell him? The official story or the real story? He told me about his brother and his parents. I can trust him with this. "My mom broke out the windows of her asshole boyfriend's car after he hit her. He was going to hit her again, so I picked up the bat and was swinging it over my shoulder to hit him when the cops showed. Mom is on probation, so I took the fall for the destruction of property. My aunt called Scott to bail me out so..." I wave my hand in the air. "Here I am."

Silence. I hate silence. Silence means thinking and thinking means judgment.

Ryan edges closer to me and flips my hair from my face. "You let the police arrest you instead of your mom?"

Missing my shirt, I draw my knees back up. "Wouldn't you?"

"Beth." I hear the tense hesitation in his voice. "What you did is admirable, but it's not normal. You shouldn't have to take the fall for your mom. You shouldn't have to pick up a baseball bat to defend her...or anyone."

He straightens and I watch as our trip into Louisville clicks into place. "In fact, you shouldn't even be taking care of your mom. You knew she would be at the bar, didn't you? You knew what you would be up against. This is screwed up. Your mom should be taking care of you. Not the other way around."

My throat tightens. There is no way he could ever understand. "It's what I do. She needs me."

Ryan runs a hand over his face and shifts off the bed. His body pulsates with a dangerous energy as he paces the floor. "What were you fighting about with Isaiah that night outside the coaching facility?"

"Nothing." I give the answer too quickly, and the pointed glare from Ryan tells me he knows I'm hiding the truth.

He continues his circle of the room. "I heard him tell you that you belonged in Groveton, and that's when you went nuts. You were going to run away that night, weren't you? That's why you were mad at him. He stopped you from going."

Panic surges through my body and I hop off the bed. Where did he throw my shirt? I have to go before he figures it out. A black blob lies in the corner. I take two steps and strong arms grab my waist.

"I already said you aren't running." Ryan's light brown eyes bore into mine. "From the moment I began to care for you, I've always felt like you were slipping away. Sometimes when you kiss me I feel like you're saying goodbye. I kept telling myself that was in my head. That you're scared to love me so you retreat. It's more than that, isn't it? Scott won't let you near your mom so you're planning to run away with her."

Ten minutes ago, I wanted nothing more than his body close to mine. Now his closeness is too much. I need space and I can't move.

His fingers press tight into my skin. "When?"

My mouth becomes dry and I stare at the floor. This isn't how tonight was supposed to go. Ryan raises his voice and yells, "When?!"

I don't want to lie to him. "Soon."

Ryan moves his hands off my hips and curls me into his body. A body that a few seconds before stood solid in anger. My heart breaks from the desperation of his defeat. His forehead rests against mine and his hand grips my hair. "Stay, Beth."

I close my eyes and wrap myself around him. I'm going to miss this: Ryan's strength, his warmth, his love. "I love you, Ryan," I whisper, half hoping he doesn't hear it. Why does everything hurt so damn bad?

His body stiffens and my heart stops. Maybe he did hear me. Ryan places his hands on my shoulders and gently pushes my body from his. His eyes dart over my face. "I don't lose. Do you hear me? I don't lose and that includes losing you. I'm done being kept in the dark. I'm done feeling like you're slipping right past me. You are not saying goodbye to me. I'm in love with you and you love me back. You're staying."

Ryan says it as if it's an easy decision. Like I could forsake my responsibilities. Like these chains that have been strangling me for years can easily be cast off. "I can't."

The anger and confusion drains from his face and the calm and control I've only seen while he's on the pitcher's mound take command. "I won't let you go."

I blink. As if he could stop me. "You won't let me go."

"No, I won't let you go. You're mine and I don't lose." He rests his hands on his hips and I see the same cockiness from Taco Bell, as if telling me to leave my mother to die is no different than asking for my phone number.

"This isn't a game to be won or lost. There are things in my life that were set in motion before I took my first breath. I don't have a choice in this."

"That's bullshit. Everyone has choices and I've made mine. There is no way you're leaving."

He's so confident that part of me believes him. "I'm not?"

"Nope. Three months ago you had no roots here, but now, you've got them."

"Roots."

"Roots," he repeats. "You're on the homecoming court and starting to do well at school. My friends love you. You're closer to Scott. You have a best friend in Lacy."

My mind races and so does my breathing. I made a life here—in Groveton. A life I enjoy. A life I could keep. Ryan draws me into him. He lowers his head as his fingers leave a burning path across my cheek. "You have me."

The pure emotion in his voice causes me to shiver. I could try to build a wall, but the intensity of his gaze tells me he'd see through anything. The seconds stretch between us. His lips come dangerously close to mine, yet he keeps them away. With his hand warm on my face, his nose skims my jawline and I try to inhale to steady my pulse.

Ryan tugs at the loops on my jeans and guides me back onto the bed. Taking my hand, he urges me to stretch out beside him. His jeans hang right along his hip bones and I swallow.

I'm in love with him. Tonight I was going to give him a memory of me. I found the confidence and I was in control. My heart stutters. I lost my control. I lost my confidence. My hand shakes as I touch his bare chest.

"I want you to trust me." Ryan brushes his hand down my arm and I tremble. The signals he sends are unmistakable. There are times when you stand on the cusp of moments so huge, you know you'll remember them forever. This is that moment for me and for Ryan. I'm not seducing him. He's not seducing me. Instead, we're choosing to be together.

I suck in a breath and rush out the words before I lose the courage to say them. "I trust you." And please, please don't use that against me.

"I'm in love with you," he whispers.

"Are you scared?" I ask him. Because I am. Terrified. Earlier I was anxious, but not frightened. This isn't me giving him a memory. This is me giving him my heart.

"I don't want to hurt you. Tell me if I do and we'll stop." Ryan slides his thumb over my lower lip. The warmth he creates melts the fear.

Unable to speak, I nod. In painfully slow movements, Ryan lowers his head closer and edges his body over me. His lips press gently against mine and as I gasp for air I whisper the words to him again. "I love you."

RYAN

I'VE NEVER BEEN THIS CLOSE to a person. Skin touching skin. Legs and arms wound tightly around one another. Lying on my bed, Beth's tucked close to my chest and she slowly runs her fingernails up and down the inside of my arm.

I kiss her head again, revel in the scent of roses, and fight the urge to shut my eyes. Every single muscle has fallen asleep and my mind wanders lazily, but I want to hold on to this moment a little longer. "Are you sure I didn't hurt you?"

She's answered before, but the anxiety still creeps deep inside. Beth glances at me from under long dark eyelashes. "I'm okay."

The anxiety level increases. We went from fine to okay. "I hurt you. Tell me the truth."

"It burned some, but I'm okay. It's not like you were..." And she drifts off.

Heat scorches my face and neck. It's not like I was in for that long. "I'll get better. It'll take some practice and then we'll both feel good."

Beth giggles and her happiness eases the anxiety. "Practice? Do you ever turn off the jock?"

"We should create a schedule. Maybe stretch beforehand."
She laughs loudly and the sweet sound squeezes my heart.
Beth rarely lets happiness overwhelm her and as if on cue
she releases a weighty sigh. Her body grows heavier against
mine and I pull her tighter to me. Beth is dead wrong if she
thinks she can leave me.

"I was thinking..." Her fingers begin tracing my arm again,
but this time her touch is stiff and apprehensive. "Maybe I
could talk to Scott about my mom. Maybe he could help me
help her."

I kiss her head again, close my burning eyes, and clear
my throat. I get to keep her. My Beth. "That's a great idea."

"You need to go to sleep," she groggily murmurs into my
chest. "The writing competition is tomorrow."

"I love you," I whisper into her ear. She cuddles closer to
me and I realize what a dick I am. I'm telling my parents
about Beth as soon as they come home and I'm walking out
on that homecoming field with her on my arm. Screw what
Mom and Dad think. Screw the rest of the town. Screw perfection. This girl is mine.

BETH

I AWAKE TO THE SOUND OF BIRDS chatting happily and beams of sunlight highlighting the dancing dust particles in the air. A cardinal rests on a bush outside the window of my room in Scott's house. The bird flaps its wings and rises into the sky—into freedom. I wonder if the bird in the barn ever escaped.

The scent of bacon and onions drifts in the air. Scott promised to cook hash browns this morning. I hop out of bed and I'm surprised by the image in the mirror. I'm smiling. It's more than that—I'm different. Last night made me different. My eyes shine like Scott's do when he's around Allison. In fact, my entire face glows and I'm hungry. Starving. For more than food. I want to ask Scott if he can help Mom. Hope floods my body and makes me feel high. I can get used to hope.

I toss my hair into a bun and go out into the kitchen. Scott glances at me as he hovers over the stovetop. "Good morning, Elisabeth."

"Good morning, Scott." I almost giggle at how cheerful I sound. Me—giggling. That's funny in itself.

He does a double take as I sit at the counter and the annoying I-know-everything grin stretches from ear to ear. "Whatever side of the bed you rolled out of this morning is the one you should roll out of every day."

"Very funny."

From the other side of the island, Allison studies me, but not with nearly as much contempt as normal. She looks like she's on the verge of saying something, then focuses on the newspaper in front of her.

Scott's cell rings. He reaches into his back pocket and holds the phone against his shoulder to answer as he flips the hash browns in the pan. "Hello."

His face darkens and he pushes the pan onto an unlit burner before switching off the stove. He turns and his troubled blue eyes find me. My hope slithers away.

"We'll be right there," he says.

RYAN

THERE'S A LOW BUZZ of conversation as the auditorium fills. Today's been both exhilarating and torturous. I've met college professors who gave me incredible feedback on "George and Olivia." I listened to lectures on writing, learned new techniques, and I've spent the whole day sweating this upcoming moment.

I'd take a cold rainy day on the mound over this—wearing my Sunday best while waiting to hear whether or not my story is good enough.

I hunch forward in the folding auditorium chair with my hands clasped together. My feet won't quit moving. The only things keeping me halfway sane are my memories of last night. The moment I get out of here, I'm buying two dozen roses and I'm heading straight to Beth. I want to show her I'm nothing like the bastard who broke up with her the next day. I'm the guy that will be around forever.

Mrs. Rowe yanks the placeholder off the seat next to me and plops down. "Are you nervous?"

I glance at her in response and rub my hands together. It's scary how much I want this. It's even more terrifying to think what happens if I do win. If I lose, then I know my path: pro baseball. If I win...it opens up possibilities. Possibilities that I'm good at more than just ball, that I'm good at writing too. Then I'll have choices to make.

"It's too bad your parents couldn't be here for this," she says. "I bet it's killing them to be away."

"Yeah." Possibly killing them to be near each other. My hopes aren't high that a week's vacation will fix the issues between them. Divorce isn't an option on the table, especially since Dad's considering the run for mayor. Maybe I should be grateful, but I'm not sure how much more frozen silence I can take.

"I'm sure they're proud of you," she continues.

"Sure." Even though they have no idea I'm here.

Through the squeal of feedback, a woman in a black business suit asks the audience for silence. As she thanks us for our entries, Mrs. Rowe leans over to me. "Regardless of what the results are, Ryan, it was a huge honor to final."

I nod, but what she doesn't understand is that I don't like losing.

"...so, with that, we are ready to announce the winners."

I inhale deeply to calm the nerves. Fifty of us made it to the last round. All of us entered the final, only three spots left for a win and, to be honest, I'm only interested in first.

"The third place winner is Lauren Lawrence."

The crowd applauds and I lean back in my seat, antsier than I was before. The girl walks unbelievably slowly and it takes even longer for the people onstage to hand her the award.

The announcer clears her throat before beginning again. "The second place winner is..."

Part of me craves to hear my name and the other part doesn't. First is the best. First is what I desire, but for the first time in my life, I think I could be happy with second.

"...Tonya Miles."

Everyone applauds again. At least this girl is faster. I hunch forward again, wondering what a loss like this would feel like. I could have been happy with second. Possibly third. And, I finally realize, I don't want the easy path...I want the choice. I want to possibly go to college.

Or not. I don't know. But I do know that I want this win.

"...and our first place winner is..." She pauses for dramatic effect. I lower my head as my gut tightens. What if I'm not good enough?

"Ryan Stone."

Adrenaline rushes through my veins as I lift my head to stare at the stage. The crowd claps and Mrs. Rowe gestures for me to go onstage, saying words I don't understand. I stagger forward, wondering if I heard it right. Is this happening? Did I really win?

Onstage, the lady shakes my hand and offers me a plaque and a certificate. They feel heavy in my hands—heavy and amazing. I did this. I won a writing competition.

Mrs. Rowe is on her feet. So are a few of the college professors who had read my story. And while their applause is appreciated, a lump forms in my throat and drops. My parents aren't here. And even if they did know about the competition, they still wouldn't be here.

I nod to the crowd, then turn toward the stairs. The applause dies except for a loud clapping in the back of the room. A deep booming shout gains my attention and the part of me that was sinking suddenly flies higher.

I pause on the stage and Mark smiles. He cups his hands to his mouth and yells, "Way to go, Ry!"

How could I have been so blind? He never left me. My brother—he never left.

BETH

THERE ARE MEMORIES THAT EXIST in my mind that are so clear that if I focus on them enough I could practically relive them. The sky was ocean-blue and two doves sat on the roof of Grandpa's trailer when Scott taught me how to throw a ball. Lacy's dad's callused hand was cold the day he led me to the back of his police cruiser. Mom bought me a Hostess cupcake the first night we spent alone in Louisville.

What ingrained those moments was that when I lived them, I knew I would remember them always. When Scott taught me to play baseball, time lost all meaning. I held the ball in my hand longer than needed so I could remember the feel of the threading. I hesitated when Lacy's dad told me to hop in the car so I could take a mental snapshot of our trailer. I spent a half hour nibbling at the icing of the cupcake before taking a bite, knowing that Mom gave all her money to our new landlord.

The emergency room takes on the same slow-motion quality as I run through the sliding doors. Scott brushes past me and talks to a nurse at the station. My heart beats loudly in my ears. An orderly passes by and stares at my head. I didn't brush my hair. I didn't do anything.

The nurse looks up from her computer and motions toward the closed doors of the emergency room. Large letters on big signs warn me to stay out, but if that's where my mother is, no one can stop me. My hand aches as I slam on the swinging door and I barely register my name being called behind me. Both sides of the corridor are filled with curtained areas. Machines beep and people softly whisper.

Walking in the hallway, the hulking figure that torments my dreams turns a corner. I chase after him. Trent. Anger courses through me and propels me forward. Past the beds. Past the nurse asking if I need help. Past anything that is sane or rational.

At the end of a long, desolate hallway, he enters a room. The other rooms surrounding it are empty. No nurses or doctors are on guard. Trent stands near my mother's bed. He doesn't see me, nor does he see the fist that strikes out and punches him in the jaw. "Fuck you!"

My knuckles throb and pain shoots through my wrist, but it doesn't stop me. Everything is a blur. My hands hit again and again. Trent slaps me across the face, yanks at my hair, and I cry out when a knee hammers my stomach. He tosses me like a rag doll and air slams out of my lungs when I crash into the wall.

I try to refocus and go after him again. If I give him enough time he'll hit me and I'll go down. On the floor with Trent is a bad place to be. He prefers to kick. I hear a smack followed by the sight of Trent stumbling across the floor.

"Elisabeth, are you okay?" Scott keeps his back to me. He

holds his arms slightly out to his sides waiting for retaliation. "Elisabeth!"

"Yeah." I shake away the stupor. "I'm fine."

Blood seeps from Trent's nose. Good for Scott. He broke it. Trent glares at me, causing Scott to step toward him. "Touch my niece again and I'll kill you."

Trent ignores Scott and the bald asshole keeps staring at me. "I know you're trying to take what's mine. Put those thoughts in her head again and the paramedics won't be able to save her next time."

"You fucking son-of-a-bitch." I leap toward him and Scott wraps his arms around my waist, practically lifting me off the ground to prevent me from mauling Trent. "I should have hit you with that bat when I had the chance." I wish I had taken the swing. "I wish you were dead."

"Get out of here before I call security!" Scott yells at Trent.

Trent's eyes go flat and he half smiles as he walks past. Scott tightens his hold as I try to go after him again. Trent won't forgive me for trying to run away with Mom. He'll want revenge and if he can't extract his revenge on me then he'll use Mom as payment.

Scott releases me and blocks the doorway. "What the fuck is going on?"

My hand snaps out and points into the hallway. "He hits her. He hits me. He's a fucking drug dealer who uses my mom and if it weren't for you and your stupid rules and your stupid blackmail she wouldn't be here because I would have been there to protect her."

A nurse appears in the doorway and I turn from both of them.

"Is there a problem here?" she asks quietly, quickly, and

in a tone that indicates she knows everyone in this room is fucked up.

"Everything is fine," Scott says.

He talks some more, but his voice and the nurse's become muffled as I stare at the pathetic creature on the bed. A few hours ago, my entire world was right. Ryan held me in his arms and I convinced myself that everything was going to be okay. This is what happens when you believe in hope. Karma comes around to destroy it.

I sit on the bed and touch Mom's cold fingers. This is what death feels like. "Did she die?"

The chatter behind me stops.

"She stopped breathing," says the nurse. "But the paramedics gave her naloxone and it counteracted the effects of the heroin."

Heroin. My heart stops and my lungs ache. Heroin.

My fingers follow the line of her IV, but I purposely skip the track marks that dot her arms. "How long has she been using?"

The blood pressure cuff swooshes as it releases. The nurse clears her throat. "We don't know."

"When can she go home?"

"She's asleep now. The doctor will check her when she wakes and as long as she's still fine, they'll let her go." She whispers something to Scott. Scott whispers back.

"Elisabeth," he says, "I'm going to go fill out some paperwork."

Meaning he'll pay her bills. For now. How could I have not noticed the marks on her arm before? "Okay."

The room becomes very still except for the steady beat of Mom's heart monitor. From the moment my aunt Shirley called Scott, I've felt like I've been spinning in the Gravitron from the fair. If I could, I'd crawl right into oblivion and disappear. I'm tired and all I want is to get off this damn ride.

"Which one of you punched Trent?" Shirley asks behind me.

"Both of us. Nice job taking care of your sister." I knot my fingers with Mom's. Does she know I'm here? Probably not. Mom doesn't even notice I'm with her when she's somewhat coherent. "Where have you been?"

"Smoke break." Shirley hacks her smoker's cough and Mom flinches in her sleep. "Who do you think found your mom and dragged her ass into the alley before I called nine-one-one? If the police went into your mom's apartment we'd be in a bigger shit pile than we are now."

Mom stirs and I wish she'd wake up and tell me she's sorry. "Thanks for calling Scott."

"He's got money. Make sure he uses it to pay the bills." Shirley's light footsteps come closer to the bed and she rests a hand on my shoulder. I keep my eyes on Mom, terrified if I glance away she'll disappear.

"Two days ago your mom told me a funny story. It was the type that could start with once upon a time," says Shirley. "She said you were coming soon to take her away. Sad part was she also told the whole bar and someone there told Trent. He got a little pissed."

A little pissed? Fresh bruises cover the right side of Mom's face. Knowing her, she took the heroin to forget the beating, to relieve the pain.

"You know I don't believe in fairy tales." I should never have left Mom. Never. I should have found a way to leave weeks ago. This is my fault.

"That's a shame," she says. "Because I would have paid to see that one."

I jerk my head to look at her.

"Cash," says Shirley. "She's not going to last much longer the way she's been going. The decision is yours. She's your responsibility."

Shirley walks out of the room. I try to inhale, but it's virtually impossible with the burden weighing me down. Ever since I was eight years old, the responsibility of my mother has been on me. I've taken care of her. Moved her. Fed her. Made sure she went to work or helped her find jobs. But right now, what I want more than anything is for my mom to take care of me. I'm done being the grown-up. For a few minutes I want to be the kid. I want my mom. I just want my mom.

A light touch moves across my hand. "Don't be sad, Elisabeth," my mother mumbles.

I sniff. "I'm not sad."

"I dreamed of you. You and your daddy. I miss him." Her fingers lightly grasp my wrist. "I miss you. You were a beautiful baby."

"Why?" A tangle of anger and sadness and happiness weaves around my soul and strangles the scream fighting to leave my throat. She's alive, but she almost died. "Why do you have to make everything so fucking hard?"

"Come here. I like you better sad. I hate it when you're angry." She tugs on my wrist and ignores my question. "I want to hold my baby."

I feel like I'm five as I crawl on the bed and rest my head between the crook of her arm and her chest. Her fingers weakly pick at my hair. "You were born on a Tuesday."

I close my eyes and will the hurt to leave, but it doesn't

go away. It stabs at me over and over again. I'm so tired. So damned tired. I don't want to think about Trent or heroin or running away or about the responsibility I thought I could abandon.

"It was an awfully hot day. You were so beautiful, but so tiny. The doctor wouldn't let me hold you for three weeks because you were early. Your daddy loved you then. He came by the hospital twice before your grandma brought us home. Scott was excited to hold a baby for the first time."

Her bony fingers relax against my head and I wish she'd tell me she loves me, because I love her. She may be a drug addict and an alcoholic and she's probably a whore, but she's my mom. My mom.

"I loved to take you to the mall. People would stop me and tell me what a beautiful baby you were. I'd let them hold you and they'd try to guess your name. You were so cute and you never cried. You were my own personal baby doll."

I wrap my arm around her and cringe when I feel her ribs poking through her skin. Mom sighs and continues, "I named you after my momma, hoping if I did she'd change her mind and love us both. My momma left me, Elisabeth, but I never left you. Never."

No, my mother never left me and that is the reason why I owe her. I grew up knowing the sacrifice she made on my behalf. I hold my breath to keep my body from shaking with sobs. My mom needs me and I can't be soft any longer. I did this to her. I left her behind.

"You're still coming for me, right, Elisabeth? On Monday?"

RYAN

IN A WRINKLED POLO and a pair of jeans, Scott leans against the wall at the end of the emergency room. He raises an eyebrow when he spots me, but then lowers it as if he's too tired to care. "How did you know she was here?"

"Your wife told me." I came straight from the competition to Scott's house so I could share my news and give Beth the roses. My world came crashing down when Allison said those three words: Beth's mother overdosed.

I glance into the room and immediately look away. The sight of Beth curled up on the bed with her mother is too intimate for anyone to witness—including me. "How long has she been in there?"

"A while." Scott kneads his eyes with his fists, just like Beth does when she's had all she can handle. I see a lot of Beth in Scott. "How did the writing competition go?"

And just like Beth, he'll avoid the bleeding elephant in the room. "I won."

If he weren't so tired, the smile on his face would appear natural. "Congratulations. How did your team do against Eastwick?"

"They won too." Just like I knew they would. They're a great team and I'm proud to be a part of them.

"Good."

Difference between me and the Risks? I have no problems discussing elephants. "How is Beth's mother?"

"She's alive."

I pause. "How's Beth?"

Scott shakes his head. Silence falls between us, but we both jerk our heads toward the room when we hear a muffled sob. Beth is breaking my heart and from the pain tearing across Scott's face, she's doing the same to his. More silence between us. A sniff comes from the room and my fingers itch to hold Beth and somehow right her world. I won't let her use this as an excuse to run. I'll talk to her and make her realize that now is the time to involve Scott.

"Elisabeth says that you're trying to decide between college and pro," he says.

I nod. The choice is harder now that I've won the competition.

"Can I give you some unsolicited advice?" he asks.

I tilt my head up. "I'd love your advice."

"Decide what baseball means to you, because if you're playing to make money, then you'll be sadly disappointed. Only a small percent of drafted players ever play a day in the majors and you'd make more working at McDonald's than you will playing in the minors."

A nurse passes between us and I let the back of my head hit the wall. "You went pro."

"When I was eighteen, baseball was my only option. From what Elisabeth says you have several options. If baseball is what you want more than anything, then it will be worth the sacrifice. If going pro is a means to an end, I'm telling you the odds are against you."

Then Scott gets that crazy gleam in his eye. The gleam I understand. "If baseball is what you live by, breathe in, and die for, I'm telling you that you'll need the rush of running out onto that field. I've never experienced anything else like it."

"Thanks," I tell him. His comments are well received, but not helpful. I'm nowhere closer to making a decision. Out of the corner of my eye I peek into the room. Beth's eyes meet mine.

"Spend time with her," says Scott. "But Elisabeth goes home with me."

BETH

SCOTT'S HAND ON MY BACK urges me forward as I watch my aunt Shirley drive away with my mom. It's late, I guess. The sun has set. Stars twinkle in the sky. Ryan has come and gone, though I could tell he didn't want to leave. He loves me. I know that. I somehow wonder if his love is the only thing that's kept me from losing my mind.

"Let's go home," Scott says.

Home. My room with my clothes and my box of Lucky Charms in the pantry. Home. It can be my home if Scott will help my mom. The red taillights of Shirley's car disappear as she turns left onto the main street.

I exhale all the air out of my body and turn to Scott. "We need to talk."

He nods in agreement as he hooks an arm around my shoulder. Three months ago, I would have decked him for touching me. Now, I welcome the embrace. With exhaustion weakening my knees, I lean into my uncle.

"We'll talk tomorrow." Scott continues to lead me to his car. "You're dead on your feet."

We're halfway to his car when a moment of déjà vu hits

me. Like I'm seeing something that I've seen before—a memory in slow motion. I jerk my head to the right and realize that it's not a memory, but reality.

I flinch to a stop and Scott halts along with me. "What's wrong?"

"Isaiah," I say not to Scott, but to myself. My best friend is here.

Leaning against the hood of his black Mustang, Isaiah watches Scott and me from a distance. He dips his head when he spots me looking at him. I step toward him and Scott grabs my arm. "No, Elisabeth."

My head whips. "Just for a second. Just one second. Please."

His grip loosens at the word *please*. When he finally releases me, I sway. I'm worn out—physically, emotionally, but I dig for strength. I have to talk to Isaiah.

Isaiah stays where he is, not even bothering to meet me halfway, and speaks before I reach him. "Shirley told me about your mom. Are you okay?"

His question stops me about a car's distance from him. Hurt pours out of his eyes, and every muscle in my abdomen clenches. My close proximity actually causes him pain and that fact slaps me in the face.

"Yes," I answer, then think about it. "No. She's addicted to heroin."

Isaiah glances away and a lead ball drops into my stomach. "You knew."

He meets my eyes again. "She's bad news, Beth. You're not going to change her."

She will change. Scott will help me. I know it. "How are you?"

"I'm surviving." Isaiah surveys the night sky, then pushes away from his car. "Have a nice life."

"Isaiah…" I say, unsure of how to make us better. "This isn't goodbye."

"Yeah," he answers as he unlocks his driver's-side door. "It is."

"If you believed that you wouldn't be here now." I'm energized by a second wind as my words sink in. "We're friends. For life."

He rubs a hand over his face before sliding into his car, shutting the door, and turning over his engine with an angry growl. The brief burst of energy drains from me, starting in my head and seeping out through my toes. It hurts to know that I've caused Isaiah pain, but someday he'll really fall in love and discover that all we've ever been is friends.

I open my eyes and curse. This is twice I've gone pathetic, fallen asleep, and Scott has had to carry me in. Just like the first night in this house, the blanket is tucked around me and my shoes are neatly placed near the bed. It's dark and I don't bother looking at the clock. I toss aside the blanket, climb out of bed, and head into the foyer.

In the kitchen, Scott sits at the island and stares at the countertop. I flop onto the cushy leather couch. I've lived in this house for three months and I've never sat here. "Nice couch."

"It's about time you tried it out," Scott says. He wears a Yankees T-shirt and a pair of jeans. Scott acts so grown-up at times I forget that he's not even thirty yet. He slips off the stool and joins me in the living room. "Want to fill me in on Trent?"

"No."

"Let me rephrase. Fill me in on Trent."

Scott did hit the bastard. I wipe the sleep from my eyes and try to find the simplest and fastest explanation. "The fucking asshole is the spawn of Satan and someone needs to stake the bastard in the heart, shred him to pieces, then set the pieces on fire."

"Or take a swing at his head with a baseball bat?"

"Or that." I smile weakly and Scott gives the same weak smile back. I told Ryan I'd stay. I finger the smooth material of the ribbon tied around my wrist. "Why did you leave us? You didn't just leave me. You left Mom too."

"Are you ready to discuss this calmly or are you looking for a screaming match?"

"Talk." I think.

"When I left Groveton, I meant what I said. I fully intended to come back for you. I know I was young, but I loved you as if you were my own."

I loved him like he was my father. I draw my knees up and wrap my arms around them. "Then why didn't you come back?"

"Because..." He starts and stops several times as the words catch in his mouth. "Because I wouldn't have made it out if I did. I couldn't take you on the road with me and if I chose you then I would have had to quit baseball.

"If I stayed in Groveton, I have no doubt I would have become my father. Your dad swore to me he'd never be Dad, and the day he graduated from high school he turned into the same bastard our father was. I didn't want trailer parks and I didn't want girls hooked on drugs and I didn't want to spend the rest of my life hurting the people I said I loved. If I stayed, I would have become my father and one day I would have hurt you."

I shake my head. Scott would never have hurt me. He wasn't capable of it.

"I was so damned scared that when I began to run, I couldn't stop. I was scared to face you again. Scared if I saw you, I'd stay and turn into my father."

Scott swears and holds his hands together as if in prayer. I bite my lip when his voice cracks. "When you first moved here—every time I looked at you I saw the old man. I saw his anger coming out of your eyes. I saw your father's bitterness wrapped up inside of you. As much as I've hated myself for leaving you behind, I don't regret it. If I'd stayed I would have never broken free and all of that anger and bitterness I see in you would have been inside of me."

I know the anger and bitterness he's talking about. They're the chains that weigh me down and threaten to drown me daily—at least until I found Ryan. But those chains returned with one phone call from Shirley and they're slipping tighter around my throat. "Yay for you. You broke free and I got screwed."

Scott leans forward. "I know it seems that way, but I broke free for you too. I fucked up. I should have come back when I signed with the Yankees and dragged you to New York with me. I didn't and I'm sorry, but I'm here now and this..." He holds his hands out and motions at the house. "This is your break, kid. This is your baseball. All you have to do is trust me and take it. Whatever you want, it's yours, but you have to let the past go."

Scott is talking about hope and hope is a myth. He acts like it would be easy to leave Mom. As if I could effortlessly hand over the demons in my nightmares and somehow with the swish of a magic wand, everything would be okay. "What about Mom?"

He doesn't answer immediately. Instead, he stares at a thin scar on his right hand where he told me Grandpa had cut him with a knife when he was a kid. "She's not my responsibility and she's not yours either."

"No. That's where you're wrong. Mom is my responsibility. It's my fault that she's miserable."

"You're wrong."

"Whatever. I've been thinking, maybe you could give her some money. We could put her in one of those rehab places and when she's clean we could move her someplace nicer. Mom used to work and we could get her another job. She's been down for so long and I know she keeps Trent because he has money. If you help her, I'm sure she can get better."

"I can't."

My head snaps back as if he slapped me. "What do you mean you can't?" I did it. I came to him for help. I'm trusting him and he's throwing it back in my face?

"I made myself and Allison a lot of promises when we moved to Groveton and more importantly when I brought you back into my life. Your mother is a line I can't cross."

No, no, no, no. NO! This isn't how our talk was supposed to play out. "But you have to." The room becomes suddenly restrictive and I stand. I need to get out. Everywhere I turn there's a window or an entrance to another room. There's not a damn door to the outside in this huge fucking room.

"Elisabeth," says Scott real slowly, "why don't you sit back down?"

"You have to help her!" Because I can't, and the realization cracks my sanity. "Send her to a rehab. Get her clean. She'll be better then. You don't understand. She never had a shot. We never had anything. No one ever helped us."

"I sent her money," Scott says softly.

There's a roaring in my head and I freeze midstep. I'm in the kitchen and I have no idea how I made it here. "What did you say?"

Scott walks over to the island. "I sent your mother money every month. I opened a bank account for her and every month she drained it. I wasn't man enough to call you, but I was man enough to pay for my mistakes. Allison found the account a couple of months ago and thought I was having an affair. I brought her here, to Groveton, to prove to her that I wasn't lying about you or your mother and when I got here I didn't like what I found. So we stayed, but I promised Allison I would cut off your mother. She obviously wasn't using the money to help either one of you."

"You're lying." I slam my hand against the counter. "You're fucking lying!" He has to be.

"I can show you the statements if you'd like."

I can't breathe. I can't... I can't breathe. I can't.

"Elisabeth," says Scott, "sit down."

I try to suck in air, but my lungs won't expand. Grabbing on to the side of the counter, I bend over in my search for oxygen. Scott's wrong. He has to be wrong. Mom would never have done this to me. Never. Why can't I fucking breathe?

"Elisabeth!" Scott shoves a stool out of the way and catches me as I fall to the floor. He sits beside me as I lower my head into my hands.

"Just breathe," he commands.

My intake sounds like a wheeze and I feel as if my mind is splitting into halves.

"It's okay," Scott tells me.

But it's not. Nothing is okay.

RYAN

BETH DIDN'T SHOW LAST NIGHT. I'm not surprised. My parents are back in town, plus Beth spent the whole day and into the evening at the hospital Saturday and needed a day to rest. I hoped she would come though. I only saw her for a few seconds on Saturday and that was in front of Scott. She seemed so broken. I need to hold her and tell her I love her and I need to hear the words back.

I'll catch her before school begins and spend the day trying to put a smile on her face. Lacy, Chris, and Logan will want to help. Between the four of us we can distract her.

I open the fridge, pull out a Gatorade, grab my keys from the counter, and swerve to avoid steamrolling my mother. "Sorry. I'll see you at the game later."

And officially introduce Beth as my girl to my parents. There is no way either of them would make a scene in public.

"It's early. Sit down." Mom brushes past me. She's polished for the day. Dress pants. Sweater set. Pearls. Mom will be on the social club prowl by lunch. Dad walks into the kitchen from the formal dining room and barely glances at Mom. The vacation was supposed to save their marriage. Last night they slept in separate bedrooms.

My keys jingle in my hand. "I have some stuff to take care of before school. Can we talk later?"

Mom eases into a seat at the table and gestures for me to follow. I cock my hip against the frame of the door instead.

"Fine." Mom opens her right hand and like an accordion my condoms fly onto the table. "Would you care to explain?"

My keys dig into my hand as I try to keep my anger in check. "You went through my room?"

"We're your parents. We have the right."

I survey Dad and he patiently stares at me from the other side of the room. Panic combines with nausea and adrenaline, but I'll be damned if they see it on my face. How much did they go through? Did they find my plaque from winning the writing competition? Did they turn on my computer? Did they find my stories? This is exactly how they treated Mark when he first came home from college this summer. Right before he told them he was gay.

"I counted them," Mom says. "There's one missing."

I've never hated my mother before and, right now, I do. "What do you want?"

"Who is the girl?"

"I'm not telling you." Not when Mom is going to downgrade Beth to the girl I used a condom with. Mom will take something that was beautiful and twist it into something dirty.

"Is it a girl?" Dad asks.

My grip on the Gatorade tightens. "What is wrong with you?"

Dad pushes away from the door frame with muscles

tensed. Mom hops out of her seat and directly into the path of me and Dad. "We heard a rumor yesterday when we went to dinner. I know it has to be untrue because you would never go against our wishes. I would have discussed it with you yesterday, but you were out. I did what I had to do to get some answers."

"You wait for me, Mom. You don't go through my stuff."

"Are you dating Beth Risk?" she demands.

"Or is she the girl you're experimenting with?" asks Dad.

Mom spins. "Andrew!"

"Some girls you date. Others you have sex with. Boys do this."

"I'm aware of your behavior in high school," Mom says. "But my son will not be sleeping with one girl and dating another in public. Gwen deserves better than that. I deserved better than that!"

"Stop it!" I'm tired of the fighting.

"It was one night, Miriam!" Dad yells. "Twenty-five years ago."

I throw the Gatorade in my hand across the room. Glass shatters in the china cabinet and Mom holds her hands over her head. "Do you guys even hear yourselves anymore? Did you even bother listening to Mark? Do you even hear me? I'm not dating Gwen and leave Beth out of this!"

"Ryan!" Dad bellows, but Mom puts her hand up to silence him.

"Ryan," she says slowly. Her hand plays with the pearls around her neck. "Beth Risk isn't who you think she is. Gwen grew concerned when you continued to date Beth at school even after we forbade you to see her, so she went to her parents...again."

I swear under my breath. Gwen doesn't even understand the destruction she's created.

Mom continues, "Don't be mad at Gwen. She cares for you and she did the right thing. See, her father knows the truth about Beth. She didn't move to New York with Scott all those years ago. Her father went to prison and her mother moved herself and Beth to Louisville. Gwen's mother knows the attendance clerk at Beth's old school in Louisville.

"I'm sorry, Ryan, but sometimes children are destined to become nothing more than their own parents. Beth is a drug user. She's been arrested and her reputation with boys at her old school..."

I don't wait to hear anything else. "Does Gwen know any of this?" Because she didn't before. Otherwise, she would have told me in order to break Beth and me up.

"Yes. She was there when her parents told us yesterday."

With my keys tight in my hands, I turn my back to her.

"Ryan!" Mom calls from the kitchen. "Come back!"

She's too late. I race out to the garage, start the Jeep, and peel out of the driveway. If Gwen knows, then that means she'll tell the rest of the school.

BETH

SCOTT PULLS INTO A SPOT next to the front entrance of school and places the car in Park. We're early. Neither one of us said much during breakfast. I didn't eat. Neither did he.

"Are you sure you want to go today?" he asks for the tenth time. "I'm okay if you stay home. Allison and I heard you pacing downstairs so I know you didn't sleep the past few nights. She's worried about you and so am I."

I'm too damned tired to even roll my eyes at the lie of Allison being concerned over me. Mom and I were supposed to leave today. I was going to cut school and take a cab into Louisville. Then Mom and I would have left. My insides feel tormented, battered, and bruised. Sort of like if Trent was allowed free rein over my organs. The worst sensation is the tightness in my lungs, the feeling of drowning.

I touch the ribbon on my wrist. "No. I want to go to school." I need to see Ryan. He said I had roots here. I need to hear him say it again. I need to laugh with Lacy. I want to smile when Logan and Chris egg each other on. I want to nail the anatomy quiz in science. I want to know that I'm not making the worst mistake of my life by leaving my mother behind.

My backpack sits on the floorboard and I hold my science book to my chest. I'm good at science. Really good. My teacher likes me. Instead of yelling at me when I accidentally cursed while giving an answer, she laughed and winked. After class she told me to watch my fucking language. I earned a B on my last progress report and last week my teacher told me that I'm close to an A. Me, Beth Risk—I could get an A.

"I never wanted to tell you about the money."

I shake my head and Scott stops talking. I'd rather not think about that. It still hurts too much. I try to wipe out the thoughts of Mom and money and how I'm leaving her behind with Trent. Instead, I try to focus on Lacy. She called me her best friend and she asked me to stay the night next weekend. Since I left Groveton at the age of eight, I've never had a sleepover with a friend. She said we'd eat frosting and watch movies. I have a best friend who's a girl.

"You don't look good, kid."

I hit Trent Saturday, which means he'll hit her. I choke as I attempt to breathe. How can I do this? I can't leave her behind. "Mom swore to me she'd never do heroin."

"I'm sorry," he says in a simple way. Kind of like when a child finds out that Santa Claus or the Easter Bunny doesn't exist. He's sorry that the fantasy is over, but happy I've entered reality.

Mom doesn't fight back when Trent hits her. I should go into Louisville. "Dad shot up heroin. He sold it too."

Scott turns off the car. "I didn't know."

I'm leaving Mom behind, but I owe her. She never left me. "He wasn't bad when he shot up. Mostly he slept. The needles scared me. Mom got real nervous if I played too close to them."

"What happened?"

Why didn't Mom tell him? Or Shirley? Why do I have to do it? "Dad didn't want me."

"Your dad was young. He didn't know what he wanted. It had nothing to do with you."

True. Dad was seventeen when I was born. Mom was fifteen. Dad knew he wanted her. He took her and made me. But Scott is missing the point. "He told me that himself because I, uh...made a mistake." I am a mistake.

Scott stares at me with those blue eyes that are much gentler than Dad's and much more full of life than Mom's. I don't want anger and bitterness in my eyes.

"When I was in third grade, a guy came to the trailer and at first everything was fine, but then he and Dad began to argue. The guy reached to the back of his jeans and he pulled out a gun." A shiver runs through my body. My eyes dart in front of me. I see my backpack, the floorboard, the stereo in the car, but my body reacts like I'm back in the trailer.

"He pointed it at Dad and when Dad laughed he pointed the gun at me. It was so close." Very close. Close enough I could feel the metal on my forehead. Mom screamed and warm urine streamed down my legs onto the floor.

"Elisabeth," Scott softly urges.

"They argued some more and he cocked the trigger." It made a frightening sound—click, clitch. I rub the goose bumps forming on my arms. I knew I was going to die and I remember praying to God that it wouldn't hurt. Mom screamed and screamed and screamed. "Dad threw a sack of money at him. He uncocked the gun and lowered it." I ran. Past Mom, who collapsed on the floor crying. Past Dad, cursing the man out. Past the bathroom and into Mom and Dad's bedroom. "I hid under the bed and I called the police."

Scott shakes his head as he stares out the windshield to the entrance of my school. "How much heroin was in the house?"

"I don't know," I whisper. "Mom found me on the phone and she realized what I had done. Dad was still trying to flush the heroin down the toilet when Lacy's dad placed the handcuffs on his wrist." They cuffed Mom too and she cried so hard that her body shook. While they searched the house, Mom and Dad were on their knees in the living room.

"Elisabeth." It's a plea, but I'm not sure what he expects from me.

"Elisabeth is dead, Scott. Please stop calling me that." I remember my father's glare as Lacy's dad walked me past them. I died to him in that moment. "Mom was put on probation. Dad served six months. After he got out, he drove into Louisville to see me. He got down on his knees, looked me in the eye, and told me I was the worst thing that ever happened to him." He stood. Faced my mother and asked if she was coming with him. Mom decided to stay with me. "And he left."

And Mom didn't leave, because she chose me. Even though she loved my father, she stayed. I owe her.

Scott turns the car back on. "I'm taking you home."

"No!" I need to get an A in science. I need to see Ryan, go to his game, and know I'm making the right decision. I have a life here in Groveton and I need to be okay with letting my mom go. "I have a test today, then Ryan's game after school. Let me do this."

"If it's what you want, fine. But we're talking about this when you get home."

Home. I have no idea what that word really means.

★ ★ ★

The bell rings as I slip into the building and I weave through the hallway filled with students. My own skin feels strange on my body. Almost like it's too tight and needs to be shed. For years I focused on skipping class and today I fought to go to school. What is wrong with me?

A girl runs into my shoulder and laughs the moment she sees who she's collided with.

"It's her," her friend loudly whispers.

The hair on the back of my neck stands on end. It's me. What does that mean? I continue down the hallway and a group of guys stop talking and watch as I walk past. I clutch the science book as a shield. I didn't even garner this much attention on my first day.

Screw them. I want to find Ryan and go to science. He won the writing competition and he has his last game this afternoon. I haven't even properly congratulated him. I round the corner and stop the moment I spot a crowd of people near my locker.

An underclassman nods her head in my direction. "She's here."

The whispering and laughing cease and people distance themselves from me and my locker. Dread forces all hope to abandon my body. Written on my locker is the word I fear the most: *whore*.

Whore.

I slept with Ryan on Friday night.

Whore.

But he came to the hospital Saturday. He texted and called on Sunday, but I was too exhausted to call back. Ryan cares.

Whore.

I spin on my heel and try to escape down the hallway—away from my locker, away from the whispers and the laughter. I round a corner and slam into a friend of Gwen's. "Well, look who it is—Beth Risk. Is it true you were arrested in Louisville?"

The only person I told about that was Ryan. "Go to hell."

Her friends laugh and she smiles. "Gwen tried to warn you. Ryan and his friends take dares very seriously. What made you think you were anything more than that?"

Ryan gave me a bottle of rain. He told me he loved me. He wouldn't tell people that we slept together or that I was arrested in Louisville. He wouldn't call me a whore. "I'm not a dare."

"Really? Then how come Ryan's parents didn't know that you guys were dating? In fact, his mom told my mom that they forbade him to date you weeks ago."

The ice pick straight to my heart leaves me speechless and I step back, but my retreat isn't enough. She glances at her friends, then narrows her eyes at me. "Not only were you a dare, but you were Ryan's dirty little secret."

RYAN

I PARK THE JEEP behind Chris's truck and hop out. I've got
to find Beth and I need to find Gwen. I'll hand Gwen homecoming. I'll tell her that Beth and I will drop out, as long as
Gwen keeps Beth's secrets. Chris and Logan lean against
the tailgate and smile when they notice me. Today could be
a nightmare for Beth and I'm going to need their help. "Have
you seen Beth?"

Both of them shake their heads.

"Have you seen Lacy?" asks Chris. "She was supposed to
meet me here."

I scan the parking lot and spot Lacy bolting out the side
doors. "There she is."

Chris straightens as he watches her hurry to us. "Something's wrong."

She bypasses Chris, reaches out, and slaps me across the
face. The pain sucks, but the worst part is the tears stream-
ing down Lacy's face.

"How could you?" she chokes out.

Lacy's never hit me before. She's never hit anyone before.

Chris places himself between me and Lacy while Logan

yells at the people loitering to witness the show to keep moving. "Lace, what the hell?" Chris says.

Lacy shoves Chris and the shoves turn frighteningly close to hitting. "What the hell?" she screams. "What the hell is wrong with you? You were supposed to be her friend."

From behind her, Logan pulls her hands to her sides. "Slow it down, Lace. Tell us what's wrong."

Tears overflow from her eyes while she stares at me. "You promised me you wouldn't hurt her. You promised she was no longer a dare."

Beth. She means Beth. "She wasn't. I mean, she was, but you know I called it off."

She jerks her arms out of Logan's grasp, but he stays near in case she decides to attack again. "Everyone is saying Chris and Logan dared you to sleep with her. They said you won when you took Beth into the woods during the last field party. They said you slept with her and that she told you about her past. Everyone knows what happened to her in Louisville. Everyone knows."

Gwen. I smack my fist into the side of Chris's truck. "Have you seen Beth?"

Lacy shakes her head. "Tell me you didn't do it. Please."

Chris hesitantly touches her cheek. "No, baby. The dare ended the night Ryan fell for her."

She wipes the tears from her face. "Someone wrote *whore* on her locker."

Logan runs both hands over his face while Chris swears. The nightmare has already begun.

I search the hallways for Beth and I come up empty. The first warning bell rings and from the opposite end of the hallway Lacy shakes her head. Dammit. They can't find her either. Logan taps my shoulder. "She just walked into class."

Finally. I take off down the hallway and step into class right when the tardy bell rings. Lacy, Chris, and Logan trail behind me. Chris claps my back and the three of them head for our seats. Someone shushes the whispering and laughing as everyone watches me. I study Beth. She's reclaimed the seat in the corner of the room instead of the one she took next to me weeks ago.

Just like the first day of school, Beth's hair hides her face and she doodles in her notebook. My ribbon no longer graces her wrist.

An adult I don't know clears her throat. We must have a sub today. "Do you mind taking your seat?"

Beth glances up at me, then immediately looks back down. It's as if I swallowed knives. She's heard the rumors and she believes them.

Perfection. It's what everyone expects from me. Take my seat. Do my work. Go to practice. Play ball. Keep everything bottled up and let your insides rot as long as the outside looks perfect. "Beth."

She keeps her head down and the substitute steps into my line of view. "Either find a seat or find yourself in detention this afternoon."

"Ryan," Chris says, "the game."

The game against Northside. I promised Chris I wouldn't miss another game and detention would bar me from keeping that promise. Reluctantly, I take my seat and turn to stare at Beth, willing her to look at me.

"We'll catch her after class," Chris whispers to me from across the aisle.

★ ★ ★

The bell rings and it's a race of who can get out of their seat faster. Beth is out the door first and her size makes it possible for her to duck and weave through the mass of bodies crowding the hallway. My next class is in the opposite direction of where she's headed, but I don't care.

She runs down the history hallway and I grab her arm right before she enters the safety of the classroom. I lean in and look straight into her eyes. "You know I love you."

Her eyes search my face and she appears as broken as she did two days ago at the hospital. "Did you fuck me to win a dare?"

I fight the urge to shake her. "I didn't fuck you, I made love to you. Don't do this, Beth. Don't take what was beautiful between us and make it ugly."

Water fills her eyes and my heart slices into a million pieces. Beth isn't a crier and I'm making her cry. I thought making love would prove how much I loved her. Prove that she could trust me, and it's killing me to know that one act could be what's tearing us apart. "I gave you my word that the dare was over. When have I ever lied to you?"

"On the front steps of Scott's house you promised me I wouldn't be a secret."

I'm standing here breaking the PDA rules by holding her close to me. How can she believe I lied? "I've told everyone at school. I've brought you to games. I've taken you to parties."

"Tell me you told your parents. Tell me that when your parents confronted you about us, you told them we were a couple."

My grip on her loosens and she jerks her arm away. How could she know that? Over Beth's shoulder I spot Gwen skulking at the end of the hallway. She glances at me, then immediately averts her gaze. Dammit.

Beth kneads her eyes with her hands. "I fell for the jock again. The worst part is I told you how to play me. Convince me you love me and I'll fall into your bed. I'm so fucking stupid."

The warning bell rings and I watch in shock as Beth turns. No. She can't believe that. "I do love you."

Beth pauses in the door frame and I pray she'll say she believes me. "No, you don't. You don't want to feel bad for winning the dare." She walks into class and the tardy bell rings.

Beth's second-period teacher assesses me. "Get to class." Then closes the door in my face.

Feeling numb, I turn in the direction of my next class. I made love to Beth and I lost her. I swallow as my own eyes sting. It was too soon. She didn't trust me enough. What we did together, it was too much, too fast. I run a hand over my head and try to comprehend how everything blew out of control.

"Ryan!" calls Gwen from behind me. "Ryan! Please wait!"

Rage shoots through my veins as I spin in her direction and tower over her. "Are you finally happy, Gwen? Congratulations, you've bagged homecoming. I hope it was worth it."

Her eyes widen and she steps back. "I didn't do it for homecoming."

"Then why? Why would you hurt me like this?"

She blinks. "Hurt you? I've said nothing about you."

"If you hurt her, you hurt me. I love her."

Gwen's face pales. "You only think you love her. I just...I just told a few people. Just enough so word would get back to you, because I knew you wouldn't listen to me. I didn't know that they'd call her a whore. I didn't know about the locker. I swear, Ryan. I feel awful. I do. I had no idea it would go down like this."

When I angle my body away from her, she tries to reach out to me. "Please, you have to believe me. Ryan..."

I move out of range and her fingers hover in the air for a second before dropping to her side. "She's all wrong for you. I thought if you heard it, maybe from other people, you'd see what she really is and then you'd..."

Nausea crawls up my throat. "What? What did you think I'd do?"

Tears pool in her eyes and she shrugs. "Come back to me."

I pop my neck, trying to relieve the tension, but find the act did nothing to help. "We were over long before Beth came to this school. If you can't understand that, try this—I love her, Gwen. I love *her*."

I turn my back and head in the direction of my next class. This school isn't that big and, because of that, Beth won't be able to hide from me for long.

BETH

I KNEW THIS MATERIAL LAST WEEK. I know I did. I studied every night and Scott quizzed me most mornings. But I'm drawing blanks. The words jumble as I read them, which means my paper's blank. The bell rings. "Please bring your tests to me," says Mrs. Hayes.

The hand clutching my pencil sweats. I've written my name. That's it. My head falls forward. I failed. Again. This is who I was meant to be.

"Beth," says Mrs. Hayes. She walks back to my seat after everyone else turns in their tests and leaves. "Are you okay?"

"No." I'm a whore and I'm stupid. I snatch my backpack and leave the blank test on my desk. "I am not okay."

I burst out of class. Groveton is a mistake. I'm a mistake. Ryan lied to me. He used me. I was a dare. I'm nothing more than a stupid whore who makes mistake after mistake after mistake. Just like my mom.

People laugh as I pass. They're judging me and their judgment is spot-on. I don't belong here. I never have. I can't go to lunch and I can't handle the thought of gym. I don't want to listen to Ryan lie so he can make himself feel better, to

Gwen's laughter because I'm the trash she wants me to be, or to Lacy's pleas to talk to her.

Ryan rounds the corner and I duck into the hallway where I saw Isaiah on my first day of school. God, I've fucked everything up. I lost my best friend because I fell in love with a stupid jock who doesn't love me back. My fingers tunnel into my hair and I pull hard to cause pain. Stupid, stupid, stupid me.

Why couldn't I do one thing right in my life? If I'd left with my mother weeks ago, none of this would have ever happened.

I stop breathing. I can still go. I packed my remaining money and a change of clothes in my bag last week. The backpack weighs me down. The books I can ditch in my locker. The other items that I kept as reminders can also be left, but not here. I know exactly where I can unload them on my way out of town.

RYAN

SMACK. THE BALL COLLIDES with my glove. Bottom of the sixth and the game is tied. I wiggle the fingers of my throwing hand to keep them from becoming stiff from the cold. Late October and it's the coldest day of the year. Cold-weather games bring strange sensations. The wind burns my cheeks and fingers, but sweat forms from the heat trapped beneath the mock turtleneck of my uniform.

"Let's go, Ryan!" Dad calls from the stands. Playing the perfect wife and mother, Mom sits right beside him with a fleece blanket covering her legs. My eyes scan the bleachers again. Beth's not here and she won't be showing.

A high-pitched whistle originates from home plate. The new batter is taking his time for the third pitch in what I assume is an attempt to freeze me out. Logan steps to the left of the batter's box and motions for me to throw. He wants me to keep moving so my muscles will stay warm. I'm distracted and have pitched the shittiest game of my life. My arm winds back, releases, and I curse when the ball flies two feet to the left of Logan's glove.

Logan pulls the catcher's mask to the top of his head and walks toward the mound.

"We'll find her," Chris says as he approaches me from the right. "Lacy's already looking for her and after the game me, you, and Logan will do whatever we have to do to get her to listen."

Beth skipped class. I should have gone after her then, but Coach would have kept me from playing. "I can't focus."

"Yeah, you can," says Chris. "You have ice water in your veins when you pitch. Go to that place and you'll be fine."

How do I explain that I never had ice water in my veins when I pitch? That there is a constant burning pressure that threatens to destroy my pitch even when I'm not distracted.

"Your pitch," Logan starts when he reaches the mound, "is everywhere. Rein it in and you'll get to her faster."

He's right. I will. Chris swears under his breath and I follow his troubled gaze to the first baseline fence. Lacy stands on the opposite side with Beth's pack dangling from her shoulder.

Logan gets in my face. "One pitch. One more pitch."

"We've got another inning," Chris protests.

Logan throws him a glare. "One pitch."

They return to their spots and the batter digs his cleats into the dirt. This one's for Beth. Logan flashes two peace signs in a row. I nod, glance over my left shoulder, and spot a shadow of movement. Crossing my right arm over my left, I throw the ball to the first baseman, and hear the sweet word come out of the ump's mouth: "Out!"

The crowd cheers and I run off the field, into the dugout, and out to the other side. Lacy's eyes are wide with panic and she extends Beth's backpack to me. "I don't know what it means."

I tear the pack open as Lacy continues to talk. "I drove by her house, but no one was there. Then I drove around town and came up with nothing. So I went home, hoping that maybe she dropped by or called the landline, and I found this."

The pressure that always threatens me explodes and I toss the pack to the ground. My hand clutches the bottle of rainwater with the ribbons tied to it. I suck in a breath before unfolding the note tucked into the ribbons: *I thought I could, but I can't.*

Dammit. Her mom. She's gone after her mom and Beth has had enough time to find a way into Louisville by now. I race back into the dugout and grab my bat bag.

"Ryan?" Coach calls from the other end of the dugout.

"I'm sorry. I've got an emergency. Put Will in for me."

I slip the bottle of water into my bag and toss it over my shoulder. Chris wraps a solid hand around my arm. "Where are you going? We have one more inning and the game is tied. Will can't hold these batters like you can."

"Beth's running away. If I don't stop her, I'll lose her."

Chris tightens his grip. "You promised me you'd never walk from another game."

The ice water Chris prayed for finally enters my veins. "Let me go before I physically remove your hand from my arm."

"You're choosing her over us?"

Logan angles himself between me and Chris. "Let him go, Chris. He'd never dog you if you chose Lacy over a game."

"That's different," yells Chris. "I love Lacy."

"Take a look at him." Logan gestures to me. "He's in love with Beth. You and Lacy don't own the emotion."

Chris eyes me and I see the war inside him. He yanks the hat off his head and turns from me. I'm letting him down, but I let Beth down first. Logan nods at me and I give him a quick nod of thanks back.

The crowd buzzes with conversation as I exit the dugout. I keep my head down and ignore how people stare and even the occasional shout. The perfect Stone is doing a very imperfect thing and I don't give a damn what anyone thinks about it. I hear loud thumping footfalls striking the metal bleachers. If I'm lucky, I can hightail it to my Jeep before Dad reaches the parking lot.

Like the rest of today, I'm not lucky. "Ryan!"

I don't have time for this. I open the Jeep's door and toss my bag in the back. Dad grabs hold of the door. "What are you doing? You have another inning to play and the game is tied."

"Beth's in trouble and I'm going after her."

"No, you're not. You're going to finish that game." Dad's face reddens and he places his hand on his hips. In twenty-five years, I'll be his clone if I continue on my current path. My entire life I desired nothing more than to be him. It's funny how life changes.

"If I don't go after her, she'll be gone."

"Let her go. She needs to be gone. Since she entered your life you've lost focus on everything that's important. You're letting down your team, Ryan. You are single-handedly destroying your career in baseball. Everything I've worked so hard for!"

A strange mixture of ice and heat fights through my veins as I go toe-to-toe with my father. "You haven't worked hard for it! I have. This is my life. Not yours. If I want to play base-ball, I'll play. If I want to go to college, I'll go to college. If I want to talk to my brother, I will. If I want to go after Beth, I am. You are not making my decisions anymore."

Spit flies out of his mouth as he yells at me, "You're going to destroy your life over a drug-using waste of life?"

Power surges through me and my fist connects with his face. Adrenaline shakes my body and I watch as my father stumbles back. "Don't you ever call her that again."

I jump into the Jeep, turn on the engine, and push the ac-celerator. I don't lose and I'm not losing her.

BETH

I RUB MY HANDS TOGETHER and blow into them for possibly the thirtieth time. Hiding in the alleyway behind the bar, I stare at Mom's apartment. Trent entered right after I arrived and he's been in there for three hours. I have no choice but to wait. He'll kill me if he sees me again.

The door to the apartment opens and the bald asshole finally stumbles out. Fucking fabulous. He's tweaking, which means he'll be in a kicking babies mood. I'll take a heavy heroin user over a tweaker any day.

Resting his weight against his car door, Trent fumbles his keys, drops them, and dips low to pick them back up. Yeah, asshole, you belong behind a wheel. I hope you drive into a wall and die.

His car doesn't start immediately. The engine whines as he turns it over twice. Come on. The third time the engine groans to life. The car trembles when he backs it out and eases onto the main road.

I dash across the parking lot and bang on Mom's door as I try the knob. It doesn't give, but I hear Mom undoing the chains on the other side. She opens the door and wavers when she spots me. "Elisabeth."

I push in. "Did you pack?"

"No," she says. "I'm not sure we should do this."

God, this guy is a slob. His clothes are everywhere and so are the little empty packets that hold his meth. I grab a garbage bag and head into the bathroom. "What do you need?"

She follows me and rubs her bare arm. I remember Dad doing that. It means she's craving a hit. Withdrawal with her is going to be a bitch.

"Trent took care of me after I came home from the hospital. He says he's sorry for how he treats me and he wants to start again."

"Trent's full of shit." I pitch into the bag her toothbrush, hairbrush, then pause when I notice a small brown bag behind Mom's tampons. "What's this?"

"I don't know." Her hand moves up and down her arm again. "Shirley put it in there when she brought me home."

I snatch the bag. "I thought you said Trent took care of you when you came home."

"I meant to say he came by here this morning."

Inside the brown bag are a roll of fifties and a prescription bottle of the drug needed to help Mom detox from heroin. *Thank you, Shirley.* I try not to think about what she sold or what she did for the money. It's here and I need it and that's good enough for the moment. I throw everything into the garbage bag and go into her bedroom. The pickings are slim in the clothing department and I toss the less stained and torn clothes into the bag.

"Elisabeth," Mom says in a whine. "Maybe we should put it off—by a day or two."

"We are not putting it off by a day or two, we're leaving. Where are the keys to the car?"

"I...don't...know." Which means she does know.

I swing the bag full of stuff and knock her liquor bottles off the bedside table. Glass shatters against the wall. "That's what Trent's going to do to your head one of these days. We're getting out of here!"

Frustrated, I stalk out of the room and quickly glance toward the spare bedroom. The door is open for once and I freeze. "You have got to be fucking kidding me."

I rest my head against the door frame—too dizzy with disappointment to stay upright on my own. On an old coffee table I found near a Dumpster a couple of years ago are several bags of white powder. Smaller baggies and balloons lie on the floor. I can barely whisper the words. "You're selling heroin."

Mom shoves me out of the way and shuts the door. "No. Trent does. I used to let him keep it here overnight at times, but after the night you busted out his windows the police got nosy with him so he brought it here for good. It was the least I could do."

My fingers open and close. "*You* busted out the windows of Trent's car. I took the fall so they wouldn't send you to prison."

"Pretend you didn't see it, Elisabeth. Trent will be mad you know. He thinks you ratted him out to the police."

"What the fuck is wrong with you?" I shout in her face. "Do you not remember the outcome of our last heroin experience?" Forming a gun with my fingers, I point it to my forehead. "He was going to kill me, Mom. I was eight years old! He pushed the gun against my head and cocked the damned trigger."

Mom shakes her head too quickly and won't stop. "No, he wouldn't have. Your father said he was just trying to scare me and your dad. Your father said you were safe the whole time. He swore it."

How can she lie to herself so easily? How can she continue to turn away from the truth again and again? Then Mom rubs her arm. I stumble back and hit the wall. God, I'm no different. All the signs of a heroin user were there, for weeks if not longer, and I ignored every single one.

But I'm not ignoring the truth, not anymore. I go into the living room and start throwing crap off the kitchen counter to find her keys. I'll drag her out by her hair if I have to. The knob on the front door turns and my heart squeezes and drops. I've taken too long and Trent is going to kill me.

RYAN

BETH BLINKS RAPIDLY when I walk in. Standing in a tiny kitchen, she holds a garbage bag. I've never been so relieved to see anyone in my life. Nor have I ever craved to shake someone so badly.

"Going somewhere?" I focus on remaining calm. Beth doesn't react well to threats or anger or anyone standing in the way of her doing anything.

Beth turns her back to me and throws papers and trash onto the floor. "Get out."

"Fine with me. Let's go. We've come into Louisville twice for dinner and we have yet to have that date."

Beth leaves the kitchen and rummages through a card table. Her hands shake and her face is too pale against her black hair. "I'm not playing, Ryan. Mom and I are leaving today. That's been the plan the entire time, remember?"

"It was." My eyes dart around the confined room trying to pinpoint the threat that has Beth terrified. Adrenaline pours into my bloodstream, preparing me for the unseen attack. "But you changed your mind on Saturday."

A woman enters the living room. Too thin. Stringy blond

hair. It's the first time I've seen Beth's mother up close. "Who are you?" she asks.

I force myself to look into her flat eyes. They're the same color as Beth's, but without the shine. "I'm Beth's boyfriend, Ryan."

Her lips struggle into a weak smile. "You have a boyfriend, Elisabeth?"

Beth tosses an empty plastic two-liter onto the floor. "Ex-boyfriend. He fucked me and then he told his mommy and daddy he hated me. Where are the damned keys, Mom?"

My calm snaps. "I didn't do that to you. If you'll give me a chance I'll explain about my parents."

"Mom!" Beth screams and her mother flinches. "Keys. Now!"

"Okay," she says and shuffles down the hallway.

Beth whirls and her nostrils flare. "Get out, Ryan."

"Not without you."

Her fists curl and she smacks her leg with the words. "My. Mom. Is. An. Alcoholic. And a heroin addict. Her boyfriend's favorite pastime is beating the shit out of me and if I'm not around he has no problem taking his aggressions out on my mother. I have maybe minutes to get her out before he comes back and kills us all."

An eerie calm courses through me. Nobody hurts my girl. "He hits you?"

"Yes, Ryan. He hits me and kicks me and slaps me. I'm his own personal violent video game. If I don't get my mom out of here he's going to kill her and if he doesn't, then the heroin will."

Every word Beth says is probably true, but I don't care about her mother. Beth is my only concern. "What's going to happen to you if I let you walk out this door with your mother? Do you honestly think that getting in a car and driving to a different town is going to make anything better?"

BETH

"YES," I AUTOMATICALLY ANSWER, but a voice in the back of my head screams no. "It has to."

Looking out of place in his baseball uniform, Ryan takes up almost the entire living room thanks to his large body. "You know what I think?"

"I think you lied to me." He did and I try desperately to hold on to that.

"I screwed up. I'm not perfect. I lied to my parents about us, but I've owned up to dating you. They know I love you."

It's the right words, but... "You're too late."

"Bullshit!" Anger blazes out of his eyes. "For months I thought you were the most courageous person I knew. You've never apologized for being yourself, but standing here right now, I realize you're a coward. You're so terrified of feeling anything that you'd rather give up everything good in Groveton in order to feel safe."

My head jerks to the side and my eyes narrow. "Safe? I'm standing here in a fucking drug den trying to save my mother from a boyfriend who will be thrilled to kill me, then torture her. There is nothing safe about this."

"This is your safe. You'd rather struggle in this life than live in Groveton." He glances at the squalor of the apartment. "You *feel* in Groveton. In this life, you don't have to feel a thing and that makes you a coward."

I drop the bag in my hand and raise a shaky hand to my forehead. He's wrong. He has to be. That's not why I'm running. I need to save my mom because if I don't, who will?

Ryan closes the gap between us. My heart stutters when he places a hand on my waist. "I wish I could say that I'm the one that drove you away, but I'm not. I don't have that power. You've been running from the moment I met you and I'd bet you were running before that.

"You're a lot like that bird in the barn. You're so scared you're going to be caged in forever you can't see the way out. You smack yourself against the wall again and again and again. The door is open, Beth. Stop running in circles and walk out."

His other hand brushes the hair from my face and my lower lip begins to tremble. "If I leave her she'll die." My gut twists and my eyes burn.

He cups my face with his hands and I lean into his touch. Ryan can always do this—make me feel safe. He continues, "If you stay it'll kill you. Maybe not physically, but you'll die on the inside. If you don't want me, I'll give you your space, but you have built so much more in Groveton besides me. Give up on us if you need to, but don't give up on you."

The instinct is to flee. Instead, I grab on to his arms. Fear claws at me and I don't like how naked it makes me feel. "I'm scared."

Ryan lowers his forehead to mine. "So am I, but I'll be less scared when we leave here."

The front door opens. Bright sunlight blazes through the door and a gust of cold air announces the entrance of the devil. Trent's looming figure stalks into the living room. Losing control of my body, I feel my hands drop to my sides as my heart jumps to my throat. Ryan edges his body in front of mine.

Trent slams the door behind him and chuckles when he sees me. His eyes dart to the bag by my feet. "You should have stayed away."

Behind me, I hear the soft shuffles of my mother. "Elisabeth was just leaving."

Urging me in the direction of the door, Ryan presses his hand into my back. My mind screams *run*. My feet cement to the floor. It doesn't matter if I move or not. Trent won't let me walk out that door again.

"Let Ryan go." I say it as a plea and Trent flashes a smile. It's the first time I've asked anything of him and the bastard enjoys it.

Trent opens a box of cigarettes, puts one in his mouth, and lights it. He sucks in a long drag and blows out the smoke as he stares at me. I shiver as I watch the glowing ashes. The last time, Trent enjoyed listening to me scream when he burned holes in my arms. "Go ahead, boy. Get out. My problem isn't with you."

"Not without Beth." Rage shakes Ryan's voice.

I love Ryan despite everything, and if it weren't for me, he wouldn't be here. Shoving my hands against his chest, I push him away. "Go!"

Ryan sizes Trent up and Trent does the same to him.

"Walk out the door, Beth," says Ryan. "He's not going to touch you."

Trent laughs. Ryan is sturdy, strong, and young. Trent is larger, older, and a mean bastard. Last year, Isaiah and Noah took him on and the two survived because my uncle threatened Trent with a gun. My uncle isn't here and I'm not lucky enough to own a gun.

Ryan inches toward me and the door. His eyes never leave Trent. "Let's go."

My pulse pounds in my ears. Maybe we can walk out. "Mom?"

"Don't you dare move, Sky," Trent says.

I hold my hand out to her. "Come with us."

Ryan yells my name as his arms fly out in front of me. Pain slices my head. The ground rushes toward my face. A combination of darkness and light flickers from behind my closed lids. Noises blend into a high-pitched buzzing as warm liquid trickles from above my eyebrow to the bridge of my nose. I lick my lips and flinch at the salty taste of blood.

My eyelids flutter and I fight to keep them open. The room shifts and spins. Forcing my eyes to focus, I see the shattered remains of Mom's table lamp on the floor next to me.

The buzzing fades and I turn my head to the sound of a struggle and grunts. Ryan shoves Trent into the front door by tackling him at the waist. Trent quickly responds by punching Ryan in the stomach.

Ceramic cuts into my hand as I crawl toward them. "Stop." My voice comes out soft and hoarse. Ryan stumbles but is able to block a hit, then buys himself seconds by socking Trent in the jaw. I force pressure onto my legs so I can stand, but I fall.

Sitting in the fetal position on the other side of the room, Mom rocks back and forth on the floor. I swallow and force words out of my raw throat. "Help Ryan, Mom."

"I can't."

"He's going to kill us!"

Mom lowers her head to her knees and continues to rock.

"Mom!" I scream. "Please!"

Mom hums loudly and my heart breaks open. She's never going to change. No matter what I do. No matter how I try. My mom will always be this poor pathetic waste of life. I won't be her. I can't. I grab on to an overturned chair and force myself to my feet. Trent tackles Ryan and they both go crashing to the floor. "Leave him alone!"

Trent rises to his knees, punches Ryan in the face and Ryan falls once more. Panic tears at me. He's going to kill Ryan in front of me. The fucking bastard is going to take away everything I love.

I launch myself at him and smack and hit and claw. He bends my wrist and arm in a way not physically possible. Bones in my arm snap and pop. A scream tears through my body as pain blinds me.

He lets go and I fall to my knees in agony. My scream becomes silent as Trent squeezes his fingers around my neck. I gag and try to suck in air. Nothing happens. Thoughts flash through my head at a frenzied pace. I need air. He's going to kill me. My hands go to the fingers crushing my throat, but I can't pry them off.

He's stronger than me and powerful and he's going to win.

Trent jerks and his fingers loosen. Ryan holds Trent in a headlock as I collapse to the ground and draw air into my burning lungs. My hands flutter near my neck and cover where his fingers marked my skin.

"Baby!" Mom's hand joins mine on my throat. "Are you okay?"

Dazed, I nod.

Mom snatches my biceps and yanks in an effort to get me off the floor. "Let's go."

Ryan curses and I unsuccessfully struggle to stand. "Help him, Mom."

Ryan locks his other arm around Trent's neck and yells, "Go, Beth!" Trent battles against Ryan's hold and Ryan's face strains as he fights to keep his grip.

Mom shakes her head. "Let's go. Now. He'll hurt me."

Trent elbows Ryan in the gut, swings around and lands a blow to Ryan's face. Ryan falls.

"No!" Screams and pleas fly from my mouth. Blood covers Ryan's face. Trent stands and kicks Ryan in the stomach. I scream out in pain when I place weight on my left arm. "Help him, Mom!"

"We have to go now, Elisssabeth." Mom calmly slurs my name. "I want to leave. I'll go with you now."

I turn my head and stare at the eerie image of my mother. Her tired eyes with their constricted pupils look at me as if I'm a shadow instead of her daughter. Mom squeezes my hand again. For the first time, she's not rubbing her arm.

Cradling my left arm close to my body, I grip the table and pull myself to my feet. "You shot up?"

As I stand, Mom drops to the ground. In shame? In exhaustion? Too high? I don't know.

Refusing to watch Ryan die, refusing to make eye contact with me, Mom covers her head with her arms and rocks over and over again.

Blood pours over my eye and my sight wavers as my body sways to the side. My fingers accidentally hit Mom's cordless phone near the edge of the table.

Heroin.

It destroyed me nine years ago and one phone call cost me my father.

Heroin.

If I call, my mother will go to jail.

Heroin.

My finger slides against the numbers and like nine years ago I listen to the phone ring once, twice, a third time. The world turns black, then reappears in a fuzzy tunnel. My knees buckle and I force consciousness for a few more seconds.

"Nine-one-one, what's your emergency?"

RYAN

I SET MY CELL TO THE LOUDEST ringtone and place it on my chest before I rest my head on my pillow. Beth's supposed to come home from the hospital today and because of that I've refused pain medication. I want to hear her voice on the other end of the line and know that she's only a mile down the road instead of thirty minutes away in Louisville.

Then, for the first time in more than a week, I can sleep deeply.

My body is one slow, throbbing ache. Every pressure point pounds in time with my pulse. Broken ribs, bruised everything, and cuts. Each and every injury worth the cost of saving Beth.

"Can you tell me why?" My dad's voice carries into the room.

My eyes flash open and I turn my head to see him leaning against the door frame with his gaze pinned to the floor. It's the first words he's said to me since I hit him. He's been around. Present, but not speaking. I don't feel bad about it, because I haven't talked to him either...until now. "Why what?"

"Why you risked it all for that girl?"

"Because I love her. And her name's Beth."

No response. Sometimes I wonder if Dad knows what love is.

"Scott called," he says stiffly. "He wanted to remind you that there are rules now. He's angry with both of you and he won't be letting her out of the house anytime soon."

I return my focus to the ceiling. I can deal with rules as long as I've got Beth. Scott's been a mixture of grateful and pissed. In hindsight, maybe I should have called him when I found Beth's note, but I don't think Beth would have listened to him. She needed me.

"I don't think you should continue to see her," Dad says.

"Don't remember asking."

There's silence and when I glance out of the corner of my eye, Dad's gone. Who knows if the two of us can fix what's been broken.

My cell buzzes and my stomach plummets when I notice Beth's name above the text. She promised she'd call. Friends, right?

I half chuckle. It's the first text she ever sent me. Always.

The doorbell rings and I rub my eyes. I'm too exhausted for guests, but they keep coming: my friends, the baseball team, my coaches, teachers, my parents' friends.

Mom and Dad's slightly raised tones indicate that they're disagreeing over something, and I don't care enough to figure out the issue. I expect them to continue the argument, but what I don't expect is Mom's voice at the door of my room. "Because I said so."

She throws a glare down the hallway before addressing me. "Ryan, you have a guest."

Before I can ask who, Beth walks into my room with her left arm in a sling. The breath slams out of my body. She's here. Forgetting about my injuries, I rush to sit up—and wince. The smell of roses overwhelms me and I glance up to see Beth by my side.

"You look like hell. Have you been resting at all?"

The right side of my mouth quirks up. "It's nice to see you too."

"I'm serious." Beth doesn't wear worry well and the ache on her face bothers me.

I capture the hand she uses to try to push me back down, bring it to my lips, and kiss her palm. God, I've missed her.

A clearing of a throat and I notice Scott standing beside my mother at the door. "A few minutes, Beth, then we're heading home."

Beth nods and I watch my mother's reaction to a girl in my room. She studies us, almost like someone seeing a painting they don't quite get. There's no malice in her expression, just curiosity. "I'm leaving the door open."

"Thanks," I say and I mean it. Mom's trying now—not only with me, but with Mark, and I have Chris to thank for it. He called Mark when EMS brought me into the emergency room. Mark and Mom talked for the first time while I was in X-ray. Both are silent about the conversation they had, but they're speaking again. It's a start.

Scott leans his head in when Mom leaves and stares straight at Beth. "Behave."

She rolls her eyes. "Because the moment you leave we're going to go at it like wild animals. Please." She motions to her arm. "Broken bones and bruises are so attractive."

Scott shakes his head as he follows Mom to the living

room and Beth mirrors his movements. Do they have any idea they're clones of each other?

Beth sinks onto the bed and turns her head toward me. I don't like how she looks. Beyond the cuts on her face and head, plus the bruises, she's too pale and dark circles outline the bottom of her eyes. Wondering if I'm dreaming, I reach over and rub her hair between my fingers. It's silky and real. I let the strands fall and meet her gaze. "How are you?"

I hate the way her forehead crinkles and the pain weighing her features. She closes her eyes briefly. "I'm so sorry. It's my fault he hurt you."

"Nope, not going to hear it." I grab Beth's hand and coax her to lie with me on the bed.

She resists. "But your mom—"

"What's she going to say? I'm hurt. You're hurt. We got tired and lay down. I want to hold you so for once in your life can you not fight me?"

"Wow. Someone's cranky."

"Damn right I am." But the knots twisting my gut begin to unravel when I lie back and Beth wraps her body gingerly around mine. She's hesitant, testing areas first to confirm the contact won't make me sore, and I'm gentle when placing an arm around her so that I don't jostle her arm.

When we're settled, I exhale and close my eyes. I've dreamed of this for seven days. Who knows, I'm probably dreaming now. If I am, maybe Beth will do something that's hard for her; maybe she'll give me answers. "Why did you believe Gwen over me?"

BETH

I READJUST, SNUGGLING CLOSER to Ryan, but braced for signs that I've hurt him. I can hear his heart now and the inhale and exhale of air through his lungs. If I weren't so damn tired, I could possibly cry. I thought I lost him at my mom's apartment.

Ryan runs a hand through my hair and I lick my lips, searching for courage. He deserves an answer. If not because he risked his life to save me, then because I love him. "I didn't trust you."

His heart beats several times before he speaks again. "Why?"

Because I was stupid. "I don't know...." I don't have Ryan's way with words. They're hard for me. Difficult. At least words that have emotion. "I guess it was easier to believe that you used me rather than loved me. To be honest... I don't get it. Why would someone like you want to be with someone like me?"

Ryan tips my chin up so that I have to look him in the eye. "Because I love you. Beth—you're everything I want to be. You're alive and live without apology. I never would have made love to you if I thought you didn't trust me...or love me. And I never would have done it if I didn't trust and love you."

I lean up on my elbow and my heart is practically yanked out of my chest by the hurt in his eyes. "I do love you, and I want to trust you.... It's just that...I try.... And..."

Just damn. I slam my good hand on the bed. Why can't I explain it? Why am I so impaired?

"Hey." The authority in his tone causes me to meet his gaze. My heart stalls when Ryan caresses my cheek with one finger and, under his touch, my skin turns red. I miss this. I've missed him. Maybe I'm not fucking this all up.

"Breathe," he instructs. "It's okay. Take your time, but just keep talking."

Keep talking. I actually stick out my tongue in disgust and Ryan fights a smile. If he weren't so battered already I'd sock his arm. I blow out a rush of air and try again.

"I don't know.... I just don't...trust...me." I blink and so does Ryan and it feels sort of scary and exposing to have said something so raw. He rubs my arm, urging me to continue, and I don't know how to continue. That's bull. I just don't want to continue. But this is beyond what I want. This is about me and Ryan.

"I don't want to make bad choices anymore." I glance at him, hoping I'm making sense, because I'm not sure that I am. "And I sort of think that any choice is bad because I'm making it and then I meet you and you're great and you're wonderful and you love me and I love you and I'm just so damned scared I'm going to screw it all up...."

I slam my eyes shut and my lower lip trembles. "And I did. I messed it all up again."

Ryan cups my cheek with his palm. I lean into it and open my eyes. "I'm glad it happened," he says.

"I thought they ran an MRI on your head."

His eyes laugh. "They did. Just answer me this—before Trent arrived, were you going to leave with me?"

I swallow and I'm nodding before I answer. "Yes."

"Why?"

My eyes narrow as I try to understand the question.

"No, Beth. Don't think about it. Just give me the first answer that comes to mind. Why were you going to leave with me?"

My eyes flash to his and my mouth pops open. No, it's not possible, because if it is, then it's a first for me.

The same hope I've seen a million times from Ryan builds on his face. Is it possible he's known all along? "Say it, Beth."

"I love you." Those used to be the hard words, but now they're easier. I exhale and the air shakes as it comes out of my mouth.

"Nice try," he says. "The other thing. Say that."

"Ryan..." My throat dries out and sweat forms along my hairline. "I'm scared."

"I know." He tucks my hair behind my ear. "But it's okay."

His fingers slowly trail down my arm, over my sling, and he rests his fingertips against mine. A warmth unfurls within me, starting in my heart and flowing through my bloodstream. It creates a weird sensation of chains unlocking and breaking free. It's almost as if I'm floating.

"I trust you," I say. "I was going to leave with you because I trust you."

Ryan's silent, but the small, peaceful smile on his face causes me to smile in return. I wonder if my smile looks like his. I trust him. Ryan. It's a little scary, but not as much as I thought it would be. Maybe this is it; maybe this is the beginning Scott's talked about for months—the clean slate.

"Was that so hard?" he asks.

"Yes."

Ryan touches my hair again. It's like he requires the contact to confirm I'm not a ghost. "You need to learn how to start trusting yourself."

I flop down so that my head rests on the pillow beside him. Ryan's slow as he shifts. Our faces are so close that our noses almost touch. My arm begins to ache and I have a feeling Scott will show soon because he's timed my pain med schedule into his phone. "Do you mind if I heal first before I tackle any more long-lost resurfacing emotional issues?"

Ryan tilts his head and I silently swear. Apparently we're not done yet. "You're kidding me, right?"

"Scott said Isaiah came to the hospital," he begins.

I nod, preferring not to go into this now...or ever. Noah visited me several times while I was in the hospital—once with Echo, and twice on his own. He told me that Isaiah paced the waiting room until he heard I was going to be okay, then he left. My best friend left.

"I think we should talk about it."

The fingers of my left hand try to tighten, but the blast of pain keeps me from making a fist. I hiss at the sting and Ryan edges closer. "Are you okay?"

"Yes," I bite out. "It's just...I already told you that it's not like that for me with him."

"I believe you."

My brow begins to lift and I stop when the stitches on my

forehead pull. Dammit, I'm never going to be able to move again. "Then why bring it up?"

Ryan sucks in a breath and I can tell this conversation is eating at him as much as it is me. "Are you going to see him again?"

No. Yes. "If he'll let me. But he left the hospital without talking to me. I don't know what that means." Screw that. "Yes, of course I'll see him again. Isaiah and I are friends and he's going to realize that even if I have to take a two-by-four to him."

He looks torn between a smile and a sigh. "And you wonder why I'm concerned."

"What's that supposed to mean?"

"You've got to admit, the life you lived in Louisville is different than the one you have now. I'm scared that if you have a place to run, a person to run to, when things get tough you'll go." Ryan stretches out the fingers of my left hand that had begun to retighten. "There's always going to be someone doubting us, Beth, and I can't be in this if you're always running."

"No more running. I promise." It's almost painful to step past my pride to say the rest. "You were right...in Louisville... about me having a life in Groveton. I have you...but I also have Scott and Lacy and school. I like who I am here."

"Me too," he says as if proving his case.

"But Isaiah and I go back too far for me to abandon him. I'm here. Heart. Soul. Body. Groveton's my home, but I will never abandon a friend, especially my best friend." I stare at the comforter beneath us. "I need you to be okay with it, because I'm not budging when it comes to him."

After a few moments of silence, I risk a glance. Ryan eventually caves. "Fine. He's your friend. If you're going to trust me, then I'm going to trust you."

I kick off my shoes and rub my toe against his foot. It's the best I can do with an arm in a sling. "Deal. I love you and..." I swallow my fear and push through. "I trust you."

"Good." Ryan's muscles visibly settle and his eyelids flutter.

"Good," I repeat, allowing myself to relax along with him. "You know I want to hear it again."

Ryan moves closer, wraps a protective arm around my waist, and shuts his eyes. "I trust you."

"Nice try." I softly mock elbow him with my padded cast and his chest moves as he chuckles. It feels so good to tease him again. "The other thing. Say that."

"I love you."

Enjoying his warmth and strength, I melt into him and close my own eyes. "Again."

"I love you," he whispers.

"Again." But this time my mind drifts as I hear his soft declaration. I mean to demand the words again, but then my head finds his chest. His heart beats steadily in my ear and I have my answer. Both Ryan and I lose ourselves in each other and sleep.

RYAN

A YEAR AGO, I HAD MY LIFE completely mapped out. It turns out, no one knows the future. I slip my arms through the suit coat and readjust my shoulders so the jacket will fit properly on my body. The bruises and cuts faded, but my ribs still ache by the end of the day. Especially if I've pushed myself too hard.

"Your tie is crooked." Mom leans one shoulder against the door frame and gives a disapproving nod as she looks at my throat. "Come here."

I inch away from my dresser and Mom undoes the knot.

"You look nice," she says.

"Except for the tie."

Mom's lips tilt up and she slides the tie to measure it against my chest. "Except for the tie. How do you feel?"

"Good."

Lines worry her eyes and she strains to hold the smile. "I know the doctor cleared you to start practicing, but I think you should wait another week or two. Just to be sure everything healed correctly."

Mom expertly weaves the tie into a knot and tightens it

up to my throat. She stares at it for a second before letting her hand touch my cheek—a rare physical gesture for both of us. "I'm glad you're okay."

She withdraws. "I talked to your brother again this morning. He asked how you were doing."

Mark knows how I'm doing. We've talked on the phone every day since I was released from the hospital. Mark must still be feeling awkward talking to Mom and looking for the easiest conversation to have. I busy myself with buttoning my cuffs. "What did you tell him?"

"That you're stubborn like your father and wouldn't tell me if you were in pain."

"I'm fine, Mom."

Mom fiddles with her pearls. "If we had listened to you that morning... If we had listened to you weeks before... If I had stood up to your father when Mark told us...none of this would have happened."

"It's okay." I wish they had listened to me the morning Beth ran away. I wish they had listened to me weeks before when I told them I cared for her. I wish Mom had stood up to Dad and kept Mark in our family, but none of that happened. Even if it did, there's no telling if it would have stopped the nightmare in motion. Beth ran away because living in Groveton terrified her. She would have run regardless of what happened between us and because I love her, I would have followed.

Mom sighs and falls into social mode. "Mark's coming home for dinner on Sunday. I thought we could keep it simple. Just me, you, Mark...hopefully your father."

"Sounds great." Even though we both know Dad will go into town while Mark is home. Dad still refuses to acknowledge Mark exists. Nothing much has changed in my parents' marriage. Mom's choosing me and Mark, and Dad dropped the idea of running for mayor. But he's still home and they're still going to counseling. As I said, who knows what the future might bring.

"Don't forget the corsage." Mom slips out of the room.

I grab my car keys, the red rose wrist corsage, and head out to the garage. From the corner of my eye, I see Dad sitting behind his desk in his office. We haven't talked since that day in my bedroom and I guess today won't be the day either of us breaks our silence.

As I open the door to my Jeep, I hear the squeak of his chair and footsteps against the cement floor. Dad walks to his tool bench and sifts through the boxes of bolts and nuts. "Your mom told me you signed a National Letter of Intent to play for the University of Louisville."

My muscles tense in preparation for a fight. The letter required a parent to sign with me and I asked Mom for help. "Yes, sir."

"She said that you're planning on playing with the team for a year, then reassessing whether or not you're ready to go pro."

Feeling naked without my cap, I rub the back of my head. I could go the easy route and give him a simple yes, but I'm done saying or doing whatever it takes to appease him. "At the end of my freshman year, I'll decide if I'm good enough to go pro. I'm also going to major in creative writing. I love writing and baseball and I want to give them both a shot."

Dad slides a drawer full of nails closed and nods his head. "Did you get her a corsage? Girls like flowers."

I hold the clear box in my hand. "Yeah," I say, and lift it up so he can see. "You taught me that."

BETH

SCOTT AND ALLISON'S BEDROOM is too gaudy for my taste. The curtains are blue silk and frilly things like flowers and paintings of flowers decorate every available space. The bed is beyond massive. Scott and Allison don't have to go to separate rooms if they fight; they can roll over a couple times and be in different zip codes.

I sit on the overly cushioned chair in front of Allison's vanity and watch as she pins the hair onto my head. I hate the updo, but I can't complain. An hour ago, she dyed six stripes of temporary black color in my hair. Now my hair is an inch and a half of golden-blond at the roots, black flows over my shoulders, and black stripes even it out. "Scott is going to be pissed."

"Yes," she says. "He is, but I'll deal with that."

My lips curve and when Allison catches it in the mirror she smiles too. We've had an uneasy truce since I came home from the hospital and sometimes I'm scared I'm going to say the wrong thing and send her over the edge. "Why are you being nice to me?"

Allison lifts the curling iron again and shoots me a glare

when I fidget. She twists a few strands that refuse to be a part of her plan. "Because Scott loves you."

He loved me before, but that didn't keep her from hating every cell in my body. Not like I helped. "I'm sorry I accused you of trapping him."

The curling rod pulls at the roots of my hair and I bite my lip. She releases the hair and little ringlets dance on the back of my neck. Okay, I deserve the pulling—and the ringlets. Maybe now we'll be even.

Allison sets the iron back on her vanity. "I'm sorry...well, I'm sorry. I didn't want you here."

I blink. That was blunt, yet honest.

"Scott told me about his past, but it was easy to pretend it was a story until you came into the picture. I prefer life clean and simple. You made Scott complicated."

"Scott was always complicated."

Allison spritzes hair spray on me. "I know that now."

Scott clears his throat and both Allison and I turn to see him entering the room. I stand and Scott grins when he sees me in the black strapless dress with a skirt that ends at the knees. He frowns again when he sees my hair.

"I did it," says Allison without a hint of guilt.

Scott's eyes widen. "You did that?"

"You told her last weekend she could wear those God-awful shoes with her dress and I told you that you'd regret it."

I fidget in my official Chuck Taylors. "I'm wearing panty hose." That was a major concession on my part.

"You should put on a sweater," Scott says.

"She's not wearing a sweater." Allison swats at him. "That would look wretched."

"I don't care how she looks. I care how much skin is showing."

Allison leans forward and Scott kisses her lips. I glance away. They do this more since I came home from the hospital. Not just kissing, but kissing like they mean it. Kissing because they truly love each other. She steps out of the room and Scott shoves his hands in his pockets.

I resist the urge to scratch my healing temple. "She covered the cut with the makeup."

"I noticed." He gestures to my left hand. "How's it feeling?"

I shrug. "Fine." The black cast is temporary. Trent shattered lots of the bones in my hand, wrist, and arm. I'll have to have another surgery in two weeks. My nondamaged fingers drum against my leg. I thought I could go without asking, but I can't. "How did Mom's court appearance go?"

Mom and Trent had preliminary hearings yesterday. I told Scott that I didn't want to know what happened, but the curiosity is eating me alive.

"It's okay to want to know." He meets my eyes while I wrestle with the millions of emotions tugging me in different directions.

I nod and he continues, "She accepted the plea bargain and will be serving six years. Trent pleaded not guilty against his lawyer's recommendation. The D.A. thinks they can get him to serve fifteen years."

A ball of dread forms in my stomach and I sink back into the chair. "Then there will be a trial."

Scott lowers his head. All of us had hoped to avoid this. "Yes."

Ryan and I will have to face Trent again when we testify. I take a deep breath to calm myself.

"Did you talk to Mom?" I ask.

He shakes his head and I'm not sure how I feel about that.

I'm not sure how I feel about my mom at all. Six years. My mom is going to prison for six years and I'm the one who put her there.

"You did the right thing, kid."

"I know," I say softly. I do know, but it doesn't mean that it sucks any less. The doorbell rings and the dread starts to fade. Ryan's here.

A good-natured smile settles on Scott's face. "And Prince Charming awaits."

"Hey, Scott?"

He motions for me to continue.

"How could you keep the heroin to yourself? I mean, that's a pretty big secret. I know that you wanted something to blackmail me with, but it was heroin."

Scott scratches behind his ear. "I was in the process of hiring private detectives to find you when your aunt called. When I got to the police station, there was no way you were going home with anyone but me. One look at your mom and I knew things were bad."

He sighs. "She was so jumpy around the cops that I figured she was hiding something. I would have said anything I had to in order to keep you. But I never used the word *heroin* with you or your mom and I never went into your mom's apartment. I guessed that she had a secret and I bluffed."

And I sort of feel like an idiot. A happy idiot, but an idiot nonetheless. "Well played."

He smirks. "I think so."

At the two-minute warning, my hands begin to sweat, including the one in the cast. Indian summer in Kentucky has a strange way of making November feel like July. As we walk to the open field behind the scoreboard, Ryan holds my hand and he doesn't seem to care it's cold and wet. People yell and scream from the bleachers and the announcer informs the crowd that our team is at the first and ten—whatever the hell that means.

The other couples nominated for homecoming court stand closer to the lamppost, but I hesitate farther back and Ryan plays along.

"Gwen won't bother you," he says.

"I know." He's right. She won't. Since Ryan and I returned to school, she's been less than her normal stuck-up self, quiet and withdrawn. She apologized to both me and Ryan. I accepted it, but it doesn't mean I have to like her or be near her. Perfectly groomed, Gwen stands off to the side of the group. I sort of feel bad for her. Guilt is a horrible emotion. I should know.

"We could go talk to Carly and Brent," Ryan teases. "She's a big fan of yours."

I roll my eyes. "Carly and I were paired as lab partners today."

"See, best friends already. Lacy will be pissed someone is encroaching on her territory."

"That's exactly what's going to happen," I say sarcastically.

"Carly's nice."

"She's chipper."

"Same thing."

"Nice is nice. Chipper is annoying."

"We should double-date with them."

My eyes almost pop out of my head. "Are you kidding me? I'm about to walk out onto that football field and make a fool out of myself and you want me to consider double-dating with Mr. and Mrs. Chipper? Have you lost your mind?"

Ryan chuckles, then winks. "I just wanted to see you get aggravated."

I wrinkle my nose. "You're annoying."

He lets go of my hand, slips his arms around my waist, and pulls me close to his strong body. "You're beautiful."

The corners of my lips turn up and I slide my right arm around his neck. "I miss touching you with both hands."

"It's weird seeing the ribbon on your other wrist," he says.

I shiver when Ryan caresses the sensitive skin above my cast and rubs the small of my back. Joyous and devious warmth spreads throughout my body. "I never take it off."

"I miss you in my bed," he murmurs so only I can hear.

My smile grows and Ryan's face reddens. "That's not what I meant. I meant I miss sleeping with you."

I know what he means. "It's a little hard to slip out with a broken hand."

He lowers his head to mine and his hold on me tightens. "I'm sorry I didn't protect you better."

"Ryan, no. I would have died if it wasn't for you."

"It's over now," he whispers against my mouth.

I expectantly part my lips for his kiss. "It is."

"Mr. Stone. Ms. Risk," calls the assistant principal. "A little more space between you and a lot more paying attention. It's time for you to get onto the field."

I deflate and wrap my hand on Ryan's bent arm so he can escort me out underneath the glaring lights. I wanted Ryan to kiss me. I needed him to kiss me.

Over the PA system, our names are announced and Ryan leads me to the fifty-yard line. People yell and scream, the loudest cheers coming from the section where we left Lacy, Chris, and Logan.

"When you win," says Ryan, "don't forget you said you'd keep that tiara on your pretty little head all night."

My eyes widen as I realize how I can get exactly what I want. We stop in the middle of the field and I turn to him. "Kiss me. Not just a peck. The real deal."

Ryan glances around at the bleachers full of hundreds of people. "Excuse me?"

"I, Beth Risk, do double dog dare you to kiss me in front of all these people."

Ryan's eyes brighten and the arrogant smile that makes my heart trip over itself spreads across his face. "Are you forgetting dare etiquette? You have to dare before you can double dog dare."

I roll my eyes. "Fine. I dare you to kiss me."

"And if I do?"

"If I win homecoming, which I won't, I'll wear that damn tiara for a week straight."

He cradles my face with both his hands. His lips whisper against mine and I ache for him to kiss me. My mind whines that he won't do it, but then he nibbles on my lower lip. His mouth parts and the two of us move our lips hungrily in time with one another.

In between gasps of air our names are called as the winners. I feel Ryan's lips tug into a smile before he says one word: "Can."

★ ★ ★ ★ ★

ACKNOWLEDGMENTS

To God—Isaiah 61:1
For Dave—Because I still own
the first baseball cap I ever saw you in.

Thank you to...

Kevan Lyon—Everybody should have someone like you in their corner. Your advice and guidance have been extremely valuable to me. Thank you. I will never forget that this all began with you.

Margo Lipschultz—Thank you for caring as much about my characters as I do. You are absolutely brilliant and I'm a better writer because of you.

Everyone who has touched my books at Harlequin Teen, especially Natashya Wilson. You guys have made this experience fantastically memorable!

Matt Baldwin and Mike Baldwin with Future Pro: Thank you for welcoming me into your indoor training facility and for taking the time to answer my questions on baseball.

Angela Annalaro-Murphy—Thank you for loving Beth first. It was your faith and friendship that kept me writing.

Shannon Michael—How many times did I end up on your back porch with my head in my hands wondering if I was headed in the right direction with the story? Thanks for the laughs and friendship.

Kristen Simmons—I couldn't have done this without you. It's amazing when I think of the laughter and tears we've shared since we met. This book is for you.

Colette Ballard, Kelly Creagh, Bethany Griffin, Kurt Hampe, and Bill Wolfe—You guys are more than a critique group. You've become family. Kelly and Bethany, thank you for holding my hand through my debut year. Kurt and Bill, thank you for pointing out when "a guy wouldn't do that." Colette, thank you for the endless hours of laughter, support, and extra reads.

Louisville Romance Writers: It was you guys who first put me on the path toward publication. Thank you for continuing to light the way.

Again, to my parents, my sister, my Mt. Washington family, and my in-laws...I love you.

My biggest thank-you is to the fantastic authors I've met, the booksellers, the librarians, the teachers, the book bloggers, and my readers. Thank you for taking the time to spread the word and for the messages, tweets, and emails you've sent to me. You remind me why I write.

To A, N, and P. You know who you are and you know that I love you more than my own life.

Don't miss Isaiah's story,

CRASH INTO YOU

available now
from Katie McGarry
and Harlequin TEEN!
Turn the page
for a two-chapter preview....

Rachel

THE DRIVER'S SEAT OF MY MUSTANG is one of the few places where I find peace. I guess I could go on some tangent about how my older brothers influenced my love of cars, but I won't, because it's not true.

I get cars. I like the feel of them. The sound of them. My mind clears when I'm behind the wheel, and there's something about the sound of an engine dropping into gear as I press on the gas that makes me feel...powerful.

No fear. No nausea. No brothers to boss me around. No parents to impress. Just me, the gas pedal, and the open road. And a big, fat, fluffy dress that reminds me of a flower. Shifting in this getup was a nightmare.

The fluff from the ball gown pops out of my brother Ethan's old gym bag and I try to shove the overflowing lace back in as I exit the gas station bathroom. I wind through the aisles and out the automatic doors into the cold winter night. My parents would kill me if they knew I was in the south side of town, but this isn't my destination. Just a pit stop. The county south of here contains backcountry roads that are flat for several miles. Perfect for maxing out the speedometer.

Two college-age guys in jeans and nice winter coats chat as one pumps gas into a 2011 Corvette Coupe. She's impressive. Four hundred and thirty horses are compacted into that precious V-8 engine, but she's not as pretty as the older models. Most cars aren't.

On the opposite side of the pump, I insert my credit card and unscrew the gas cap. My baby only receives the best gas. It may be more expensive, but it treats her engine right.

I suck in a breath, and the cold air feels good in my lungs. My stomach had settled when I left the country club and the nausea rolled away when I turned over the engine. I'd made it through the speech with shaking hands and a trembling voice. When it was over, my mother cried and my father hugged me. That alone was worth the trips into the bathroom beforehand.

The guys stop talking and I glance over to see them staring at my baby. "I like your Vet," I say and decide to test them. "V-8?" Of course it has a V-8, but some guys have no idea what sweet cargo they own under the hood.

The owner nods. "3LT. Got her last week. Nice Mustang. Is it your boyfriend's?"

Loaded question. "She's mine."

"Nice," he says again. "Have you ever raced her?"

I shake my head no. It feels strange to talk to guys. I'm the girl who hangs on the periphery. The other girls who attend the most expensive private school in the state don't want to discuss cars, and most guys get intimidated when I know more about their cars than they do. When it comes to any other type of conversation, my tongue often becomes paralyzed.

"Would you like to race?" he asks.

Our gas nozzles click off at the same exact time and my

heart flutters in my chest with a mixture of anxiety and adrenaline. I'm not sure if I want to faint or laugh. "Where?"

He inclines his head away from the safety of the freeway
and down the four-lane road—deeper into the south end. I've
heard rumors of illegal drag races, but I thought they were
just that—rumors. "Are you for real?"

"It doesn't get any more real than where I'd be taking you.
Stick with us and we'll help you get a nice race."

I have four brothers, and one is the type that mothers warn
their daughters against. In other words, I'm not that naive,
but to be honest, his proposal intrigues me. But I'm also sure
this is how horror movies begin.

Or the best action flicks on the face of the planet.

I scan the guy's car out of the corner of my eye. A University of Louisville student parking tag hangs on the rearview
mirror along with a maroon-and-gold tassel. Only my school
has those God-awful colors.

But to be safe… "Where did you go to high school?" I ask.

"Worthington Private," he says with the arrogance most
guys from my school use when saying the word *private*.

"I go there." And I don't bother hiding my grin.

Neither do they. The car owner continues to be the spokes-
man for his duo. "What year are you?"

"A junior."

"We graduated last year."

"Cool," I say. Very cool. My brother would be a year behind him, but West has made it his business for people to love
him. "Do you know West Young?"

"Yeah." He brightens. This guy thinks he is so close to
scoring. "Do you guys party together?"

I laugh and I can't stop myself. "No. He's my brother."

Their smiles melt quicker than a snow cone on a summer's afternoon. "You're his baby sister?"

"I prefer to be called Rachel. And you are?"

He runs a hand over his face. "Going to get my ass kicked by your brothers. Forget I said anything about racing or that we even saw each other."

As he inches to his car, I spring over the small concrete barrier. I only meant to make sure the guy would keep his distance, not sprint for Alaska. "Wait. I want to race."

"Your brothers don't play around when it comes to you, and aren't you supposed to be sickly or something?"

Stupid, stupid brothers and stupid, stupid rumors and stupid, stupid hospital visits when I stupid, stupidly was so panicked my freshman year I had to stay overnight twice. "Obviously the whole sick thing is wrong and if you don't take me to the drag race, I'll tell West about tonight." No, I won't, but I'll try bluffing.

Owner Guy looks over at his friend hovering near the passenger door. His friend shrugs. "I bet she'll keep her mouth shut."

"I will," I blurt. "Keep my mouth shut."

Owner Guy curses under his breath. "One race."

Isaiah

I LEAN AGAINST MY CAR DOOR and assess the group illegally loitering in the parking lot of the abandoned strip mall. Green, blue, and red neon lights frame the bottom of different makes and models. A few of us puritans remain on the streets, refusing to decorate our cars like Christmas trees. The bass line of rap rattles frames and a couple drivers are brave enough to blare the screeching electric guitar of heavy metal.

Clouds cover the sky, leaving all of us in a dark pit. Close to a week after Christmas, the presents have been opened, the turkey dinners have been demolished, and mommies and daddies are either tucked in bed or sucked into a bottle of Jack. Time for the rats to hit the streets.

"Isaiah!" Eric Hall abandons two girls in short skirts and faux fur jackets and heads for me. Most people underestimate the bleach-blond, skinny son of a bitch, but that mistake could prove lethal for your billfold and your health. On the streets of the south side, this nineteen-year-old is king. "Merry belated Christmas, my brother."

I accept his outstretched hand and the half hug.

Eric is who I came to see, and if I don't watch myself,

I'll end up indebted to him. My goal in life is to be free of everyone—foster care, school, social workers. Eric Hall may not be official, but he's an organization all his own with the street business he created. He even has "employees": guys with bats and tire irons that willingly beat the hell out of anyone who doesn't pay.

He motions to the two giggling girls. "Santa brought me twins and in the spirit of the season, I'm willing to share. That is, if you drive for me tonight."

This is the reason why I'm here. Noah and I need cash and Eric can make that happen. If I play this right, I'll rake in money and stay free.

While sucking on a lollipop, the twin with black hair stares at me longer than her sister. "Ho, ho, ho," mumbles Eric.

My thoughts exactly and I turn my back to them. I have a bad track record with girls with black hair. "You know I don't street race."

Typically, I don't. Street racing can put my ass in jail and cost me the setup I have with Noah. I have no intention of being placed in juvie or worse—a group home. I race legally at The Motor Yard, but The Motor Yard is closed for the holidays. Tonight will be a one-time deal.

He leans in close as if what he's saying is a secret. "I'll give you twenty percent of what I make on top of the Christmas cheer. I'm giving my other boys ten."

Eric has never offered anyone such a commission, but if he's starting off high, maybe he'll go even higher. "Twenty percent isn't going to cover my bail if I get arrested."

"I know you, my brother," says Eric. "You need speed and I have the need for green. Say yes and you can race my recently acquired suped-up Honda Civic with two full tanks of nitro."

I cross my arms over my chest. "I'm looking for a one-time race, Eric. That is, if we can come to an understanding."

The sweet purring of an engine grabs not only my attention, but that of every hot-blooded, car-worshiping male in the lot. Jesus—that's a 2005 Mustang GT. And unlike the other muscle cars parked on the strip, not a piece of her looks like it's seen the inside of a body shop.

A flood of male bodies surround the beautiful pony. I drop back and let the wolves have first crack. A car like this is here for one reason—to race, and any new piece of machinery has to pass Eric's inspection. Someone is going to have to approve the engine and I have no doubts I'll be the one caressing that soft underbelly.

The driver shuts down the engine, opens the door, and a halo of sunshine slides out of the car and into the light of the only working streetlamp. Fuck me. God does exist and he sent an angel in a white Mustang to prove it.

Angels are small—at least this one is. She stands barely a foot taller than the top of her car. Her long golden hair curls at the ends and she has a slender frame. Her leather-gloved hand grips the top of her door and she uses the door as a shield between herself and the street rats.

"Nice car." Like a vulture, Eric slowly circles her.

"Thanks." She glances at two guys exiting a Corvette. Those college boys belong here even less than she does. All three of them are easy prey.

The angel tucks her hair behind her ear. "Is this where I can drag race?"

I wince internally at her words. Asking for anything on

the streets is a cardinal sin. Asking nicely is basically serving your soul to the devil. God didn't send this angel to save me. He sent her as a sacrifice....

Overall theme:
"Dirt Road Anthem" by Jason Aldean
"F**kin' Perfect" by P!nk

Taco Bell dare:
"Summertime" by Kenny Chesney
"U + Ur Hand" by P!nk

Beth's mother in the bar:
"Farmer's Daughter" by Crystal Bowersox

Beth wakes in Scott's house:
"Heart Like Mine" by Miranda Lambert

Ryan in town:
"Back Where I Come From" by Kenny Chesney

Isaiah offers to run away with Beth:
"Somewhere with You" by Kenny Chesney

Isaiah betrays Beth by taking her away from her mother:
"Hurt" by Nine Inch Nails

Ryan takes Beth to a field party:
"My Kinda Party" by Jason Aldean

Ryan dances with Beth:
"Just a Dream" by Nelly

Beth stays the night with Ryan:
"Don't You Wanna Stay" by Jason Aldean and Kelly Clarkson

Beth sings her mother to sleep:
"Free Bird" by Lynyrd Skynyrd

Beth tries to scare Ryan away with the truth:
"Don't Let Me Get Me" by P!nk

Ryan teaches Beth to float:
"Broken Arrow" by Rod Stewart

Beth and Ryan are briefly happy:
"Teenage Dream" by Katy Perry

Beth's final showdown with her mother:
"25 to Life" by Eminem

This song perfectly describes Beth and Ryan's relationship:
"How Country Feels" by Randy Houser

Songs written for *Dare You To* by Angela McGarry:
"Ribbons and Bows"
"We Weren't Meant to Be"
Check out the songs at:
www.reverbnation.com/AngelaMcGarryMusic

What inspired you to write *Dare You To*?

In high school, my best friend and I would spend our evenings riding around in her car with the windows rolled down and music turned up. At some point, we would always find ourselves at a late-night fast-food restaurant.

Some of the most interesting things in my life happened between bites of greasy food.

Those memories pushed me to write the opening scene of *Dare You To* and, from there, Beth and Ryan became full-fledged characters who demanded their story be told.

Your first book, *Pushing the Limits*, takes place in an urban/suburban setting. What made you decide to set a majority of *Dare You To* in a rural environment?

I grew up in a fringe neighborhood south of a large city. While we had a city zip code and all the conveniences of a larger population area, we would run into farmland if we traveled a few miles south. Because of that, I grew up with a mixture of friends. I knew people who owned lowrider cars with hydraulics along with guys whose tires on their four-wheel-drive trucks were almost as tall as me.

Beth was definitely a city girl and I liked the idea of shaking up her world by placing her somewhere different. Ryan was then born!

What type of research did you do while writing *Dare You To?*

Ever since I've known my husband, I've spent a good majority of my Friday nights during the summer up at the ballfield watching him play. It's amazing to see how a group of guys work, and sometimes don't work, together on the field.

I knew immediately that Ryan would play baseball and while I learned quite a bit from my husband, I wanted to understand baseball in the context of a teenager chasing a pro career and/or an athletic scholarship. I visited an indoor baseball training facility and was able to talk to trainers there. I also spoke with teens and parents of teens in similar circumstances as Ryan.

Everyone was extremely helpful and their answers and experiences helped shape the situations that Ryan faced.

Why did you choose not to have Isaiah and Beth end up together?

What if I told you that when I wrote *Pushing the Limits,* where they appear as secondary characters, I did see them together? I'm sure no one would be shocked by that answer.

When I began to examine Beth and Isaiah closely, I realized that in order for them to find peace they needed to be challenged by someone else. Beth and Isaiah are very similar and Isaiah completely enables Beth's behavior. The two of them had a lot to work through, and as I began plotting, I realized they couldn't grow as individuals as long as they were together.

I love Beth and Isaiah as if they are real live people and I truly want them to be happy. Unfortunately, I just didn't think they could find true happiness as a romantic couple. Ryan, on the other hand, is Beth's perfect match.

Beth doesn't see who she really is and because Ryan has no history with her, he's able to see her very clearly. He falls hard for the wonderful person buried deep inside her. Beth holds on to a past she can't change and Ryan helps her learn how to let the past go and look toward the future.

Now, one of the many wonderful chain reactions that stemmed from writing Beth with Ryan was the joy of writing Isaiah's story, *Crash Into You*. My heart broke several times for Isaiah while writing *Dare You To* and I can't tell you how excited I am for my readers to see who Isaiah ends up with and how this will change his life forever.

I promise—you won't be disappointed!

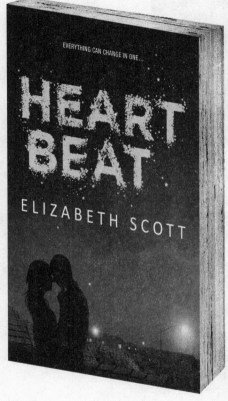

THE SECRET DIAMOND SISTERS

by
MICHELLE MADOW

Savanah, Courtney and Peyton Diamond are three sisters who grew up never knowing their father. But it looks as if their luck is about to change when they find out the secret identity of their long-lost dad—a billionaire Las Vegas hotel owner who wants them to come live in a gorgeous penthouse suite. Suddenly the Strip's most exclusive clubs are all-access, and with an unlimited credit card each, it should be easier than ever to fit in. But in a town full of secrets and illusion, fitting in is nothing compared to finding out the truth about their past, and holding on to the most important thing of all—sisterhood.

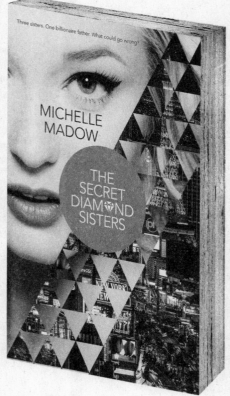

Coming March 2014

www.HarlequinTEEN.com

HTSDSTR